MW00779051

SLOW
FADE

a novel

Kate G. Philips

KATE G. PHILIPS

SLOW FADE

ISBN 978-1-66789-659-5 (Print)
ISBN 978-1-66789-660-1 (eBook)

Cover Illustration by Jason Phillips

Thank you to my family and friends for always
being supportive, loving, and encouraging.

Thank you Ms. Tripp for your law enforcement expertise.

A special thanks to my husband, Jason.
I could not have journeyed here without you.

Thank you to the countless friends and family members
who supported me by providing feedback
to help make this what it is.

The WHY Behind the Novel

People who know me probably use words like "assertive," "loud," "strong," "outspoken," and maybe even "intense" when describing my personality. But I wasn't always this way. So why am I now? Domestic violence has silenced so many people who aren't able to speak from the grave … from the hospital room … from the prison they are currently trapped in at home. I found my voice before it was too late.

I so often hear, "It's her own fault she went back to him. She knew he would hit her again." People also say, "I would never stay with someone who abused me. It's her own fault she's staying." They even say, "I never knew. There were no warning signs." Victim blaming is too common when it comes to domestic abuse, and so is the theme that others never would have guessed it was happening with someone they knew. I was never warned about how domestic abuse starts. What I can say is that it doesn't start with a fist to the face.

I came from a tight-knit family; we all lived in one house. I had a solid faith as a Christian and a strong sense of right and wrong. We were an average family living in the suburbs of Minnesota. I trusted others freely as I had never really been given a reason not to. While I was made fun of through most of my school years by being called unkind names or having rumors made up about me, my life was still pretty easy. It was quite privileged.

I had recently broken up with my second boyfriend when my friends from work told me about a guy who would be perfect for me. I agreed to meet him. I'll never forget the night I met him: butterflies bounced around in my stomach when an older guy told me I was pretty. The compliments were not something I was used to, aside from those given by my friends. On our first few dates, he was a complete gentleman. Kind. Funny. He complimented me. He held my hand. He was smooth, so smooth that I never saw a change.

Then one night, as we sat in his car alone in a rural park, he cried, yet no tears came down his face. He shared a story with me that played on my empathy and giving nature. He made it seem like no one would love him. I promised him I wasn't going to judge him. I promised I wasn't going to leave him. I promised I would never do something to violate him. My heart hurt for him. I wanted nothing more than to help him, nurture him, and take care of him. Thinking back, my emotions and empathy blinded my logic.

One day shortly thereafter, I had not had a chance to eat before I got to his house. My stomach loudly growled. I said I was hungry. He made a comment about how he was glad I noticed it too. I didn't understand. He acted surprised, like maybe he shouldn't tell me, but then was more than happy to tell me that he thought I was trying to skip meals because, you know, I was getting kinda pudgy. I was five feet four and weighed 106 pounds. One hundred six pounds is anything but pudgy. But I didn't eat that night or many times thereafter. I wanted to remain beautiful. As my bones protruded more, his reassurance of my beauty motivated me to double down on my hunger.

When we hung out with my group of friends, we had a fun time together. But after we left, he told me he felt uncomfortable, like they were judging him. I assured him they were not. But when he told me he wanted to hang out just the two of us next time, I read it as insecurity; with everything he had been through in the past, I didn't want to put any kind of pressure on him. Before I realized it, we stopped seeing my friends.

I remember clearly stating I never wanted to do more than kiss before marriage. Some people called me a prude or uptight, but that was supposed to be my choice. Instead of listening to the hairs that stood up on the back of my neck each time he "forgot" my limits, I rationalized his actions. I clearly recall his hands groping me where I specifically told him not to. The empty air stifled my words. I vividly recall thinking I could scream, but it was just him and me in his house, so no one would hear me. No one was coming. No one would save me. Plus, I would look stupid screaming when I'm with my boyfriend, someone who loves me.

I remember one specific night like it was yesterday. I was sitting in my car, shaking, crying, and alone. My body was acting as if it was in danger, but my body, brain, heart, and mind were in all different areas. I couldn't comprehend why my body was trembling when my brain told me I was selfish and a tease. My heart knew something wasn't right, but my mind told me I was also overreacting. It was all so confusing. This was the first time I recognized my story may not be the fairy tale I believed it was.

Between compliments, he convinced me I was selfish, extremely flawed, and not a great person. I was lucky he loved me. He was more experienced and knew what love was. He convinced me that if I really loved him, I would let him do whatever he wanted to me. Let me say that one more time. He convinced me that if I really loved him, I would let him do WHATEVER he wanted to me, regardless of what I wanted.

My soul knew something was off, but my brain believed him. I wanted to be loved. I had never been in love, so I didn't know what it felt like. Any time I brought up the fact that I didn't want to do something or that maybe we should go separate ways, he would threaten to hurt himself; his death would be on my hands. So I went back. I doubted my own instincts because he was just that good at manipulating my reality.

I'm not going to get into how I got away from him—that's a story I'm keeping to myself. I will say all of our mutual friends told me I was a terrible person for breaking his heart. They made me the villain in my own nightmare.

Like many people who escape an abusive relationship, I didn't realize the reasons I sought to get drunk, starve myself, or gamble away thousands of dollars were because I had somehow completely lost myself in my own mirror without ever noticing my identity fading.

The first time I saw the power and abuse wheel, it was like I could finally see something I never knew was there. It unveiled just how bad and toxic that relationship had been. I had lost all my self-worth. He had convinced me I was too pudgy, too much of a hypocrite, ugly, a liar, a devil, and just overall unworthy, when, in reality, he was the serpent in the garden all along.

So why doesn't a person leave when they are hit? For many, the emotional and psychological abuse is so sneakily hidden between the good that they never realize the pot of cold water is now boiling.

While this story is fictional and not based on any one person or thing, it illustrates how a strong person can rationalize away even the most absurd experiences. Any parallels in the story to my own life are purely coincidental. Domestic abuse can impact anyone, which is why it is so crucial to pay attention. Research and share the power and abuse wheel with your friends, with your family, and with your colleagues. I share this story in hopes that it will save others from the serpent in the Garden.

CHAPTER ONE

Officer Kipton Pierre

I pull over this supped-up, wannabe thug car, knowing I'll find intense pleasure in ticketing this young punk for running the red light. I snap on the video cam to make sure no funny business ensues. Gun in holster, check. Taser in holster, check. Pad of tickets and pen ready to go, check. I adjust my hat to make sure it's on just right and begin the twenty-foot walk toward this shady car.

I lean over and peer in through the window, which this rude kid never bothered to roll down. My hand remains on my holstered gun. As I crouch down to look in, I'm shocked to find a woman in the front seat. She's about my age—early to mid-twenties—with blonde hair brushing her shoulders. She's looking into her rear-view mirror, oblivious to me standing here. I wait a second to see if she will look over. She doesn't.

I tap on the window. "Ma'am, please roll down the window and then put your hands on the steering wheel." She obliges and then returns her left hand to the steering wheel. She has yet to make any sort of eye contact with me.

"Ma'am, I'm going to need your license and registration for this vehicle. Do you know why I pulled you over?" I wait for her to answer.

She hesitates, then whispers, "No." She stutters, "I ... I'm sorry. I don't know where the registration is, but here is my driver's license." As this tiny woman digs into her apron to pull out her license, I notice her hands trembling. I've never seen someone this nervous about being pulled over. Is she on drugs? What is she hiding?

As her shaky hand reaches out to give me the license, her voice squeaks, "This is my boyfriend's car. I'm getting cheese. I got the wrong cheese. I need to get ch ... cheddar. American isn't burger cheese."

Cheese? What is she talking about? But her voice, her voice alarms me, like she's in some kind of danger. Concerned something bigger may be going on, I try to remain calm.

"Ma'am, I'm going to need you to look at me." I hold my breath because I'm afraid of seeing her eyes. I can tell by how shaky she is that her eyes will reveal what her words do not.

She slowly turns towards me, hesitant to show me her eyes.

"Am I being ar ... arrested?" She is hiding half of her face.

What is underneath her hair? Is she hurt? Is she scared? Is she on drugs? What is she hiding? I need to maintain professionalism but get a better read on her. I take my hand off my holstered gun. "Ma'am, I need to see your entire face. I need you to look at me." I add, "And no, you aren't going to be arrested. You ran a red light, so that is why I pulled you over." I don't want to add to her fear.

Her right hand trembles. I resist the odd urge to reach out and embrace her shaking hand. My job is to protect, and by getting all the information, I can do just that. Part of me suspects what is behind her shielding hair, and the other part of me hopes I don't know—hopes it's nothing. She slowly pulls her hair behind her ear, tucking it there. She turns to me.

My heartbeat stops. I swallow what air is already inside my lungs. Her face is swollen from her forehead down to her lips. I'm not even sure she can see out of her right eye. A trickle of blood stretches from her eyebrow to her chin. Again, I restrain my arm from reaching out to hold her delicate face. Anger boils inside me. I feel immense guilt for forcing her to look at me, exposing her in such a raw state. Her eyes quickly retract behind her tears.

Realizing I've been staring at her for twenty seconds without saying a word, I refocus.

"Are … are you okay, ma'am?" I ask without trying to sound too disturbed.

Her slight nod yes is not convincing as a new tear glistens, sliding down her cheek.

"Did someone do this to you? Did someone hurt you?" I try to contain my worried tone. She stares at nothing and nods "no" as she sits quietly in her seat. Her hands are still tightly gripping the steering wheel. I see her knuckles turning white.

She looks innocent and fragile. I need to keep my emotions out of this to see if I can help. The academy never trained us on how to deal with this. We're trained on procedures when we arrive at domestic disputes or bar fights, but not for this, when we stumble upon them by accident. Millions of thoughts run through my head. Was she raped? There have been five recent cases of date rape in town this past month. Was she beaten at work since she appears to have a waitress outfit on? Wait, she mentioned a boyfriend. I take a slow, deep breath before asking, "You said this is your boyfriend's vehicle? And you have permission to drive this?" I need to make sure I'm not just trying to pry; I need to make it sound like I'm still concerned she is the one who broke the law. On the other hand, I don't want her to realize my stunned state is because I hadn't expected a woman to be driving, much less a battered woman.

"Yes, yes. I'm getting him cheddar cheese," she says so matter-of-factly. I can see her whispering something else but can't quite make it out.

Her boyfriend must be the problem since she sounds like she just came from his home and is driving his car. "Let me just run a few things. I'll be back." I walk to my squad with her license. I shut off the dash video without thinking twice. She isn't dangerous. I quickly scribble her name and DOB onto a piece of scratch paper. Next to it, I jot down the license plate number for the souped-up piece of crap she is driving.

I can't make it look like I'm writing down her information or processing a ticket, so I stuff the paper into my right pocket and walk back to her car. "Here is your license, ma'am. I'm going to let you off today with just a warning. Just don't try to make any late yellow lights." I put my business card in with her license. I know I should have given her the domestic abuse hotline number, but something tells me it wouldn't do any good. I want her to know that I can help her too, that I want to help her. I keep staring at this frail woman. Inner beauty radiates from her broken body. Nobody should be a victim of domestic assault.

"Thank you," she says with a loud sigh of relief.

My soul feels lighter. I walk back to my car, not wanting to leave her side. I still have her image vivid in my mind as I open my squad door and slide into the seat. My eyes focus forward on the vehicle and the small body in the front driver's seat. Is it because she is likely in danger? Is it because she was hurt? Is it because she was so scared? Why do I have such a strong yearning to wrap my arms around her and embrace her, keep her safe? I need to get to know this woman more. My job is to protect; I must protect her.

I pull out the small paper I had tucked in my right pocket and study my note.

"Sara Olivia Scott. 4-13-85. BAG666."

CHAPTER TWO

Sara Olivia Scott ~ Age Seventeen

Nine months earlier.

This is it. The last of my most precious belongings neatly stacked inside a cardboard box. I'm surprised my life fits in so few boxes. After seventeen years, I thought there would be more than six cardboard cubes to document my existence.

"You get everything you need all packed up, Sara?" Momma joins me in my now-empty room, empty aside from the small twin bed huddled in the corner and the three remaining boxes hiding in the closet.

"Yep, Momma." I hold in my insecurity. I don't want her to know I'm petrified of leaving.

"You know, your father and I don't care about having a guest room. Really. We don't want you to feel like you have to move all of your stuff out of here just because you're going to college."

I know they wouldn't mind if I kept my artwork up and other décor out to accompany the now bare sage-colored walls, but they've spent their whole lives giving me everything I needed; I feel compelled to give them the luxury of a guest room. And if they don't have any guests, at least this is a room where Momma can sleep in peace when Daddy's snoring rumbles their small master suite.

"I know, Momma. But it's time for me to take the next step."

"We're so proud of you." Her arms embrace me. "You'll be just fine in the cities. You're a strong woman. And you know that this will always be your home, no matter what. You'll always have your bed to sleep in when you come home."

"I know," is all my voice allows me to muster before my composure begins cracking. Momma senses my quivering nerves and hugs me tighter.

"Everything is going to be okay. I promise," she reassuringly whispers into my ear.

I nod in agreement. I hope she's right. I'm not sure I'm ready to be on my own. My parents are more than just my parents; they are some of my best friends and the people I confide in.

Momma's words force me back into reality. "Okay. Let's get this last box packed up in the car so we're not late."

I carry the surprisingly light box out to the car and make room for it next to my suitcase in the trunk. Daddy is already outside checking the tire pressure and the oil.

"Everything okay with the car, Daddy?"

"Absolutely. I just wanted to make sure we won't have any problems on the drive down to the city."

Bummer. I was hoping we'd have to cancel or at least delay the journey.

"You guys got everything?" Momma yells from the porch.

"Yep," Daddy hollers back as he puts his tire gauge and oilcloth back in the garage.

"What I can," I quietly reply to Momma, knowing no one can hear me but me. I can't fit my home in the dorm, and they aren't moving in with me. So no, I don't have everything.

Don't get me wrong. I look forward to the new adventures that are expected with moving away from home and attending college; it's what I'm leaving behind that has me anxious. I fumble around for my seatbelt buckle as my eyes follow Momma. She locks up the house and hustles out to the passenger seat to join me. Daddy isn't far behind as he presses the button inside the garage to close the garage door and hurriedly runs through the opening, jumping over the sensor so it doesn't reopen. I sure am going to miss them and all these trivial moments.

As we pass the farmland on either side of the road, my heart races. St. Paul is over an hour and a half away from home, and I won't have a car. What if I don't like it? What if my roommate is crazy? What if I need Daddy or Momma?

"Sara, we are so proud of you." Daddy's eyes glance through his rearview mirror at me, interrupting my panic.

"Thanks, Daddy."

"This is a big step for you—for anyone."

Momma breaks Daddy's slow train of thought. "And you know that if you need us, we are only a phone call away." *And a hour-and-a-half drive.*

"She won't need us." Daddy smiles. I wish Daddy would share some of his faith in me with me.

"You know, Sara," Momma says, her eyes glistening as she turns around in her seat to look at me, "your Daddy and I met in college."

"Don't give my little girl any ideas." Daddy still isn't willing to accept I'm at the age Momma was when they met.

"Oh hush. She's a beautiful woman, and she can't help it if her prince charming finds her sooner than later." Momma is such a romantic. I blame the countless corny romantic movies she's made us sit through. Although I'll admit I wouldn't mind if I met my future husband.

Even though I've heard the story of how they met a million times, I hope Momma starts retelling it for the one millionth and first time. She doesn't. Instead, she inquires as to what kind of man I'm looking for. "I know you are capable of finding someone good, but do you know what qualities you are seeking in a man?"

"Honestly, Momma, I haven't thought about it a ton."

"Well, sweetheart, you are going to the big city, where there are lots of good men but also some crazy ones." Of course, she is worried. "I just want to make sure you filter out the bad ones."

"Don't worry. I've had you guys as my role models for seventeen years." Momma's hand reaches over the center console and rests on my father's arm as he continues his ten and two o'clock wheel grip. I catch a glimpse of his smile. "I know that I'm not going to date someone who is arrogant or selfish. I guess I assume I'll probably just know, like you guys did when you met."

"Just know that people in the city aren't always as sweet as the people of Duelm. But I know you'll pick only the good ones." Momma reassures herself.

"I'll be fine, Momma."

"Of course, you'll be fine," Daddy pipes in. "You're my little girl. You're smart."

"Thanks, Daddy."

I know Momma's tears are just waiting to spill from her eyes, so I quickly change the subject. "Are you guys going to do anything fun when you get home?" *Like decorate the new guest room.*

Momma answers before the last word falls from my mouth. "We don't have anything planned, but we might see if Judy and Bob want to come over for dinner next week."

Momma is going to have to fill her free time so she doesn't worry. Judy and Bob have been friends with my parents for many years. Judy and Momma met in college when they were sophomore roommates and have been close ever since. Bob, Judy, and my parents used to double date frequently before they had three kids of their own and my parents had me. Their kids are a few years older than me, so they've been empty nesters for a while.

"That would be good for you guys. Tell them I say hi."

"Of course. I know Judy has wanted to get together for a while, but life's just been so darn busy. It will be fun to see those two again."

Our conversation changes from Bob and Judy to autumn. With all the rain we've had this summer, fall's colors are bound to pop. My heart sinks knowing that I'm going to miss my favorite tree, the fifty-year-old silver maple outside my bedroom window, change from green to red to orange to yellow. At least St. Paul has an abundance of old trees that I'm sure will be a new kind of beautiful.

We arrive at the dorm hall sooner than I had hoped. After check-in at the front desk, I'm forced to take a mug shot for my ID card. Hard to have a great photo taken when you are scared half to death. I put on my brave smile.

Room 409. I open the door to find the room empty. I wheel in my suitcase, and my parents follow me in and set my boxes down on the floor. I'm relieved that my roommate isn't here yet; now I have first pick between the two beds. I choose the bottom bunk, assuming it will be easier to get in and out of bed. I quickly toss my worn maroon shoulder purse on the mattress to claim my spot.

We all feel the inevitable goodbye that lingers in the quiet room. No one wants to make the first move to acknowledge our future is now a reality. As their only child, I know my parents are just as nervous to drive back to their childless home as I am to be left here alone. Yet, they realize that staying will only make it harder to say goodbye. It's like ripping off a Band-Aid; you don't want to rip it off, but you know it's best.

"Let me walk you guys down." Momma's eyes no longer hold back their tears, and I sense Daddy starting to get choked up. Neither say a word.

We silently ride the elevator down to the ground floor. Our walk through the corridor is strange. It feels as if we are walking in slow motion.

Outside the glass door entrance, I hug Daddy. "I love you, Daddy. Thank you for everything."

"I love you, Sweet Sara." His voice cracks. For being a fifty-year-old, 210-pound, silver-haired man, he's a softy.

I hug Momma last. "I love you, Momma." Her contagious tears spread to my eyes. Momma's five-foot-seven frame is a powerhouse of love; she can make the most stoic spill their soul.

"We love you, Sweet Sara. Remember, you can call us anytime." Her words are strong even as she struggles to speak through her tears.

After a few more hugs and kisses on the cheek, I wave goodbye to them as their blue Impala leads them away from me. I sense a few odd glances coming my way from strangers, but I don't care what people think of me waving. The most important people in my life are starting a new journey of their own as I am here.

Once their blue Impala is out of sight, I use my mug shot ID badge to get back into the building. I take the stairs up to Room 409 to give me a bit more time to compose myself. I open the door, relieved that my roommate still hasn't arrived. The room feels much colder with the cement floors and ceiling than it had when my parents were here.

Of course they make us take mug shots; this feels like a prison cell. Desperate to ease my rising panic, I open my boxes to find some "home" at my fingertips. My sentence for the crime of wanting further education: four years at St. Alyssa's College.

CHAPTER THREE

Sara Olivia Scott

College classes are unquestionably easier than most movies and gossip make them out to be. My high school teachers talked about college like it was a war between peer pressure and maintaining good grades; they also tried to scare my graduating class into believing we had a 50 percent chance of failing out of school in the first semester. I have been going here for a month and a half now and think the "work" is much less stressful than high school. Sure, the coursework is more advanced and challenges my brain at times, but with a couple hours invested in reading the material, I find the classes to be fairly straightforward. There is rarely busy work because most of the grades are based on tests and papers, both of which I like to think I excel in. Maybe the people who flunk out are the ones who get sucked into the social world, the world my roommate knows more about.

I was assigned my roommate by the college, and I couldn't love Melanie more. She and I come from a similar background: we are both close with our families, spiritual, and aim to excel in our studies. Even though she is more social than me, from the moment she wheeled her four suitcases, one dedicated entirely to shoes, into Room 409, I knew we'd be friends.

We had our tiny dorm room decked out with all of our décor by midnight the first day we moved in. Our unique styles oddly complement one another. My bed, which is on the bottom, has a black and white floral comforter with three matching pillows. Her top bunk has a royal purple comforter with two oversized, bright blue pillows.

To warm up the faded black-stained wood of the bunk beds, built-in dresser, and two closets, Melanie taped a bunch of calendar men dressed in firefighter clothing around her computer and bed wall. I decided to go a bit more traditional by displaying an oak-framed picture of my family from last summer, a pressed leaf from one of our many hikes, and a painting my mother did as a child that sits on my desk—no half-naked men.

Believe it or not, it's the abstract painting that pulls the room together. It exudes tranquility with its beautiful oranges, blues, and yellows swirled horizontally over one another. Ironically, these are also the colors Melanie's firefighter models chose for their boxer briefs.

Aside from the slightly promiscuous photos taped on her designated walls in the room, I look at the other girls on campus and am ever so grateful I was paired with her. We both like to run together after class a few times a week. We eat dinner in the cafeteria at the same table just about every night. We also stay up late talking about Melanie's current crush of the moment.

She has more crazy dates than anyone I have ever met. She keeps asking me when I'm going to share my crazy dating stories with her; I prefer to live vicariously through her without having to actually go through the uncomfortable situations she finds herself in. However, I assume it won't be long before she tries her hand at matchmaking, forcing me to participate in these crazy date talks.

Melanie is much more stylish than I am. Her hair changes colors every couple weeks; when I met her, she was sporting a short blonde bob, then she was briefly a redhead, and now she shows off long, rich brown curls that are definitely extensions. Even though I'm not willing to let her touch my hair, I have borrowed a few of her clothes.

Most people see me next to her and think *scrawnier pale blonde with stick-straight hair and wide blue eyes.* My "small"-sized clothing hangs baggy on me, but I do not want to get the XS stuff that would cling to my skin. She, on the other hand, only wears name-brand jeans and expensive T-shirts or sweaters that show off her, um, I'll call them assets.

Melanie is also clearly better at accessorizing outfits than I am. Her necklaces alone fill up our vanity, and her earrings dangle from one of those department store holders one sees on the display counters. If it weren't for Melanie, I would be without any style or social life.

She is one of those extroverted people who others just flock to. One can't help but love her spunky and lively personality. I tend to be quiet in bigger groups because I'm just not used to gatherings with dozens of people. Baker's Hall, the restaurant my family frequented in our hometown, on its busiest night would have fifteen people, whereas the lunch hall here has hundreds. I've never had an issue being the person in the background, the one lost in the group. This is why it's so great to live with Melanie. She is always the bright light that sticks out; she is always the life of the party. This allows me to follow in her shadow from a safe distance while still enjoying the chaos.

"Are you going out tonight?" I already know what she is going to say.

"Heck yes! It's Thirsty Tuesday," she declares, like I should already know this.

"I thought Thursdays were the thirsty days." Melanie has been trying to "spread my wings," as she calls it. Where I prefer to curl up with a good book or study for an exam on a Thursday night, she participates in what she calls "Thirsty Thursday," which is a group of underage kids drinking in the basement of a frat house; I keep promising her I will join her before the semester is up at least once. I'm prolonging that "once" as long as I can.

"Well, they are too. But this week, we decided to have a Thirsty Tuesday as well. Are you going to join us?" She plucks some long, black-beaded dangling earrings from the display on the vanity.

"Nah, not tonight."

"Come on, Sara. I'm going to get you to come out with us one of these nights!"

I watch her paint her lips bright pink. "I need to study for my sociology exam tomorrow."

"Sociology smociology. We all need a break." She adjusts her assets in her low-cut black lace blouse.

"Maybe next week." Gosh, I hope she forgot I just said that.

"I'm holding you to it." She smiles as she grabs her purse. "I'll be out late. I'm leaving my dorm key here, so please leave it unlocked. Have fun studying! Don't wait up." She runs out of the room.

"I won't." I chuckle under my breath, but she is already halfway down the hall.

I know I've only been away from home and in the Twin Cities for about a month and a half, but I immensely miss my parents. I talk with them daily about my classes, the crazy trouble Melanie has gotten into, and what I'm going to be up to that night. Last night, Melanie snuck in some wine coolers and hid them in her socks—literally, in her dresser. Of course, I had a few sips myself; after all, the disguises were *clean* socks.

Even though Melanie is close to her family, she doesn't talk with them daily. I'm sure people probably think it's abnormal for a college kid to talk to her parents daily, but my parents are different. I like being around them for the most part. I like hearing them tell me about their days and what furry animals were picking at the breadcrumbs they had thrown outside that morning; it is almost always squirrels and pesky rabbits. I smile as I picture Momma running after the rabbits and squirrels like a crazed woman trying to scare them off; she leaves food crumbs for the birds, not four-legged creatures. I grab my phone and tap "Momma" on my Favorites. The phone rings twice before she picks it up.

"Hey, Sara!" Momma chimes in on the phone.

"Hey, Momma. I wanted to give you a quick call before I started studying. What are you and Daddy up to?"

"We're just watching the news. How was your day?"

"It was good. Nothing eventful. I'm just procrastinating on studying."

"Is that Sara on the phone?" I hear Daddy's voice through the phone.

"Yes, it's Sara. Who else would it be?" Momma laughs.

"Tell her I say hi."

"Hi, Daddy. I can hear you through the phone." I laugh. Even though my parents are only in their early fifties, they don't always understand how advanced technology is these days.

"Hey, Sara!" I hear him take the phone from Momma. "I hope you are having fun. Just a couple more weeks, and you'll be here for Thanksgiving. Now that you're a college woman, I bet you'd even like some wine with your turkey."

"Daddy, that's like a month away. Just because I'm in college doesn't mean I drink now."

"Your mother told me you had some wine coolers with Melanie last night."

I do a mental head-bang. "It was a few sips, Daddy. I'm not a lush."

"Well, I can get wine coolers if you'd rather have those." What I assumed would be a small lecture is quickly turning into bait to get me back home.

"With or without wine or wine coolers, I'll be home for Thanksgiving, Daddy. I promise." I stifle my giggle.

"Okay. I'll get wine then. Here's your mother."

"Sara, what kind of wine do you want? Your dad wants to know if you want white or red."

I can't contain my laughter anymore. "You guys crack me up. I don't need wine. If you have some with dinner, I may have a glass."

"Okay, we can figure it out when you are home."

"Well, Momma, I better get going. I'd love to chat more, but I need to cram for my sociology exam tomorrow morning." For some reason, tomorrow's exam is stressing me out more than any previous exam this year; maybe it's because it's my midterm.

"Sleep well, my Sweet Sara." I love that phrase my parents coined for me at a young age: Sweet Sara. When they want to show me how much they truly love me, they always call me Sweet Sara.

"I love you guys." I assume she'll relay this to Daddy, who is still probably sitting right next to her on the blue couch in the living room.

"We will talk to you tomorrow. We love you too. 'Night."

CHAPTER FOUR

Sara Olivia Scott ~ Tomorrow Comes

It is 5:23 p.m. My cell phone vibrates just as I walk into my dorm room. I don't recognize the number, but I should probably answer it just in case it's Melanie, who tends to frequently lose her cell phone and call from other people's phones. To my surprise, a strange man is on the other end.

"I need to speak with Sara Olivia Scott. Is this she?"

"Yes. Who is this?" *Why would a guy be calling my phone? Melanie has never used my cell to make a call to any of her boy prospects.*

"Ms. Scott, my name is Counselor Vesbetty. I am the counselor here at your school. I need to speak with you as soon as possible. Do you have some time right now?"

Why would he be calling me? "Did I do something wrong?"

"Oh no, not at all. I just need to go over some things with you. Do you have some time right now?"

"I guess … do you need me to go to your office?" My heart trembles, sensing something is wrong.

"If you can."

I don't know what provokes me, but I ask, "Can you just come to my dorm room?"

"If you would feel better talking there." *Better?*

"Can I ask what this is regarding?" I try to hide the fear in my voice.

"We would just like to discuss a matter with you."

"And I'm not in trouble?"

"Not at all. I can be there in a few minutes. Will that be okay?"

"I guess."

"Okay. Thank you." Click.

That was surely odd. I wonder if Melanie did something wrong. What if they found out about the wine coolers she's been sneaking in here? I rush to her dresser and dig through her socks. Just socks. *She must have finished the wine coolers.* Just as my panic calms, I look in the top-less trash can and see six empty wine cooler bottles.

Searching the room for a place to stash the evidence, I feel like an escaped convict looking for a place to hide. My eyes rest on her pink and blue bed pillows. I quickly grab the bottles and hide them in the bottom of her pillowcases. I carefully set the heavy pillows back down on the bed. A sigh of relief sweeps over me as I stare at perfectly normal pillows on the top bunk. No one will know.

A knock at the door startles me.

"Who is it?"

"Hi, Sara. It's counselor Vesbetty."

I open the door to find a slender man in his late fifties with gray hair; he's wearing black pants and a button-up shirt. It's not him that I'm surprised to see. Standing next to the counselor is my town's sheriff, Sheriff J. Ryan.

"Sheriff J. Ryan, what are you doing here?" My shock is transparent in my voice. He works in Duelm, nowhere close to here.

"Hi Sara. Counselor Vesbetty and I would like to talk with you. Can we come in?"

Why is he being so formal? Our small town is one big family. Sheriff J. Ryan is practically family. "Of course."

As they walk in, I close the door behind us.

"Sara, dear, would you like to sit?" Sheriff J. Ryan's face is solemn.

Why is this counselor having Sheriff J. Ryan do all the talking? "Why?" My suspicion is quickly inflamed.

"We're here because we need to talk about your parents."

"Not Melanie?" The words pop from my mouth before I can stop them.

"I'm afraid not. Would you like to have a seat?"

What could they possibly need to talk to me about Momma and Daddy for? "I want to stand." I feel the need to be defiant.

Sheriff J. Ryan begins, "You know that Rose and Scott are like family."

"Yes." I choke on my own word.

He takes a slow deep inhale. "This is never easy …" Everything stops around me. *Never easy?* Those are not good words. It is 5:30 p.m. I don't call my parents until later. *Why are they here?* My heart starts to throb, and my sight blurs. I put a hand on the dresser to steady my dizzying self.

"Ma'am, are you sure you don't want to sit down?" The counselor's worried tone makes me woozier.

I try to force words to come from my mouth, but they are getting stuck. "Mmhm." I feel my tongue go dry like a tumbleweed swelling in my mouth. I sense the dooming words on the tip of Sheriff J. Ryan's tongue.

"Sara, there is no easy way for me to tell you this." I hear the clock ticking as each second drags on. "Your parents were in a single vehicle accident …" Tick-Tock. Tick-Tock. "… I'm sorry …" Tick-Tock.

Tick-Tock. Tick-Tock. "… They didn't make it." Tick-Tock. Tick-Tock. "They're dead."

Dead. That word hangs there, echoing over and over in my ears. *Dead* rings like a bell I can't quiet … *dead.*

But I'm supposed to call them soon to talk about my day.

I feel Sheriff J. Ryan's hand on my back in an effort to comfort me. "Is there anything I can do to help, Sara?"

My eyes swell with tears as I try to hold back my choking sobs. "NO!" I curtly yell. "Get out. I want you both out of here now!" I scream.

"Sara, we're here to help." The counselor's attempt at soothing me makes me angrier.

"Get out! NOW!" I put my hands up in the universal get-the-hell-out-of-here sign.

"Sara, please, we're here to help." Sheriff J. Ryan remains tearless but clearly struggles getting his words out.

"Get out!" Something in my voice pushes them to open the door and step outside. I slam the door shut. They stand outside the door. I assume they won't be leaving their posts for a while. I know they weren't done talking, but I am. No more words are going to escape my mouth. *Dead.*

I call Momma's cell. No answer.

I call Daddy's cell. No answer.

I call home. No answer.

What should I do? Should I call someone? I don't have anyone. I don't have any aunts since Aunt Kathy died a few years ago of breast cancer. I don't have any uncles. I don't have any grandparents since they all died before I was thirteen. They are all dead. *Dead.* I'm all alone.

I feel so small. My room is growing, and I'm getting swallowed up in it. My shirt's wet, my sight's blurred, and I can't breathe. Maybe they got the wrong person; Scott is a common last name. But Sheriff J. Ryan …

I call Momma's cell. No answer.

I call Daddy's cell. No answer.

I call home. No answer.

I rock back and forth, now sitting on the cold floor, as my silent sobs grow louder. *Dead.* My parents were going to call me tonight, but they are dead. My ears close, pushing out all noise. I don't even hear Melanie open the door. I can see a blur out of the corner of my eye—the counselor and Sheriff J. Ryan standing with Melanie. It can't be Momma and Daddy.

I call Momma's cell. No answer.

I call Daddy's cell. No answer.

I call home. No answer.

They always answer.

"NOOO!" With the realization that they weren't mistaken, my tears shatter what little hope I had left.

Melanie rushes to my side and sits down next to me on the cold cement floor. I feel her warm arms wrap around me. She doesn't ask what's wrong. All I hear are my gasps for air. I keep rocking because I can't do anything else. *Dead.* I cry harder, rocking back and forth faster.

She rocks with me. Her warm arms tightly wrap around me, holding me close—the way Momma used to wrap her arms around me when I was a child. Except she isn't Momma.

Minutes morph into hours. There is no talking. I can't speak and breathe simultaneously. Melanie doesn't question. I can feel her saddened eyes looking at me. I avoid them. The air around us is still as neither of us knows what to do.

The word surfaces and bursts from my throat: "Dead!" I gasp with a sob. "My parents are dead!" The words barely escape before my tragic realization plants itself forever in my soul.

She doesn't say anything. It's like she already knows. I'm glad. I cannot bear to hear the words that follow someone's death: they are in a better place; I'm so sorry for your loss; or blah, blah, blah. Melanie merely holds me tight. I shrink in her arms as my brain processes this forced reality.

More hours pass before exhaustion and defeat take over. My eyes, too tired to squeeze another tear, dry and swell. My breathing remains sporadic as I hiccup for air. I feel my body continually shrinking while everything around me grows bigger. I have no more energy to fight, to change reality. I close my eyes and surrender to what *should have* been: conversations with my parents, Daddy walking me down the aisle at my future wedding, having my future kids know their grandparents, hugging my parents and hearing their voices … it's all fading. Forever gone.

CHAPTER FIVE

Sara Olivia Scott ~ Dreaming

Giggles roar in my belly. Not wanting to keep them locked inside, I let them break free through my lips. My loud laughter startles Momma. She is getting married today, and I am her one and only flower princess!

"Ha-ha!" her laugh echoes throughout the bedroom. "My little bundle of joy getting excited?" Momma glances over her shoulder to get a better look at me twirling in circles. "Sara, I'm excited too! Daddy and I are going to renew our vows in just a little while"—she pauses, still smiling at me—"and you're going to be the most beautiful flower girl!" she beams.

Since I was a baby, Momma and Daddy put their change into a big glass jar that always sat in the corner on the kitchen counter. Daddy said the jar was filled with ginormous pickles before they started putting coins in it. Momma ate a lot of pickles when I was still in her tummy. I smelled the jar once, but it didn't smell like pickles to me. It smelled like metal. The jar was labeled "Special Day" in black permanent marker. When I turned seven, I put some of my own saved money into the jar because I wanted to make the "Special Day" come sooner. I think it helped.

For all the years in my life, whenever the jar was filled to the top, we went to the bank to put the coins in a safe hiding spot. I used to think the bank people hid the coins behind the big metal door in the middle of the bank, but I never got to see behind it because I didn't have the key to turn the wheel handle. Last week, Daddy, Momma, and I went down to the bank, and the people in suits gave them a pile of green paper. I cried because I thought the people in suits at the bank lost all of the coins we saved, but Momma assured me the pile of green paper was way better than the coins.

Daddy told me that before I was born, they went to a courthouse to get married. I think they got married by a guy named Justice Peace, who was dressed in a robe and hit a wooden stick on the table. Even though Daddy said they are married, Momma wanted to have a wedding party so now they are getting married again. I think it's because they need me to be a flower princess since I wasn't born yet for their last wedding.

Yesterday, we got on a big airplane and flew over the world. Poor Dude, our dog, couldn't come with us here because the plane doesn't have a seat for dogs; instead, my parents found a dog hotel for him to play with other dogs while we are gone.

I held MeMe, my yellow blankie who's been with me since I was born, for the entire three hours we were in the flying spaceship. When we got back to earth, MeMe and I explored this island place that has fruit up in the trees. I wanted to climb the tree to grab a banana, but MeMe isn't a good rope anymore. When I was six, I tried to use MeMe as a rope to climb a big tree at home. It didn't work because she ripped almost in half, and I didn't want her to be broken. Instead, we played in the sand, making castles and burying my feet. When Momma saw that MeMe was filled with sand, she made me put MeMe safely in bed for the rest of the trip. I plan to tell MeMe tonight when I go to sleep what my adventures were today so she doesn't feel left out.

We don't have sand like this in Minnesota. Daddy says it's because Florida is a special place reserved for special events. I'm happy we got to come here for this very special event.

"Momma, when do we get to do my hair? Is yours done yet?"

"Sara, I'm going to have Aunt Kathy do my hair in just a few minutes after I finish my makeup. When she is done with mine, she'll do yours and make you look just like a real princess." Momma's smile is contagious and spreads to my face.

The wet and sticky air outside the beach house is making my hair frizz. It frizzed up a lot yesterday too, after MeMe and I played in the ocean. Momma spent hours scrubbing my hair and MeMe to get all the sand pieces out from when we did a somersault. I hope Aunt Kathy can still make me look like a princess today.

"How long until my hair looks like a princess?" my seven-and-a-half-year-old voice squeaks.

"Soon, Sara, soon. Maybe you should practice your walk again before Aunt Kathy gets here to do your hair because then you'll have to sit very still." I nod in agreement.

I jump down from the counter and start practicing my walk, dropping imaginary flowers as I try to walk in as straight of a line as I can. I have a big part in Daddy and Momma's wedding; my job is to drop the blue flowers from my basket onto the white ground before Momma walks down after me. I've been practicing for weeks to make sure I don't trip. Momma is even letting me wear high heels for the first time because this is such a special day. Good thing we aren't walking in the sand because it makes me wobbly.

Another giggle escapes my tummy, and Momma joins in. She wraps her arms around me, giving me a big bear hug, before returning to the bathroom mirror to finish her "face." I join her there, where she lifts me up and sets me on the counter to watch her paint her lips pink.

What seems like forever passes before Aunt Kathy arrives with a bag full of hair stuff. Her hair is curled in ringlets and pulled back into a low bun at the bottom of her neck. Momma says she is still a princess looking for her prince; I don't know why she hasn't found him yet because she's already a grown-up.

I watch as Aunt Kathy plays with Momma's beautiful long brown hair. Aunt Kathy's hair is short and blonde. I like Momma's more, but my hair is like Aunt Kathy's. Momma says I got Aunt Kathy's hair because she is her younger sister. I wish Momma had given me her hair instead of Aunt Kathy's.

"Momma, I want to be a queen when I get married one day, just like you."

Momma's hazel-green eyes sparkle as she smiles into the mirror at me. Her smile widens, and she throws Aunt Kathy a glance before looking back at me through the mirror. "You are a princess already, sweetheart. You will be the most beautiful queen when your prince charming finds you."

I hope she's right. "What will he look like?"

"Well, your prince charming could be tall or short, big or little. No one will know what he looks like until you see him, but I do know that he will be nice and caring, and he will treat you like Daddy treats me."

"So he will make me coffee in the morning?"

"Ha-ha." Momma's laugh echoes throughout the room. "Yes, Sweet Sara, he will make you coffee."

"But I don't like coffee." I scrunch my nose thinking of the time I tasted Momma's coffee; it tasted like cough syrup.

"Well, then he may get you juice or milk with your breakfast."

I nod my head in agreement. I like juice and milk. "How else will I know it's him?"

Aunt Kathy wraps another piece of Momma's hair around the hot iron. "He will never be mean to you."

"Not like some of the kids at school, right?"

Momma's face grows serious. "Your prince charming will never say a hurtful thing or do anything hurtful to you."

"Nope," Aunt Kathy agrees. "He will protect you from the mean people because he will be your best friend."

"Best friend? But Marie is my best friend!" I shriek.

"No, when you meet your prince charming, he will be your best friend too. He will be your best boyfriend," Aunt Kathy reassures me.

"So I can still be friends with Marie AND my prince, right?"

"Yes, Sara." Momma calms me.

"Oofta." I shake my head back and forth. "I can't imagine having to tell Marie I can't be her best friend because I met my prince!"

I watch Momma smile through the mirror at Aunt Kathy.

"Sara, why don't you practice your walk some more before I finish Momma's hair?"

"All righty." I go back to practicing my walk until Aunt Kathy calls me over to do my hair.

Momma's hair is in a million slinky curls. I've never seen her hair so pretty before. "I want my hair like Momma's!" I can't hide my excitement.

"Okie dokie, curls it is." Aunt Kathy gleams. "Now be careful and don't move around too much; this curling iron is very hot. It will burn if it touches your skin." I sit still forever as she twirls my hair around the hot iron. Once she finishes burning my hair into place, I close my eyes to get sprayed with hairspray. Aunt Kathy told me this spray will keep my slinky curls from "poofing."

"Auntie Kathy, can I get my face done like Momma's?"

"I think we can do that. Just don't tell your mother," she laughs. Aunt Kathy pulls out a box containing shimmery glitter and rubs it on my eyelids. Then she pulls out this tube of sparkly clear gloss and paints my lips. "Now be careful not to get this on your dress, missy, or your mother won't be happy with me."

"I'll be super-duper careful, I promise," I declare as I hold my breath, hoping I do not get my *face* on my dress.

Momma comes back into the room with her dress on, and Aunt Kathy finishes zipping up her gown. Her dress is almost white with lace that covers the back of her dress and stops at her lower back. I think Momma called it satin. Maybe they call it that because she wore it and sat in the sand, because it's not very white anymore. She has the same colored heels on, but they stay hidden under her dress. I know they are the same color because we picked them out together.

Twirling, Momma smiles. "How do I look?"

"P-R-E-T-Y," I exclaim.

Momma and Aunt Kathy giggle. "Amazing big sister, absolutely stunning." Aunt Kathy dabs at her eyes. "Now let's hurry up and get downstairs. I can see everyone waiting on the deck," Aunt Kathy says as she looks out the window in excitement. I peek out the window as well. People are already sitting down in their white folding chairs on the deck, which is a big wood stage surrounded by ginormous trees that have coconuts and bananas on them. I shoot a glance at the ocean; it keeps trying to get closer to the ceremony, but it can't seem to get past the sand. I've been watching it all day to make sure it doesn't ruin our day.

Daddy is standing by the minister, talking with him. I can't hear what they are saying, but they are both smiling. I don't think he can see me through the window, but boy oh boy is he going to be surprised at how princessy I look!

We rush to the front entrance of the building and get ready to walk on the white cloth. Aunt Kathy arranges my hair and hands me the basket of flowers before opening the two connecting doors with a soft push. She nods at the violinist, and the music starts. Turning to look back at me, Aunt Kathy smiles. "It's time to walk down the aisle, sweetheart." I take a quick glance at Momma, who is smiling at me.

"Remember, Sara, you are our princess. You'll do great. I love you."

"I love you too, Momma." I move forward and look out the doors to see a hundred eyes smiling at me with flashing lights bouncing around the flower-covered beach. I take a deep breath. The flower smell tickles my nose. I really do feel like a princess.

Carefully, I put one foot in front of the other and walk down the aisle. My feet quickly lead me to Daddy, whose arms are stretched out for a hug. "You look beautiful, Sweet Sara. You did a great job walking down the aisle," Daddy whispers into my ear. I knew he'd be happy with how princessy I am. I give him a hug before turning to walk to the left, behind where Momma will stand, just like we practiced.

The music changes on the violin. Momma walks up the aisle towards Daddy and me, and everyone stands. A hundred pairs of eyes follow her every step. Momma's eyes have tears in their corners. She warned me that if this happened, it meant she was happy and not sad. She must be really happy. Her gown flows behind her steady steps. She looks like an angel.

Momma turns and hands me her bouquet, which is filled with bright blue and pink or-kids—I think that's what she called them. They must be baby kid flowers. It is my job to hold them during the ceremony. Momma and Daddy talk to each other using big words and then kiss each other. Everyone start clapping. I can't clap because I must hold Momma's bouquet with both hands. Momma and Daddy turn to me, and Momma takes her bouquet with one hand before they each hold one of my hands; Momma has my right hand and Daddy has my left hand as we walk back up the aisle. I'm grinning so big my cheeks hurt. Aunt Kathy told me to be sure to smile the whole time because people would be taking pictures of me nonstop. Princesses always smile.

We walk over to the other side of the beach deck, where tables are setup for the dinner. The people dressed like penguins bring me a grilled cheese sandwich and fruit right away, while the grown-ups must wait for their food. Momma tells me princesses are always served first. Once I'm done eating, their food comes. It looks nasty with lots of vegetables. After dinner, the grown-ups get up and dance on the wood floor in the middle of the tables.

Daddy and Momma, the king and queen, dance first. They look like one person as they float across the floor. Daddy twirls Momma around and around before holding her closer in his arms. When the music ends, Daddy kisses her. Lights flash across the floor as people click their cameras.

After their special song, Daddy grabs my hands and pulls me onto the dance floor. Just like we practiced, I stand on Daddy's shoes as we dance to our song. Our song ends, and Daddy lifts me up above his head and twirls me. "I love you, my Sweet Sara, my little princess."

"I love you too, Daddy," I giggle as he kisses my cheek before setting me down on the dance floor.

After Daddy's and my song, I run over to Grandpa Mel. His table is right next to the floor, where Daddy and Momma are talking and dancing with the other grown-ups. My new white shoes hurt my toes, so I take them off and throw them under Grandpa's table. Grandpa Mel lets me sit in his lap so no one steps on my bare toes.

Lots of people laugh and dance all over the wood floor as well as on the sand as they sip their adult pops. Grandpa pours me a glass of my bubbly wine from its glass bottle. It tastes like apple juice, but Momma said it is only used for celebrations like this. I finish my glass before a yawn takes over.

I take a quick glance behind me. Oofta, the ocean is still in the same spot it was earlier. I'm glad it can't get any closer. Another yawn steals my attention. I wish MeMe were here to see this with me.

We had to get up super-duper early to get ready for today, so now I'm sleepy. The white lights strung around the trees and hanging from the branches over our heads dangle in the night's cold breeze. Grandpa wraps his suit coat around me. My eyes grow heavy as I sit in the safety of Grandpa's lap, watching the rainbow of colors swirl around us. What a perfect night for a ball!

A flash of bright light momentarily blinds me. I can't see anything but whiteness. Then all of a sudden, I'm sitting in the chair where Grandpa was holding me. Except I'm sitting alone. The plastic feels hard and cold against my skin. Grandpa is gone. My parents are gone. The dance floor is empty.

I whip my head around, looking for anyone. There is no one. There are no sounds except for the ocean rumbling behind me, crawling towards me. Darkness is closing in.

I feel myself getting smaller and smaller. I'm shrinking. I can feel the panic surge through my body.

I scream as loud as I can. "HELP!"

I snap my eyes open as my own scream pulls me back to consciousness. My gasps for air make my chest heave up and down. Melanie is by my side.

"It's okay, Sara! It was just a nightmare. It's okay!"

I try to get a sense of where I am. I see the dorm room walls with the half-naked firefighters. I feel the sheets beneath my hands. I'm soaking wet, drenched in my own sweat. My sheets are damp. I recognize this is college. I'm in college. My gasping subsides.

"It's okay, Sara. That's it. Take slow, deep breaths. You're safe. I'm right here."

Her voice helps ground me.

It was so real. I could see their smiles. I heard their laughter. I felt every detail. It had to be real. With each passing moment, I realize none of it's real. I can't hear their voices. I can't feel the warmth of their embrace.

"Are you okay?" Melanie whispers.

"Yes." I keep my eyes closed so no more tears can escape. My eyes throb as the salt water stings my already swollen lids.

I hear Melanie crawl back into her bed. I'm glad she didn't ask me anything further. I don't want to talk.

I listen to my breathing, praying I can fall back into the dream. Their renewal of vows was my favorite memory. I'd give anything to go back there again. I close my eyes tighter in an attempt to force my mind back to the moment. I imagine us dancing under the white lights hanging from trees in a rainbow of colors. Momma, Daddy, and me. Together.

I pretend I'm there with them, listening to the priest go over the only Bible quote I have memorized: 1 Corinthians 13:4–7.

Love is always patient and kind; love is never jealous; love is not boastful or conceited, it is never rude and never seeks its own advantage, it does not take offence or store up grievances. Love does not rejoice in wrongdoing, but finds its joy in the truth. It is always ready to make allowances, to trust, to hope and to endure whatever comes. Love never comes to an end.

CHAPTER SIX

Sara Olivia Scott

I stand alone in the small cemetery with two orchids in my hands: a bluebonnet orchid for Daddy and a fuchsia calypso orchid for Momma, their favorite flowers. The exhaust from the last car carrying the other mourners floats away from the cemetery. I asked to be alone, so Melanie went with the others to the restaurant for the post-funeral meal. I'm not hungry.

Finally, I have a chance to be alone: Daddy, Momma, and me.

I can feel darkness hanging in the air around me as I stand here. Alone. I feel as if my soul is wandering in purgatory as I'm not sure which way to go or how I even got here.

The road back home seems the easiest. Thinking about my childhood doesn't make me sad; rather, it awakens my soul, making me believe I'm young again … with my parents by my side. It's coming back to the present that hurts.

Most people have never even heard of this township, where I spent the first seventeen years of my life: Duelm, Minnesota. There are only twenty or so homes in the area, all at least an acre apart. This cemetery is right in the heart of the town. I've never thought about it until now, but I'm ever so grateful this community remains unscathed from major commercial development. I want my parents to rest in peace.

Duelm boasts a Catholic church, one gas station, some other small stores, and one restaurant. We fit the stereotype of a small town: everyone knows everyone else. The twenty families in this township are one big family, the Duelm family. Sheriff J. Ryan is like the town "dad" in the sense that he's the man of the town; we go to him when we need legal or manual labor help. Mary J, the owner of Baker's Hall Restaurant, is our town "mom." She fills our tummies with delicious food and listens to our problems. Obviously, there are many more, but they are the "aunts," "uncles," and "cousins" of the town. If someone in town doesn't have a place to go for Thanksgiving or Christmas, nineteen doors open for him or her. My heart sinks. *My parents' door won't be open.* Quickly brushing the thought away, I concentrate on today. Most of my town family was here today.

My swallow gets stuck in my throat. It feels like just yesterday that Andrew, my only boyfriend, and I went out to see a movie. It was the last week of high school for us. When I had gotten home, Momma had wanted to know all the details. I couldn't keep from smiling when I recalled how nervous he was to kiss me on our one-month anniversary. Two days later, Momma comforted me as I cried. We had agreed, more him than I, that we wouldn't take our relationship further than that kiss at the movie as he was leaving for Duluth to go to college and I was going to the Twin Cities.

Daddy and Momma cheered me up by bringing me out to Baker's Hall. They have the best salad bar and BLT in town. Yes, it's the only restaurant in town, but the food is still delicious. I took that night for granted, eating dinner with my parents; now, I can't help but wish I could relive that day just once more.

A teardrop escapes my eye and falls into Daddy's bluebonnet orchid. I'm captivated by its sliding movement down the petal into the heart of the flower. Poetic. He would have said something like, "A tear nourishes the heart of a mourning beauty." My intellectual and quirky Daddy. He loved being life's commentator.

If I could rewind time, I would. Then I'd hit pause. I truly had the best childhood. I love my parents' fifteen hundred-square-foot, blue vinyl-sided house with maroon shutters. It is my safe place. Well, at least it was when my parents were there.

Not wanting to focus on the empty home, my mind drifts. I bet Daddy and Momma are playing with Dude, our Irish setter who passed away years ago. Poor Dude was never allowed in the house, but he usually found his way into our small pole barn on the colder nights. I think Dude just liked being close to the chickens because they had their own heat lamp. He was my pal. I miss him too.

I spent most of my young years outside in our backyard, which is an acre of the softest green grass. It isn't like the hard, sharp grass at school that hurts to sit on. Our green grass felt silky. And our trees! I smile as I picture our home surrounded by enormous elms, magnificent maples, and wispy willows. I would be out there from dawn until dusk playing dolls, flying my rainbow kite, and running through the sprinkler on hotter days. Dude was my sidekick.

Knowing I'm delaying saying goodbye, I give myself permission to keep daydreaming just a bit longer.

I was never allowed to go into the thick woods that surround our home by myself, but we had our weekly Sunday wood-walk at two in the afternoon. Daddy, Momma, and I would go hiking for a couple of hours through the winding paths we'd created over the years. Daddy pointed out the different types of plants and trees while Momma paired the song of a bird with its species. *I wonder if I can still identify the correct plants or songbirds.* I shake my head, not wanting to think too much about it.

We saw hundreds of deer, ducks, frogs, birds, and other furry two-legged and four-legged creatures throughout the years, but my favorite is when we found a black bear hiding in a tree about half a mile into the woods from our home. I was never so excited and frightened in my life. Momma quickly snapped a few photos of the bear from a hundred feet away before making us return to the safety of our own home.

My fondest memories of childhood, outside of their wedding renewal, are our yearly summer vacations. We would pack up our six-person tent, bag of groceries, and Dude before driving up to Bemidji to spend a week sleeping among the animals in the state park. At night, our tent's four side windows were unzipped from the top, allowing the cool night's breeze to dance against our faces as we identified the constellations that lit up the night sky. I close my eyes tight, trying to relive those moments.

Our sleeping bags were our cocoons. During the day, we found our wings and spent hours hiking through the state parks in the area. Inner peace always accompanied nature's soothing music on those trips. I need to immerse myself in raw creation now … I can't seem to find my peace with all this noise.

My parents taught me at a young age that family was all we needed to make it through life. Even though we had rough times where we spent weeks eating tuna (cold tuna sandwiches, hot tuna sandwiches, cold tuna salad, hot tuna salad, and so on), my parents never focused on what they didn't have; they taught me to always be thankful for what we do have. All we needed was each other. My smile grows cold. All we needed was each other, but now my family is gone.

I watch my breath float in front of me before vanishing in the cold, dense air. I close my eyes, not wanting any more tears to escape. I have nothing more to give.

Life wasn't always easy. My parents earned everything they had by never giving up. That reminds me of a quote by Thomas Edison that Daddy loved to recite: "Genius is 99 percent perspiration, 1 percent inspiration." I can't help but smile recalling his favorite follow-up line: "Boy, did I go through a lot of deodorant!" I couldn't have asked for better parents. They taught me what is important: family, God, and how you choose to live your life with what you are given. The last bit of knowledge weighs on my soul.

"Daddy and Momma, I promise to try and hold onto these values for the rest of my life." My whisper escapes my chattering teeth in the brisk fall breeze.

It was nice to see Marie and her family today. I haven't seen them in a couple years. When her dad, Mr. Dettger, got a job in Alexandria, they moved away before our freshman year of high school. During high school, I often wondered how high school would have been different had Marie not moved away. I would like to think she and I would have spent our senior year inseparable.

We were best friends growing up; our houses were across the gravel road from one another. We spent countless hours on our bikes, riding all over town. Dugley's Deal, the town's gas station, was our favorite hangout because on the last Friday of every month, the new candy shipment came in, which meant the old candy was being sold for half off.

When we weren't gobbling down our candy from our week's allowance, we were playing dress-up for our future weddings. We spent hours every week walking down a fake wedding aisle lined with wild flowers we picked from a nearby field. I laugh as I think back to us fighting over who got to be the bride and who had to be the groom. When my parents renewed their vows at their "wedding," it was single-handedly the most special day of my life. Even Marie's parents flew down to Anna Maria Island for the ceremony. Everyone I loved was in one place for one magical night I'll never forget. I can still picture it as if it were yesterday.

A sharp breeze whips against my face, pulling me from memory lane. "Pretty cool that the Dettgers were here, huh?" I whisper to my parents' flowers, not wanting to look directly at their coffins lowered beneath the earth's surface.

I recognize all of the sacrifices my parents made over the years. Even at age seventeen, I felt so loved and empowered by their selflessness. They were my heroes. No, they are my heroes; their teachings transcend this world.

"The last time I was home, we were getting ready for me to go to college. Momma, this is where you tell me that college is where you and Daddy met," I say out loud. Another tear manages to find its way down my cheek. "Daddy, this is where you say I'm too young to talk about men."

"I promise to tell you about my prince when I meet him." Even though I have no clue what I want to do career-wise, I'm hoping I find my prince charming sooner rather than later. "Feel free to help," I add, trying to throw some humor into the situation like Daddy would have done if he could. For the first time in a week, a smile spreads across my face, giving me a moment's escape.

"Don't worry about me. Your little girl is all grown up."

Even though I am nervous to leave the only living "family" I have left, I can't stay here. Without Daddy and Momma, this place is an open wound. I need time away to heal.

Stepping forward, I drop their flowers six feet below the frozen grass. The petals perfectly fall on top of their caskets. I allow a few tears to forever nourish their open gravesite before turning away to face this world. It truly is painful coming back to the present. But it's time to start a new chapter, the chapter where I become an adult.

I know I won't be alone forever. I know Momma and Daddy's spirits are out there, guiding me. Having watched my parents over the years, I'm fairly certain I know what I will be looking for in my prince: a man who has a close relationship with God, whether it be outwardly apparent or not; a man who gives more than he takes; a man who will never intentionally hurt me; a man who will always protect me; a man who will love me for me and not try to change anything about me; and, most importantly, a man who I can call my best friend.

I'm hopeful for what is yet to come, as it can only get better from here.

CHAPTER SEVEN

Sara Olivia Scott

I glance out from my dorm window and see a couple walking down the paved road. They are holding hands, sharing laughs, and smiling. I assume their eyes are twinkling as snowflakes gently fall upon them. I want that twinkle in my eyes, the same twinkle my parents once held for one another. I need happiness again.

"Earth to Sara. You done cleaning the window?" Melanie teases me.

"Yes." I wipe the window down, slightly embarrassed for half-stalking strangers outside.

Melanie and I clean the last speck of dust from our small dorm room. My college roommate, well, soon-to-be ex-college roommate, and I became very close friends over the last three months. Unfortunately for me, she decided to move back home to California and go to school there in order to be closer to her family. After seeing how short life can be with my parents dying at ages fifty-nine and fifty-eight, she's determined to cherish every moment she can with her family. I don't blame her.

Melanie has been by my side for this dark month and a half since my parents' deaths. She's the one who held me as I cried the night my parents left this earth, and she's the person who supported me as I mourned for weeks thereafter. She's my rock. She's my best friend. I'm devastated she's leaving me, but I understand why she wants to go home. If my parents were here, I'd be moving home to be closer to them as well; all I have is a vacant home in Duelm I can't bear to even acknowledge.

Because she is leaving in a few days, to celebrate our friendship, I am throwing her a "goodbye" party. Honestly, I just bought the streamers and food. I gave her money to buy the alcohol, and she invited all the guests. I'm just going to treasure tonight's party and our remaining week together.

"People are gonna be here any minute." The excitement in Melanie's voice pushes me to hurry. I rush to the bathroom to finish getting ready.

I hear a knock on the dorm door.

"Come on in guys! I hope you brought me gifts or at least some champagne," Melanie laughs. There is a shuffling of footsteps outside my bathroom door as I hear a bunch of her friends scattering throughout our dorm room for the party. I'm sure glad the RA is out of town this weekend, as I know there will be plenty of forbidden behavior taking place: males in the dorm room and alcohol consumption, two things that will get you kicked out of the dorm hall.

I quickly pin my naturally straight hair into a low bun because I don't have time to curl it. Had I realized it was already seven o'clock, I would have stopped cleaning thirty minutes ago. At least it is spiffed up in my bun. I wish I had glasses; buns always look better on people who wear glasses. I briefly think about the fake pair Melanie keeps by her books. *Maybe I'll grab them when I get out.*

My hands shake, like they always do when I'm rushed. I try to steady them as I brush on my black mascara, skipping the eyeliner altogether. After three coats, my eyelashes look exquisitely long. I cake on concealer under my eyes to hide the circles before brushing on some foundation. I never used to wear makeup, but that's another thing Melanie taught me. Makeup only makes you look prettier—well, as long as you don't look like a clown when it comes to putting on the blush. I lightly feather some blush on my cheeks and add some dark gray eyeshadow. The eyeshadow gives me a mysterious look. I can make that work.

I give myself one last glance in the mirror. *Something is missing. Ah, lip gloss.* I search through my makeup bag and find a bright pink sparkly gloss. Perfect.

I'm nervous to open our bathroom door and join the party, not only because there are many people out there, but also because Melanie told me she had a *friend* in mind for me. I'm not sure I'm ready to date. I have no one to bring him home to, and I don't really have any—I mean, ANY—experience dating. One boyfriend probably doesn't make me an expert.

Melanie has told me about this guy she's wanted to set me up with for the last month, but I've declined every time. Last week, she said she wasn't waiting any longer and invited him to the party tonight. *I wonder if he's going to show up.* My nerves anxiously flinch, but excitement dances in my veins at the thought of meeting my so-called perfect man.

I can't delay my future anymore, so I open the bathroom door and find a dozen people laughing and drinking champagne in our living room. Yep, both forbidden activities are activated: men and alcohol. Here's to living on the edge. *What do I have to lose? Okay, don't really think about that one, Sara.*

Just as I let out a sigh of relief that the party is still somewhat small, I glance back to the dorm room door and see two guys walk into the darkly lit room. I'm drawn to the guy who walks in first. *This has to be him.* He is wearing a light brownish-tan jacket with blue jeans. An oversized baseball cap shadows his eyes, but his reddish-brown curly hair sticks out from under his hat. He is slim, and I assume he's five feet nine.

He lifts his head ever so slightly and smiles. His eyes twinkle. I notice a little chip in his right front tooth, which seems rather cute in a flawed sense. His cologne lingers in the air, finding its way into my nose for a few seconds as he walks past where I stand. *He smells like an expensively dressed mannequin in a department store. Wait, what did I just think? A mannequin? Uh-oh. This must be how love stories start, by sputtering nonsense.* I shake my head at my own internal dialogue.

I can't help but look at him again. My stomach gets fluttery. After all, per Melanie, he is perfect for me, right? He is with another guy who seems to be about the same age. However, the other guy is much taller, maybe by half a foot or so, and appears to be a bit fuller around the waist. He is cute as well, but not nearly as attractive as the other guy, the one who immediately caught my eye.

This other guy is also wearing a cap, but he looks too much like a worn-out partier, something I am not attracted to in the least bit. He has bags under his eyes, his hair is a bit crazy, and he has on those high-priced name-brand clothes on. I hate brand names for two reasons: I cannot afford them, and usually the type of people who like to wear them are those who like to flaunt their wealth. Melanie is an exception to this stereotype, of course.

Melanie comes and stands next to me, nudging me to go over and talk to the shorter guy sitting on the couch. "So, what do you think? Huh? Huh? I was right, wasn't I? He is such a good guy, Sara! My friend Tom was his neighbor, so that's how I met Doug. I hear he's just the best, a true gentleman." She smiles as she brushes her shoulder to show off her matchmaking skills.

I, of course, am too shy to even look his way after my initial twenty-second stare. I mean, I'm only eighteen years old and can count the number of guys who have had crushes on me on one hand—actually, I can count them on one finger. But when he walked in, there was just something about him. When I made eye contact with him, the feelings that took over … love at first sight? Why else would my stomach flutter and my heart seem heavier?

Melanie asks me, rather loudly, "Do you have a boyfriend?" when she notices I am not moving from the bathroom doorway.

"No," I announce equally loudly. I can feel my cheeks turn bright red. I'm talking clown-red red. She is setting me up. Classic Melanie. Everyone knows we are roommates, and of course she knows I'm single!

She whispers in a not-so-soft voice, "Go over and make conversation with the guys sitting on the couch."

I give her the look. I appreciate a little push, not a big push. At least I can feel my cheeks returning to their normal color.

I feel my legs begin to move towards the two men. I smile and blurt out "Hi," but I'm so nervous that my "Hi" is more of a karate-chop greeting. It's one of those moments where so much adrenaline runs through your body that you react without planning, and then when the adrenaline diminishes, you can't recall what happened. The shorter man, my future husband-to-be, reaches out his hand and introduces himself.

"Hi. I'm Doug, but I go by Dougie."

What a cute name. "I'm Sara" is all I can summon. *Where are the rest of my words? What should I say?*

"Well, Sara. How do you know Melanie?" asks Dougie.

"She's my roommate."

"Ah, so this is your place too?"

"Yep."

"Nice."

Oh my goodness Sara, talk! "So … have fun." I feel my cheeks change from blushed pink to bright red again. I quickly glance at my feet and hope he doesn't see my embarrassment.

I don't know what to do, so naturally, I feel the need to run from my overwhelming emotions. Before I can finalize my plan to escape, I hear Doug comment on how parties "get ya every time." I start giggling at his stupid comment. I internally roll my eyes at the cliché scenario playing out. A young woman laughing at what an attractive man said even though it isn't even funny. Honestly, I have no idea what he meant, and I'm fairly confident my cackle sounded like an injured hyena.

"Bye." Oh great, another karate chop. I hear my heart pounding in my chest.

I scurry across the room to chat with someone else, anyone. There isn't really anyone else that I want to speak with, but I feel so overwhelmed and anxious that there is this fabulous-looking guy in the same room as me. As I'm walking, I see Melanie. All I can do is smile.

No words are needed, as she saw me talking with Dougie.

I immediately regret saying "bye" to Dougie. *Why didn't I just excuse myself and go to the bathroom to collect myself for a moment? If I had done that, I would have at least had more time to study his beautiful face.*

I see Brenda and Erick, two of Melanie's friends, walk in the door. We've never really talked without Melanie being an active participant in the conversation, so this will be a first. I opt to make small talk with them.

"Hey guys. How's it going?"

"Hey, Sara." Erick smiles.

"Hi. It's good." Brenda answers. "I hope we aren't late."

"Not at all. People just started showing up about fifteen minutes ago or so."

"Nice." Erick looks around. "What about the RA?"

"She's gone for the weekend. Went home to see her parents or something," I answer.

"Gosh, I'm gonna miss Melanie." Brenda finds the champagne and pours herself a glass.

"You're telling me. I'm gonna be bored out of my mind in this empty room."

"Don't worry. You'll just have to hang with us more often." Erick gives me a half-smile. Melanie told me he was the nicest guy in the world. I can see why.

"Hey!" Melanie joins our conversation, clearly buzzed. After giving Erick and Brenda hugs, Melanie demands, "You guys all better hang out when I'm gone. Don't let Sara become a recluse!"

"Of course we expect her to hang with us," Brenda says with a cheerful smile.

"She's always been and will be invited," Erick reassures Melanie.

It's sweet of them all to make sure I don't become a recluse.

I feel eyes on my back while Erick, Brenda, and Melanie continue talking. I glance over my shoulder and find Dougie smiling at me. Fluttering butterflies fill my stomach as I catch his eyes. It is so tempting to skip out on the rest of this conversation I'm having so I can just talk with him, but my nerves keep me from walking back over to him the rest of the night. I babble and nod to conversations people are apparently having with me. My mind is elsewhere.

An hour passes as I talk with Melanie's other jabbering friends, whom I don't know, before Dougie and his friend get up to leave.

As Dougie passes me in the hall, he smirks and whispers, "I hope to see you later, hotness."

Wow! Did he really just say that? I can't believe he called me hot!

Even after he leaves, his image sticks in my head for the remainder of the night.

Finally, the party ends. People disappear from our room and the hallway. I hug Melanie goodnight as she follows the crowd to a frat house for some additional partying. I crawl into bed with little fairies dancing in my stomach, sprinkling their dust all over my heart.

Just as my eyes become heavy, Melanie texts me: "Doug thinks ur cute. He textd me." Wow! I'm unable to articulate the excitement I feel as I read the words over and over again. *Cute.* That came from his mouth. The image of his face stays vivid in my mind.

I fall asleep to the dream of Dougie falling head over heels for me and us being together for a long time—a long time meaning forever and ever. I dream of having someone intimately close to me. I dream of having someone to call family. I dream this guy, Dougie, will never hurt me; he will always respect me; he will call me just to tell me he is thinking about me; and when we cannot talk to each other, he will still be thinking about me. I know I'm getting way ahead of myself and acting somewhat crazy, but he just may be my prince.

My brain continues to fill in Dougie's blanks: he volunteers in his free time to help others; he's down-to-earth; he never lies; he never pressures me; and he is absolutely perfect! I place Dougie into the shoes of this made-up guy of mine, and he magically fits each characteristic down to the one where he always shuts the toilet lid. There is only one end result: he is my perfect match. Drowsiness overcomes. Peacefulness sweeps through me. I sleep well knowing I have a promising future, with the hope that happiness is waiting at my doorstep.

• • •

A few days go by, and Dougie runs through my brain during the day and my dreams at night. Melanie has been on hiatus, spending most of her nights with her other friends here on campus. I don't pester her about Dougie even though he takes over most of my thoughts.

I hear a key opening the dorm door, and I get out of my computer chair to rush and open it. Before I get there, Melanie bolts open the door with a smile. "Miss me? I've been having a bit too much fun these last few days." She throws her jacket in her opened closet before looking back at me. "Gosh, I am really going to miss you!"

"I'm so going to miss you!" I push back the urge to ask about Dougie, but she doesn't make me wait.

"So,"—she pauses—"I've heard a bit more from Dougie. He told me that he wanted to see you again." The smirk on her face widens.

I can't believe this guy thinks I am cute, even with my hair in a bun! This must mean that he is not shallow like most guys. I mean, for a guy to think I am pretty at my worst—that has to mean something, right?

She continues, "Well, I thought you might like to know that Doug texted me this morning and wants us all to meet up before I leave."

"What did you say?" I try to hold in my excitement.

"I said I wouldn't have time."

"WHAT? But you are here for a few more days!"

She bursts out with laughter. "I'm kidding, Sara! I couldn't help myself. I told him I'd talk to you and see when we can all meet up."

"You turd! You had me. I can't get him out of my head!" I wrap my arms around Melanie, giving her the biggest hug I can.

"I told you that you two would go well together." She hugs me back. "Now let me get some sleep because this being hungover thing is a bit overrated."

• • •

I continue to imagine Dougie's personality until Melanie and I meet up with him and a different friend of his, Chaz. We meet at BeerTap, the local dive bar and restaurant just off campus. Chaz sits across from Melanie, and Dougie sits directly across from me.

"Good to see you again, guys," Melanie greets them. "Sara, I don't think you've met Chaz."

"Nope. Hi, Chaz," I squeak.

"Hey. Nice to meet you." His voice is surprisingly low for his 150-pound body.

"Oh, sure. You say hi to Chaz, but I don't get a hi?" Dougie's voice teases.

"Hi." I smile, already blushing.

Melanie kicks up the conversations from there. We discuss college, sports, the weather, new movie releases, and some other forgettable small talk. Dougie and Chaz both graduated and are already working their forty-hour weeks. They are living the real, full-blown adult life.

We order nachos to share. I continue to let Melanie do most of the talking. I answer when asked direct questions, most of which are from Melanie. We all know she is trying to pull information from me so Dougie can get a better idea of what sports I like, what I do in my free time, and everything in between. She is as obvious as she was when she bluntly asked me if I was single at the party.

Dougie's eyes hold their sparkle, the same sparkle they had the first night we met. The butterflies keep fluttering their ticklish wings in my stomach. He's funny and sort of goofy as he tells us stories of his college experiences. He also tells us what it's like to work in the real world, having to work from nine to five.

I try to do the math in my head. He works in the real world after college, so what—that must make him about twenty-one years old? I'm not too concerned about his age; he has a job and a home, which both equate to being a respectable and responsible man, even if he is like four years older than me. As I'm settling up on the math, I feel his foot rub up against my shin. I'm not sure if it's an accident until my eyes meet his. He winks at me and rubs his foot up and down my shin once more before putting his feet beneath him again. *Should I have played footsy back? I've never played footsy.* Before I can overanalyze my non-response, he gives me another wink and a slight chuckle. My cheeks feel warm as I glance down at my hands. I feel so inexperienced with flirting that I'm not sure I'm doing it right.

Dougie interrupts Chaz and Melanie's gambling talk with his love of horse racing. I smile and nod my head like I'm following their conversation, but I can't stop thinking about Dougie playing footsy with me and the sly little smile he gave me.

"Have you been to the races, Sara?" Dougie asks.

That sounds dreadfully boring. I lie and say, "No, not yet. That sounds fun, though." Dougie mentions he likes to bet on horse races at the local casino. I can't gauge if he is good at it or bad. He talks like he wins a lot, but I'm not a gambler. Gambling turns into fantasy football. The guys are making an argument as to why the Vikings are still a great team while Melanie is defending her state's team. I try hard to concentrate on what they are discussing, but truthfully, I can't get over the fact that someone so good-looking thinks I'm cute.

When our eyes meet, I imagine mine twinkle as brightly as his. We smile until one of us looks away before it becomes awkward. Usually, I'm the one who turns away and blushes first. His eyes have a deepness to them—some sort of mystery. I don't want to stare too long for fear I may get lost in them. I'm quite confident my quiet nature is already making this somewhat awkward. I sure hope I'm doing this right.

A couple hours pass, and I decide I need to call it a night. I am getting tired and still want to review my notes one last time before tomorrow's final. Melanie and I say goodbye to the guys.

As we get up to leave, Dougie looks right at me. "What do you say about joining me Saturday night for a movie premiere that I have some extra tickets for?"

Melanie looks at me, forcing me to answer.

"That would be fun. I would like that very much."

"Great. Well, I'll need your number to call or text you the details." Our eyes hold, and Melanie and Chaz momentarily disappear from our gaze.

"That would help, wouldn't it?" I chuckle. I put my number into his phone as the butterflies flutter in my stomach for this new beginning, for some good in my world of sadness. I can't help but sense this is the start of a whole new chapter.

CHAPTER EIGHT

Sara Olivia Scott

As much as I'd like to see Dougie's sparkling eyes again, I just can't ask Melanie to spend her last night in Minnesota accompanying me on a date. I know that if I asked her to go out tonight, she would, but I won't do that to her. Plus, I kind of want some quality one-on-one time with my best friend since I don't know when I'll get to see her next.

Before we can crack open the bottle of wine, I can't procrastinate any longer. I need to cancel on Dougie. Knowing a text would be rude, I pull my phone out and call him. *Ugh, I hate the sound of the other line ringing. What if he doesn't answer? What if he does—*

"Hello?"

"Hey, Dougie. It's Sara."

"Hey Sara! How are you doing?"

"I'm good. You?"

"Better now that I'm talking to you. I didn't expect you to call me."

I hope he can't sense through the phone that I am blushing.

He asks, "Are we still on for tonight?"

"I'm sorry, but I didn't realize this was Melanie's last night. I have to take a rain check on the movie."

The pause makes me wonder if he's still there. "Oh … I see." His letdown tone makes me feel more awful.

"I'm so sorry. I truly am. I didn't realize until today that this was her last night. I thought she was here for another day." I immediately regret putting this off. I should have canceled earlier.

"No, I understand." He doesn't sound like he believes me.

"I just completely forgot tonight was her last night here."

"No worries. I'll be fine. I can call up some of my guy friends to go out with me."

"Thanks for being so understanding." Not that saying this will make him feel any better, but I do appreciate him being so nice about this.

"Well, have a great night. Tell Melanie hi for me."

"I will."

The silence on his end of the line feels awkward.

Uh-oh. I don't want him to think I'm not interested! Breaking my comfort zone, I quickly add, "And, uh, Dougie?" without fully forming my thoughts.

"Yeah?"

"Maybe we could hangout next weekend?" *I can't believe I just asked him out. Please say yes. Pretty please, say yes.* The static on the phone is painful as I wait for him to answer.

"Yeah! That'd be great. I'll shoot you a text later this week."

"Perfect. Thanks again." I hear his phone go silent. *That didn't go so bad.* My mind brings me back to a verse my parents used to quote: "Love is patient." Indeed, it is.

As soon as Melanie returns to the dorm room after saying good-bye to Erick, Brenda and some other friends, our party begins.

"I've got the wine ready to go." I hand her a plastic Twins cup from an old baseball game with half the wine bottle's contents. Thank goodness Melanie saved these cups from the Twins game we went to in September; otherwise, we wouldn't have anything to pour the wine into!

"You're the best, Sara." She smiles, taking a sip.

"Even though I've never done a Thirsty Thursday with you, I figured we could have some fun of our own." I went to my computer and cranked up the station to popular 80s music.

"I love this song!" Melanie jumps up on the couch, grabbing the empty bottle as her microphone. I join her on the couch, looking completely silly and holding my hairbrush as a backup microphone. We belt our lungs out, making up most of the words as we go. When the song comes to an end, we play it again.

Out of breath from all the jumping and half-singing, half-screaming, we fall to the couch laughing. Our giggles turn to tears. I speak first. "I'll miss these moments."

"Me too!" She holds up her plastic cup. We clink our plastic cups together, promising one another to never forget the bond we share: a sisterhood. Our night is filled with reliving only the good memories we've shared over the past three months.

Sunday morning brings with it the moment I've been dreading. I hug Melanie goodbye outside the dorm building. I don't want to let go. She's become what I imagine a sister to be. "I love you, Melanie."

"I love you, Sara. I'm sorry."

"Don't be. I'll come and visit you."

"You'd better." She wipes her tears away.

The taxi cab driver stuffs her last suitcase, the one filled entirely with shoes, in the backseat since the trunk is filled with her clothing suitcases. I'm going to miss Melanie and her fashion.

I wave goodbye as the yellow taxicab drives further and further away. It turns the corner and leaves my sight. Melanie is gone.

I knew Melanie was leaving, but I hadn't let reality sink in. My memory of my final wave to the blue Impala that once turned that same corner surfaces—it is a blessing and a curse. Now, I can't help but face what I've feared all along.

Everyone I've ever loved is gone. Why do they keep leaving me?

CHAPTER NINE

Sara Olivia Scott

After days of being alone in an empty dorm hall since most students are home for winter break, I receive a glimmer of hope. Dougie texts me: "Hey. Wanna go out tonight?"

I respond, "Yes!" Okay, maybe that's a bit too strong, but I've spent the last few days trying to fight the loneliness that keeps creeping into my every thought. Waiting for his response is painful. I should have asked at what time. He doesn't make me wait long.

"I can be there in thirty minutes."

"Sounds good," I reply. *Thirty minutes before our official first date? Eek! I better hurry.* Since I already showered this afternoon after my workout, I immediately start curling my hair and painting my face.

I'm ready to go in record time. I wait in silence, staring into my bathroom mirror. My blonde locks are tightly curled and hair-sprayed to ensure they stay beautiful. The pink lip plumper tingles my lips as it transforms them from ordinary to irresistible. As I stare at my mirrored image with curled hair, I'm reminded of Momma's curled hair that day long ago. I try to concentrate on my brown eyeshadow accentuating my teal blue eyes. My long black lashes flutter as I hold back tears remembering my parents' renewal of vows.

I blink away the tears, trying to concentrate on my perfectly curled hair. Next, I focus on my glittered lips and flawlessly painted face. I'll have to be careful not to smear makeup on my dress since I tend to be overly clumsy. Unable to keep my mind from wandering, I think back to that special day. Even though I dressed this beautifully at my parents' renewal of vows, I don't feel like a princess anymore. I feel like an empty vessel looking for something to fill me with happiness. Something—anything—is better than nothing.

Before my memory can replay my walk down the aisle, I hear a knock at the door. I deeply inhale and try to forget the painful, loving memories. Dougie is here. Someone must have let him up, as men can't usually get in through the locked front door, nor are they allowed to.

"Just a moment, please," I holler politely as I do a double take of myself in the mirror. I need to look stunning in this purple dress so I can take his breath away. Admiring the tight fit of the dress on my lean body, I smile. Melanie gave me this dress as a gift before she left because I needed, in her words, "spicing up." I don't have much to hold the dress up, but that is what miracle bras are for—also something she gifted me.

I rush to the dorm door on tiptoe. As I open the door, I try not to over-smile; I don't want him thinking I'm too eager. He's breathtaking with his faded blue jeans and a bright blue collared shirt. His black peacoat jacket hangs over his right arm.

"Why hi there, sweetie. You look hot!" He smiles, leaving his mouth half open in an effort to catch his breath.

I feel the pink rising in my cheeks. *He called me sweetie!* My ears play the echo of his words while my brain reminds me of my parents calling me Sweet Sara.

"Why, thank you. You don't look too shabby yourself." I softly giggle as I lock up the room behind us.

"I just can't get over how hot you look! I can't stop staring." He smiles. "I'm sorry. I should stop saying that. I just … I just feel so plain next to you. The princess and the toad," he chuckles.

"Oh stop it. You are quite handsome yourself, mister." I blush. I'm not used to giving compliments or receiving them. "I'm excited to see this movie, and you again," I add.

"Oh yeah? I'm excited Melanie introduced me to you. I didn't think you would meet us at the restaurant because you were so shy the night we met."

"I'm sorry I'm shy. I wanted to talk to you that night; I was just nervous." What was I saying? Why would I tell him I was too nervous to talk to him? I need to zip my mouth shut. I don't remember taking any truth serum.

"I think it's cute you're shy. I'm just glad you met up with us. I wanted to see you again. This has been taunting me for days! Like I said, I just wanted to see you again." He grins before getting into his vehicle.

His vehicle is bright red and low to the ground. It has big chrome wheels and a bunch of decorative pieces that hang low toward the ground. When we open the doors, blue neon light glows under the dash. His seats are made of leather and are slippery. The gear shifter is different from any I have ever seen before. Its top piece is shaped like a spinning wheel, so the center part spins like those fancy wheels on high-end SUVs. I get into the passenger seat and buckle up.

He is quick to get the engine up and running along the dimly lit streets. Music I don't know plays on his radio. We zoom past my dorm room and the campus as my dress slides up my back against the seat. Not sure what to say, I pretend to be interested in looking at the city as we speed along the winding roads. He turns down the volume. "Oh, you don't get out much, do you?" He attempts to make the silence less deafening.

Not sure what he means, I'm not sure how to respond. "Well, I don't have a vehicle, so I pretty much stay on campus all the time." I smile at him. Was that what he was asking?

"Well, then I'm glad I get to rescue you."

The fluttering starts again as I replay the word *rescue* in my head. Rescue. That definitely has to be a characteristic of a prince charming; I'm surprised I hadn't thought of that one before. He is rescuing me more than he knows.

We pull into the theater parking lot before I'm ready for the ride to be done. I was hoping we would have some more time to talk before the movie. We get out of his car and start walking through the slushy roads, where the snow is melting. I can feel the slush soaking in through my worn black heels and beginning to wet my toes.

As we get closer to the theater, I hear him beep his vehicle twice to ensure it's locked. "My car is my baby," he explains. "It's been with me for six years. I've spent a lot of time working under the hood and polishing her look. Do you know anything about cars?"

"Not really. But I've heard Hondas are the cars to have." I add, trying to show interest. As we approach the theater, he skips ahead of me to open the door.

"Ladies first." His eyes sparkle, and he flashes me a big grin.

"Thank you!" I can feel my cheeks blush as I walk through the doorway. I like a chivalrous man.

Continuing our prior conversation, he adds, "Yeah, Hondas are nice. They race better than others, and they look better." We walk up to the counter at the theater. Dougie shows the employee his VIP tickets, and they let us in through the door. After I wasn't able to make the premiere for the free tickets he had, he wanted me to still be able to go to the movie, so he purchased the $32.00 a piece tickets for the leather recliners in the "special viewing" room.

"I've spent thousands on my baby, getting her to run like she does. I used to race her, but I got into a bit of trouble, so she and I are laying low." He laughs.

"Trouble?" I ask.

"Not really trouble. I was given a misdemeanor for racing back in the day. The law changed, so it's a felony to race. I don't want to take the chance on getting a felony, so I just keep her polished and looking beautiful. My sexy red dragon."

I nod and smile because I'm not sure how to comment on that. Racing? Every guy I dated—who am I kidding? Andrew, the only guy I've dated, thought staying out past curfew was risky, but racing? I've never even been around anyone who did anything that … that *wild*. My stomach skips a beat; I am both curious and intrigued by Dougie's bad-boy past. I guess my prince charming could be a bit of a daredevil.

"What would you like, my lady? Popcorn? Candy? Pop?"

Candy. I do have a sweet tooth, but I should probably act like a grown woman. "I wouldn't mind a pop." His words reverberate in my mind. *My lady.*

He's such a gentleman. He orders us a large popcorn and a pop—my choice. As he grabs the popcorn and hands it to me to hold, he grabs a straw for the pop. I notice he only grabs one straw, not two. He sure is cute, already planning to share germs through one straw. It's practically our first kiss, right?

We balance our munchies and take our seats in the back of the full theater in the roped-off VIP area. Halfway through the movie, with his left hand, he takes my right hand in his. His skin is hot to the touch as my hand is enveloped in his. I turn to look at him, a smile coming to my eyes. He gives me a half-smile and turns back to watch the action-packed film.

I am quite surprised this isn't a chick flick, but I honestly don't mind the action-packed movie. I jump a little—okay, a LOT. I scream when a guy onscreen pops out from behind a wall with a machine gun.

Dougie laughs as I jump in my seat. "It's okay, sweetie. I won't let them get you," he whispers. His deep, dark eyes accompany his smirk as the grip of his hand briefly intensifies around mine.

He wants to protect me. My heart smiles. As I'm still relishing this moment, he turns my chin and kisses me. His warm lips cup mine as we turn French. I've never been French-kissed before. Honestly, it's hard to get my lips and my tongue to work at the same time. Just as I think I'm getting the hang of it, he pulls away and smiles.

"You have the softest lips I've ever felt. I just want you to know I couldn't wait anymore. I've been waiting to do that since I picked you up."

Euphoria intoxicates me. I don't believe it. My prince has found me. I have someone to hold me again.

The rest of the movie is a blur, a blur that was spent trying to contain my excitement. After the movie, Dougie holds on tight to my hand as we walk back to his car. "That was a really good movie. Thank you." I try to keep the overpowering excitement out of my voice.

"Well, I enjoyed the hot company." Dougie smirks. He walks me over to the passenger side of the vehicle and pushes me up against the car. His arms grab my waist, and he pulls himself closer to me. With our bodies held close by his strong pull, he kisses me again. I feel his tongue inside my mouth and concentrate on trying to make my lips and tongue work together. He pulls away and smiles. Did he notice I don't know what I'm doing?

"I'm not very good at this kind of kissing," I inform him.

"That's okay, sweetie. I can teach you and make you better." Darn, he noticed too.

I feel my cheeks blush as he pulls away because the other people in the parking lot probably thought the kiss lasted five seconds too long. He walks back around to his side of the car as I open my door and get into the passenger seat. He slides into his seat and glances over at me again.

"I just want to make sure I imprint this image of you in my head."

His words paint a smile on my face. The drive back to campus goes a lot faster than the drive out. He takes the turns quickly as my butt slides from one side of the seat to the other. The music fills the silence.

"You're so cute sliding around."

"I'm trying not to, but my dress is really slippery," I giggle.

The rest of the drive back is quiet, neither of us wanting to say anything to remind us the evening is about to end. We cruise up to my dorm room and stop in front of the main glass doors. My heart doesn't want to leave him. I just want to sit here and have someone physically close to me for a few more hours. I can't tell if I should lean over and hug him, kiss him, or just get out. Knowing that it's awkward to just sit in his car as he waits for me to get out, I turn to him and say, "Thank you for such a fun night. I hope to do this again soon." I smile.

"We most definitely will have to do this again soon." He winks.

He doesn't reach for me, so I get out of his prized car and gently shut the door. Unable to control my smile, I give him an index finger wave before turning toward the building, hoping he is still staring at me as I walk away. As I'm halfway to the door, I hear him rev up his engine and take off. I resist the urge to glance over my shoulder and see him speeding away.

What I wouldn't give to have him stay a few minutes longer. I momentarily fantasize about him holding me in his arms, of feeling loved. Shaking the premature hopes from my head, I open my dorm door.

I half expected Melanie to be inside. *Oh, how I wish Melanie was still here so we could chat about my date with Dougie.* She is probably still at dinner with her family due to the time difference. I'll just have to text her about my excitement. I message Melanie a play-by-play of the night.

With nothing left to do on a Friday night at midnight, I fill it with dreams of how Dougie and I may quite possibly live happily ever after. I don't care that I'm acting like a child by believing in fairy tales, because fairy tales had to stem from something like this.

• • •

I force myself to crawl out of bed at one in the afternoon on Saturday. Saturdays are for sleeping in. I look at my phone only to be bummed that there are no messages. I was hoping Dougie would have sent me a follow-up-date text. *I wonder if he had fun. Will he want to see me again?* Trying to ease my thoughts, I put my workout DVD into my computer.

Twenty minutes later, my shirt and shorts are dripping with sweat. I check my phone. Still no message. *I wonder why he hasn't texted me yet.* Melanie had once mentioned to me that there is some sort of timeline on when a person can respond to or follow up on a date, but I haven't a clue what it is. Was it the next day or three days? Maybe it was two days? As my brain starts fighting itself, trying to remember, I hear my phone beep.

"Hey, Sweetie. I just wanted to say I had fun last night. I hope you'll want to see me again soon." As my lips read his words out loud, I try to calm my excitement. Heck, why bother? I jump up and down inside my empty dorm room, flailing my arms about to let all the exhilaration out of my hands before I respond.

"Hi! I'm so happy to hear from you. You are too sweet. Of course I want to see you soon. Like today. Lol." I hit send before I can proof what

I wrote. The remaining exhilaration pumping through my veins disappears. *Did I seriously just text him that? Oh my gosh! I sound completely desperate. That's like saying, "Hey, I have no plans ever. Please give me something to live for."*

What should I do? I start texting Melanie about my text to Dougie, but before I can finish, my phone beeps with a new message: "Ha-ha. Hot and sweet. I wish I could, but I'm going home to Wisconsin for Christmas."

Bittersweet. I delete my message to Melanie as my crisis was averted, but I'm reminded I have no one at my home waiting for me to have Christmas dinner. "Have fun. We should hang out when you get back." I hit send.

I forgot tomorrow is Christmas Eve. Sheriff J. Ryan had called me last week, inviting me to his home for the holiday; he even offered to pick me up. I lied and said I was joining a friend on campus for dinner. I wish I hadn't lied.

Last year, I never would have imagined I'd be eating microwaved meals on Christmas Eve and Christmas day. Then again, I never would have imagined Momma and Daddy… No, I can't go down this road. I set my phone screen-side down on my bed and replay the workout video. Working out always calms my soul.

• • •

A thousand texts and a week and a half later, Dougie finally gets back from Wisconsin and is able to take me to the dinner he told me he so badly wanted. He told me to be ready by 6:45 p.m. It's 6:25 p.m., and I'm ready to go. I wait out in front of my dorm hall in a black dress cut just above the knees and just above my collarbones. Melanie always said to show legs or boobs, not both. Legs seem like a safer bet. The minutes roll by slowly as I keep glancing at my reflection in the window of the lounge. I want to make sure I take his breath away this time too. Getting anxious, I look at my watch: 6:45 p.m. Glancing outside, I see an empty street. Most kids have already left for the weekend or are already at parties. I really hope he isn't going to stand me up.

Since our movie date, Dougie and I have texted one another at least thirty times a day. He definitely isn't afraid to call me Hottie or Sweetie. We talked on the phone three times this past week, with each conversation lasting about an hour. I could have talked longer, which is rare for me!

I start replaying what he told me, like I'm studying for a test. What if he quizzes me? He told me that he was raised in Wisconsin with three brothers. His father was strict, and Dougie doesn't really talk to him too much now that his parents divorced. His mom still lives in his childhood home out in Wisconsin, and two of his younger brothers, still in high school, live with her. His oldest brother has a wife somewhere in Utah or something. Dougie doesn't really keep up with that brother, but he goes home every couple of months to see his Mom.

Dougie went to the University of Minnesota, Twin Cities, to study engineering. He graduated two years ago and has been working at his "in-between" job until he finds the job he wants. I'm not sure what job he has in mind as his dream job, but it's probably something with engineering.

I told him a little about my life growing up. He basically knows that I am an only child. I've never talked about my parents, and he has never asked me. During our phone calls, I let him do most of the talking. I'm not ready to talk about my childhood or how close I was to my parents.

My phone reads 6:59 p.m.

I look out the window, and through the sleeting rain, I see a red Civic speeding up the road. I feel my own unconscious sigh of relief. I give one quick glance in the window to make sure my reflection is still in order. Pulling my rain jacket's hood over my head, I rush outside and climb into his car.

"I am so sorry! I seriously hit every red light. I even left ten minutes early. I'm so sorry!" he blurts out as I buckle up.

"It's okay. I'm just glad you came!" I give a nervous laugh. Thank goodness. I was worried he was going to stand me up.

"Well, of course I came! I've been dying to see you all week, sweetie!" Looking me up and down, Dougie smiles. "You look even hotter than before, and I didn't think that was possible!"

My smile grows too large and shows way more of my gums than I want, but I can't help it. He makes me feel seen. I'm delighted to simply see him again. Because we had talked or texted every day, I knew I was falling for him—and falling fast.

"Well, hotness, I'm sure glad you waited for me," he says matter-of-factly.

The short drive to the restaurant is filled with his apologies for being late. We pull into the parking space, and we both run inside to escape the ice rain. I spent an hour curling my hair and don't want the moisture to make it frizz. Success.

A high school hostess, whom Dougie seems to take notice of, seats us in a booth in the back of the restaurant per Dougie's request. "It will be more romantic this way." He winks. I'm slightly uncomfortable with the way he smiles at the hostess, but I suppose he's just being polite. He did tell me he couldn't stop smiling when he picked me up.

Dougie sits across from me, and his smile widens. I forget my previous concern about the hostess; he must just be smiling because of me. *Love does not envy.* I feel ashamed for even thinking twice about the hostess.

"I've been thinking about you a lot. I'm so lucky to have such a hot, sweet lady in my life. I've never met anyone like you. I seriously think about you all the time; it's been so hard to not just get in my car and come surprise you at school."

Love is kind.

"I definitely haven't met anyone as sweet as you either." I try not to smile too big again. Hearing words of affirmation makes me feel like I'm wrapped up nice and cozy in love.

The waitress comes up and asks for our drink orders. Dougie orders the house beer on tap, and I ask for water.

"So, Sara, I know we've talked a lot about me and my family this past week, but I don't know too much about yours. Where do your parents live?"

I feel the words pierce my heart. I try not to let the words break my composure. I look at my hands and take a deep breath. Hold it in, Sara. Fail.

Unable to hide my sadness, I feel my eyes well up with tears. I continue to stare down at my hands, which are nervously fidgeting with one another. "My parents died last fall in a car accident." I try to keep a steady voice as I stare at my hands. I feel his eyes glued to me and sense his loss for words. Looking up, tears drip from my eyes. The drops burn as they crawl down my cheek. "I probably should have told you sooner, but I …" I don't know what else to say.

We sit there looking at one another in a momentary stillness. The waitress's words shake us from our temporary limbo. "Are you guys ready to order?"

Dougie looks up at her. "We need a few minutes." She sets our drinks down before turning and walking away.

I take a sip of water. "I'm sorry to have sprung that on you. It's just hard for me to talk about it." I take another sip of water. "I'm not ready to talk about it yet. Sorry." I avoid his eyes. I hate seeing the pity in people's eyes when I tell them my parents died.

"You don't have to apologize. I'm sorry, I didn't know. I know Melanie said you guys got really close over the past few months, but I just figured it was because you were roommates. When you are ready to talk about it, I'll be here for you."

I sense he is forcing a smile as I glance up. "Thanks" is all I can muster.

Dougie quickly changes the topic. "Have you eaten here before? I heard they have some great burgers."

"Never. I know a lot of people talk about it, but this is my first time. Have you been here before?" I discreetly wipe the tearstains from my face.

"A few times. I recommend you get a burger. I've never been disappointed."

"Well, you've sold me on it." I chuckle. "Very convincing argument."

We both laugh. My tears dry.

The waitress comes back, and we both order the Tapp's Home Burger with fries.

"Well, I'm glad you are here with me. Now everyone here knows I am on a date with a superhot chick." Dougie scans the room, smirking.

Chuckling, I can't help but add, "You better have someone take a picture for evidence."

"Great idea! But I broke the camera on my phone."

"Bummer for you. Now no one will believe you."

"Ouch!" He fakes a hit to the gut.

"I'm kidding. Who else would I be with?" I try to stroke his pride.

"So you saying you want to be my lady?" he asks.

"Aren't I already?" I smile back.

"Well, I guess it is official then. You are MY lady."

I smile, knowing that I am officially his lady. I actually have a boyfriend. I have someone to call mine, and I'm someone's. I'm not all alone.

Our burgers are delicious, just as he had promised. When we finish our meals, he pays the waitress, and we walk back to his car. The rain has stopped, and the air feels cleansed. I feel cleansed now that he knows of my deep sadness.

We get into the car, and he turns up the music. We both stay quiet and let the music fill the silence for the two-minute drive back to the dorm room.

"I had fun tonight. Thanks for letting me *in*," he says in a monotone.

"Thanks for not asking questions. And the burger lived up to its expectations, as did you."

I smile. "Call me later? After all, that is what boyfriends have to do, right?" I chuckle.

"I'll call you, sweetie. Sweet dreams. Dream of me."

I nod. I want him to reach across the seat and hug me. I realize he isn't going to, so I speedily get out of the red dragon before my lingering feels awkward. Walking up to the door, I glance over my shoulder to see him texting someone on his phone.

He speeds off. My phone buzzes: "You look hot from behind, sweetie :)" My dimpled cheeks hurt in unison with my growing smile.

As I crawl into bed, my mind races through the events of the night Sheriff J. Ryan told me of my parents' deaths. The harsh reality is that I have been alone in this world for months, with no one to call mine. But now, now Dougie says I'm *his* chick. There is someone here who wants me. I have someone I can tell I'm studying for an exam, someone I can tell I've aced my test, and someone I can ask how his day was. Someone cares about me.

Maybe Momma sent me this prince charming to help me through this darkness. Tears stream from my eyes as I am overcome with sadness over my parents' deaths and happiness over Dougie finding me. Salt water burns my cheeks and swells my eyes until exhaustion conquers reality. Calmness sweeps through my body, and blankness stops all emotion, allowing me to finally find solace.

CHAPTER TEN

Sara Olivia Scott

In the weeks that follow our burger date, nothing is mentioned about my parents other than a bouquet of red carnations Dougie has delivered to my dorm. They come with a little card that reads, "I'm here for you." I'm relieved Dougie doesn't ask me any questions about my past. In fact, he rarely asks me questions about me at all. I sense he doesn't want me to feel like he's prying, so he's waiting for me to volunteer information.

He's been texting and calling me so frequently that I've rarely had time to spend with my other friends at college. Not that I have many, but I do have a few friends whom I've rarely seen since I met Dougie. Okay, by few, I mean two.

It's been two weeks since we became "official." I'm still smiling. My dimples are permanently indented in my face as I walk to Brenda's dorm room. Brenda wanted to know where I've been, so we're going to spend the night in her dorm room having a girl talk about my prince, Dougie.

I give a quick and soft knock on Brenda's door. She opens the door before I can finish my third knock.

"Hey Sara! I'm so glad to see you."

"How's it going?" I ask as I step into her neatly decorated room. I try not to look around too much as I don't want to look nosy.

"Oh, you know. Same old, same old. What about you?"

"You know, just spending a lot of time studying and with Dougie."

"I hope I get to meet him soon. I mean, I'm seriously happy you found someone who makes you happy, but you know, we want to see you too. We haven't done anything for weeks. How often are you guys hanging out?"

"We haven't been together a ton because he works a lot. But we talk or text a lot. I'm really thinking he may be *the one*."

"Whoa! The one? Don't you think you're moving a bit fast?"

"Well, I know it's a bit fast, but I feel different with him. I feel happy, I feel safe, and I feel … loved," I say, thinking aloud.

"Like I said, I'm totally happy for you, but I'm worried too. Just don't forget about us too, you know? Maybe we should all go out this weekend, and we can meet this Dougie." They didn't officially meet at Melanie's party.

"Yeah, that does sound like fun. I'll talk to him and let you know."

"Johnny is having a party Friday night at his apartment, and I know everyone wants to see you again and meet Dougie too."

I really only talk with Brenda and Erick, but I'm an acquaintance of their friends as well.

"I want to see everyone too! I'll for sure be there, but I need to make sure that Dougie isn't working. I'm sure he'll want to meet everyone as well!"

We chat for another hour about my dates with Dougie before switching to Brenda's interest in Hubbard. Hubbard is a German guy studying engineering here at the university, and he's the one she sits next to in her physics class. She's been dropping subtle hints to indicate she's interested in him, hoping he catches on.

"I think I'm going to invite him to Johnny's party this Friday. I don't think he knows too many people here." She smiles.

"I want to meet him. You should definitely invite him! Well, it's almost nine, and Dougie and I talk at nine every night. I'll text you later and let you know if he'll be able to make it Friday night." Just as I leave Brenda's room, my phone rings. It's 9:01 p.m., and it reads, "Dougie calling."

"Hey, hotness. What are you doing?" His voice sounds so smooth and husky.

"Hey. I'm just leaving my friend Brenda's dorm room. I haven't really had a lot of time to see her lately, so we were catching up."

"Were you talking about me?"

"Of course! She really wants to meet the guy who's making me fall head over heels in love. Or rather, the guy I've jumped into a relationship with." I laugh, mocking her. I'm not sure why I said that. I like Brenda. I didn't mean to mock her, but she doesn't know Dougie yet like I do.

"Oh yeah, she say that?" He asks in an emotionless voice.

"Yeah, but she is just worried about me because she hasn't met you. I haven't dated much, so she is just surprised I'm so in like with you."

"Got ya. Yeah, we can't let others define our relationship. I want to meet her too. Well, I just wanted to give you a quick call here. I am actually still at work and have to get back. But I'll talk to you tomorrow, sweetie." I hear some guys laughing in the background.

"Ah, I wish you didn't have to go. I miss your voice already." Reluctantly, I say, "Night."

"I know. Tomorrow, hotness." The line goes blank before I can say anything more. I had already made the short walk from Brenda's second-floor dorm room to my fourth-floor dorm room. Wishing I had known Dougie couldn't talk longer, I contemplate going back to Brenda's room. Too lazy to walk back downstairs, I get into a tank top and shorts and crawl into bed. My phone beeps with a kissing face emoji from Dougie. It makes me smile that he is still thinking about me even when he's working. I'm not sure how I lucked out finding him. The quiet is too deafening to sleep, so I turn on the television before drifting off with a smile on my face.

• • •

"Sweetie, I hope your friends like me." Dougie gives me puppy eyes.

"How could they not like you? I like you, so they will have to like you." I give him a playful wink.

"Thanks, thanks a lot."

We knock on Johnny's door.

"HEY!" Erick shouts, slightly intoxicated. "Come on in! Hey everyone, look who's here! It's Sara! She's alive!" he jokes. Erick is one of Johnny's best friends, so he acts like this is his place too.

"Ha-Ha. I had to prove to you all that I'm still alive," I joke right back. "And this is my boyfriend, Dougie. Dougie, this is everyone." I notice Erick give Dougie a quick glance, but he doesn't acknowledge him. Must be a guy thing.

"Hey," Dougie says, nodding at everyone. We walk through the crowded apartment and find our way to some space on a loveseat.

"I'm going to go grab a drink. You want something, Dougie?"

"A beer."

"Okie dokie. I'll be right back." On my way to the kitchen, I find Brenda. "Hey, girlie!"

"Oh my gosh, you came! Good to see you! Did you bring him?" Her eyes grow wide.

74

"Yep. He's sitting on the couch, saving me a spot. I'm going to grab us some drinks. And who might this be?" I point to the tall, dark, and handsome man standing next to her.

"Why, this is Hubbard. He is actually from Germany and is here studying engineering." She introduces us. She winks at me, making it clear she doesn't want him thinking I've heard about him.

"Nice to meet you, Hubbard. Hope you find the USA … charming." I give a quiet giggle, shooting a glance at Brenda, whose face reddens. "I'd love to stay and chat, but my man needs a drink." I excuse myself and find two beers. Walking back to the couch, I run into a few other acquaintances from math and English class. I quickly exchange greetings, trying to hurry back to Dougie.

"Where have you been? You get lost?" Dougie uncomfortably chuckles. I can't tell if he is serious or joking. His voice sounds serious, but the chuckle makes me think he is kidding.

"I'm sorry. I kept running into people who wanted to talk. Everyone wants to meet—" I can't even finish my sentence before Brenda walks up to us.

"So you are Doug, the guy Sara is always talking about, the one who stole her from us." Brenda gives an awkward half-truth, half-lie laugh while extending a hand to Dougie.

"I guess that would be me. And you are who?" Dougie asks.

"I'm Brenda. Sara and I met through Melanie last fall. We had a bunch of classes together last semester, and then she disappeared. I understand why now." Brenda smiles at us.

"I told you he was a catch!" I blurt out.

"Well, nice to meet you, Doug. I have to excuse myself because I have a gentleman waiting for me who doesn't know it." She glances over her shoulder at Hubbard, who is talking with some girl I don't know a few feet behind us.

"You better hurry!" I whisper. Brenda dashes back to Hubbard to regain the conversation. "He's from Germany, and she's had her eyes on him for a while." I catch Dougie up to speed.

"Well, from the looks of it, she better hurry and make that clear because he just got that other girl's number."

The night passes quickly. I introduce Dougie to my friends at the party, and we drink a few more beers before calling it a night. I thank Johnny for having us, and we make our way down to the red dragon.

I hold onto Dougie's arm to steady myself, as I feel like I just stepped off a carousel. I don't normally drink, so three beers was a lot. I know he enjoys beer, so I wanted to show Dougie that I'm grown up like him and can keep up. I'm not sure if it worked. He doesn't say anything as we walk through the apartment to the parking lot.

"Thanks for coming. I know my friends can be kind of crazy." I give an uncomfortable laugh, trying to gauge how Dougie feels.

"Yeah" is all he mumbles.

"Is something wrong, Dougie?"

"Well, you know … nah, nothing."

"What is it?" I ask as we climb into his car. My heart beats in my chest as I wait for him to speak.

"Well, I just don't like going to college parties with kids like that. I got the feeling a lot of them didn't like me."

"What do you mean? I'm sure they all loved you! Did someone say something to you?"

"No, no one said anything to me, but it was a feeling I got from them."

"I'm sorry. I really think they liked you, though." I attempt to convince him. "If they didn't, they would have told me." I try to reaffirm my own beliefs.

"Sweetie, there is something you don't know about me. Something that happened a few years ago, something very few people know about me."

"What is it? You can tell me anything."

My heart hurts, wondering what could be so bad he hasn't told me. *Is this why he didn't have fun tonight at the party? Is this why he loathes college parties? He seemed to be having fun. What could it be? Did I do something to hurt him? Didn't I pay enough attention to him?*

We sit silently for a moment in his car.

"When I was in my third year of college, I liked to party. My friends and I had gone to a party like the one just now. In fact, that Brenda girl reminds me a lot of this chick, Jane. Maybe that's why tonight has been difficult for me. I feel weird talking about this; I've never told anyone. I don't want to scare you, but I feel so close to you."

"You can tell me anything. I'm here for you. I care about you," I reassure Dougie. I can feel myself blink a few times to try and focus my attention, as I still feel like things are spinning.

"Are you sure? I don't want you to judge me. I just like you so much."

"I'm not going to judge you. I promise. You can tell me anything. I'm your girlfriend."

"If you insist." He takes a deep breath. "This was a few years ago. I had had quite a bit to drink, so my buddies and I just spent the night at the party we were at; we slept in the spare bedroom. Well, next thing I know, this chick Jane is on top of me … raping me." His voice squeaks as his eyes glance to the left out of the car window and then downward at his fumbling hands.

I feel as though the air has been sucked out of my lungs. I don't know what to say. My mind is blank. I know I need to say something, but I don't know what the right words are.

"I tried to get her off me, and she was so angry. She slapped me and then ran out of the room. I haven't seen her since. I didn't tell anyone because I was so embarrassed. But a few days later, she started telling people I had raped her. I tried to tell people my side, but people called me a liar. No one believed me. My buddy had been sleeping next to me and never awoke; he never saw anything." Dougie's face looks cold, almost like it's made of stone. His words are matter-of-fact.

The hairs on the back of my neck stick up as soon as he says *raped*. My stomach suddenly has a black hole that feels like it's sucking my insides into it. I shake my head ever so slightly, as it must be the alcohol. He is still staring at his now-steady hands. My heart aches for him. I feel scared. He seems deeply troubled by this. "I'm sorry. I believe you," I add. I grip onto my seatbelt in an attempt to steady myself.

"I didn't tell you because I was afraid you would stop seeing me."

"Why would I stop seeing you? What happened to you was awful, and I'm so very sorry you had to go through that. But that doesn't impact how I see you. You are still the same man I fell for." I pause, waiting for him to talk, but he says nothing. I add, "Also, I don't want to do anything more than kiss before marriage, so don't worry about that either. I don't expect you to have sex with me." I can't read him. *Should I keep talking or just be quiet?*

I want to ask more questions: did he know Jane before this? Why didn't he ever press charges? Can a girl rape a guy? Did she press charges? I quickly erase the interrogating questions from my mind. It isn't appropriate for me to be questioning him about something so traumatic.

With dry eyes, he looks at me. "Thank you. Thank you for believing me." He pauses. I sense he has something more to say.

He lets out a sigh. "I needed to hear that, especially after tonight."

"Of course I believe you. Why wouldn't I?" Before I let him answer, I blurt out, "What about tonight?"

"Well, when you are around your friends, you act differently."

"What do you mean?" My brain searches for what he could mean. How do I act differently? I'm the same me I've always been.

"You know, you just act like you are better than other people. I know you don't do it intentionally."

I'm shocked. "I'm … I'm sorry. I've never meant that … I've never thought I was better than anyone else. You know that, right?" I cringe as I hear my own insecurity.

"I guess so. It's just that sometimes … it's like you concentrate on yourself and your own needs above other people's."

I close my eyes momentarily to make sure I keep the tears inside. "I'm sorry." I can't lose him. And I can't have people thinking I view myself better than everyone else. "I never would think that. Especially with you. I don't even feel like I'm enough." As soon as the words escape my lips, I regret saying them out loud. Stupid alcohol dulled my senses.

"That's good to know. I don't know what I would do without you either. I need you. You make me whole."

Hearing those words from his lips quiets my fear. I watch as he plays with his hands, which are sitting in his lap.

"If I ever lost you … I don't know. I would probably end up cutting myself."

"Don't say that!" I yell at him. "Don't say something so stupid like that. I am not going to leave you, so don't even think like that. You can't hurt yourself because I need you. Please, just don't think like that." I can't bear to lose him too. I would be all by myself in this world.

"I'm sorry. I didn't mean that. I'm not crazy. It's just—I don't know what I would do without you."

"You won't need to find out because I'm here for you." I reach over and hug him tight. *Here he is thinking I will leave him, yet I'm wondering how I even got someone so amazing to like me!* My arms start to quiver from holding him with all my might.

"You promise?"

"I promise," I whisper into his ear.

We sit in total silence as I hold him.

After a few moments, Dougie pulls away. "Sweetie, Sara, do you think I could come up to your dorm room for a while?"

"I'm sorry Dougie, but I can't have men up in my room past nine. It's midnight. I'll get into trouble."

"Oh, I see. I just don't want to be alone. It's been a long day. I met your friends, and I know they don't like me. And … I told you about my past, and I'm just afraid you'll leave me because of your friends or my past." He looks down at his lap, glances up with deep, dark, saddened eyes, and then looks back down. I think *actor* for a fleeting second before my thought is replaced with guilt.

Feeling guilty for being so selfish when he so badly needs me, I agree to have him come upstairs. "Okay. I'm sorry. I know you shared something that was difficult for you. I'm sorry." I think for a moment. "You need to park your car in the main lot and walk by yourself to the dorm room. Wear a hood so you look like you live here. I'll let you in." I get out of the vehicle and walk up to the front entrance. I feel my body sway beneath me with each step. I hope it isn't noticeable.

I can't believe I'm going to break the rules. With each step—each slight stumble—I take towards the front door, I feel as if the cameras around campus are spying on me.

My nerves about getting caught are quickly quieted by the guilt I feel for not considering how fragile he is right now. He needs me, and I hadn't even thought about his feelings or his needs. Maybe he was right. Maybe I've been so absorbed with my own feelings that I've not paid enough attention to the people around me. Just as the guilt begins to swell again, Dougie walks up to me with his hood shadowing his face.

I open the door, acting as if this hooded mystery woman is someone who lives in the dorm hall. He pauses at the open entrance until I walk ahead. I hear him walking up the stairs ten feet behind me. I look around the hall and find it empty as I push open my dorm door. I get inside, and he sneaks in after me. Locking the door, I tell him, "We need to be quiet. If anyone hears your voice, I'll probably get reported."

"I'll be quiet. I just want to be close to you. I want to smell your beer breath and listen to your beautiful heartbeat."

I have beer breath? My eyes scan the room; there are no mints in sight. I run my tongue along my teeth in a last-ditch effort to clean the beer breath from them.

I make Dougie turn his head as I change out of my black dress and into my comfortable flannel pajamas.

"Why can't I look?" He pleads.

"Shhhh—Because. Because you aren't supposed to," I whisper back. "Okay. I'm dressed. Now you can look." He looks at me and crinkles his forehead.

"Those are your pajamas? They make you look like an old lady." He wrinkles his nose.

"Hey now. You weren't supposed to spend the night, so you weren't supposed to see these," I say, feeling slightly uncomfortable. I love these pajamas. This is the blue checkered flannel set my parents gave me the Christmas before last. My heart briefly sinks as I recall spending this past Christmas in my dorm room, eating a frozen dinner after midnight mass.

"Don't you have anything sexy? I'm feeling a little vulnerable and could use some cheering up." His puppy eyes make me feel guilty for being dressed in grandma pajamas.

"I'm sorry. I don't have any other pajamas. We can still snuggle," I say, hopeful, trying to cheer him up and change the subject.

"I guess so. But just so you know, I sleep in my boxers." He smiles.

A shot of fear shoots up my stomach, and I clench my gut. *Sleep.* I thought he was just going to stay for a little while. Before I can even clarify what he means, he's in his boxers and crawling on my bed.

"Come on, sweetie. I need some cheering up, so come to bed."

I have a weird feeling in the pit of my stomach again. This evening has escalated very quickly. Is this normal? Or wait—this must be the alcohol. How do people enjoy this side effect so much?

"There is something I have been meaning to tell you, Sara …"

I'm still standing in the same spot, staring at him.

"Well, aren't you going to get into bed so I can tell you?"

"Yes." I start to walk over to him. My stomach feels slightly uneasy. I'm not sure what

I'm doing or what is going to happen tonight. I can't stop worrying about the RA hearing us, or worse, having campus security kick me out of the dorm.

"Well, shut off the light before you crawl in. I don't want to have to get up."

On autopilot, I turn around and shut off the light. I walk back to the bed and crawl under the covers. *This is the normal progression of a relationship, right? It must be. He's like five years older than me, so he clearly has dating experience. Sleeping next to one another isn't the same as "sleeping together."* He interrupts my internal discussion.

"So, do you want to know what I've been waiting to tell you?"

I nod, indicating yes. I haven't a clue.

"Olive juice."

"Huh?" I whisper, confused.

"Olive juice. What does it look like I'm saying?" He mouths the words to me. I see his lips move in the moonlight spread across my bed.

"Really?" I ask. He loves me? No man has ever said that to me. I haven't heard those words from anyone since my parents died. Well, Melanie and I said it, but not like this. This feels different. "Really?" I ask again.

"Of course." His deep, dark eyes pull me in.

"How do you know, though?" I ask him. How does one know what love is?

"Because. I am six years older than you. I know what love is, and what we have is love. Don't you olive juice me, sweetie?"

Time momentarily stops. I never stopped to think of love. "I don't know. What does love feel like?"

"You don't know? That hurts me because I know. I know olive juice, and I know that you olive juice me. I can tell by how you look at me. I know these things. Like I said, I'm older, so I know."

Trusting he knows what he is talking about, I whisper back, "Olive juice too, Dougie."

Dougie pulls me in close and starts kissing me. My jaw tenses up because he is being so forceful. Or maybe it's still those weird side effects from the beer. I never want to drink beer again. I follow his lead physically.

Do I olive juice Dougie? What does that feel like? Of course, it's not like loving your parents or your friends, is it? I don't know, but he must know. After all, he told me he knows what love is, and he is six years older, so why wouldn't he know? *Love is always patient and kind … love is not boastful …*

"Passion, sweetie," he commands with a smirk on his face. He flips me over onto my back and continues to make out with me. Thrusting his hips into mine, he tells me, "This is how people who olive juice one another show it." I don't know what he is talking about. I am not quite comfortable making out like this—a bit more physical than Dougie has ever been. I feel like he may be crossing some sort of boundary I've never verbalized. But if I verbalize that I'm uncomfortable with skipping the hugging and going straight to sexual acts, he is going to think I don't love him. My gut briefly tells me to think more deeply, but the shock that he loves me promptly devours that instinct. Someone loves me.

"Can we just kiss tonight, please?" I hear the words shakily pop out of my mouth.

"Sure. Because you drank too much?"

I nod my head. We haven't ever done more than kiss, and I don't know if I want to do more than kiss before I'm married. He will understand since he was ... *raped.* The word echoes in my brain. I pull away from him as the word reverberates through my head.

"What?" he curtly asks.

"I'm just really tired. And I think that beer is getting to me. Can we go to sleep?"

"Sure." He looks at me with his puppy eyes. "I guess we can fall asleep now."

Thirty minutes pass without another word being said. His leg feels heavy as it lies across my legs. His arm is growing heavier as it rests over my chest. I can't tell if he is asleep or not. The beer I drank earlier is wearing off and making the room spin even more than before. I close my eyes and pretend to be asleep so he doesn't ask me any questions. After what feels like an eternity, I drift away.

I awake in the morning to an empty room. I rub my eyes. *Was that a dream?* There is no sign of Dougie. I get out of bed and check the mirror; my grandma pajamas are still on. I go to my phone buried in my purse. I unlock it. No texts. *Hmm. How much did I drink last night?* I dial Dougie's number.

"Good morning, Sweetie," he says.

"Hey! Where are you?"

"What do you mean where am I? I'm at my house. Just woke up and am getting some coffee. Where are you?"

"I'm in my dorm room. When did you leave?"

"Huh? What do you mean? I dropped you off last night after the party and came home. I even called you when I got home to say goodnight."

"Wait, are you kidding? Don't you remember? You came up to my room and stayed in bed with me."

"No, hotness, I didn't. Now that I know you are dreaming of that, I wish I had." I could hear him smiling.

Did I really dream that? It was so real. He was in his boxers, he had his puppy eyes, and I felt guilty because he was so vulnerable.

"You really didn't spend the night last night?" My forehead begins to hurt.

"No. I was at my place. Ask Chaz. Sweetie, you are sounding a little crazy. I know you drank a bit last night. Maybe you had too much. Come to think of it, you may have stumbled into the dorm and slurred your words a bit."

"I'm sorry. I just could have sworn. Must have been a dream. I was wondering where you were when I awoke. I was sad you weren't here."

"Well, we can change that. You know, you haven't really been making a lot of time for me since you have been so busy with school, so maybe this dream was you feeling guilty for not taking as much time for me as you have for school. Your semester is almost done, and you'll need to find a place to live for the summer. You know, you can come stay with me in my guest bedroom, and this way it will be a win-win for us both."

I can feel myself pausing, waiting for him to laugh. I never hear him laugh; it's just static on the other end. "Really? You want me to spend the summer with you? Like moving in and sharing a closet and everything?"

My gaze falls upon my dorm room door—it's unlocked. I must have been really drunk not to lock up behind me; I always lock my dorm room door to keep the crazies out.

"Of course, you're my girl. Plus, I need to make sure you don't keep having dreams of our dates without me being there; that's just not fair. You can make it up to me this summer by always being here for me."

"That sounds awesome! But … don't you think we are moving a bit fast?"

"Relationships move a lot faster when you meet the right person. We are right. Have you ever met someone where you just know? That's how I feel about you. I just know."

He is right! "Agreed! Well, classes will be over in mid-May, so that's still a month away.

You must be planning on keeping me around, huh?"

"Who else would I have around?"

"I hope no one."

"Well, I got to run and meet up with Chaz. Olive juice." He disconnects before I can say anything.

We must have said olive juice on the car ride back last night. I had to have been extremely drunk to be getting all these details jumbled.

Douglas J. Adams

Sara's an upgrade from Monica.

She's pure. She's a virgin. Not a slut like Monica.

She's in love with me. She won't leave me. She needs me.

And soon, I'll have her all to myself.

Sara Olivia Scott

I vow to myself not to drink the next time I'm with Dougie. I'm still quite uncomfortable with how I let myself drink so much last time at the party. Being drunk is not something I am proud of, and it's definitely not something I want him thinking I do all the time. I get an uneasy feeling in my stomach when I think about how I literally invented an entire scenario. I shake out my thoughts as I see Dougie walking up to me as I stand outside my dorm hall.

He is carrying a grocery bag.

"What do you have there?" I ask as he approaches.

"Oh, you know. Just a little surprise."

"I love surprises!" I wrap my arms around him and give him a kiss hello.

"Let's go find a spot in the grass to sit. I packed us a picnic."

"Ah, I haven't been on a picnic since … in a long time!" I try to push the memory of my last picnic out of my mind before it can fully form.

We walk hand in hand to a little spot behind my dorm hall, under a massive oak tree. He pulls out two of everything: peanut butter and grape jelly sandwiches, apple juice, mini bags of chips, and chocolate bars. Just as we are about to open our chocolate bars, his phone rings. I try not to eavesdrop, but I can't help it.

"Do I really need to come in to fix this?" He pauses to listen and then says, "Fine. I'll be there as soon as I can."

I look at him, longing for that call to have ended differently. "Do you need to leave?"

"Yeah. Sorry, but work needs me to go in and fix a problem some idiot made." He packs up the bag. "Sorry, but I need to run. I'll call you later." He gives me a quick peck on the lips and takes off. I stay sitting in the grassy area, as I still plan to enjoy my chocolate bar, even if the sweetest thing in my life isn't here to enjoy it with me.

A week passes quickly before we can get together again. This time Dougie can't pick me up until after dark, so we go to another movie. We kiss briefly during the movie, but Dougie is really into the action-packed film, so we just hold hands for most of the show. He surprised me again by opening all the doors and buying snacks. It feels really nice to be taken care of again.

Since he lives about twenty minutes out of town in the middle of nowhere, it's never convenient for him to take me back to his place after our dates. But seeing that we've been talking and dating for quite a while, we are ready to take our relationship to the next step. I'm not entirely certain what I physically feel comfortable with yet, but emotionally I'm ready to give him my heart. Like he said, when you know, you know.

I have not had time to dissect our relationship with friends since most of my friends are doing their own thing. The only person I really talk to is Dougie, and of course I'm not going to dissect our relationship with him.

Could I live my life without Dougie? I'm not sure. I would be all alone if it weren't for him. I try not to think of this too much because my core shakes easily with the fear of having no one. I guess that's what love is: putting your faith in the hands of the man you trust. Why would Dougie ever be dishonest with me? He's the one who first realized we were in love and helped me see it so we'd be on the same page. I have a good feeling that we're moving this to the next level.

I do feel bad because I've had so many study groups on nights Dougie doesn't work, and on the nights I'm free, Dougie is working or out with his guy friends. We talk daily via text and over the phone at nine every night. I feel like I know him so well. I've been waiting to talk to him tonight, but this is my last week of class this year as finals are done Friday morning.

My phone rings. It's Dougie. "Hey! I miss you! I can't wait to see you!" My smile jumps through the phone.

"Yeah, I can't wait to see you either. You've been so busy. I've felt so lonely lately. Now we'll have the entire summer, uninterrupted."

Uninterrupted? What does that mean? Hmm. "Sorry, sweetie. I do feel bad, but my finals are almost over!"

"I know. I just miss my girlfriend."

I can tell Dougie is making his puppy face on the other end of the phone. "I promise it will change when I'm done with classes. I have two finals tomorrow, one on Wednesday, one on Thursday, and my last one on Friday morning."

"I suppose. Hey, sorry, but I actually need to go. Chaz needs some help with his car, so I told him I would take a look at it."

"No problem. Tell him I say hi. Oh, wait. For Friday, want to pick me up at noon?"

"I'll be there. Can you have your stuff ready because I hate trying to find a parking space there? Olive juice, sweetie."

"Olive juice too, Dougie."

CHAPTER THIRTEEN

Sara Olivia Scott

Dougie cannot wait for Friday, so he surprises me outside my dorm hall Tuesday as I'm walking back after class.

"Hey, hotness."

"Hey! What are you doing here?" Butterflies jump around in my stomach with this unexpected surprise. I run up and give him a big hug. His arms pull me and my backpack in close.

"I have a little gift for you." He hands me a little box.

I love gifts. I open it and find a key. This is getting very real.

"You like it? I figured we could get you a tour of your new home tonight."

I look at my watch. Even though I haven't studied for my final tomorrow, I'm already getting an A- in that class, so my final shouldn't have a big impact on my grade. Dougie's excitement quickly makes my decision for me.

I've never been to his townhouse, but he tells me it's nice. Plus, by driving up there tonight, I can get more acclimated to living there before the big move-in day. That's okay with me.

"Thank you. Yes, that sounds great!" I hear my stomach grumble in rebellion. "What about dinner?"

"I already ate. Hop in."

Darn. I'm starving. I try to think of what his home looks like instead of focusing on the rumbling in my stomach.

We pull into his driveway, and he leads me inside.

"I've been thinking about you all day, sweetie; I just can't get my mind off what a sexy thing you are. Olive juice, sweetie, olive juice." His lips plunge into mine, forcing my head up against the hall's wall. He is being a bit more forceful, which I assume is his way of telling me how much he "olive juices" me. We stand in the hallway for fifteen minutes before I complain that my legs are getting wobbly. I don't dare tell him it's because I've barely eaten all day, as I don't want him to feel bad for misinterpreting my earlier dinner inquiry.

"Sure, we can move this to the couch. But why are your legs wobbly? You been working out?"

"No, I just probably haven't eaten enough today."

"Well, I think you look good. Your stomach is nice and flat, and you look hot."

I wasn't sure what to do with this flattery. Maybe skipping a meal wouldn't be so bad if it really made a visual difference in how I looked. "Thanks. Maybe I'll watch what I eat more."

"Well, I wasn't going to say anything, but I'm glad you noticed. I could tell you had put on a few pounds. I'm not trying to be mean; I'm just glad you noticed too."

What? I didn't notice anything. I am pretty sure my scale still reads the same weight it did a month ago. Sure, I haven't had the most time to work out, but I haven't been gorging myself on donuts and junk food. Why am I getting so defensive? I take a mental pause. Maybe I did gain some weight. I can't believe he noticed!

"Why aren't you kissing back?"

"Oh, sorry. I was just thinking about my weight."

"Like I said, sweetie, you look good. But it won't hurt you to tone it back up." He smiles, like he is giving me a compliment instead of a suggestion.

We make out for a few more minutes before Dougie gets annoyed with my distant thoughts and decides to show me the rest of his house. Walking back to the front door, Dougie shows me the entrance and where he puts his keys, on the stand under the mirror directly to the right of the front door when you walk inside. Down the small hallway, which is about seven feet long, his kitchen is a small room off to the right. The cupboards look like they are from the seventies, and the countertops are a stained tan. He has a small fridge, microwave, and stove, but no dishwasher.

"They always say you can tell a lot about a man by what's in his refrigerator." I smile as I walk over to his white 90s fridge. Pulling back the handle, I can't hide my eagerness to see what items he stores in this icebox. Squinting, I look at the half gallon of milk, two random eggs, butter, jelly, some lunch meat and cheese, and a bag of microwavable burritos, and my eyes rest on what took up most of the fridge: about thirty cans of beer. "Ha-ha, really? Your fridge has been overtaken by beer!" I chuckle.

"Well, I eat a lot of frozen pizzas and sandwiches, and those only taste good with beer."

"Whatever works for you. We may, however, need to add some food that actually has some nutritional value, like veggies and fruit." I play it off as a joke, but I'm serious.

"Well, I have burgers and some steaks in the freezer next to the pizza, so I don't eat all that bad. You don't need to judge me, jerk." He playfully nudges me with his hip.

"Oh, I'm so sorry, Mr. Douglas," I say, playing along.

We walk out of the kitchen, which also connects to his living room. It's a small living room with a fifty-inch TV, a three-person couch, and a glass coffee table. I'm actually quite amazed at how well the home is decorated. The dark blues and greens complement one another.

We walk back up the small hallway and toward the front door to go up the steep stairs. I swear there are about thirty steps that go straight up, no gradual slope upward. I hold onto the railing to ensure I don't fall backward; it's like climbing a ladder. At the top of the stairs, to the right, there is an even smaller, narrow hallway. Standing in the hallway, I see a very small guestroom on the right that has a twin bed mattress lying on the floor. Dougie shows me the bathroom, the only bathroom in the entire home, which is also quite small.

"Now, here is my bedroom. If you are nice, I may let you sleep in here with me." I can pinpoint the tone in his voice, but his eyes sparkle.

For a brief second, I worry we are moving too fast. *How can I live with someone I've only known a few months? But when it's the right person, there is no timeline.* My mental debate is interrupted by the whoosh of him opening his door.

I'm not sure what I expect, but he opens the door to unveil a large king-size bed with a bright red comforter and three oversized maroon pillows. He has a tropical leaf-sculpted wooden blade fan that hangs from the twelve-foot vaulted ceiling. Two bedside tables lie on either side of the bed, each with a lamp that looks like it is out of a magazine. Straight out from the bed is a double French door closet. There is also a five-drawer dresser to the left of his bedroom door. "Wow, this is a lot bigger than I would have expected. This is really nice, Doug."

"Yeah, what did you expect? I told you I lived in a really nice home."

"No kidding, that wasn't a lie. Now I'm even more excited to move in." With my words, my stomach drops for a fleeting second.

"Me too. Want to go back downstairs and watch a movie and get some popcorn?"

Hmm, popcorn. My stomach, angry that I have not fed it, kicks me. "That sounds perfect."

The movie is somewhat boring, so we spend most the time making out. At ten o'clock, we decide I should probably get back to the dorm room since I have a week left of finals, one of which starts at eight o'clock tomorrow morning.

On the drive home, we discuss what it will be like for me to move in. Dougie holds my hand and with a gentle squeeze says, "Just think, babe, we can be a lot more intimate now that we will be able to spend so much time together."

• • •

Finally, the last week of finals is behind me. I barely saw Brenda or Erick because I was so busy studying for finals. On the other hand, I didn't have a ton of time to talk with Dougie either. We haven't spent a night together in one bed, aside from the dream I had, but that is about to change. It was so difficult to concentrate on studying for my finals knowing I would be moving in with him for the summer—well, until the dorm hall reopens for the following fall semester.

Looking around my dorm room, it looks so empty, so lonely, so dead. *Dead.* I shake the thought from my mind before it can fully form.

"You ready?" reads the phone text. Dougie is waiting downstairs, parked at the curb. I packed up all of my belongings into two suitcases earlier this morning.

I do a double take of the room and whisper, "Goodbye," before turning to leave. I quietly close the door behind me—the door that muffled my cries, the door that bounced Melanie's and my laughter around the walls, and the door that stood between me and the rest of the world.

As I walk outside, the sun is hot. The reflection off the red dragon is blinding. Dougie is sitting in the car, smiling at me. "Hurry up, sweetie! What's taking so long? I can barely wait!" He grins. I set my suitcases into the trunk of the car and jump into the seat.

Giving Dougie a quick kiss, I ask, "What took you so long? I've been waiting forever!" I have been waiting a long time for my prince to save me from my dungeon of loneliness.

"Well, buckle up, because now you are in my possession, hotness!" He revs the red dragon before peeling out of the parking lot and far away from campus. I can't help but feel I am leaving something behind, but I know I double-checked the room before I left. The impending feeling of losing something important lingers for a moment, but then it's gone. All I am left with is the present.

The drive seems a lot longer than twenty minutes; it feels closer to thirty minutes. As we pull up to this townhome, Dougie looks over at me: "Welcome to your new home … for the summer."

"Why thank you, sir." I smile back. "Are you going to help me with my luggage or make me do it myself again?" I chuckle.

"I got to get the door for my hottie, so use those muscles." He runs up to the door and unlocks it.

I peel my legs back from the sticky leather, praying my skin hasn't melted to it. Why anyone would have black leather seats is beyond me. The red splotches where my legs were glued to the seat start to throb once I stand up. I creak open the trunk and struggle as I pull my suitcases out, being certain not to scratch the dragon.

"Be careful of the paint!" I hear Dougie yell.

"I am. That's why it's taking me so long!" I huff as I heave my first suitcase out of the trunk.

"Well, hurry up. I don't want all this heat to get into the house."

I finally manage to get the second seventy-pound suitcase out of the trunk and onto the driveway. These were a lot easier getting into the trunk than out. Trying to wheel two suitcases up a wobbly driveway at 110 pounds is not an easy task. When I get to the door, Dougie whips it open and proceeds through the hallway to the television. *I guess I'm on my own with the suitcases now too.* I haul the suitcases inside and leave them by the bottom of the front staircase, which is thankfully five feet from the front door. I take a deep breath; this is a new chapter for me. I'm with the man "olive," and now we will get to see each other every day. I can't help but let my smile brighten my face.

I brush away the feeling of disappointment that he didn't make a big deal about my being here. Guys just don't think like that. Plus, I know sports are really important to a lot of guys. Probably as important as my studies are to me.

I join Dougie on the couch. He's already sipping a beer with his feet up on the coffee table, watching sports. I kick off my shoes and put my feet up on the couch as I curl up next to him. "Thank you for letting me stay here with you. It means a lot to me, Dougie." I nestle in close to his neck.

"Of course, that's what you do for the people you care about." He hands me a beer. I crack it open, not sure why we're drinking beer at one in the afternoon, but why not? We are celebrating a new chapter. "So, have you thought anymore about picking up a job? There is a restaurant up the street, about a ten-minute walk away, that needs waitresses. You should try for a job there."

"I haven't really had a chance to think about it." My cafeteria job on campus ended with the semester's end. "But maybe I'll head over there later today or tomorrow and see if they want me."

"I'm sure they'll take you. They want hot people working to draw in more people. They'd be stupid not to take you. I'll even drive you over there to apply, but we'll have to wait till tomorrow. I know the manager."

"That works for me. So what are your hours for the summer?"

"The same as always. Monday through Friday, from eight in the morning to six at night. That's the life of construction. I'm just lucky to have a job since most of the guys Chaz and I usually work with have been laid off."

What do I say in response? I'm at a loss for words. Thankfully, Doug continues his thought process.

"Thursdays after work, the guys and I have a work outing for happy hour at the restaurant up the street, the one I want you to work at. You can be our waitress!" The excitement in his voice booms. "Because then I don't have to tip!"

"Oh, so you think you won't have to tip me, huh?" I laugh. "Well, I guess me living here will make up for that."

"It better. I may need some help paying for the extra bills around the house here. I'm sure my utility and food bills will go up. But we can work that out once you start working."

"I guess I really hadn't even thought about that. Of course, I'll pay my share of the bills." I take a bigger swig of beer. The gulp hurts my throat. *Why didn't I think about bills? Of course he'll need me to pitch in money for them. How else would he be able to afford his place?*

"Like I said, I'll take you down to the restaurant tomorrow, and we can get you hooked up there."

I can't quite put my finger on it, but it feels like there is awkwardness in the air tonight. I'm not sure what Dougie's expectations are for me living here, and I guess I never really asked him. I assumed it would be like dorm living, with each of us in our own bedrooms and a shared space. I take another bigger gulp than normal of my beer. The more I drink, the less scary it feels. *Love does not seek its own way.*

A shiver runs down my spine as I awake to dancing light from the TV bouncing around the walls. *Where am I?* Panic momentarily consumes me as my brain searches for understanding. Once the confusion wears off, I remember I'm at Dougie's. He must have gone up to bed because he isn't curled up next to me on the couch anymore. I rub my eyes to try and clear the sleepiness from my vision. I shut off the TV to go upstairs, but my suitcases are still camped at the bottom of the staircase. I debate whether to haul them upstairs and dig out my comforter but opt to go back to the couch instead. In the dark, I reach for Dougie's gray fuzzy blanket from where he was sitting. I wrap myself up like a burrito and try to get comfortable as thoughts start further disrupting my sleep.

How much are these bills going to be every month? What if I can't afford to live here? What did I do by moving in with him without knowing any of this? Should I have moved back to my parent's home and faced the terror of going through their stuff?

When they passed away, their life insurance policies took care of the bills for their small home, so it is now mine, but I'm not allowed, per their wills, to touch a penny more of money until I complete college. I never told Dougie that my parent's house was now mine; in fact, I never told anyone, not even Melanie. I haven't been home since their funerals. I just can't bear to open the door without Mom baking cookies or without Dad reading his almanac by the front window, half-sleeping in his brown recliner. I'm really lucky Bob agreed to keep an eye on the house for me.

Shaking my head, I kick the painful thoughts from my mind and focus on my current home before drifting into a dark sleep. Dougie's clock continues to sing me into oblivion with "tick-tock, tick-tock …"

The smell of fresh coffee floats into the living room. I open my eyes to see the light shining in through the drawn curtains, warming my face. I hear Dougie clanking coffee cups in the kitchen.

Summoning the energy to get off the couch, I wobble over to the kitchen. The stove clock says it's 10:15 a.m. "Wow, I didn't realize it was already so late. Morning, sweetie." I wrap my arms around him and push my face into his back. He clearly hasn't showered yet, as the smell of his sweat sticks to my nose.

"Morning. I didn't want to wake you. And since you were drooling, I figured you were still in a deep sleep."

"I was drooling?" I'm mortified.

"Yeah, so I let you be. No biggie though. Want a cup of coffee? I figured we can head over to the restaurant at about two o'clock for you to get a job."

"Yes on the coffee, and sounds good about the job." I join him at the table for two in the kitchen, and we drink our coffee in silence as he reads the paper. It's cute he still reads an actual paper. He is so mature.

My head pounds from all the beer I consumed last night, so the silence is welcomed with open arms. I really need to stop trying to keep up with him. I hate beer.

After my shower, we head over to the restaurant. It is about a seven-minute drive, which probably equates to a fifteen- to twenty-minute walk. When we walk in, most of the staff shout hello to Dougie. He must be somewhat popular here.

I trail two steps behind Dougie up to a tall, scrawny, pale guy in his thirties. The guy has bulging blue eyes, bushy brown carpet hair on his head, big lips, crooked teeth, and a chicken pox scar right under his right eye. He looks like a weasel. Dougie introduces Brian and me, calling me his woman. Butterflies flutter briefly in my stomach at hearing those words from his mouth.

They excuse themselves from me and disappear into the back of the kitchen, out of my sight. I'm left standing here, looking around at the small setup. They have a bar that looks to fit fifteen people comfortably, and maybe around twenty tables, six of them booths. I pass the time by counting the chairs. I don't want to look weird, but I'm not sure if I should sit down or just stand here. A few minutes later, Brian and Dougie return to the front. Dougie's grin is contagious.

Weasel puts out his hand in front of me, so I shake it. He offers me a job!

"Welcome to the team. I'm giving you this job because Dougie strong-armed me into it. You can start ASAP as we just lost one of our waitresses."

I start tomorrow. My schedule will be six in the morning until three in the afternoon Monday through Wednesday, four to whenever I get cut on Thursdays, Fridays six until two, and potentially an occasional Saturday shift to be determined. Dougie requested I be allowed to work the evening shift on Thursdays since that is when he usually hangs out here. Of course, that is because my Dougie just wants to see me all the time. My heart bounces with joy. The uniform is tight black pants and a white oxford button-up short-sleeve polo. I will get the apron tomorrow when I arrive.

We take a seat at the bar, and Dougie places an order for two burgers with fries. Dougie tells me that he told Brian I had serving experience in the past, so I would start waiting tables next week after a quick training. This is concerning because I don't actually know how to serve, but how hard can it be? Ask people what they want to eat and bring the order to them. I think I'll be quite good at this. We eat a quick lunch, and I meet some of the staff before we leave.

Our trip into town after lunch to the local store proves a success; I find a fitted white oxford shirt in the little boy's section and some stretchy black pants in the young female section. My new work outfit is lying on the ground next to the mattress. I'm not sure if I'm more nervous or more excited. I guess Sundays are slower for the restaurant, so it should be easy to get mostly trained tomorrow.

The spare bedroom is quite small but comfortable. The mattress is on the ground against the far wall and across from the only window in the room. Dougie told me I could sleep with him in the king-size bed, but I thought it would be better for me to sleep alone since I have to go to work and train tomorrow. Plus, I don't know if I am ready to sleep in the same bed with him; I've only been in one other relationship—if it can even be called a relationship. That didn't grow past holding hands. Maybe in a few weeks, I'll be ready to fall asleep under the same covers as a man, but only time will tell.

I crawl beneath the mattress sheets and turn off the lights. The top sheets slightly stick to my body because of the humidity. My eyes rest upon the window, which has no shades. The moon's light spreads across my face as the stars sparkle in the darkness of the night. I'm really happy to be somewhere where I can see the stars sparkle like diamonds in the darkness. At school, there was too much light pollution to see more than a couple stars. Everything has changed so much in the past year.

My throat tightens as I remember my life a year ago. I had just graduated high school. My parents were so proud of me. We spent my last summer at home playing board games, watching movies, and talking about my future. My mom had a gracefulness about her presence ... I could tell her anything and everything. My father was his usual self, cracking jokes and just enjoying life. They were so proud of me for getting into college and even earning some academic scholarships.

My eyes bounce from a dull star to the really bright star that seems to twinkle down at me. I hope my parents are out there, watching over me. *What would they think of me now?* I finished my first year of college with passing grades, have a summer job, and met a man who might just be my prince charming. Dad would be impressed Dougie has his own place. Mom would be surprised he has it decorated so beautifully. The star blurs in the distance as my eyes surrender to tears. What I wouldn't give to hug them, to feel their unconditional love.

True love must grow into what my parents had after years of getting to know one another. Dougie and I are in "olive," but I'm not sure there is any love like the one between a parent and a child.

"Momma and Daddy, if you can hear me, I love you. Don't worry about me. Dougie, he is going to take care of me."

I close my flooding eyes and admit defeat to the grieving wounds tearing at my heart. Tomorrow will be a new day, a new chapter. "Goodnight," I whisper into the silence.

CHAPTER FOURTEEN

Sara Olivia Scott

The alarm clock squeals from across the room, forcing me to crawl off the mattress and shut it off. Five o'clock has come too early. I dress in my serving outfit and go to the bathroom to apply some makeup. Seeing the circles under my eyes, I brush on another layer of mascara to accentuate my eyes and take the focus off the dark circles beneath them.

Dougie is still sleeping, so I quietly sneak down the stairs. Pulling a sweatshirt over my outfit, I'm ready to see how quick this walk really is. I quickly grab the key Dougie made for me and tuck it safely in my pocket. It's chilly outside, enough to make me shiver when the air brushes my warm face. That is one thing about Minnesota summers: days can be hot and humid while nights and early mornings can be brisk. I hustle alongside the road through the residential neighborhood.

There are only ten other townhouses in the same neighborhood as Dougie's, and then there's a long stretch of wooded, undeveloped land on either side of the neighborhood. I quickly get through the neighborhood and reach the main roadway, a somewhat untraveled highway. It's a winding road with tall oaks and pines hugging the pavement. I walk on the side of the road opposite traffic with my hands in my hoodie's pocket. I think I'm going to grow to like this walk ... time to just float in the quiet and be one with nature. I've grown familiar with my alone time, which I assume will be rare now that I'm living with Dougie.

I can hear the wind rustle the leaves. The cold hair makes my nose tickle. Nature's music sprinkles some peace in my soul.

Twenty minutes later, I arrive at the restaurant. I check my phone. I'm still about fifteen minutes early; I wasn't sure how long the walk would take and didn't want to be late. I meet Stephanie as soon as I walk in through the doors of the restaurant. She's the main waitress at the restaurant; she's been doing this job for years. Her uniform is so tight her butt and chest look like they could burst out at any moment. I am acutely aware of my eyes focusing on her clothing.

"You'll learn that the tighter and sexier the clothing, the better the tips. Don't worry, I'm the one training you today."

I force a small smile. I'm not really into wearing clothing that accentuates intimate parts of my body. "I guess that makes sense."

"Don't worry, hun. You'll get used to things quickly. The job itself, waiting on people, is easy. Just smile, flirt with the men, compliment the women, and don't piss off the manager, and you'll be good to go. Follow me. I'll show you the break room so you can hang up your coat and purse."

"I met the manager. My boyfriend is friends with him. He seems nice."

"Like I said, hun, as long as you don't piss him off. Sure, he's sweet on the outside. If he thinks you're hot, he is nice, but if you ever play into his attraction, you've already ruined your job here. Don't repeat this, but this girl, Michelle, used to work here. She was young and pretty like you. She was just dumb." Stephanie looks around and then whispers, "One night after work, she went home with him. She came into work the next day bragging about it, like she would get special treatment or something. I shook my head because I knew better. As soon as Brian came into the place, he expected Michelle to be perfect and serve not only the customers' every need but his as well. And I mean *every* need. She got fired last week for 'failure to obey rules' by none other than Brian. Like I said, be careful. Oh, and I never told you nothing." She looks around again to make sure no one heard our conversation. I opt to just listen.

"Well, here's the room. Not much to it. Shove your coat into one of the lockers and hide your purse behind it. May not be a bad idea to keep your personal money and phone in your apron pocket. Ya know, sticky fingers seem to be everywhere here."

"Yeah. Thanks. About that Michelle—"

"SHH! Keep your voice down. Most of the gals here have big mouths. Like I said, we never had this conversation."

"Well, my boyfriend is really good friends with Brian, the manager, so I don't think I'll have any problems like … you know." I try to reassure myself as I shove my small purse into the back of the beat-up gray aluminum lockers.

"Yeah, sure, hun. Like I said, be careful. That little man is kind of a snake. Hurry up so we can get you clocked in. You don't want to clock in a minute late with him around."

The training portion of the job is simple. Get people's orders, ring the order into the computer, pick up the food from the kitchen, and deliver the food. Pick up drinks from the bar.

Stephanie is nice. I can tell I'm going to like working with her. She was right; most of the other females here are blonde bimbos. I will get to work with Brian because he typically works mornings during the week with an evening shift on Thursday—pretty much my schedule. The confidence I had in having him as my manager is lessening slightly after my conversation with Stephanie, but I think I'll be okay since Dougie is my man.

My walk home is about twenty minutes. I'm just grateful the wind is on my back. I don't have any tips yet, but that will come shortly. I'm so happy to have another girl I can talk with. Too bad Stephanie and I won't work together more often, but I'm happy she still works there because our paths are bound to cross.

As soon as I walk through the front door, I see Dougie kicking off his shoes. I hear him over my shoulder as I close the door behind me.

"Long day, sweetie? Mine sure was. I had to work with some pricks. My boss was riding my ass all day. Not to mention, they are forcing us to leave work early because business is slower than usual." Dougie has been working overtime on Sundays for the last couple of weeks since so many of the regulars were laid off. Now his job has gone to the other extreme, forcing him to leave early. I'm so thankful I'm not in the construction business.

"Yeah, my day was long, but it was definitely fun. Sorry your day was so crummy. What do you want to do for dinner? I can make us some sandwiches," I offer, hoping to make his day better.

"We don't have any stuff for sandwiches. You going to go get something?" he grumbles as he opens the fridge and grabs a beer.

"I can," I offer.

"I'm sorry. Olive juice, sweetie. I'm just tired. I'm fine with beer and a pizza. You make any cash today for us to get some pizza?"

"No. I don't get to keep any of the tips until my first day actually serving on my own, which is Thursday. I can order some pizza and put it on my credit card if you want pizza." I smile.

"Yeah, do that. I could use a good, greasy slice of pizza."

I brush away the monotony of our interaction. He is having a bad day, and I'm drained from all the learning. Thank goodness for ordering pizza via an app, as I'm talked out.

The pizza arrives forty-five minutes later. We both enjoy a beer and the artery-clogging heavenly treat. I retreat to the guestroom after dinner to get an early night's sleep. I have a big couple of days ahead of me. Dougie decides to fall asleep on the couch watching television, which is fine by me because I'm still not ready to share sheets with him. I'm also very grateful he hasn't asked. *Love does not behave itself inappropriately.*

The rest of the week goes by quickly. Tuesday and Wednesday, I follow Stephanie around the restaurant and practice using the computer system. Each night I come home to find Dougie in a crummy mood because work was long and arduous. We spend both evenings cuddling on the couch while the television plays mindless shows. Hopefully, things will get better at his job so he can relax at home instead of worrying about money.

Dougie is awake before I leave this morning. He sends me off to work with a kiss. The morning is crisp and cool as I start out on my walk. It feels good to inhale the fresh air since it will likely be a toasty seventy degrees by noon. Tonight is going to be my first night of actual waitressing. I have one last morning of training with Stephanie today, and my evening shift starts tonight with Brian managing. I get to have real customers all on my own.

Brian is happy when I tell him that I am available to work a double today because they really want me to start taking my own tables tonight. Even though I'm starting out on his good side, my nerves are on edge because I'm still nervous regarding what Stephanie told me about him.

The morning flies by. Stephanie wishes me luck at four o'clock when she leaves. I am all on my own now. Well, there were a few other gals working, but none of whom I really feel the desire to know personally.

A short blonde I haven't met yet bounces up to me in a shirt that is literally two sizes too small and very low-cut. "Hi, I'm Ashley. I hear you are Dougie's girlfriend."

"Hi. Yeah, I am."

"Well, I'm pissed you're going to be getting him in your section tonight because his group of boys were my best tippers. You better treat them nicely. Don't worry, you can make it up to me and hook me up with his friend Chaz."

"Well, I'll see what I can do. Sorry I'm taking that group. It was Dougie's idea I work here."

I feel her eyes looking me up and down. "Yeah, I bet."

She seems delightful. Hopefully, this isn't indicative of Thursday nights to come.

"Girls, come here for our pre-dinner meeting. I want you all to meet the new gal, Sara. Don't pick on her too much. Her boyfriend is our good boy Dougie."

I squirm as I see everyone's eyes on me. I can feel the judgmental energy directed my way. I try to smile in the most non-threatening manner possible, if that's even a thing.

"Girls, I want us to start upselling the new beer. We aren't meeting quotas, and the district manager is chewing my ass and handing it back to me. I'm not going to deal with this. Use your ta-tas or whatever sales talent you have and get those people to buy the beer. If you aren't making the quotas, I'm taking some of your tips. There, how's that for motivation. Now get to work. Oh, hey, Sara, come and see me a sec."

I walk over to Brian, and he motions for me to follow him to his office.

"Yes, sir?"

"I like that—calling me sir. Keep it up. Look, you got this job because Dougie and I go way back. I know Stephanie was training you in this week, but do you feel ready to get out there and make us some money?"

"Yeah. I think so."

"Good. Don't mess up. 'Cause I'll report you back to Dougie." He gives me a crooked eerie smile.

"Ha-ha!" I say in an exaggerated tone of voice. "I'll try not to, sir." Being in a room alone with this man is uncomfortable. I think I can see what Stephanie was talking about.

I come out of Brian's office to find two of my five-table section already seated. I greet both groups, ring in their orders, and deliver their food with a smile. My tight pants and tight oxford shirt are looser than the rest of the waitresses', but my customers still seem to like me. I'm reassured of my skills and relieved to find out one of the old men at my tables told Brian it was a good thing they had a new face in here.

Now that I'm getting the hang of it all, this waitressing thing is much easier than I anticipated. I'm finally getting tips on top of my $6.75 base wage (which is paid to me biweekly). Let the money roll in.

The rest of the evening is spent running from table to table with drinks and food. I'm getting slightly overwhelmed when Dougie shows up with some of his buds, most of whom I've never met before. I know Chaz, but then there are Brendon, Ian, Mike, and Joey. I can feel Ashley's eyes piercing my back as I seat the men.

Dougie has some ratty work clothes on and a smudge of dirt across his face. He looks cute in a rough way, like a hardworking man. I know my dimples are peeking through as I flash him a smile. With a small head bob, he winks at me before seating himself in my section. Not wanting to provide any of my customers bad service, I walk over to Dougie and greet him.

"Why hello, sir, welcome to my section. What can I get for you this evening?"

"Sweetie pie, I could use a Corona with two limes and some nachos right away. Why don't you get that cute behind over to that bar there and fetch me my food." I can hear his playfulness.

With a joking backhand tap to his shoulder, I whisper, "You be nice, or I'll spit in your nachos, mister." I chuckle at my server humor before I go to the machine to punch in his order. Just as I'm at the screen, typing in Corona and nachos, Brian sneaks up on me, startling me.

"Now you make sure you take care of my best man Doug out there, little lady. I don't want him getting bad service with a new waitress and whatnot." His hot breath in my ear pulls goosebumps from deep within my skin.

"Ha-ha. I'm going to give him the best service."

"You'd better. You can give Doug your employee discount of 50 percent off unless you decide to get a meal yourself. If you choose not to eat tonight, you can give the discount to him. Just don't go giving two discounts out, lady."

I do the I-understand-that's-awesome head nod as he walks away, and I finish typing in Dougie's order under "employee meal." I can just eat when I get home. I don't even get my server's book back into my apron pocket before the bartender hollers over to me that Dougie's drink is ready. They sure don't waste time here.

I collect the beer and deliver it to Dougie. I think it's cute he asks for two limes versus one. I like learning these little things about him. By the time I get back to the table, a few more of his friends are there. He introduces me to each of them and advises that I will be taking good care of them from now on because I'm his girl. Their eyes critique me as they wander from my face down and back up to my face. I push judgment from my mind because I know these people are important to Dougie.

I take their orders with an obligatory smile and go back to the computer to punch in their requests. By the time I am done typing in the last order, my light (number 13) comes on, indicating one of my food orders is up. I bring Dougie his nachos after I throw a few extra scoops of cheese on top. He is clearly pleased with my "extra" service.

Dougie shoots me glances as I wait on other tables. He winks at me or gives me a half smile, which ends up with me biting my lower lip to keep from giggling while I take strangers' orders. I see Ashley walk past the men multiple times, trying to flirt them all up, including Dougie. Cute Dougie merely entertains her with his laughs at her stupid comments. I know he is really looking at me. I remind myself that *love does not envy.*

Every time I walk over to their table, he puts his hand on my butt and proclaims he can't keep himself from doing it. Normally, I wouldn't allow him to put his hand on my butt, but I don't want to embarrass him in front of his guys, so I just smile and try to nonchalantly step out of his reach. I've never really seen this side of Dougie. He's very touchy-feely with all these people around. I also don't think he has ever touched my butt before.

The night goes by quickly. I have many more tables, but I always keep an eye on Dougie. He's already had five beers and is getting a little loud. I'm concerned because he's getting somewhat aggressive playing darts with his buddy. Trying to be discreet, I tug on his arm and whisper, "Sweetie, are you drunk?"

"WHAT?" he yells. "No, I'm not drunk, miss THANG. I want another beer, woman," he yells at me with a chuckle.

I feel uncomfortable. Is he kidding or being serious? His face has a snicker, but his eyes are cold. Not wanting to make this anymore awkward, I turn to get him a beer. Before I can take a step, I feel his hand slap my butt. The noise draws his entire table's attention. I ignore the sting and shoo his hand away without turning around to see their eyes. My eyes immediately want to fill with water, but I push that response down—way down. Why do men get so testosterone-y when they drink? Note to self: have a talk with him when he is sober.

I reluctantly bring Dougie his last beer for the evening. I don't even get a thank-you. *Is he upset with me or just too occupied with his friends to notice I set it down?* I ignore the ongoing stinging in my butt from his friendly butt slap. Maybe I need to just loosen up a bit. I keep an eye on him as he milks the bottle for the next hour. At 11:30 p.m., he and his friends get up to leave.

"I'll see you home." His voice is void of emotion and his speech slightly slurred.

I notice Dougie forgot to pay his tab when I collect the bills from the table. I don't have the heart to tell him he forgot to leave money, so I'll just pay his tab. Surprisingly, his tab takes up most of my tips from the evening. But OLIVE JUICE him, so why wouldn't I help him enjoy a carefree night?

I'm the first server "cut" from the floor, aka allowed to clean up my section of tables and do my side work before I can leave for the night. By the time I finish rolling what seems like a hundred silverware sets, mopping the floors, re-stocking the cooler, and cleaning the food prep area, I'm allowed to clock out … at 12:45 a.m.

Exhausted and sore from all the running around I did today, I pull on my neon pink rain jacket to walk home. It is chilly outside now that the sun has gone down. I never walked home so late at night when it was dark out, and to be honest, I'm a bit scared knowing it will take about twenty minutes of walking down the windy road with the tree branches clanking and the leaves whistling.

I hear a bark in the distance. Shivers race up my spine. *Is that a dog or a wolf? Can coyotes bark?* The shivers crawl up my neck and penetrate my body with fear. My walk turns into a giant's speed walk, which for me is a run. I make it home fifteen minutes later, safe behind Dougie's closed door. Exhaling, I feel the fear seep from my pores.

The television flickers. I meander down the hall to find Dougie with another beer in his hand, half-passed out.

"It's about time. Where you been?" His voice is husky, like he's been sleeping for hours.

"I've been at work, silly. It took forever to clean up after my shift." Now probably isn't the time to share with him that I didn't appreciate the slap on my rear. I don't even feel it anymore. "I think I'm going to head up to bed since I have to get up early for my shift tomorrow." I walk over and bend down to give him a kiss. I can't put my finger on it, but his eyes look different again, like they did earlier. Not scary, but cold … distant. "Everything okay?"

"Why wouldn't it be? It's not like I'm drunk or anything." His voice carries a twinge of anger in it but appears mostly sarcastic.

"I'm sorry, sweetie. I was just getting worried. I care about you a lot and get worried something could happen to you. I didn't ask if you were drunk to be mean. I asked because I wouldn't want you to get in a car accident. Olive juice, sweetie. Olive juice. You know that." I attempt to mend his hurt feelings. *What did I do that was so wrong? I don't think I did anything wrong.*

"Well, it just cut me deep and unmasculated—no, demasculated— whatever. It made me look like an idiot in front of my guys. You can't be saying things like that when I'm with my boys. You need to chill and be a cute waitress, not my mom." His eyes soften as the anger diminishes.

"I'm sorry. I won't do that again." I wrap my arms around him. *Does he care about them more than me?* He doesn't say anything more, so I get up and go upstairs to get ready for bed. I've never seen Dougie this way, exuding sadness like he has been deeply hurt. *How could he think I was trying to mother him when I was just a concerned girlfriend?* I give up trying to understand a man's brain and crawl into bed.

Sleep quickly falls upon me as my aching calves spread to my heels and thighs. Tomorrow morning will come quickly.

CHAPTER FIFTEEN

Sara Olivia Scott

A loud beeping rips me from my sleep as my eyes search for the disruptive intruder. My eyes fall upon my alarm clock, which shows the time: 6:37 a.m. CRAP! I slept through the alarm or hit snooze in my sleep! I was supposed to be up twenty minutes ago. There is no time for me to shower. I force my hair into a messy bun and yank on my wrinkled clothes. Thank goodness they are tighter than what I usually wear because the tightness will iron out the wrinkles on its own, hopefully.

I dart out the door and hustle to work. The cool air swirls around me as I attempt to dab some eye shadow on while speed walking. I try combing on my mascara as I take steady, quick steps. I feel the brush slip and hit my eyebrow. Ugh. This is not the way I wanted to start out my Friday. I rub at my eyebrow and then check my hand to make sure there is a black smudge confirming I aimed correctly, making contact with the damaged zone. Success.

I get to the restaurant just in time. I clock in with one minute to spare. I knew the day would be *off* since everything about this day so far has been *off*. I keep getting confused on small things, like where we keep the OJ and what the table numbers are. I can't seem to focus and keep things straight. I know my body is still exhausted from a stressful week and a very long day and night yesterday, but I keep treading through the minutes. Thankfully, Brian doesn't seem to notice my inability to stay focused.

Lunch is busier than I hoped. I only have time to eat a few bites of the salad I made myself because Brian seated my section with new guests. *I suppose it's for the best he isn't letting me eat; Dougie did say I could drop a few pounds.* I won't be able to get out of here anytime before two o'clock. Mental sigh. The minutes drag by as I make little slip-ups here and there on orders. Luckily, no one seems to notice but me. Four thirty rolls around, and I'm finally cut from the floor. I hurry through my side work and rush through rolling my share of silverware. Just as I'm about to walk out the door with a hazy day behind me, my phone beeps with a text: "Wanna grab me a chzburgr with what I like?"

I give myself an imaginary head bang before realizing maybe this will help smooth things over with Dougie. We haven't really had a chance to find closure on our talk about yesterday yet, so this may be a good opportunity to make sure we are okay. My calves are on fire from being on my feet the entire day. Without allowing myself to give into my crying calves, I turn around to input my "employee" cheeseburger order. *What temperature does he like his burger? Does he like toppings?* Too tired to overthink, I go with a standard burger: medium-well with American cheese and the typical toppings of lettuce, tomato, and onion. Ten minutes slowly creep by before I hear my order is ready to go. I grab the burger and head home. I walk faster than my body prefers so that Dougie's sandwich doesn't get cold. This can be my peace offering for yesterday's misunderstanding.

I feel my body shutting down from pure exhaustion. Not willing to allow myself to relax, I walk faster. The faster I walk, the less the aching in my calves radiates up my legs. I just need to get this sandwich home before I can crash on my bed for a long-awaited and much-needed nap.

I finally get into our development, and I feel my spirit lighten knowing my bed is only three minutes away. Two minutes away. One minute away. Here. I open the front door and find Dougie waiting in the kitchen for his food. I'm too fatigued to even think about eating. My appetite is sleeping like the rest of my body should be. I give Dougie a quick kiss hello.

As I lean in, I smell alcohol on his breath. "Have you been drinking already?" I laugh.

"Rough day. What's the big deal?" His answer is short and defensive.

"I'm just kidding around. I could use a beer, but I'm pretty sure I'll fall asleep before I even get it opened." I recall last night …

I quickly hand him my peace offering and turn to head upstairs. "I need a nap, sweetie. Enjoy your burger." Probably best to let him be for a bit. I'm too tired to have a real discussion.

"WAIT!" I hear him holler just as I'm about to climb the stairs. At least he hollered before I took the first few steps; I would hate to waste any bit of energy, as my body is about to shut down. I turn around and walk the few steps back to meet him in the hallway. We stand under the awning that leads into the kitchen.

"Yeah?" A yawn escapes my mouth. I feel like a lion as I tilt my head back and let the yawn take over. Another strong odor of alcohol from his breath stings my nostrils.

"What the heck is this crap? Are you freaking kidding me? I asked for a cheeseburger with real cheese. Not this!" He holds the opened to-go box in front of me steady in his hands. "Did you intentionally do this?" His voice gets louder. I swear his eyes darken with every word.

Huh? "It's a burger." *I'm so confused. Why is he so mad?*

"You gave me American cheese? That's not burger cheese! Where the hell is my cheddar? Are you seriously so stupid you can't even get me a burger without messing it up? You intentionally tryin' to mess with me just because you're tryin' to lose weight? Then you interrogate me for drinking a frickin' beer! Well, excuse me if I want a beer after a hard day at work, at work providing for YOU!"

"Sorry?" My tone comes out incorrectly. I meant it more as a question, but it comes out sarcastic. My tone echoes in my ears. Before I can correct myself, his left arm rises and shoots sideways in slow motion. I'm unable to react, frozen in place. His fist smashes against my jaw and eye, thrashing my head to the left with a snap. The force pushes me back a couple of steps. I attempt to balance myself but fail to do so. My legs become tangled noodles. My body slumps backwards out of my control until my back hits the floor, and my head follows with a loud THUNK. The skin on my face burns like alcohol on an open cut. The burning causes my eyes to immediately fill with tears. Dizziness overwhelms me. Reality feels speckled, like static on a radio.

Dougie drops his boxed burger on the ground beside me. He nonchalantly tosses his car keys into my lap with the same left hand.

"If you actually care about me, you'll go buy me the correct cheese and make me the food I deserve."

I don't understand. The pain crawls into my jaw, my cheekbone, and my ear. The crawling keeps spreading, now around my ear to the back of my head. I search, I search Dougie, I search the entryway, I search for anything that will help me understand what is happening. I'm distracted by my face's heartbeat … THUD … THUD … I'm deafened to the world around me. Everything is static: the noise, my sight, my sensations, the taste in my mouth—only static.

As I search the static around me, my eyes gaze down on the keys sitting in my lap. The keys are all I can focus on. They don't move. They stay still in my lap as the static consumes everything else around me. Keys mean car. Car means store. Store means cheese. Cheddar, not

American. Static distracts me again. My face. It aches. I so badly want to hold it in my hands, but I'm afraid to acknowledge I'm hurt.

The static gets louder. *Purgatory? No, I'm here. I'm alive.* I try to stand up but fail. I look behind me to see Dougie flip on the television in the den as his shadow leaves me. *When did he walk away from me? How long have I been lying here?* Warm tears start to blur my vision again, making the static louder.

I push through the pixelated picture of my legs lying in the hallway. I make my noodles lift me up, so I'm standing against the wall. The door is five feet away. I look down at my legs and command that they move. I watch as I put one foot in front of the other. *I'm controlling a foreign body. I'm robotic.*

Closing it softly behind me, I manage to walk out the front door. My legs, still wobbling, proceed toward the car. There is less static out here. I can hear my unsteady breathing. I tell my brain to focus. *Car, store, cheese. Car, store, cheese.*

I slide into Dougie's seat and turn the ignition. The static is back. It's so loud in here. It is deafening. Blinding. *Why is everything so fuzzy?* I tilt my head from side to side; I get dizzier, so I stop. I watch my hand pull the gear changer into reverse. Everything is blurry. Every aspect of my life, every movement, is in slow motion. I feel the hot, steamy salt trickle down my cheekbone … further, further, until it loops under my chin. The red dragon reaches the side road. I push on the accelerator to try and fast-forward out of the static that is following me. *Hurry, hurry, hurry. Car, store, cheese.*

I see a splotch of red out of the corner of my right eye. *Why do I see red?* My flooding eyes begin to empty, mixing in with the red invader. *Who is pushing down my right eyelid? What is forcing it shut?* I can barely see through the slit in my right eye; the picture is small and blurry. I don't know how I got here, but I'm now on the freeway. The freeway means I'm closer to the store. *Store, cheese.* I'm on autopilot. My eyes must know where I'm going. My mind is almost blank as the static keeps stealing my thoughts. Almost blank. *Store, cheese.*

I see the store three exits up. *Store, cheese.* I hear a horn trying to break through the static. I can feel the horn shoot through the static. I feel the horn close by, but I can't find my way out of the static.

My jaw is tight. My skin burns. I don't know whose body I'm in, but it's a struggle getting it to move, to feel, to be present. The static is like quicksand; I feel myself sinking deeper into it. The horn tries to pierce through again but can't find its way to me.

A bright flash of white flickers in the rearview, mirror puncturing this other dimension. Suddenly, a loudspeaker arouses my ears: "Pull over!" Pull over? This time, the noise finds me through the static. I look in the rearview mirror and see a cop with his lights on; he's right on my rear bumper. I watch my hand turn on the right turn signal as my right foot presses on the brake. Whose body am I in?

I catch a glimpse of what appears to be my face in the rearview mirror as I slowly awaken from this fog. I hear my body take a quick burst of air. I hold it tightly in my lungs until it hurts. My right eye is swollen and turning blue. *Why is it turning blue?* Salt trails down my face. A pink line is colored on my right cheek. My right eyebrow has an half-inch laceration. I don't recognize the girl in the mirror. *It's not me, is it?* The lights flickering in the mirror distract me from the face staring back at me.

I take my hair out of my ponytail and strategically arrange my long bangs over the right side of my face. My left forearm dries the left side of my face. I steal a quick glance in the rearview mirror. I don't see the cop anywhere.

My eyes are suddenly drawn to my window. He is bent over, looking in at me. I jump enough in my seat that the seatbelt's safety locks, holding me in place. I never saw him leave his squad car. *How long has he been here?*

"Ma'am, please roll down the window and then put your hands on the steering wheel," he says through the closed window.

I listen. I roll down the left window all the way and then put my left hand back on the wheel right next to my right hand. My hands are at twelve o'clock, side by side, together. I watch my still hands, avoiding him.

"Ma'am, I'm going to need your license and registration for this vehicle. Do you know why I pulled you over?"

His voice is warm but stern.

"No … no." I hear my own words fall from my lips in a whisper. "I … I'm sorry. I don't know where the registration is, but here is my driver's license." I pull it out of my apron, which I never got around to taking off. I fumble through my wallet, trying to find my license. "This is my boyfriend's car. I'm getting cheese. I got the wrong cheese. I need to get ch … cheddar. American isn't burger cheese." My voice trails off.

My eyes are glued to my shaky left hand holding my driver's license, reaching out for him. *Why is my hand wavering so much? Is it because this is the first time I've ever been pulled over by a cop? Is it because I'm not even entirely sure how I ended up here, driving Dougie's beloved car, going to a store I have only passed once?* He takes my license and my hand resumes its place on the wheel.

"Ma'am, I'm going to need you to look at me." His voice envelops me.

He's a cop. I better listen. I slowly turn my head without lifting it. My left eye rolls up to meet his eyes without moving my head any further. "Am I being ar … arrested?" I hear my voice trembling. *Why am I trembling? What is wrong with me? Whose voice is it echoing in my ears? My voice doesn't quiver.*

"Ma'am, I need to see your entire face. I need you to look at me. And no, you aren't going to be arrested. You ran a red light, so that is why I pulled you over." Again, his voice is warm but insistent on me showing him my face.

What will he think? I don't want to get in trouble. I don't want Dougie to get in trouble either. My right hand shakily and slowly pulls back strands of hair, tucking them behind my ear. Not knowing what to do other than listen to his orders, I look up at him. My right eye is cemented shut as my left eye begins to water as I look at him. His badge reads "Officer Kipton Pierre." He's just over six feet tall with short brown hair, a five o'clock shadow, and warm green hazel eyes. He feels like honey. Warm and comforting. Something safe. Warm honey.

A momentary peace sweeps through me as our eyes embrace. I feel naked, safe for just a moment. One blink, and the connection is severed; it's as if it never happened.

"Are ... are you okay, ma'am?"

Why is he so concerned? He couldn't actually see ...

I nod yes.

"Did someone do this to you? Did someone hurt you?"

Hurt you. The words linger in my ears and stay heavy in my chest. I feel jumbled as I begin to remember. No one hurt me. I got the wrong cheese, and my sarcasm provoked Dougie. If he was sarcastic to me like I was to him, I probably would have been upset too. *Love is not provoked.* I'm not sure what that means, but I think I loved wrong. I provoked him. My head is swirling too much for me to focus on the words from Corinthians. I realize I got lost in my own thoughts as he is just staring at me.

I nod "no" for fear my voice will quiver too much. A hot droplet skips down my left cheek and onto my shirt. I avoid eye contact and rest my eyes on my hands. My knuckles are white from gripping the wheel for my life. If I get a ticket … if they take this car away, Dougie will never forgive me. I can hear the officer breathing steadily; he is unchanged from the same crouched position he was holding two minutes ago.

"You said this is your boyfriend's vehicle? And you have permission to drive this?"

"Yes, yes. I'm getting him cheddar cheese." I look straight ahead at the grocery store, where the cheese is waiting. "His burger is getting cold," I whisper to myself.

"Let me just run a few things. I'll be back." He takes my license and walks back to his squad. I pull my bangs back down over my face. My palms rub at the streams of water stinging my cheeks. I pull the visor down and peek at myself in the mirror. My eyebrow has stopped bleeding. I see the top layer crusting over. I flip the visor up. I see Dougie's ball cap in the front seat. *Do I put it on? What if I stain it? I'd better not.* Before I can further evaluate whether or not to use the cap, Officer Kipton comes back to my window.

"Here is your license, Ma'am. I'm going to let you off today with just a warning. Just don't try to make any late yellow lights." I take my license back, which also has his business card with it. I stare at his card. "That's just in case you have any questions that I could help you with. Now or later." He lingers by my window. He gives me a half-smile. I now realize the static has disappeared. *When did it disappear?*

"Thank you." I glance at his warm eyes once more before I start the car. He turns and walks back to his squad car. I look in the rearview mirror, and other than my makeup being a bit streaky, I look halfway decent. My hair keeps me protected. I see the officer just staring at me from his front seat. He must be waiting for me to leave. I shift the signal lever to indicate a left turn to get back into traffic and make the fifty-foot drive to the store. A smile pokes through my numb face. I just escaped a ticket!

I pull into the parking space furthest back in the parking lot. I would hate for something to happen to Dougie's car. I contemplate double parking the vehicle but opt to just park next to the last curb toward the rear of the store. I don't know if I could escape a ticket twice in one day. I run in, find the cheddar, pay the two dollars and fifty-three cents for the eight pack of cheese, and jog out to the car. I jog carefully so as not to jar my hair or aching head.

CHAPTER SIXTEEN

Sara Olivia Scott

The drive home is in fast forward; the universe is attempting to catch me up from my brief stint in slow motion. All I yearn to do is get home, fix the cheese on Dougie's burger, and see how he's doing. The second all four wheels are in the driveway, I cut the engine. I vow not to allow myself to think about the past, ever. From this moment on, I only look ahead.

I take a deep breath, trying to convince my body to get up and go inside. *Why am I so nervous? I know Dougie is waiting for me. I'll make him happy by fixing his burger.* "Sara, there's no reason to feel tense," my whisper responds to my thoughts. Finally, I sound like me again.

I pause a bit longer. Now that the shock is wearing off, I feel a rage growing in my stomach. I feel it pulse through my veins. *I'm not a punching bag! I don't deserve that. I'm going to give him his cheese and tell him to make his own dang burger!*

My legs wobble beneath me as I step out of the car. This must be how marathoners feel after they cross the finish line; after all, I've been on my legs all day at work. I struggle to put one foot in front of the other, but my anger propels me forward. I reach out for the front door's handle, resting my hand on the cold metal. *Should I knock?* Before I can make my own decision, the door swings open. Dougie's red, swollen eyes plead with me. I stand there, not sure what to do. The anger vanishes from my heart as I see him so vulnerable. A few long seconds pass before I hold the cheese out as an offering, speechless. My hands are steady.

"I'm so sorry, babe. I think I was just overtired and drank too much before you got home. That will never happen again, I promise." His hands firmly grasp my biceps as he pulls me in and wraps his arms around me. He is extremely and convincingly sincere.

For all the studying I've done the last eighteen years of my life, I can't focus enough at this moment to fully understand what's going on. I'm still holding the cheese, which is now being pressed tightly against my abdomen and his. I have so many emotions swirling around I'm not sure which one I actually feel. He holds me without saying another word. I let him do so.

I feel the cheese starting to get warm between our body heat. *How long do we stand here like this?* It should be okay to interject now that a few minutes have passed.

I pull away slightly and stare him in the eyes. The anger is gone, but my voice is steady. "The cheese is getting warm." I feel my bravery. "And don't you ever strike me again."

"I promise. That will never happen again. I'll do whatever you want me to. I will stop drinking if you want me to. I can't lose you." He looks like a sad puppy. His hands tremble as he pulls away. All I want to do is take care of him.

"Let's go in and fix your burger."

"No sweetie. You relax, and I'll fix it. Thank you for getting the cheese. Why don't you go take a bubble bath and just relax? It's been a long emotional day for both of us."

I see a tear glistening down his cheek as he tries to hold in his emotion.

He looks at me with his big, sad eyes. "I'm sorry. Olive juice forever."

"Olive juice too." I give him a peck on the lips with such elegance so as not to rustle my bangs, still perfectly placed over the right side of my face.

"I don't deserve you." His tears cover his cheeks as he gasps for air in between his words.

"Don't be silly." I give him another hug. "I don't deserve you. You have given me so much. I'm so blessed. Let me fix the burger for you, and then I'll take a bath, okay, sweetie?"

He gives me a half-smile. "I just felt like you were insulting me. I got scared you were purposefully trying to do that to me. I'm so sorry."

Only think about the future, Sara. "We've both had a long day."

I'm in control of my thoughts. My jaw tightens with my smile. I hope my hair didn't move just now; I don't want him to see me like this. He is already so angry with himself; I don't want him to feel worse.

Gingerly, I step inside the kitchen, fix his burger, and deliver it to him on the couch. We don't say another word, tiptoeing around something we both want to forget.

I got charley horses. I force my legs to bring me upstairs. A bath will help fix all of this.

My eyes are fixed on the water crashing into the porcelain tub, drowning out the television downstairs. As I undress, I don't dare look in the mirror. Instead, I slip into the hot, steamy water without ever taking my eyes off of it.

As I slide deeper into the water, my tears mix with the bubbles, leaving no trace on my face. *I was so mad, but now I feel so bad for Dougie. His eyes were so sad. He's beating himself up over this. We all make mistakes. No one is perfect. I'm not perfect. I did provoke him, and I should have asked him what he likes on his burger. Why did I assume? This is my fault too. I didn't communicate well.*

My heart hurts. My heart hurts not for me but for Dougie. His eyes were so swollen. I bet he has been crying since all this happened. I wish I could take away his guilt. I know he didn't mean it. It was an accident, in the heat of the moment. I know he "olive juices" me; he wants to take care of me. He saved me.

Think only of the future, Sara. Love does not rejoice at wrongdoing, but finds its joy in the truth.

My bath water turns cool. I delicately pull on my "grandma" pajamas. My eyes avoid the mirror … *I don't need to see this anymore. This all just needs to be done and over.* Thankfully, I don't work tomorrow. Maybe a good night's sleep will just erase all of this.

The right side of my face throbs in unison with my heartbeat as I hang my towel up on its hook. The sheets weigh heavily on my fatigued body. My left eye closes to join my right, and my thoughts pull me in, consuming me in their mystery. Utter exhaustion eases my physical pain as I quickly surrender to sleep.

CHAPTER SEVENTEEN

Sara Olivia Scott

I wake up to the sun shining on my face and warming my cheeks. I attempt to open my eyes, but my right eye is partially crusted over. My heart skips a beat as I remember why. I slowly reach up to touch my face. It feels almost normal, except it's more tender than usual. I lie there with my hand on my warm cheek, staring outside at the sun streaming in on me. *Today will be different; this is going to bring us closer together.*

Before I can completely gather my thoughts, Dougie taps on the door with a slight knock before entering. His eyelids are swollen, proving he spent the evening crying.

"Hey, sweetie. I thought I'd make you breakfast." He places a cookie sheet next to me on the ground, along with a glass of orange juice, two misshaped pancakes, and scrambled eggs.

"That was really sweet of you." *I can't believe he made me breakfast. I've never had breakfast in bed!*

"I just wanted to do something nice for you. You deserve this." I see him glance at my face. Before I can shield myself, his swollen eyes fill with tears. "I'm so sorry. I'm so sorry," he sobs as he curls into a sitting fetal position.

I sit up and wrap my arms around him. I just hold him as he cries, sitting on the ground next to my mattress. "It's okay. Shhh. It's okay. I'm okay. I know it was an accident." *Why do we have to keep discussing this?*

"I don't deserve you. I can't believe I did that. I never want to hurt you." His cries turn into wheezes for air. "I'm so sorry. Forgive me."

"I forgive you. I know you didn't mean to hurt me. It's okay, sweetie. I'm okay." My pancakes and eggs turn cold as I console him.

The tears finally stop, and Dougie returns to himself: the confident construction man I've missed. He retrieves his cold breakfast from downstairs, and we enjoy our meal from the comfort of my mattress. I pick at the meal as Dougie gorges himself to my left. I purposefully had him sit to my left so he couldn't see my face. We are using the bed like a couch, with our backs up against the wall. The sun sprawls across our legs as we sit, two separate individuals sharing one space.

I don't know what to say. *Do I reassure him again that I'm okay, or should I just change the subject altogether?* He isn't sobbing anymore, but he sure has beat himself up quite a bit. My chest feels achy as I watch how sad Dougie is. *I'm strong. I don't cry. My voice doesn't quiver. I need him to know I'm okay. I just want to take his pain away.*

"What do you say we spend today together, just you and me?" The sun warms my face as my words come out cheerfully. My eyes remain staring out at the bright blue sky as I speak. I feel his eyes on me.

"Yeah, I think that is exactly what we need." He wipes his mouth before leaning over and pulling me close to him. His lips kiss my left temple.

"What would you like to do?" No need to turn my neck. My eyes stay focused on the cloudless blue sky. Hopefully, he chooses something where we don't need to be staring at one another all day. I just want to forget any of this ever happened.

"What about a movie marathon downstairs? I can go to the movie rental box up the street, rent like five movies, and we can just eat junk food and watch movies all day."

I envision his eyes lighting up as he thinks aloud. My eyes focus in on the baby blue hue of the sky.

"That sounds perfect." My smile voluntarily relishes this turning point. *Thank goodness he chose something to cover us in darkness. The sun can warm my face tomorrow.*

After breakfast, Dougie zips over to the 24/7 rental box and rents a bunch of movies. We watch the three back-to-back action movies and start the horror movie; Dougie surprised me with his choice of movies as I was showering when he went to pick them up. The lights are off. The shades have been pulled. I don't turn any of the lights on after the sun goes down because I don't want us to be reminded of yesterday.

The horror movie sends chills up my spine as the main actress's lover stabs her to death after he finds her cheating on him. I close my eyes and dig my head into Dougie's shoulder to keep my mind from the horror. He senses my nerves and wraps his big arms around my body, holding me so close to him that it's hard to move even an inch. The movie ends with the unforgiving man living a life free of conviction. The fact that such an awful human being could escape jail is unsettling. Thankfully, Dougie rented one other movie as well.

I'm surprised to find the last movie is a chick flick. He's just the sweetest man. Most men wouldn't voluntarily sit through a chick flick, yet I found a man who goes out and rents one for us to watch together! Although I'm curious what the movie is about, I'm overwhelmed by his thoughtfulness. Dougie and I opt to entwine ourselves on the couch instead of focusing on the love story taking place on the plasma.

I don't even know what to call yesterday … a thing because we were both overly exhausted. We merely misunderstood one another. Yes, that's it. A misunderstanding.

Our kissing grows from soft pecks into passionate declarations of love. When his hands try to roam, I whisper, "Not yet." Our passion does not extend beyond our lips.

CHAPTER EIGHTEEN

Sara Olivia Scott

The last two weeks since the *misunderstanding* have been perfect. I narrate the last two weeks in my head, paying most attention to all the positives. Dougie's sweeter than a peach; he's even driven me to work a couple of times. Thankfully, I had some heavy-duty concealer, and I was able to cover the bruising on my face. The swelling was completely gone by the time I had to get back to work the following Monday after the *misunderstanding*.

"Sara, you're cut."

"Huh?"

"Did I stutter? I said you're cut. Clean up your section and go. It's a slow Friday, so you can take off. Make sure you get all your side work done. Come get me before you leave so I can make sure everything has been taken care of." Brian must be in one of those moods today.

"Oh. Sorry, I was …" There is no use in finishing my sentence since he is already ten feet away with his back to me.

"Hey, Carla, how late do you work today?" I'm trying so hard to be nice to her. She's a short, size double zero on the bottom and C on the top, blonde-haired, gorgeous green-eyed woman. She got hired right after me, and she didn't take Stephanie's advice about not getting involved with Brian, or maybe Stephanie didn't get to her in time. Carla and Brian have been all giggles and smiles since she started. Even though she's scheduled to be off before me, as long as Brian is managing, she gets cut when his shift is up. I'm pretty sure it's because he's giving her a ride home—probably more than just a ride.

"I don't know. I guess Brian wants to keep me on longer. I told him I needed some money so I could get a new phone since I dropped mine last week."

I'm trying really hard not to let her irritating voice get on my nerves. I have no justifiable reason to be annoyed with her voice. Maybe it's because she acts like your friend to your face, but I'm pretty sure she is cussing at me behind that smile.

"Bummer about the phone." Even though she bothers me, I do feel bad for her because none of the other waitresses really like her. I'm pretty sure she was hired because Brian wanted to get to *know* her more, but hey, who am I to judge? "You doing anything fun this weekend?" I try to make small talk as I bus the last dirty table in my section.

"Yeah. I've been seeing a guy for a couple weeks, and we're probably going to go to the bars tonight. Other than that, I'm counting on Sunday to clear up the hangover I'm intending to have."

"Cool. Well, have an awesome time." I smile as I head to the back of the restaurant to finish restocking the fridge with the salad fixings. I so badly want to ask whom she has been seeing, but I'm pretty sure she would get annoyed with me for asking. Plus, it would be too obvious that I'm prying. And to be frank, I don't really care. In the last two weeks, she hasn't really chosen to talk with any of the other waitresses because (a) we aren't men and (b) we don't tip.

I finish my side work in record time and get Brian's approval to clock out. I've barely been able to contain my excitement today. Dougie and I have a special date night planned. He won't tell me what he has planned, but he's pretty excited for six o'clock this evening to come. Work has picked up for him the last couple weeks, so he's been working longer hours. He's been happy and charming.

"Have a good weekend, Carla!" I holler as I walk out the door. She either can't hear me or is ignoring me. Oh well, I don't care. I'm too excited for tonight. The weather is absolutely beautiful today. Hundreds of birds sing in the woods surrounding the roadway. The sun is spreading its warmth everywhere. I've wanted to stop by the park that I've passed to and from work, but I haven't had time. I haven't lost myself in the woods since … since my parents and I went on our last Sunday walk too many months ago.

It's only two thirty, which means I have at least two hours before I am usually scheduled to be off work. Dougie won't be home anyway, so why don't I stop and enjoy this weather?

The park is halfway between work and our home. Its gravel parking lot is typically vacant. The only thing better than the sun warming my naked face would be if Dougie were here to explore this park with me. Hey, maybe that's his idea for our date night as well! Oh, that would be perfect—another picnic but in the park.

As I reach the gravel parking lot, I find it abandoned other than the Biffy that huddles in the corner. I try to stay as far away from the gag-smell-projector as possible. I walk to the outermost side of the parking lot. As my feet touch the parking lot, I feel the rubber soles of my tennis shoes melt into the little dirt pebbles. If walking through scorching coals is what needs to be done to explore a possible "Heaven on Earth," I will more than happily sacrifice my shoes.

For some reason, I just sense that this park will remind me of the many wood walks I used to go on with my parents. I have been dreaming of this place since my first walk past it. My parents and I used to search for crab-apple trees; Daddy's favorite hobby was to make "crape" jelly. His jelly was always the best. I hope there are crab apple trees in this place.

The day is hot and humid, and my hair is glued to my face with sweat in a matter of minutes. I can feel the sun's rays burning my pale skin. With each step I take closer to my dreamy destination, a slight breeze, ever so gentle, passes through each strand of my hair, cooling each pore on my sweat-soaked face.

At the entrance of the woods, paths wind like ribbons in between tall pine trees, shadowing the damp dirt. The trees are like selfish skyscrapers hiding the sun in an attempt to keep this mysterious beauty to themselves—and now me. Not wanting to stay on the predictable paths, I roam off onto the untouched path.

There are trees of all sorts of shapes, sizes, and colors. My line of vision is filled with vivid greens and browns—plant vegetables of all sorts. I stop. I want to breathe in all of this. Nature's beauty is always accompanied by peace.

I continue my walk through the grassy, thick patches of bushes, stepping on twigs as I go. The cracking of the twigs surely scares away any deer lingering in the distance. Birds chirp their melodic tunes as if to form some grand masterpiece even the most respectable musician couldn't create.

I come upon a lake that stands still deep within the woods. Mallard ducks float across the top of the water, relaxed and quiet. The sunlight reflects off the water's glossy layer and spreads warmth over my body. Knowing there is more grandeur to be discovered ahead in my journey, I yearn to move on; however, an hour has already escaped, so I'd better turn around and get home. I know there is grandness awaiting me at home—my sweet Dougie's surprise!

As I turn back and weave through nature's tapestry, I feel my soul being rejuvenated. I haven't felt this peaceful since before my parents died. I wish Dougie were here to enjoy this, but then again, I don't know if he would understand the deep meaning a place like this holds for me; I feel so close to my parents here. When I have time again, I may need to discover the other hidden treasures this unknown paradise holds.

I find my way back to the smelly Biffy much too quickly and cross the coals disguised as gravel. It's a good thing I'm hurrying home early so I can shower and make myself sweet for my man.

My mind is racing between the park I just discovered and what Dougie has planned. *I can't wait to tell him about the lake; I wonder if he's ever stumbled on it himself. He must have. He's lived here for … hmm … I don't actually know how long he has lived here. I bet he's been through the park before. How could someone not be tempted by the vacant parking lot to discover what is behind all those tall, beautiful trees?*

I turn the corner onto our street, barely able to contain my excitement. Dougie's car is in the driveway. *Why would he be home already? Did he ask to leave work early for my surprise? Darn, I wish I had skipped the park! No, no, I don't, because then I might have spoiled what he has planned.* My feet pick up their pace as I struggle to contain my exhilaration for my big surprise.

I open the door. "Hey, sweetie! I'm home." My shout reminds me of a husband from a 50s television sitcom. I wait for him to answer, but there is no answer. *Is he hiding as part of my surprise?* I take my sweaty apron off and hang it on the staircase railing. I meander through the kitchen, hoping my eyes don't spoil my surprise. Nothing. I walk into the den. Nothing. I return to the hallway to check upstairs. Dougie is standing in his work clothes in front of his bedroom door. His eyes are dark, and he is somewhat staggering. My heart pauses for a moment, not sure if I should be scared or surprised.

"Didn't you hear me? I was looking for you!" I rush towards him. His face is unchanged.

"I heard you." His monotone is void of emotion.

I wrap my arms around him. He puts his arms around my waist. His hug feels cold, lifeless, and obligatory.

I pull away. "What's wrong? Did something go wrong with the surprise?"

"What surprise? Surprise, I was just forced to take a week off of work because of this damn economy. My effin' boss told me to sit this week out because business is hurting." Anger rises in his eyes as we stand staring at one another.

Did he forget my surprise date? Is he kidding? "Are you serious?" My voice inquires. I sense his body tensing up with my question.

"What do you mean, am I serious?" His voice grows louder with every word.

Instinctively, I take a step back. "I'm sorry," I whisper.

"Why are you walking away from me? Can't you tell I'm upset and could use some womanly care?" He seems insulted.

"I'm sorry ... I ... I ..." Maybe it's best to just avoid the explanation for stepping back.

His eyes are growing darker. My awareness is heightened. "What can I do to help?" I ask very carefully, making sure my tone is not angry or sarcastic.

"What you can do is shower your sweaty self clean and then come back downstairs and keep me company. I'm glad you stepped back because the last thing I want to smell is sweat when I need some cheering up."

That's right, I stepped back because I'm sweaty. Duh, no wonder I stepped back ... I wasn't even sure why I had done it, but that makes sense. "Okay, babe. I'll shower quick and then help you feel better."

He turns and walks away. I hear his footsteps lead him down the stairs, into the kitchen, and to the fridge. I'm fairly certain the fridge is 90 percent beer and 10 percent moldy food.

My heart is racing, and my hands are trembling. Why? I haven't a clue. I hustle into my room and grab some clean clothes. I'm in and out of the shower in five minutes. *I wonder if he's still planning to take me on my surprise date tonight? I'll ask after I cheer him up a bit.*

I rush downstairs. Dougie is sitting on the couch with football playing on the television.

"What can I do to help?"

"Wanna grab me a beer?" There are two empty bottles next to him on the coffee table.

"Yeah, let me grab that. Can I get you something to munch on?" I want to cater to his every need.

"Nah, a beer is fine."

I grab his beer and snuggle up next to him on the couch.

"Thanks." His eyes don't move from the television.

"Of course. Do you want to talk about it?"

"No. I just want to sit and watch the game. Do you mind rubbing my shoulders?"

"Of course I don't mind." He seems *off*. He moves to the ground, and I skooch over behind him. We sit in silence for the first half of a recorded football match between Minnesota and Wisconsin, from who knows when. My hands are numb and aching from massaging his solid shoulders. "Feel better?"

"Yeah. Thanks."

Thank goodness. My stomach starts to grumble. "Um, sweetie …"

"Yeah?"

"Were you still feeling up to going on our date tonight?" I didn't want to ask, but I'm starving!

He whips his head around. "Are you kidding me? Where the hell have you been the last hour and a half? I was just told I couldn't work for a week, which means no money, honey. Are you going to take me out on a date night?" His question is aggressive.

I'm not sure how to respond. "I … I can."

"You can? Great, why don't you effin' brag about having money! Thanks a lot for making me feel crapier than before. Wow, you really know how to kick a man when he's down!" His words turn into shouts as he stands up from the floor. I feel myself involuntarily cower on the couch for a moment.

I quickly find my voice. "I didn't mean it like that!" I need to blurt out my reasoning before he gets angrier. "I just meant I want to help."

"Help? Now you think I need you to help me? You think I can't provide for us?"

This is going wrong. He doesn't understand what I'm saying.

"Well, why don't you do all of the manly things in this house since I apparently can't do nothing! Get up off the couch and go make us a living so we can pay our damn bills!"

I feel his hands grab my biceps, one in each hand. He picks me up off the couch and puts me on my feet.

"Ouch, you're hurting me, Dougie!" I yelp.

"Oh, now I'm hurting you? I just picked you up off the couch. So now I'm completely useless, huh?" His shouting makes me want to cover my ears, but his hands are still tightly gripped around my arms. I'm stuck.

"You know I didn't mean it like that." I hear my voice, but it doesn't sound like me. The words are shaky and barely audible.

"Well, WHAT DID YOU MEAN?" He yanks his arms down, forcing me to sit on the couch again. "How about this? I'll go figure out what the hell we're eating for dinner since I'm apparently no longer the man in this house. And you can figure out what the hell you were trying to say!" He stomps into the kitchen.

Is he mad because of the alcohol? How can that even cross my mind? He's barely had anything to drink in the last hour. I feel my feet pick me up off the couch and lead me into the kitchen after him.

"Stop treating me like this!" My voice progressively gets louder. "That's not what I meant! You are the man! You do provide for us! I was just trying to do something nice!" My shaky voice screams at him. *I can't believe I'm screaming. Why am I screaming at him?* I thought my words were going to sound more confident.

Dougie whips around and leans his face right into mine. His right hand shoots up from his side, and I feel his hand grip tightly around my shirt's collar, squeezing my neck in the process. He slams me back up against the wall with one quick step. I hear my voice let out a screech. I don't know if I can get any words out. His grip is getting tighter on the fabric, cinching it closer together.

His eyes are inches from mine. "I AM the man! Me! Not you!" His breath is hot against my face.

I can't breathe. What is happening?

"I am. Do you get it?" His voice shatters my eardrums.

How am I supposed to answer? I'm getting dizzy. I feel my heart thudding in my chest. I want to throw up, I want to cough, but I can't make a noise. I can't breathe! Panic sets in. I'm scared. *What is happening?*

THUD! THUD! THUD!

"Who the hell is that?" Dougie asks us both as he releases his hand.

I've never been so happy to hear someone at the door. My heart prays it's someone who calms him down. I fall to my knees and hear myself gasp for air. The floor comes back into focus as he walks to the front door.

"Who is it?" Dougie yells.

"The police. Open the door."

"What the hell," Dougie mumbles as he looks back at me.

His stare tells me to get up off the floor. I pull myself up using the fridge as a hoist. I lean against the fridge. My gasps have turned into loud inhales. My heart keeps trying to say something to my brain, but my brain won't let it talk. I'm completely emotionless as I wait to see who is on the other side of the door.

Dougie opens the door. "Can I help you, officer?" His voice is polite.

The officer pushes the door open further. "Mind if I step in?" The officer asks as he takes a step into the entryway. The officer immediately turns his eyes towards me.

Our eyes meet as I feel my lungs take in too quick of an inhale, which forces me to cough. I wasn't aware that my hand was around my neck, but now I am. I put my hand down by my side.

The officer's stare goes back to Dougie. "Everyone okay in here? Is it just the two of you?" His eyes turn back to me.

Does he recognize me?

The officer's gaze is on me when Dougie answers, "Yeah, we're okay. It's just us. Why?"

The officer looks back at Dougie. "We got a call from a concerned citizen that there was some noise coming from this unit, so we wanted to make sure everything was okay. Ma'am, are you okay?" His voice holds me for a moment before Dougie's eyes pierce my calmness.

"Oh yeah! We're watching football and got a little carried away," Dougie answers for me.

I force an agreeable chuckle.

"Are you sure you are okay, ma'am?"

I feel Dougie's eyes on me, waiting for me to answer. "Yes, of course, Officer Ki—" I stop myself. He didn't introduce himself.

"Huh?" Dougie blurts out.

"Sorry, frog in my throat." I smile. "I was saying I kinda just get into football a bit. I'll try to keep my voice down. Sorry." My gaze moves from Officer Kipton to Dougie. Dougie has a smile on his face.

"Okay. Well, you folks enjoy your football game. I'm sorry for the confusion."

Don't leave yet. I'm still scared.

I smile back and nod. I don't want my eyes to meet his again because I don't want to give myself away; I never told Dougie that I was pulled over on my way to the store.

"Thanks, officer. Have a good night. Go Wisconsin." Dougie smiles as he motions towards the door.

Officer Kipton turns around. "I'm a Minnesota fan. Go MN. Have a good night, folks."

And without another word, Officer Kipton leaves.

The room grows cold.

As the door closes behind the officer, Dougie interrogates me. "Do you know him?"

"No. Why would I know a cop?"

"Oh. That was weird. He was staring at you."

"I know. It was creepy, right?" No, it really wasn't creepy.

"Yeah. Effin' cops."

Dougie walks back towards me. "I'm sorry I got so angry. I just hate to hear you think less of me because I can't do everything for you. You want the world, and I'm giving you everything I got." He wraps his arms around me. "I'm your man, but I … I just felt like you wanted me to say I couldn't give you everything." He caresses my hair behind my ear.

"I would never think that." I close my eyes to keep them from welling up with tears. I hate it when he scares me. "You are everything to me. You provide more than enough. You are more than I could ever ask for!" My mouth is blurting out everything my brain has recalled from all the love movies I've seen. "I'm sorry I hurt you. I didn't mean it like that. I only want you. You give me everything." My voice is overly stroking his ego. My mouth just keeps spitting out these regurgitated phrases from those movies.

He inhales loudly and holds me closer. "I'm sorry too. Just please don't play those mind games with me." He gently kisses my neck. Its tenderness quivers beneath his lips. I feel him holding my rigid body, yet it all feels *off*.

"Sorry." I should have kept my mouth shut. I didn't mean to emasculate him. *Am I a horrible girlfriend who constantly puts him down?*

"Olive juice, sweetie."

"Olive juice too." I do love him. He didn't mean to hurt me. He just told me that. Right? Because he said it, it must mean he loves me. You can love someone and still have bursts of anger.

I extinguish the flicker of doubt that surfaces. I wish he wouldn't hurt me, but we all have our problems. I shouldn't doubt. Just because I feel like he may not love me when he acts out doesn't mean he doesn't love me. Men always say women talk too much about their feelings, which probably means feelings are wrong. I don't think he realizes his strength. He's not dangerous.

CHAPTER NINETEEN

Officer Kipton Pierre

I can't get her out of my head. At night, her delicate image consumes my every thought. I see her tiny body hunched behind the wheel, her hands uncontrollably shaking, and her jaw tight. My mind replays her head slowly looking up at me, with one eye nearly swollen shut and the other eye wide and searching. My body quivers as I remember her eyes, like shattered glass, broken.

It has only been two weeks since that Friday when I pulled her over. I have never seen her before around town. Now, I can't get her out of my mind. I never noted in my file that I had pulled her over. It just didn't seem right. I know what happens with the domestic abuse files. The household gets radioed in, and then once a week, some rookie cop swings by the neighborhood to see if anything is going on. The problem is most of those cases end up one of three ways. Either the woman stays with the man for a life filled with pain, the man ends up killing the woman after years of abuse lead to the deadly encounter, or the woman finally retaliates and ends up being the one who is found committing the crime. I can't let this Sara end up as another statistic. I can't live with that guilt. I need for her to choose the fourth option, freedom.

My job is to protect. I go to my desk drawer. I look around to make sure no one else is around me.

"Hey, Kip! You looking for the bagels or the donuts?" Randy's voice sneaks up behind me.

I quickly re-divert my reaching hand from the drawer to the stack of papers on my desk. "Ha-ha. Not quite. I was thinking of getting a start on this paperwork so I can actually enjoy this weekend."

"Jeesh, man. What did you do to deserve that pile of papers?"

"Minor kid tried stealing a T-shirt from the local thrift store. Not only did she already steal her neighbor's car to get to the store, she then backed the stolen car into the store manager's vehicle before fleeing. I was the lucky winner who got to pull her over two miles from the crime scene."

"Ouch! That hurts. Good luck with that, man."

"Thanks. Hey, wait, Randy. Did you mention something about bagels and donuts?"

"Yeah. Sam brought a couple dozen in this morning with some donuts. Allen was already devouring some. I'm on the hunt to snatch one before he eats them all."

"Maybe I'll join ya. I could use some sprinkles." I join Randy and grab my donut. He opts for a plain bagel.

Twenty minutes later, I find myself back at my desk. This time, I make sure no one is around before I reach for my drawer. I quickly open the drawer and reach to the very back. Beneath my framed photo of Gizmo, my two-year-old boxer, I quietly flip over a small piece of paper: "Sara Olivia Scott. 4-13-85. BAG666."

My jaw clenches as I read the plate number. I've been waiting for my pile of paperwork to stack up so I can run this plate number without any suspicion.

I type BAG666 into the database. It's probably short for douche bag. Douglas J. Adams. DOB: 11-6-80. Address: 863 Sunrise Court, Newport, Minnesota 55055. Priors: Drag racing 2003, 2002, 2000. Domestic Assault 2000, 2001 involving Monica Chant.

That sonuva—I knew it. This confirms my suspicion. I quickly exit out of the database. I have everything I need. Eight sixty three Sunrise court. That's not too far from where I live. Once I finish up this paperwork, I may just need to check this place out.

"It's four thirty. I'm out. I got some errands I need to run."

"Have a good night, Kip. See ya Monday."

"Thanks, Randy. You too."

Our office is about five minutes from this Douglas's home. No one will recognize me in my red F350 pickup. It can't hurt to just drive by and make sure everything is okay.

Five minutes later, I'm in his development. There are about a dozen or so townhouses. I drive by 863. No action. Maybe I'll just park up the street and stake out the place for a bit. I park about three blocks from 863. Time slowly passes. I switch out my cop hat for my Twins baseball cap. Less noticeable. Something catches my eye crossing the street three blocks up.

It's her. Her hair is in a ponytail. She has on black pants, a white oxford shirt, and an apron. She's hustling. She must have to walk to and from work. I watch her go into the house. Thankfully, she didn't look my way. I know I should leave, but I can't. *Is she alone in there? Should I swap my hats back and go knock on the door?*

Trying to devise the best plan, I organize my thoughts. An hour passes before I finally decide how to approach this situation. I just want to check on her and make sure she's okay. I switch my cap back. From what I can tell, no one is outside or peering out of windows. This street is dead. I get out of my truck and walk up the street. Still no one in sight.

With one block to go, I hear shouting. It's a man's voice. Half a block away, a woman screams. My heart picks up the pace. Was that her? I hear the man yell, "I am. Do you get it?" My legs want to run to their door, but I know I must keep my composure. I walk faster. My fist pounds on that door as my gut tells me that was Douglas yelling. THUD! THUD! THUD!

Inside, a man grumbles something, but I can't make it out. "Who is it?" a man's voice yells.

"The police. Open the door." Technically, I am the police. I have my uniform on.

More grumbling inside, with some ruckus. "Can I help you, officer?" His tone changes as he opens the door. He's about five foot eight, slender, brown hair. He looks like a slithery fellow.

Drag racer? Yes. Abuser? Yes. Date raper? Possibly. Trash that needs to be taken out? Definitely. If I could have five minutes alone with him, I'd be happy to take out the trash.

I push the door open. "Mind if I step in?" I take a step inside in unison with my words. It's dark in the small hallway, but the kitchen light is on. My eyes meet hers. She is holding her neck and breathing loudly. I can't take my eyes away. I want to run over to her and save her, get her away from this psycho. She puts her hand down by her side. I feel the rage rise in my chest; there is a pink handprint around her neck.

I return my gaze to Douglas. It takes every inkling of professionalism in me not to reach over and punch this guy; how can someone hurt such a small, innocent woman? I don't even believe in violence, but if it were to save someone like her, I'd make an exception.

As calmly and professionally as I can, I ask, "Everyone okay in here? Is it just the two of you?" I look back at her, nearly choking on my own words.

"Yeah, we're okay. It's just us. Why?" the snake smoothly answers.

Shoot! I look back at him, and the words spill from my mouth. "We got a call from a concerned citizen that there was some noise coming from this unit, so we wanted to make sure everything was okay. Ma'am, are you okay?" I look back at her, her tiny body leaning against the fridge. Cowering.

"Oh yeah! We're watching football and got a little carried away," he answers for her. She glances left with a chuckle. They always glance left when lying.

"Are you sure you are okay, Ma'am?" I sense Douglas is threatening her with his eyes.

"Yes, of course, Officer Ki—" Her voice stutters as she still struggles for every breath.

"Huh?" His voice cuts my thoughts.

"Sorry, frog in my throat. I was saying I kinda just get into football a bit. I'll try to keep my voice down. Sorry." Her eyes are lying to me. She was going to say my name. She recognizes me. *I wonder if he knows I pulled her over in his car.* I follow her gaze back to him.

What else can I say? I'm acting like I'm here on duty, but I can't stay. I can't take her away. I can't arrest him. "Okay. Well, you folks enjoy your football game. I'm sorry for the confusion." I smile at her, but she is looking away. *She knows it's me, right? She was going to say my name, right?* I hope there is still hope for her to get out of here and start a life without a lowlife like this guy.

"Thanks, officer. Have a good night. Go Packers!" His voice makes me want to rip my ears off. He motions towards the door.

"I'm a Vikings fan. Go Vikes." I really shouldn't have said anything, but I am nothing like this man.

Every muscle in my body is tense, not wanting to leave her with this animal. Heck, even animals shouldn't have their names associated with such scum. This just isn't right. I resist my urge to steal her from this self-made dungeon. His eyes are dark and beady as they stare out at me. I don't know what else to say, so I turn to leave. "Have a good night, folks." He doesn't waste any time closing the door behind me.

I force my legs to bring me back down the driveway and down the street to my truck. *Would he have killed her had I not shown up?* Everything in my body wants to turn around, go back inside, and take her away. I can bring her to safety. I can keep her safe. I won't hurt her.

Her eyes … I feel myself getting choked up as I shut my truck door. *What am I supposed to do?* I've never felt so helpless. "No!" I hear my own voice shout to no one as my fist hits the steering wheel. I can't save her if she won't willingly be saved. She knows I'm not trying to get her hurt, right? I just want to help. It's my duty to help.

I shoot a quick glance at 863 before I turn the corner and head home. I will figure this out. I'll fix this. I know I can save her. My job is to protect.

CHAPTER TWENTY

Sara Olivia Scott

My cramped neck awakens me. My eyes strain to focus. *Where am I?* My heart starts to race. Then I hear a snort from behind me. Dougie is asleep, curled up behind me like the big spoon. My nerves calm just as quickly as they flared.

I twist my neck to try and find a more comfortable position, but his arm is beneath my neck and stuck between my shoulder and head. His right arm is draped around my waist, making it much too heavy for me to move without him noticing. My body feels frail, but his strong body gives me the illusion of strength.

I mentally tap my brain as I try to remember last night. We had gotten into a fight because I emasculated him—not intentionally, of course, but he took it that way. That officer had shown up. *Who would have heard us?* We were just having a small fight. And then that officer showed up. I hope Dougie didn't get the idea that I knew him. Thankfully, the cop didn't say anything about pulling me over a couple weeks ago. He seems like a good guy too.

Another snore makes me jump a little. I never knew Dougie snored. Then again, I didn't even know he was a Packers fan before last night; I wasn't necessarily raised a diehard Vikings fan, but I was raised a Packer hater. It's funny how things work out.

I pause for a few moments until he resumes his regular breathing. That's so weird that Officer Kipton was the one who showed up. *Who would have called? People need to mind their own business. Of course Dougie would never want to hurt me. Would he? He promised it would never happen again after the ... incident. Last night ... would he have stopped if Officer Kipton hadn't shown up? Am I with the man of my dreams?*

His arm is so heavy lying across my body that I feel like I'm suffocating. His snoring blares into my eardrums. But he is here by my side. I'm not alone. He took me into his home. He didn't have to.

In fact, he took me to his room. How did we get up here? I know we both drank a few beers after the police drama. Dougie was crying because he thought I was going to leave him.

"Don't leave me. Please don't leave me," he begged.

"I'm not going to leave you. I'm not going anywhere. Olive juice!" *Why would he think I was going to leave him?*

"I ... I just can't live without you. It was the heat of the moment. I feel like I can't live up to your expectations of me. It's like all you cared about was going out on a date and that you didn't care that my hours were cut at work for the next week." His eyes looked so broken.

"I'm sorry. It had been a long day, and I was just so happy to get to spend time with you."

"That's okay." He kissed my neck. Still tender. "How about this, Hun? How about we stay in? I'll order a pizza, and we can have some beers and just chill. Would you like that?" His crying stopped. He was smiling at me with his arms wrapped tightly around me.

"Of course. I'll like anything you want to do." I added.

That's right. We finished our beer. He ate almost all of the pizza, but I was able to steal a piece. We drank quite a bit. He must have brought me up here after I passed out. Hmm, we've never slept in the same bed … except for the time I dreamt it.

He snores again. This time, I'm not startled. My body remains limp on his bed. *Why does my neck hurt so much? I must have slept on it wrong. It's not like last night was like that one misunderstanding. Last night, we were both angry because we weren't correctly communicating. I never knew relationships took so much work. He didn't do anything wrong. He couldn't have realized grabbing my shirt was also pinching my neck. He was just trying to get my attention. His eyes were so offended. I must have deeply hurt him.* My heart aches as I think about how mad he was and then how sad he was last night.

I'll make it up to him. I suppose my emotional intelligence needs some work. I probably shouldn't have skimmed that reading lesson in class last semester.

"You awake, Hun?" He finally moves his arm, freeing me.

"Yeah." I roll over to face him. "Sleep well?"

"Yeppers. You?"

"Yes." I softly kiss his lips. "Did you bring me up to your bed last night? I don't remember walking upstairs."

"Yep." He smirks. "I thought you'd like to spend the night together. So I brought you up here. Since last night wasn't quite the date I'd planned, I figured I had to make it up to you. How'd I do?" His eyes shimmer.

"It was perfect. I'd better lay low on the beer, though. I'm getting a headache."

He kisses my forehead. "Yeah, you are quite the party animal."

"What do you mean?"

"You know. Last night. You were definitely into making out with me, and you know." His smirk makes the hair on my arms stand up straight.

"Yeah." I feign a smile. I don't remember making out last night. I don't remember much of last night. Since I moved in, my meals have been limited because Dougie always seems to have already eaten by the time I get home. Honestly, I've been so physically exhausted that one beer can clearly push me into a complete blackout. I remember eating the pizza, and then Dougie brought me a beer—it was my second beer. *Why can't I remember anything else?*

Maybe he was having one of those dreams where he imagines what he wants, like I did when I thought he spent the night with me at school.

"I need to shower, Hun. I promised Chaz I'd drive up to the hunting shop with him."

"What's that?"

"It's a store to buy hunting gear up in Rogers. It's like an hour and a half away from here. Don't be sad, sweetie. I promised him we'd go before you even moved in. It'll just be today. We can hang out tomorrow." He pulls me in close and kisses me.

"Okay. Tell Chaz I say hi. I might go for a run or walk anyway. I haven't really had much time to work out."

"Good! I'm glad you will be getting back into a workout routine. It's important to stay in shape." He gets out of bed and goes into the bathroom. I hear the water turn on.

Yeah, he's right. It's good to get into a workout routine. Maybe that's why I've felt so off the last couple of weeks. I haven't made any time to work out. I was working out all the time at school.

"Hey sweetie, do you mind getting some laundry done around here? The clothes are starting to pile up." He peeks his head out of the bathroom.

"No problem." I washed my clothes two nights ago. "To clarify, you mean your laundry, right?"

"What?" He pokes his head out from the bathroom again. "You want to keep our laundry separate? That's a little weird."

"I guess I never really thought about it."

"It'd be weird not to wash our clothes together. We are living together."

"Yeah." I smile. *Is it really weird to want to keep my clothes separate?*

"Also, do my bed sheets too, please." He half-smiles as toothpaste foams from the side of his mouth before he pops back into the bathroom.

An hour later, Dougie is out the door and driving down the street to pick up Chaz. I've rarely been alone in his home. It's quiet. *I don't like it.* There's too much open space for it to be this quiet. I tug his sheets off his bed and throw them in the wash. *I'll deal with his clothes after my run.*

I put on my pink sports bra, black tank top, and black running shorts. I dig through my heap of clothes in the corner of the guest room and pick out two white socks that look like they may match. I dig out my running shoes from one of my suitcases and run down the stairs, trying to warm up. Maybe I'll go explore that park some more. Plus, I need to loosen up my neck; I definitely slept on it wrong.

It's already warm for only eight thirty-six in the morning. My feet feel heavy as I jog down the street. I take a left out of the neighborhood towards the park. The sun is shining through the tall trees that stand over the windy roadway. A cool breeze tickles the sweat-soaked hair on the back of my neck. It's a new and beautiful day.

I push my memory to remind me of last night, but my brain falls short of the events after my slice of pizza. It really aggravates me that I can't remember. *I know Dougie got both of us some beers after the pizza arrived; he even opened my beer for me and put it in a koozie before delivering it to me on the couch.* I push harder, but my mind is tired and absent of further recollection.

As I reach the park, I notice a red Ford truck sitting in the lot. I guess people do actually come to this park. I avoid the Biffy altogether and run along the outer path of the parking lot. I guess I'm in worse shape than I thought because the breeze brought with it the Biffy's odor, which was provoking my gag reflux. I give up on running. Walking is still exercise; plus, if I run with those fumes following me, I may barf. I step into nature's beautiful madness. I weave through the plants on a path never taken.

Walking for what seems to be miles brings me to an open field. There are three distinct hills, and the one furthest from me has a fallen tree cluttering its space. The grass has grown wild, and as I walk, thorns find a permanent new residence, embedding themselves in my cotton shorts. Daisies are scattered across the field, but in a manner that seems almost strategically placed. After I am deep in the woods, I come across the place I have been unconsciously searching for since my last trip.

There is a fence to my right that's about double my height. Barbed wire protects the top of the fence from invaders. The beauty in front of me is more than I can even mentally grasp. I guess I am the lucky one to get into this forbidden garden. To my right, there is a slight hill that descends into a valley of more trees that seem to act as a wall, a divider, to keep outsiders away.

Straight ahead, there is a thick barricade of thorn bushes entangled in one another. The leaves are barely clinging to the tree that reinforces the wall; the leaves are lively yet appear exasperated, as if just wanting the breeze to carry them away. Nature's wall is full of such beauty that I feel compelled to see what is hidden. Pushing myself through the kind-looking yet protective bushes is like digging myself out of a dirt hole with nothing but my fingers. I finally break through the wall of thickets to see an image that brings me back ten years.

I feel my parents so close to me as my eyes set upon a single tree, the brightest and boldest, standing tall in the middle of a circle of smaller trees and bushes. This is the only tree with bark so soft it could be used as a pillow. The tree is a dozen times taller than me, with the most beautiful green leaves one could imagine. The green is a cross between the sea, the ocean, the grass, and the forest. The tree speaks to me in a way only the breeze can translate. It's as if the tree is saying one can live in nature alone and survive anything. Yes, my parents must have led me here.

I step closer. I notice the tree is the only one in the area that is in the shade. Everywhere else is hit by sunlight, being exposed to all the angels' eyes. But this tree, this is the one that remains standing tall in the shade; this is the tree God hides from the world. I walk around the tree, putting my hands on its surface. The tree's body is no bigger than the circumference of my head. Brown with a light yet dark, rough yet soft bark has begun to peel in some areas, covering this mystery. This thickly covered tree is concealed by life forms invisible to the human eye. It's as if the tree has a power over the rest of the trees, none of which look the same in appearance or liveliness.

As I look down a bit further on the tree, my eyes meet three simple symbols: "D + M." It's a tree of love. The "D" looks like it was engraved many years before the "+" and the "M." It seems as if the "D" was put there to declare ownership of the tree. It's much larger than the other two symbols, taking up a fist's worth of space while the other two are merely half of that. Ants are scattered across the bark, crawling up and down, side to side, but never crossing over the symbols. The insides of the symbols are worn and exposed to the outside harshness. However, they are still smooth. Towards the trunk of the tree, black, rich soil protects its roots. The light sea green and yellow grass around the tree stands tall and uninterrupted. Five feet around the base of the trunk, the grass starts to get thicker and darker in color.

Daddy and Momma. My soul is lifted. I feel my parents so close to me. I get down on my knees and look up at the heavens. "Thank you! Thank you!" I shout upwards. I dig my fingers into the soul at the base of the tree. I feel so alive. So strong. "You'd be proud of me, Daddy and Momma." I speak to the tree. "I've grown up so much since you left. I found the man of my dreams. He's good to me.

"I don't remember you and Daddy having to work at things, but I'm sure you did when you first started dating too. Dougie has taken me in. He watches out for me. He even comes into the restaurant on Thursday nights when I work. I wish you could meet him." My soul cringes as I hear my own words. They will never meet him.

Tears drip from my eyes. I watch them fall into the soil beneath my hands and knees. Laughter suddenly builds from deep inside. "I'm watering your tree," I laugh, looking upwards. "I'll be okay. I'll be okay," I reassure my parents and myself.

The sun scatters on the earth around me. There is calmness in the woods. I sit here and soak in this moment for an hour. I breathe in this beauty, this paused moment. I know I should move on. I stand up and brush my knees and hands on my shirt. I look at the tree again. My lips kiss the "D" and the "M" as I wrap my arms around the tree, holding it close to me. "I'll be all right," I whisper into the bark.

As I walk away from my tree, it's getting harder to feel its power. I keep walking, this time following the paths. The dirt is light brown, clouded with puddles of mud. Weeds lie fallen on the edges of the path, as if the path ruined their only chance of survival. Less and less sun hits the path, and every minute, the beauty of this mystery is getting harder to see. Maybe it's the tears gently falling from my eyes or my allergies that are clouding my view.

I pick up my pace and start jogging. After all, I am supposed to be working out. The paths look like they are trails for bikes because they are narrow and sharp. I turn right, following the path.

BAM!

I'm knocked off my feet and onto my butt.

"I'm so sorry!" His voice is warm as he helps me to my feet. "Are you okay? Your legs are bleeding!"

"I'm fine," I say, laughing. "I was just startled." I look at my legs. Yep, they are bleeding. "I went through some thorn bushes," I declare, looking at the many cuts covering my legs. I look up at the man. "Do I know you?"

He smiles. "I think I know you. Aren't you the red yellow-light runner?"

Light runner? How does he know—"Oh my gosh! You're the cop, aren't you?" Small world.

"Yeah. I'm him." He smiles.

"Small world, huh?" I smile back at his widening grin. "What are you doing out here?" I ask.

"I run these paths frequently to stay in shape. What are you doing out here?"

"The same." I smile. It counts even if it is my first time doing so.

His smile quickly fades. I see his eyes resting on my neck.

"What?" I ask. *What caused the sudden change in him?*

"What happened to your neck?" His voice is serious but remains warm.

I instinctively reach up to hide whatever he must be seeing. "I … I slept on it weird. I must have kinked it."

"You bruised your neck from sleeping on it funny?" he asks. I can see he doesn't believe me.

"Why don't you believe me?" I know I'm getting too defensive. Before I let him say anything further, I add, "Hey, and are you following me? No one is ever here."

"Why would I be following you? You ran into me. I have been here for a couple of hours."

I remember seeing his truck in the parking lot when I got here. "I'm just kidding around. Well, enjoy the rest of your run."

"Hey." His voice makes me stop and turn.

"Yeah?"

"Are you sure you're okay? You know, if … if someone is hurting you, I … I can help you."

Hurting me? What is he talking about? I haven't seen my neck, but I'm certain it just looks weird from how I slept on it. "I'm fine. I just fell on my butt when you ran into me."

He smiles at my chuckle. "I wasn't referring to our crash." His face grows serious again. "Are you sure you're okay?" He takes a step closer to me. His voice is so sincere and warm. It's comforting. Just like warm honey. The tone of his voice makes me want to lean into him. I push away the urge.

"Yeah. I'm great. Never better!" I start my jog in the opposite direction as I wave goodbye to him. *It's so weird that he keeps running into me.*

He quickly fades from my mind.

My thoughts return to that tree. *I feel my parents so close to me. I know they would be happy for me. Right? I'm not alone. I have a someone. I have Dougie.*

Before I know it, I find myself back in the parking lot. I turn around to see the mystery, but it's hidden. Even if I can't see the tree, I know I'm not alone.

My legs burn as sweat seeps into the cuts on my legs. I return to my walk. My heart may burst with happiness. *This is what it must feel like to be an adult. I work hard. I have a home. And I have the man of my dreams. And now I know where I can go to feel close to my parents. I'm not sure life gets any better than this.* I leisurely meander home, doing dance twirls as I walk, basking in the warm sun.

CHAPTER TWENTY-ONE

Sara Olivia Scott

As I near home, I see Dougie's red dragon in the driveway. *What's he doing home already? I thought the store was an hour away. I don't think I've been gone that long, maybe a couple hours.* My stomach grumbles.

"Where have you been?" he shouts from the couch.

"I've been out running. Didn't you go to the hunting store?"

"Chaz wasn't feeling so great, so he didn't want to go today. We're going to go tomorrow instead. You've been out running for four hours?" His face looks skeptical.

"It's been four hours? Well, I didn't leave right after you did. I can't believe it's been that long."

"You ran for four hours?"

"I jogged and walked. I went to the park down the street."

His eyes scan me up and down and then pause on my legs. "Why are your legs cut up?"

I look down. "I decided I didn't need to take the path, and I got stuck in some of those thickets or prickly bushes, whatever you call them. I better go upstairs and clean them out quick before they harden." I give him a peck on the lips before turning to go upstairs.

"Hm. Salty," he teases.

"I'm a workout machine," I chuckle as I walk down the hall.

"Why do you have a twig in your hair?" His voice booms down the hall after me.

"Huh?" I turn back towards him. "What?"

"There's a twig in your ponytail. Why is there a twig in your ponytail?" His voice is serious. It's cute that he worries about me.

I run my hand down my pony and find the twig. "Ha. I was running on the path after my walk through the thorns, and some guy turned the corner and ran into me. I fell over on my butt. My hair must have picked up the twig too. Do I have more in my hair?" I turn my head around for him to look.

"A guy pushed you over? Who was it?" he asks as he stands up and walks over to me.

"I don't know who it was. It's not like I wanted to stay and chat with him. My legs were already in pain, and I wanted to get going. Plus, it's not like it's safe to be the only one in the woods with a strange guy." The words fall from my lips. I knew who he was, but I didn't want Dougie to get any angrier. His voice was already rising a few octaves.

His arms reach up, and I feel myself flinch ever so slightly. "My poor sweetie." He wraps his arms around me. He hugs me close. "I'm so glad you are okay. I don't want you going to those woods alone. It's not safe, especially if there are creepers in there." *Creepers? There wasn't a creeper.* "Promise me you won't go back alone."

"I promise." Kinda. *He just worries about me. There's no need to make him worry more. I'll be much safer next time. I can't promise to stay away from my tree.*

"Are there usually a lot of people in the park?"

"No. Every time I've walked by, there's never anyone there. There was just a truck there today." My stomach growls again. "I'm starving. Did you eat lunch yet?"

"Yeah, I had a sandwich. Want one?"

"Yes! I'm so hungry. I'm just going to shower quickly."

"Want me to put the stuff out for you?"

"That would be sweet. You can even make me the sandwich if you want," I giggle as I throw him a puppy face.

"I suppose I could be the best boyfriend and do that for you." He gives me a quick kiss on the cheek. "Blah, sweaty!"

"Ha-ha. Did you forget?"

"Yes. Go shower, stinky." He playfully pushes me towards the stairs.

I come down the stairs after my cold shower to find my sandwich sitting on the kitchen counter with carrots next to it. "Hmm, this looks delicious. What's in it?" I holler to Dougie.

"Turkey and lettuce, just like I had." His voice floats through the TV room and into the kitchen.

"Thanks, sweetie!" I join him on the couch to enjoy my lunch. I'm touched that he made me lunch. *That is so very sweet of him.* I smile as I take a bite while I glance at him reaching for something.

Dougie pulls out a box wrapped in newspaper.

"What is it?" I ask with a mouth full of food.

"I got a surprise for you. I felt bad last night that we didn't really get to have the date we wanted, so I got you a little something."

"What is it? You didn't have to get me anything!"

He hands me the box. "It's just a little something."

I tear open the gift, shredding the newspaper. "It's a puzzle!"

"I figured a puzzle was perfect to describe us. Sometimes an individual piece may not make sense, but once the puzzle is all put together, it's perfect. We complete one another." I haven't seen Dougie this happy in quite a while.

"I love it! So meaningful and true." My grin spreads across my face, exercising muscles I haven't used in a few days. "Let's put it together. I want us to be complete now."

"Ha-Ha. That works for me, sweetie." We finish the thousand-piece puzzle together. The picture is of two dolphins jumping in the ocean with a majestic sun setting behind the horizon. It's perfect for us: two individuals swimming through life side-by-side.

Dougie grabs us each a beer as we put together the puzzle. "Sara, I need to get something off my chest."

The concern is his voice scares me. "What is it, sweetie?"

"I can't help but worry I'm not good enough for you."

"But—"

"Just let me finish, please. I know I have some anger issues, and I'm working on them. I've been keeping a journal so that I can control my temper. It's just sometimes I get so upset because I feel like you are too good for me. You know, my life isn't perfect. After I was raped, I felt like I just wasn't worth being anyone's because I was already used. I look at you going to college, and I know you are going to make something BIG of yourself. I'm just a construction worker. When you are graduate with some big-wig job, why would you want to stay with a construction worker?" He sits staring at a puzzle piece that appears to be a dolphin's tail as he talks to me.

I don't know why he thinks he's going to be stuck being a construction worker forever; he said he graduated with an engineering degree. I'm fairly confident that it pays a lot. "Dougie, sweetie, don't be like that. You can't think like that. I don't judge you for being raped. That doesn't define who you are. I love that you are a construction worker. It tells me you are a hard worker; you are my strong man. I'm not going to go anywhere." I crawl around the coffee table to sit closer to him. "Look at me. I'm not going anywhere. You don't have to worry."

"I know, it's just, like today, you went for that long walk/run in the park without me. How do I know you aren't going to just want to keep going on long walks without me?"

"I only went alone because you were going with Chaz. I like spending time with you. You don't need to doubt that."

"I know. I just … I get so angry when I feel like I'm losing you. You know I would never want to hurt you, right?"

"I know that." *I do, don't I? Why would he want to hurt me? He "olives" me.*

"And the only reason I've gotten angry is because you do things that make me question if you really care about me too." His voice shakes.

"I'm sorry. I've never meant to make you question that. What can I do to show you that olive juice?"

"Well, you know, if you really love someone, you let them do whatever they want to you. I just don't feel like you really allow me to show you how I love you."

He said it. Love. *What does he mean, if I really loved him, I'd let him do whatever he wants to me?* "What do you mean, sweetie?"

"Well, like I said. If you really loved me, you would allow me to do what I want to you … you know, to show you I love you. Unless you saying olive juice was just that, the juice of olives."

"I don't even like olives. I love you." *Why did I say that? I love olives!*

"Then you should let me show you how I love you."

"I'm not sure I understand." *I'm so confused. Is that right? I should let him do whatever he wants to me? Is that what people in love allow?*

"Well, I know you haven't had a lot of experience in relationships, but when you really love someone, you allow them to show you how much they love you. Like, if I want to make out and stuff, you know, if you really loved me, you'd let me."

"I … I'm sorry. I …"

"I know. It's because you don't have a lot of experience. I'm older, so I know these things. But I think this is also why I've been so angry lately." His dark eyes puncture my spirit. *I can't believe I've been hurting him. I didn't know this … I was raised very … old-fashioned.*

"I'm sorry, Dougie." Guilt stabs holes in my heart. "I've never meant to hurt you … I'm just … I'm old-fashioned. We aren't married …"

"I see." He sighs as he looks down at his puzzle piece. "I'm, I'm just trying to show you that we are meant to be together, you know? Look at the puzzle. I know we're going to end up together. Don't you?"

"I guess I never really thought that far ahead."

"Ouch. That hurts. So you don't love me?"

"No, that's not what I meant. I love you, Dougie. I love you." As the words fall from my lips, I feel like I'm eavesdropping on someone else saying the words.

"So why don't you let me see if you really love me?" he says as he hooks a finger around my neck collar and pulls me in closer. His kiss is soft at first, but then he takes his hand and puts it at the back of my neck and pulls me in closer. *I'm not sure I feel comfortable, but I love him. I don't want him thinking that I don't. I would hurt him more if he knew this level of physical touching is more than I feel ready for.* He abruptly pauses from kissing me and adds the piece he's been holding of the dolphin's tail to his puzzle.

His lips return to mine with a new energy. I lie there replaying his words: "If you really love someone, you let them do whatever they want to you." He takes a piece of my puzzle and adds it to his—I mean ours. *I love him. I love him. I love him. Love never fails; it is not self-seeking. What is marriage but a piece of paper anyway?*

The sun sets, and darkness rises. Dougie is snoring on the couch as the cooking channel explores new recipes. His arms are wrapped around my body, holding me close to him on the couch. His hot breath pulls sweat beads from my neck.

I hope he knows I love him.

Nausea hits me as I lie here beneath his arm with his body steaming next to mine. I can feel tears lingering beneath my eyelids. *I feel slightly ill, but I'm not quite sure why. Is it because I've made him feel so alone the last couple of months? I don't understand what it's like to be in a relationship where two people love each other. Am I messing this up?*

I close my eyes tighter and try to control my breathing. In through my nose and out through my mouth, my breathing steadies. I listen to my own steady breathing to calm myself.

My parents were always so happy. I rarely remember them being angry or upset with one another. They may have hidden it from me, but I don't remember. It would be so much easier if they were just here with me. I could ask them.

Growing up, I recall Momma always referring to Daddy as her best friend. She would tell me that my prince charming would not only sweep me off my feet, but he'd protect me too because he would be my best friend. *Did she ever do stuff she didn't want to in order to show Daddy she loved him?* I guess I'd rather not think about that.

Dougie is holding me close, keeping me safe right now. He is trying to provide the best he can. He loves me. He has only gotten angry because he thought he was losing me. I guess he is protective, just like Momma always said my prince charming would be. That makes sense. He came into my life when I had nothing, no one. Why else would he have shown up? It was meant to be. He must be my prince charming. I'm not meant to be alone in this world.

As my breathing calms and my nausea subsides, his breath is now warm at the nape of my neck. I feel safe again in his arms, and I remind myself that he was sent to me when I had no one, nothing.

Does he plan on marrying me? He did say he knows we are going to end up together. I wonder if this puzzle was meant to be like a promise of that. I suppose there are two dolphins swimming into the sunset.

My soul dances as my mind races. Dougie wants to marry me someday. I'm not alone, not at all.

I push away my reservations. I love him … so I guess he can do what he wants to show me that he loves me too. We will put the puzzle together, one piece at a time. It doesn't matter what order the pieces are put together because they will all fit in the end. My mind rests now that it's reached a conclusion. It would be selfish of me to not let him express himself.

CHAPTER TWENTY-TWO

Sara Olivia Scott

Dougie is up and gone before I awake. He and Chaz went up to that hunting store since they couldn't go yesterday. He told me last night he was going to be gone most of the day. Again, I'm left in his home alone. I always feel like somewhat of an intruder here, like I shouldn't be here. His home is filled with all his stuff. My few items are in suitcases in the guest room upstairs.

I've never really had the yearning to snoop around his home. Then again, I've never really been alone here for long. It might be nice to see how well organized he keeps his room. I tiptoe upstairs into his man cave. I'm not sure why I am tiptoeing, but I don't want anyone to know I'm snooping around.

His bed is made with black and red throw pillows. Each pillow looks strategically placed. I pick one up. Feels fluffy. I set it back down. I look over at his dresser. He has five drawers. As I open the top drawer, my stomach flips. I know I shouldn't be looking, but I'm sure he wouldn't mind. He has probably looked at my stuff while I've been gone. Plus, what kid doesn't try to open the side of a Christmas gift when no one is looking? I'm just peeking in at the gift adult-style. His top drawer holds neatly folded boxers.

His second drawer has white and black T-shirts; these must be his undershirts. His third drawer has socks and some other random T-shirts. The socks are all neatly paired up with their matches and folded into a ball. The T-shirts are folded like they would be in a department store. The fourth drawer has pants. The bottom drawer is filled with everything other than clothing: baseball cards, pictures, actual cards, and little nick-knacks.

I pick up the pile of cards; after skimming through their covers, most appear to be love cards. I open one up and read it. "Monica, you are the world to me. I'm sorry for everything that has happened. Please forgive me. Your Dougie." At the bottom of the card, in red lettering, it reads "NO." The capitalized word written in red ink looks so angry on the black and white card. The pit in my stomach grows larger. *What has Dougie done to make Monica so angry? Should I be concer—?* I don't let myself finish my thought because I know I shouldn't be reading these. I'm not Monica. I quickly stuff the cards back in the drawer just like I found them. I quietly close the drawer and get out of his bedroom as fast as possible. *He probably just broke up with her, and she couldn't handle it. I bet that is what that was. Dougie seems like the type to want to be friends with his exes, and she probably wouldn't have any of it.* I place the Band-Aid across my mind, hoping this crack is healed.

I go back to my guest room and switch into my running clothes. *I need a run to clear my mind. What have I done? I shouldn't have looked through his things; that wasn't right.*

My feet hit the pavement as the warm air swarms around me. *I know I shouldn't have looked in his drawers, but I wasn't looking for something that I shouldn't find. I was just seeing how he organizes his clothes and whatnot.*

As much as I try to switch my mind to a different topic, I can't stop wondering who Monica is. *I don't think he's ever mentioned a Monica.*

I know he said he was in love before. She must be the person he was with before me. I know he had mentioned he was really hurt from a past relationship. My side starts to ache after five minutes of running. Maybe it is guilt for snooping that causes me to walk.

I conclude that Monica was his previous girlfriend. *She must have given him back all of their love letters after they broke up. Why would he need forgiveness? Why would she write "NO"? I should have never gone through his stuff.* I push the cards out of my head and focus on my breathing pattern.

I slow to a speed walk in the hopes that the ache in my sides will go away. There isn't a good running path in this city, unless I just run around his townhouse development. So my feet bring me to the path I take to work. There aren't many vehicles out on the road for a Sunday afternoon, so I give up on my speed walking and just walk. No one will know I'm cheating on my workout.

I approach the park. My feet so badly want to take me back to that special serene spot in the woods beneath that one protective tree, but I promised Dougie I would stay out of the park when I'm alone. My walk comes to a standstill as I look at the woods. *I am not sure I would even bring him to the tree if he were with me; I like having it to myself. It's the only thing I have all to myself here.*

My eyes fall upon the single vehicle in the parking lot, a red truck. Before I can connect the dots, I see Officer Kipton get out of the driver's door. I quickly glance back toward the road, not wanting him to make eye contact with me. My standstill turns back into a speed walk.

Even with my eyes straight ahead at the paved road, my peripherals tell me he is not alone. I hear him whistle. Why is he whistli—"AH-HHHH!" My own scream startles me, and my shoes leap two feet off the ground.

"SIT, GIZMO!" he shouts. The dog comes to an abrupt halt and plops down ten feet from me.

I finally hear my voice go silent as the little monster stops.

"I'm so sorry!" He runs over to me. "Are you okay? I'm so sorry. He never runs after people." Officer Kipton stands next to me with his hand on my shoulder. His face is pale with concern.

With his hand on my shoulder and his eyes looking at mine, he reminds me once again of warm honey. Comforting. "Yeah," I chuckle, trying to make light of the awkward and embarrassing moment.

"Are you sure you are okay? Can I get you some water or something? I have a couple bottles in the truck."

How is his dog still sitting in the same place? "No, I'm good. Thanks. Your dog, he's still sitting there. That's amazing."

"He listens pretty well, most of the time." He glances over at the dog and then back at me. "You know, I just feel so bad. Are you positive I can't get you something?"

"No, I'm fine. I was just startled. Didn't see him coming. What's his name?" I walk over to the beautiful dog. He's only about sixty pounds, brown with black tiger-looking stripes, and has a white stripe down the middle of his nose.

"Gizmo. He's two years old. He's a boxer."

"He's so cute." The dog starts licking my sweaty hand. "You aren't so scary now, are you, little guy?"

"He's apologizing to you." Gizmo licks me some more before Officer Kipton asks, "Are you sure I can't get you something? I feel really bad and would like to make it up to you."

"No, I'm good. Thanks though. I need to finish up my run anyway."

"Do you run this road frequently?"

"Well, I walk it daily to and from work, but I've run it a couple times."

"I should warn you that it's not the safest road. I get called at least once a month for car accidents on this stretch. Where do you work?"

"The restaurant up the street, Sweet Apple Pie."

"I love that place! How long have you worked there?"

"I just started a couple weeks ago." I give Gizmo a little pet good-bye. "I'd better get back to running. Enjoy your day." I abruptly end the conversation before he asks me any more questions. Without missing a beat, I take off running down the road.

"I'll see you around," he says to my back. "Come on, Gizmo. Ready for our run?" I hear them take off toward the park behind me. Officer Kipton reminds me of someone, but I can't place him. I resist the urge to look over my shoulder after them.

My run goes by quickly. I'm back at the house and showered an hour later. Without Dougie home, I have much more free time than I know what to do with. I opt to call Melanie.

"Sara! How have you been?"

"I'm great. You?"

"Never better! I'm sorry I haven't called you in a while. Life is crazy busy here. So what is new?"

"I live with Dougie now!"

"What?" Static.

"Yeah! After the semester ended, I didn't really have anywhere to go. He told me I could come and live with him for the summer until classes start back up in the fall."

"Oh my gosh! That's awesome! Are you guys sharing a bedroom and everything?"

"No. I'm staying in his guestroom. But it's nice to live under the same roof as him."

"Wow. I'm surprised. That just moved really quickly." Static. "You aren't engaged, are you?"

"No. Just living with him."

"I'm so happy for you guys. Guess what?"

"What?"

"I'm dating someone too. His name is Geilen. He's from Ireland, so he has an accent and everything!"

"Accents are the best! Where did you guys meet?"

"I met him at the grocery store. He's actually on his way to pick me up for a Sunday afternoon picnic date."

"I'm happy for you! How long have you guys been together?"

"Just a couple weeks. We've been spending every minute we can together."

"I miss you."

"I miss you too. I'm going to try and get out there to see you. You know you are always welcome here too."

"I know. Thanks." I pause. "I have a question for you." I know I shouldn't ask.

"Yeah?"

"Did you know Dougie's ex?"

"Kinda. She was weird. Kinda skittish. Why?"

"Why did they break up?"

"I don't know. Why?"

"I was just curious. He doesn't talk about his past, but I was just curious."

"Yeah, I'm not sure. You should just ask him. I'm so happy you two are together. Don't forget, I'm the one who made that happen." Melanie laughs.

"I won't forget. I owe you." I join her laughter.

"Hey girlie, sorry, but Geilen just pulled up. We'll talk later, okay?"

"Have fun at your picnic!"

"Thanks! Bye."

Melanie and I haven't talked a ton since she moved back home. She's still the closest friend I've ever had, but she has her own life now, just as I do mine.

I can't help but wonder if it's weird Dougie and I don't share a room. I don't think that's odd. My parents were as old-fashioned as they come. Maybe I'll just do something really nice for Dougie. Plus, I still feel slightly guilty for going through his stuff. I know I should not have gone through his personal cards, but I can't help but want to sneak back upstairs and read through the rest of the stack. I bet there are about two dozen cards in that pile, and I bet they are all love notes.

If they are all love notes, why did he apologize to her? Why would you send someone you love a love note after the relationship is already over? I assume she returned all of the love notes, but you wouldn't ask for forgiveness in a card if there wasn't something that needed forgiving.

Corinthians pops back into my head: Love, it does not dishonor others.

No, I can't snoop anymore. Maybe I'll just try to bring it up in conversation. It will be easier to ask him about his past relationships and have him bring up the cards on his own. Win-win.

Cleaning appears to be the perfect remedy for my guilty conscience. An hour and a half later, the house is so clean it's shining. The smell of bleach confirms how clean every surface is, except for that one drawer. With nothing else to do, I lie down on the couch and flip on the television. I flip through the stations for anything entertaining, but there isn't much on Sunday afternoons. I stop on the weather channel; this will be a good sound machine. The longer I sit, the more exhausted I become. I close my eyes and surrender to sleep.

"Sweetie." I feel a kiss on my forehead and find Dougie kneeling on the ground next to me.

"Huh?"

A smile spreads across his face. "Someone tired? Someone having a lazy day?"

I finally get oriented. "Was I sleeping?"

"I think so. At least the snoring led me to that conclusion."

"I was snoring?"

"Yeppers. Wanna see what I got?"

"Yeah." I sit up on the couch. I hold in my yawn and resist rubbing my eyes awake.

Dougie flips through the shirts and pants he got. "I also got my girl something too."

My heart jumps with excitement. *I get something too!* "What did you get me?"

Dougie pulls out a black long-sleeve shirt that has a picture of a doe on the front. The shirt, in small print underneath the photo, reads, "I've already been tagged."

"Like it? It's hunter humor. I had to get it for you when I saw it."

"Cute. I love it."

"Put it on!"

I go to the bathroom and switch shirts. The shirt fits perfectly. I walk back out to get Dougie's approval. "Well, what do you think?"

"I like it! And I looove you." He smiles as he scans me up and down.

I wrap my arms around him and give him a thank you kiss. "I love the shirt. Thank you for thinking of me."

"Of course. I'm always thinking of you." He gives me a bear hug. "Did you bleach the house?"

"Yeah. I wanted to surprise you, so I cleaned everything." I proudly smile.

"You are the best girlfriend. What do you say we go for an evening walk?"

"Evening? What time is it?" I look out the window. The sun is setting.

"It's 8:30 p.m."

"What? 8:30 p.m.?" *I can't believe I've been sleeping for hours.*

"Yeah. What time did you lie down on the couch?"

"I honestly don't remember, but it wasn't anywhere near 8:30." I smile. "I guess I was tired."

"So let's go for an evening walk and wake you up bit."

"Okay. How does my hair look?"

"Like you slept on it. But that's okay. Remember, you've already been tagged." His smile makes me smile.

"Okay. Let's go for a sunset walk."

The air is warm, but a cool breeze sweeps through the neighborhood. We walk hand-in-hand down our street. There isn't anyone out and about, which doesn't surprise me since this street is dead day and night.

"So what did you do today?"

"I went for a run. I was actually running past that park when a dog started to run after me." I don't think I need to say it was Officer Kipton's dog. Dougie was not too terribly thrilled with the officer that night someone reported the noise. "But then the owner told the dog to sit, and it did. I kept on my run and then came back here, showered, and cleaned. It was really boring without you."

"Where did you clean?"

I'd better stay clear of his bedroom. I didn't go back in there after I found the pile of cards. I didn't trust myself to clean his room without accidentally opening that bottom drawer. "Everywhere but your room." What if he notices some stuff has been slightly moved in his room? "Well, I went into your room to clean, but it looked clean, so I didn't do it. Is that okay?"

"Oh yeah. My room is kind of my place anyway. I prefer to do the cleaning in there. Thanks for doing the rest of the house though. I really appreciate it."

"I'm glad you liked my surprise." I give him a friendly hip-check. *Is it weird he doesn't want me in his room?*

"I'm glad you liked my surprise." He gives me a friendly hip-check back, but his is a bit stronger than mine. I fall on my side. "Ah! I'm sorry, sweetie." He helps me to my feet. "I didn't realize I did it that hard."

"You didn't." I laugh. "I was just in mid-step."

"My poor little sweetheart." He wraps his arm around my hip and pulls me in to kiss my temple.

What more can I ask for? I have a man who loves me, and I love him. "I love you, Dougie." We watch the sun set as it shoots purples, reds, pinks, and oranges across the darkening sky.

Monday morning comes early. Dougie is still asleep as I sneak out of the house. I feel energized for the workweek. I know I need to up my tips to keep some of the stress off Dougie while he's short on work. I didn't have the nerve to ask him about his ex-girlfriend and spoil such a perfect evening. I'll ask in a couple weeks when he's back working his full schedule—when he's happier.

I'm early to the restaurant; no one else is in sight, so I sit on the curb outside the front door. The sun is just beginning to rise above the trees that line the street across from the restaurant. The restaurant is pretty much the only proof of civilization on this stretch of road; there is a gas station a quarter mile up the road on the same side as the restaurant, but woods spread across the other side of the street for miles in both directions. Most people who come into the restaurant already know it's here, as most of them have been coming regularly for years.

I cherish mornings like this, when the rest of the world is still asleep. So calm, so peaceful. Birds sing their morning hymns while deer and other critters crawl into their hidden beds for the day. I take in a slow, deep breath. The fresh morning air fills my lungs, still cool from the evening's breeze.

I see headlights winding up the road. Brian must be running late since he's usually here by now with a cup of coffee in his hands.

"I know I'm late," he hollers as he gets out of his car. "Maybe I ought to just give you the keys to open the place, and then you can have coffee ready for me." His smile makes me uncomfortable. I step back as he unlocks the front doors. Sometimes he can be a bit creepy.

"I'd be happy to make you coffee." The real reason I want to make the coffee is because he makes it so strong! I usually pretend to empty the prepackaged coffee grounds entirely into the filter, but I keep a tablespoon hidden in the bag before I toss it into the garbage. Battery acid just isn't appealing this early in the morning.

"Well, you'd better clock in, or you are going to be late."

After I clock in, I get my morning side-work started: I reload the dishes and silverware and pull out the morning pastries from the fridge so they warm up before we open in half an hour. Mornings are typically very slow, customer-wise. One or two people roll in at about seven when my back-up server arrives, but other than that, it's usually just Brian and me for the first couple hours.

"Hey, Sara, we got a customer. Why don't you seat 'em? I'm still trying to eat my breakfast." I hear him screech from his office, which means he is watching the security cameras. I have no reason to yell back, as he will see me on the camera walking up to the front door.

"Good morning."

"Morning," he says, his face wrinkling with surprise. "I didn't realize you worked here."

"Sure you didn't, officer." I smile. "I work here most mornings. I've never seen you here before." Before he can say anything, I jokingly add, "First, you don't follow the leash law, and now you're stalking me!" I give him a smile to let him know I'm only kidding.

"Ha-Ha. Well, I guess you could request I give myself a ticket for the leash law. As for stalking, that's definitely not the case. I'm usually a regular here, but it's been about a month since I had breakfast here. I ran out of food at home today and didn't have time to get to the store." I seat him in a booth.

"What can I get ya to drink?"

"A coffee would be perfect. You guys are open, right?" He looks around at the vacant tables and chairs.

"Yeah. We open at 6:30 a.m., but we're lucky if we have one or two people roll in at 7 a.m. It doesn't usually pick up until about 7:30 a.m. or so."

I bring him his coffee. "I'm sorry. I forgot to ask. Do you take cream?"

"No thanks. I like it black. Healthier that way."

"True. I drink mine black for the same reason. I don't get why people add sugar to coffee."

"I hear ya. I usually have enough donuts to get my sugar fill," he chuckles.

"Oh, so the stereotype is accurate. Cops and donuts, huh?"

"Ha. Well, kinda, yes. Our sergeant usually brings in a box of donuts and bagels." He takes a sip of his coffee. "This is perfect. I remember this stuff usually being more bitter, but this is quite delicious."

I smile because I have my own little secret for brewing our coffee. "Well, what can I get ya for breakfast? And I should tell you we don't sell donuts." I give him a teasing smile.

"Ha. Well, darn it then. Nah, I'm kidding. May I please have two eggs scrambled, bacon, hash browns, and some dry wheat toast?"

"Not a problem. I'll go ring it into the computer system." Ah, look at me using waitress slang. "Ring it in" means transfer the order to the cook.

Edward, the cook, is in the kitchen starting up the grill as I walk back to warn him of the order. "Do we already have a customer?"

"Yep. I am just as surprised as you are."

"Crap. It's going to take me a few minutes to get everything up and running. Who is the customer? Bob? Carl?"

"A police officer."

"Are you kidding?" He cusses under his breath as he rushes to get the kitchen ready.

"Want me to tell the officer it's going to take a few minutes?"

"No! Just give me a minute."

I walk back out to talk with Officer Kipton again. "So do you work mornings, nights, or both?" After all, the few encounters we have had have been at all times of day.

"I work what the force tells me to work, which is pretty much all the time."

"Got ya. How long have you been an officer?" I try to make small talk. He's easier to talk to when I don't have a black eye. Plus, I need to maximize my tips.

"Couple years." He nods his head. "I've known I wanted to be an officer since I was a kid. My dad was an officer."

"That would be so stressful. To have someone in your family be a police officer. Always worrying if something is going to happen to them. I'm happy my Dougie is in construction, which is mostly safe." I don't know why I feel the need to bring Dougie up in conversation with him.

"Well, we always keep safety a priority. We don't typically respond to calls that seem dangerous without backup."

His cup is half empty. "Want me to top off your coffee? Your food should be up soon. Our cook was still getting everything setup."

"I'll maybe take one with my food. No point in making a trip just for my coffee."

"I don't mind." I turn and go to the back to get my special brew. Just as I finish filling his cup, I hear Edward holler that the food order is up.

"Here ya go." I set the warm plate on the table with his hot coffee.

"Smells delicious!" He puts his napkin on his lap. So proper.

"I know. It took everything in me not to take a bite out of it." I chuckle.

"Go for it." His smile is so welcoming. He actually seems half-serious.

"I'll pass. It's kinda against the rules here," I joke back. "Enjoy."

"I shall. Thanks."

I go back into the kitchen. "Is there a cop here?" Brian asks.

"Yeah."

"Well, just make sure he's happy. Does he have enough coffee? I don't want to piss off a cop."

"I just refilled his cup. He's good. I'll check back on him in a few minutes."

Brian wipes the small beads of sweat from his forehead before retreating to his office.

Is it weird I keep running into this officer? He isn't following me, is he? No, I'm being absurd. He was in the park both times before I was, and he didn't know I worked here until yesterday. It's reasonable to go out to breakfast if you don't have food in your home. I shake the curiosity from my mind. *He couldn't possibly plan to see me since he knows I'm in a relationship. He's even been to Dougie's home.*

"Morning Sara!" Stephanie's voice scatters my thoughts.

"Hey, Steph!"

"I can't believe there's actually a customer here!"

"I know, right? You're early today." I wonder how early Officer Kipton used to come here. I thought he mentioned he used to come here for breakfast a lot.

"Yeah, I wanted to grab a meal before work."

"Good call. I should probably check on him before I forget. I'm not used to being put to work this early." *Oh wait. He said he thought the coffee was better than the crap before. So he had to have been here before to know how nasty the coffee usually is.*

"Ha. Well, go get your money, honey."

Officer Kipton is already halfway through his meal.

"How's it taste?"

"Perfect. Just what I was looking for."

"Good." I smile before turning to go chat with Stephanie.

"Do you work here every day?" he asks just as I take my first step.

Turning around, I take the step back to his table. "Mostly. I work Mondays, Tuesdays, Wednesdays, and Fridays in the morning. I work the night shift on Thursdays, though, because my boyfriend likes it when I wait on him and his friends."

Our conversation is cut short when Ashley walks in. Her hair is ruffled, and her clothes are wrinkled. I unintentionally let out a short sigh. Officer Kipton nods in agreement. My face turns pink because I didn't actually mean for anyone to hear that. "Sorry," I mumble to him.

He smiles at me. It's like he realizes I unintentionally made the remark.

"I'll let you finish your meal." I sneakily set his bill upside down on the table before turning to hide my embarrassment.

In the kitchen, Ashley throws flirtatious glances at Brian. *I guess Carla is out and Ashley is his new chick. Hmm, no wonder Carla hasn't been at work this past week.* Stephanie looks at me and says everything with an eye roll. I raise my eyebrows and shoot a quick smirk back at her in agreement.

"What was that?" Ashley shoots me a wicked glance.

"Steph and I were talking about the officer," I blatantly lie. Steph keeps her back to Ashley.

"What about the cop?" Now Ashley and Brian are both staring at me.

"He's weird." *What can I say to cover this up?*

"Why?"

"He was trying to make small talk about the weather." I'm grasping for anything. "I mean, come on, the weather?" I actually feel guilty for even saying a bad word about Officer Kipton. He seems like such a nice guy.

"Well, did you entertain him with conversation?" Brian pipes in.

"Of course. It's just weird when people talk about the weather. People resort to that when they don't have anything else to say."

Ashley turns and walks out onto the floor, grabbing the coffee pot. I follow a few steps behind her to see what she is doing.

She marches up to Officer Kipton's table and says, "How about that weather, huh? Want a warm-up on the coffee? I see Sara let your cup go empty."

How dare she make me look bad in front of Brian.

"No, I'm good, thanks. Two cups of coffee is more than enough. It's nice outside, huh? Hopefully it won't be too warm today."

"Yeah." She turns and walks back to the prep area. "Fine. I believe you," she mumbles to me and tosses in a quick smile.

I smile at Officer Kipton even though he isn't looking my way. He just saved my butt from getting fired. *Why can't he be the manager here? Ugh.*

I see Brian holding a piece of scratch paper with red ink. It says, "Not today." My mind randomly jumps back to the cards in Dougie's dresser. *I wonder if this Monica was anything like Ashley?* I could see her writing "NO" on someone's love letter and mailing it back. Thankfully, her name isn't Monica.

I walk back out to his table. "You all ready?"

"Yep. Thanks. Have a good day." He hands me his tab with a twenty-dollar bill.

"Let me grab you some change." I take the money.

"Nah. Keep it. It's not everyday you get good service like this. I may just have to come here more often for breakfast."

"But we don't have donuts," I joke.

"Well, then, now I'm torn. Good food or donuts?" His smile is contagious. "Have a great day."

"You too. Thanks." His bill is only $9.59.

The rest of the day slowly passes. No one tips as well as Officer Kipton, but then again, you can't expect to get over a 100 percent tip all the time. Ashley lightens up as the day goes on. Stephanie makes my workday cheerful, as always. I'm cut from the floor at 3:30 p.m., which is much earlier than I am used to.

The walk home goes quick, mostly because it looks like it's about to rain. I don't want to get caught in it. The park's lot is empty as I speed past it. I feel safe walking by the woods. It is like I know my tree is watching over me. I have no need to thrash through the thickets to find it today. I can feel it.

I get home just as the rain starts to fall. Dougie is kicked back on the couch with a beer in hand. He's reading his manly magazine while watching sports.

"Hey!" I smile as I open the door.

"Hey, sweetie. How was work?"

"Great. I made out pretty well with tips. How was your day?"

"My day was fine. How much did you make?" His voice sounds grumpy.

"Eighty-seven, which is really good for a Monday," I proudly state, straightening as I say the amount out loud.

"Great. Wanna go out to dinner then?"

"Sure, where did you have in mind?"

"I don't know. There's this great Chinese place in the city. It's really small. Most people don't know about it."

"That'd be perfect. Let me change out of these clothes first. I smell like syrup and pancakes."

"I like syrup and pancakes." He meets me in the hall and breathes in. "Mmm, pancakes." He pulls me in close and kisses me.

"I'm glad one of us likes this smell." After I get out of the restaurant, syrup is the last thing I want to smell.

"Shhh." He pulls my head closer to his lips. We stand there kissing in the hallway. I feel my stomach flip. I can taste beer on his breath, which means he is probably going to get a little frisky. Plus, when he drinks, he seems to be a bit more aggressive, physically that is. My mind replays his words: "When you really love someone, you let them do whatever they want to you."

I pull away. "I really need to change out of these clothes. I'm not feeling so well all of a sudden."

"What's wrong?"

"I think I may be coming down with something." My stomach churns.

"You don't look so well. Why did you let me kiss you? I don't want to get sick." He wipes his mouth with his forearm.

"I'm sorry. I felt fine a minute ago. Maybe it's just the smell of syrup. I'm going to go get changed."

"Are we still getting Chinese?"

"I may need to pass. I can give you twenty bucks, though, so that you can still go out."

"That works. Maybe I'll call up Chaz and see if he wants to grab some grub."

I reach into my apron and pull out a twenty-dollar bill.

"If you want me to enjoy a beer, I may need forty, sweetie." He smiles at me with a cocked head and puppy dog eyes.

"Okay. Why do you give me those puppy dog eyes? I can't resist those." I give him another twenty.

"Thanks, sweetie."

I head upstairs and go into my room. I dig through the pile of clothing on the floor and find some old navy blue sweatpants and an oversized gray sweatshirt. I switch my socks out for a clean pair. The sprinkles turn to rain outside. I shiver as the rain's cold temperature permeates my body. I must be getting sick.

"I'm going to go pick up Chaz. I'll see ya later tonight, sweetie. Feel better!"

I holler back downstairs, "Thanks, Dougie. Tell Chaz I say hi." And he is out the door. Thunder rumbles through the home in unison with the front door closing. I watch from my bedroom window as Dougie backs out of the driveway and speeds down the road. The rain is falling rapidly, and mini-floods are forming in the roadway.

My stomach isn't churning anymore. It's just sore. I didn't have any time to eat at work today, so I check to see what is in the fridge. Beer? I'm going to pass on that. Just as I go to reach for the box of lunch-meat, thunder crackles outside the window. My body jumps before my brain can tell my nerves that the noise is only thunder.

I stuff the deli ham in my mouth and opt to turn on the television. As I flip through the channels, I can't find anything worth watching.

Dougie is going to be gone for at least an hour, if not longer, and I feel better, so I don't want to just lie down. Lightning momentarily blinds me through the patio door. I jump up and rush to close the curtains.

Before the thunder crackles, my brain reminds me of the stack of cards in Dougie's bottom drawer. My stomach churns a little. *Probably just hunger, right?* I push aside my physical warning and sneak upstairs. I open Dougie's door and peer in. Of course it's empty; he just left.

I turn on the light and go over to his dresser. I just need to know. He was so distraught over this girl. If I can look and see what happened, I may be able to help him. I know he loves me now, so I'm not worried about his ex. I know he's mentioned to me that he almost killed himself after she left him and that it took a long time to move on. I can't help but wonder what kind of power she has over my Dougie.

The rain gets louder as the wind thrusts it up against the far outside wall of Dougie's room. Flashes of light dance along his other three walls. I go to open the bottom drawer with slightly shaky hands. Thunder shakes the house just as I get the drawer opened. My nerves explode from the rumble. I scream to no one and slam his bottom drawer shut. That is clearly God's sign that I shouldn't be in here. My stomach punches my insides.

I quickly shut off Dougie's light and head downstairs. Television it is. I flip through the stations and end up on some award show. The actors look so beautiful and skinny. I look at my stomach. It's mostly flat, but I could define it more. Even Dougie noticed that I could tone it up. There is nothing like skinny models to make you want to work out. I get on the floor and do a push-up. I don't remember push-ups being this difficult. One … two … three. Okay, that's enough. I lifted trays all day. That's weight lifting in itself.

I browse through Dougie's stack of magazines. Cars, hot women modeling next to cars, muscle building, hot women next to muscle men, hunting—ALL boring. I look through his coffee table drawers: an empty picture frame, a pen, a lighter, an army knife—*wait, lighter? He doesn't smoke. Why would Dougie have a lighter?* I look around and find solace when my eyes meet a candle in the corner of the room. *Okay, duh, a lighter is for lighting candles.*

The television is more entertaining than anything else in the house. I look at my phone: 4:25 p.m. *Jeesh, I have nothing to do all night.*

I have an epiphany: Dougie has a stack of cards, all probably from his ex. I'll write him my own! It will be super romantic, and hopefully, if I write enough, they can replace the old ones he has upstairs.

"Dear Dougie,

I want you to know how much you mean to me. The moment I met you, I was at a loss for words. You literally had my heart at first glance. Even when my world seemed to be empty, you filled it with happiness. Thank you so much for allowing me to move into your home with you for the summer. I can't wait to see where we go from here. I love you.

Yours,

Sara

I run upstairs and tuck the letter beneath his pillow. It's 5:35 p.m. I didn't expect the letter to take me so long to write. I peer outside my bedroom window. No car. The thunderstorm isn't as strong, but I can hear the thunder roaring in the distance. The rain has turned into a melodic tune as it hits the pavement outside. Knowing tomorrow is going to come early, I crawl into my bed, leaving the shades open on the window. Calmness holds me even though the thunderstorm lurks outside.

CHAPTER TWENTY-THREE

Sara Olivia Scott

Thursdays are definitely the best day at work. Dougie comes in and keeps me company. It also means only one more day of work before the weekend. This week went by fast. Monday was exhausting, but Tuesday and Wednesday were very slow at the restaurant. No more surprise 6:30 a.m. customers and very little traffic flow the rest of the days. Dougie and I hung around home and just watched television on Tuesday and Wednesday. When he found his letter, he was very happy. In fact, he was so happy he made me dinner. He even lit the candles! He doesn't seem to mind having to take the week off of work as long as he has his beer and television to occupy his time.

Ashley is finishing up her day shift as I walk in the door. "Hey, Ashley."

I get no smile back, but she at least gives me a quick "Hi" in return.

Brian is also finishing up his shift, which means Jeremy is coming in to manage tonight. Brian usually works Thursday nights, but this week he and Ashley have something to go to, so Jeremy is taking over. I've only met Jeremy a few times, but he seems like a better manager than Brian. First, he isn't sleeping with any of the staff. Second, he actually cares about his job.

Jeremy follows me into the back. "Hey Sara, how's it going today?"

"Great! How about you, Jeremy?"

"Good. I just hope it picks up in here. It's been dead most of the week."

"Yeah, I know. Yesterday and Tuesday were dreadfully slow. I could use some money tonight."

Brian walks into the kitchen. "Hey, Jer. I'm heading out. Ashley doesn't have time to do her side work, so I assume Sara won't have a problem doing it as it's pretty much dead in here."

Jeremy looks at me and then back to Brian. "That shouldn't be a problem." Brian is still Jeremy's boss, so of course Jeremy isn't going to upset him. "Where are you guys going tonight?"

I eavesdrop as I start Ashley's side work.

"We have a thing. Have a good night." His voice avoids the question.

I glance over to see Brian give me a head nod with a crooked smirk. My smile back says what I'm thinking: *Oh, it's going to be a better night now that you are leaving.* Maybe I smiled too much?

Jeremy looks over to me and says, "Sorry, Sara. Please clean up this place before the dinner rush starts." His shrug confirms he is actually sorry to put the extra work on me. I don't mind picking up Ashley's slack. This means that tonight will be great because it will be me, a couple other girls, and Jeremy, which equates to no drama.

I finish restocking the fridge with the domestic beer bottles and then refill all the condiments on the tables. The restaurant has red ketchup containers and yellow mustard containers so that we can buy the generic brands and refill the containers. Just as I finish filling up the last ketchup container, Jeremy walks in. "I just seated you, Sara. Three top."

"Thanks, Jeremy." I go to see what customers are here. Three guys in their twenties dressed like cowboys. I feel my smile come naturally as

I greet them. "Hey guys, what can I get ya tonight?" I'm suddenly very aware of my Minnesotan accent.

"What beers you got here, ma'am?" The southern drawl matches their outfit. I list off our beers. "Well, then, pretty lady, we're fixing to have ourselves some Millers."

"I'll be right back." They fit the stereotype of charming southerners. I am somewhat uncomfortable being called "pretty lady" by anyone other than my Dougie. Oh well, it isn't that uncomfortable. Kinda nice. Hopefully, they tip well.

As soon as I bring them their beers, I see Dougie come in the door with Chaz. It takes everything in me not to run over and hug him. "What can I get you guys?" I ask the southern charmers as I smile over my shoulder at my Dougie. He gives me a head nod.

I quickly jot down the cowboys' order and punch it into the register before walking over to greet Dougie and Chaz. "Hey, handsome." I smile.

"Howdy." Dougie has a serious smirk on his face, and Chaz laughs in the background.

"Huh?" I chuckle, realizing he was poking fun at the cowboys.

"I thought I had to be a stupid cowboy to get my order in."

"I told him to say that!" Chaz holds his stomach as he bellows with laughter.

"Ha. I like you the way you are. Please don't ever become a cowboy." I give him a quick peck on the cheek. Dougie wouldn't look right with a cowboy hat on.

"You don't have to worry about that, sweetie." He glances behind me at the cowboys, none of whom appear to be looking our way.

"What's wrong?"

"They just seemed to be flirting with my lady."

"Pff. I don't think so."

"Well, my lady going to get me some beer? Pretty please?"

"My pleasure. You guys having the usual?"

"Yes," they say in unison.

I ring in their beer orders and bring them back. By then, a few more of Dougie's friends show up, so I take their beer orders as well. Just as I finish bringing the group their drinks, the order for the cowboys is up. I finish adding the parsley to the burgers and fries.

"Here ya go, guys." I set down their burgers; they all ordered the same thing. "Can I get you anything else?"

"We were debating which one of us you would go for," says the cowboy with the blonde hair and blue eyes. The other two have brown hair. They all have scruffy five-day facial hair.

"Well, boys, sorry to hurt you, but I'd have to say none." I glance over my shoulder at Dougie, who is staring at us. I smile at him before turning back. "You see that handsome guy looking over this way? He's my man."

"Oh, my bad," says the blonde. He gives Dougie a head nod as if to apologize. "Sorry, ma'am."

"No problem. Enjoy your meal."

As I turn to walk away, I feel their eyes following me.

"What did those guys want?" Dougie is serious.

"They were trying to flirt. Do you believe that?" I chuckle. "I told them you are my man, so they'd better not. Then they apologized, and that was that." I give Dougie a quick one-arm hug and lean into him as I'm talking.

Some more of Dougie's friends come join him at the table. I know they have all introduced themselves to me before, but it is hard to remember all of their names as different guys show up each week. I think it is Ryan, John, Alex, David, Pete, Joey, Paul, and … uh … I don't remember. Then of course it's Chaz and my Dougie.

"The usual," Paul pipes in. Everyone else is having their usual drink as well. I get all of their beer orders, and I deliver them five minutes later.

"I'll be right back, guys. I need to check on my other customers quick." I walk over to my only other table, the cowboys. They are three-quarters of the way through eating. "How is everything? Anyone need anything?"

"Nope, it's delicious. Thank you, ma'am." The blond man smiles.

"You really don't need to call me ma'am." I give an uncomfortable chuckle. "It makes me feel old."

"Sorry, ma—" Blonde stops himself. "Down south, we are taught at a young age to refer to every female as 'ma'am.' It's a respect thing. We don't mean any offense by it."

"Oh, I know that. Just like when I say 'guys,' I'm not actually trying to be sexist; we Minnesotans like to refer to everyone that way."

"Ha-ha. We noticed that. Ya'll have thick accents up here."

I burst out in laughter. "I'm sorry, it's just that we don't ever hear people say 'ya'll' up here. It sounds funny."

"Well, we are happy we 'guys' can make you northerners laugh." One of the dark-haired guys smiles.

"Well, thanks for coming in guys. Have a great trip." I set their bill facedown on the table.

I walk back to Dougie's table. "Are you guys ready to order?"

"It's about time. Don't those cowboys know you're taken? Jeesh!" Chaz is clearly trying to provoke Dougie. He is such an instigator.

"Of course, they know that. Don't be ridiculous. I have to make small talk with people in order to get tips. Being a jerk gets me nowhere as a server." Sometimes Chaz can be a real jerk. He loves to egg on the other guys and get their testosterone going.

"Well, why don't you serve us then if you are our servant?" Chaz is getting a bit sarcastic. I see Dougie notice Chaz's three-drink tone.

"Hey, watch it. That's my lady. You don't talk to her that way." Dougie's voice is very serious. I know he is somewhat overprotective of me. I can't help but smile on the inside at Dougie sticking up for me.

Chaz sinks back into his chair a bit. "Sorry, man. I was just messing around. It's the beer talking."

Doug gives him a head nod to tell Chaz "it's all good." I take their orders and go ring them in. The guys are all ready for another round of beers, so I bring those out as well. Chaz wants to order himself and Dougie a shot for what I assume is to "make up" for the way he talked to me. "What shot do ya guys want?"

"Blonde headed slut." Chaz gives me a smirk. I feel the hairs on the back of my neck sticking out.

"That sounds delicious." Dougie winks at me.

"Okay, I'll be right back." As I walk away, I can hear them chuckle. The way Chaz said the drink name and the way Dougie winked at me makes my stomach flutter. I shake my head. *I'm just thinking too much.*

"How's it going out there?" Jeremy asks, peeking his head out from the kitchen.

"Slow. I only have Dougie's table in my section."

"I was afraid it was going to be slow. I really hope it picks up in here." Jeremy is a good guy. I really enjoy working with him. "I would like for everyone to make some good tips around here. Maybe brighten up people's attitudes."

Do I have an attitude? I must have made a pondering face as Jeremy quickly adds, "Not you, Sara. The other gals."

I smile at him. "It's nice working with you, Jeremy. We have only had a few shifts together; maybe you should work Thursday evenings more often."

"I'm actually missing my girlfriend's birthday party right now. I had planned a big party for her, and then Brian told me I had to work tonight." He shakes his head in disappointment.

"I'm sorry. I would help if I knew anything about managing."

"Thanks. Not your fault. I'll bring her home some pie. I hope she's having a good time."

I shrug, not knowing what to say. Poor guy. I thought Brian was just a jerk; I didn't realize he was that cruel. I'm sure he and Ashley are just … um … well, I don't want to put any images in my head. "Sorry," I offer, as we both know Brian isn't.

Jeremy half-smiles as he accepts his predicament and heads back to the office. There isn't much for him to do on the floor, so I'm sure he is giving his girlfriend a call to see how her party is going.

Dougie and his friends' orders are up. I cart the ten plates out on two different trays. I feel my biceps working extra hard as I try to balance both trays. *I could be in the Olympics for how talented I am right now.* I can't help but beam as I successfully set the two trays down on a table near Dougie and the guys.

I pass out all the meals and go grab some more beers for them. "Enjoy!" I can hear them already inhaling their food as I turn to go greet my new table.

"Hey guys. How are you doing tonight?" *What is it with all these tables of guys in their twenties?* I take their drink order and sigh in relief that none of them are trying to flirt with me. I can feel Dougie's eyes follow me to the bar as I get this group their drinks. I resist the urge to turn around and look at him. My stomach flutters. I drop off their beverages and take their order, all while feeling his eyes on my back.

"Thanks. I'll ring this right in, guys." I smile and turn to go ring in their meal order. I see Dougie's table watching me as I make my way back to the kitchen. They are all hooting and hollering about something, which isn't abnormal for them; their alcohol consumption usually kicks in about this time.

Just as I finish ringing in the new table's order, I feel someone standing behind me. I whip around to see Dougie standing behind me. "What are you doing, babe? Need something?"

His eyes are slightly glossed. I can tell the shots and beers have kicked in. "I need my woman," he says in a flat monotone that half scares me. I can't help but notice I'm blocked between the machine to ring in orders, the wall, and Dougie's body. Claustrophobia abruptly swallows me.

"Well, I'll be cut from the floor in a couple hours. Maybe we can go home together." I smile as I start to wedge my way between Dougie and the wall to walk the few steps back into the kitchen.

He grabs my right bicep and squeezes it tight. "Oww, that hurts!" I try to keep myself from saying it any louder than a whisper. I can feel eyes on us in the restaurant.

"Maybe you didn't hear me? I want my woman. I'm sick of these dumb a-hole guys thinking you are some chick they can flirt with. You're mine." He pulls me in closer, not that there was any room to begin with.

"Dougie, I'm yours. Let go of my arm. You're making a scene. People are staring."

"I'm making a scene?" His voice carries throughout the quiet restaurant. "I think it is you who is making the scene. Why the hell do you keep getting all the tables with the young guys? Huh?"

The jealousy in his voice is starting to scare me. His hand is squeezing my arm tighter and tighter. I want to squirm because it hurts. Pins and needles start to stab at my hand on the arm he is holding. I try to gently pull away. He grabs my other arm in the same place with his other hand. He is holding me so tight I can feel tears starting to well up in the corners of my eyes. "Dougie, stop it," I whisper loudly, trying to stay calm.

Dougie slowly backs me up against the wall of the kitchen. I'm up against the wall. His breath is steamy on my face. "Don't you dare flirt with anyone but me. You got that? I don't want to deal with this again," he whispers into my ear before giving me a little push harder into the wall.

I can see Jeremy peek his head out from the kitchen. He takes a quick look at us and then returns to the kitchen.

"Sara needs to take a little break," Dougie yells into the kitchen as he lets go of one of my arms. "Hey, boss-man. Did you hear me?"

Jeremy pops his head back out. He looks at me and looks at Dougie. His eyes don't rest on me for long. I hope he didn't see the tears in my eyes.

"Okay. Sara, you can take a ten-minute break."

Dougie looks at me. "Let's go out back and get some air. What do you say?"

I look at him. His eyes are growing glossier. He grabs my arm again. His squeeze progressively strengthens. I nod yes. Without letting go of my right arm, he escorts me outside through the back hallway and out the back door. Just as we get outside, Dougie throws me, letting go of my arms, up against the brick building by the dumpster. He steps closer and grabs my arms in the same place, making the pain spread down to my knees before they buckle. He holds me up.

"Stand up! What the hell, Sara? Why the hell do you make me act this way? Why can't you just love me enough to only have eyes for me?"

He pulls me forward slightly before slamming me back against the brick. I hear a slight sloshing sound as the back of my head strikes the brick wall. Everything starts to dance. The stars, Dougie, the lights down the alley. I shake my head to try and let the dizziness subside. "I only have eyes for you, Dougie!" My own voice startles me. It's shaky with tears and loud with anger. I'm trying to focus on his face, which is completely hidden in darkness, only inches from mine.

He takes his hand and puts his palm up against my sternum, then forcefully shoves me back into the brick wall. "Don't you ever, ever speak to me that way! You got that? You treat me with respect." His eyes are wide with rage.

I feel my lips quivering. "S … S … sorry." He lets go and takes a few steps back before hitting the dumpster next to me. My knees give out, and I collapse to the littered pavement.

"Damnit, Sara. Why do you get me so angry?" His voice is filled with vulnerability. "I can't keep worrying that you are going to run off with some other guy. Don't you get it?"

The spinning around me slows. "I'm not going anywhere, Dougie. Why would I leave you? I love you." I feel myself trying to console him, yet I'm still sitting flat against the brick wall, too scared and unsteady to move in any direction. I don't want to say too much for fear of angering him, but I can also feel rage growing inside my belly for how he keeps treating me when he gets mad.

He turns to look at me. His eyes brighten as the moonlight lights up his face. He comes up close to me and squats down. I don't move from where I sit. I ignore that my left hand is in something wet on the ground and my right hand is on top of a wrapper—I want to keep myself steady. He strokes my head and rests his hand on the nape of my neck. "I … I love you too, Sara. I just get so jealous sometimes." He kisses me.

His low voice tries to soothe my shaky nerves. "You know, I know you need me, but sometimes you make this difficult for me."

"Sorry." I'm not sure what to say. I never really thought about how I'm difficult to love. I suppose if I had to watch him talk to attractive women all night, I would be a bit concerned as well. He kisses me again.

His lips are gentle against mine. My anger is replaced with fear—fear that maybe I am too difficult to love.

"I think your break is up." He smiles at me.

"I think you're right." I feel my smile quiver. Without thinking, I grab my right arm, the one he held onto the longest, and slightly rub it.

"What? I didn't hurt you!" His voice is very defensive.

"Oh, no. I know. It is just a bit chilly out here," I lie.

"Okay. Don't make me worry like that. You know I would never hurt you."

"I know, Dougie." *He really would never intentionally hurt me.*

We go back into the restaurant. The tears that flooded my eyes have been reabsorbed. Dougie rejoins his table; they are watching sports on one of the televisions, completely oblivious to Dougie's and my conversation. I walk back into the kitchen. Jeremy pops his head out. His face is ridden with concern. "You okay?"

"Huh? Yeah, why?" I state nonchalantly while avoiding eye contact.

"Hmm. Well, maybe you should take the rest of the night off. It's pretty slow in here, and we only need one server on."

I glance up to see the concern on his face; it embarrasses me. "I'm fine, really."

"I know. But we can't pay a bunch of servers if the customers aren't coming in." His face is still consumed with concern.

"Okay. I'll do my side work. What about my other table?"

"I had Darla pick it up." He smiles and walks back to his office.

I finish my side work, and an hour later, Dougie and I ride home in silence. He insisted I drive him since he may have had too much to drink. I silently agreed.

CHAPTER TWENTY-FOUR

Sara Olivia Scott

My alarm pierces my dream. I abruptly sit up in bed, on high alert. It takes me a minute to realize it's just my morning alarm—nothing to actually be alarmed about. I rub my eyes. Just lifting my arms to my face makes my arms pulsate with achiness. This must be from the heavy lifting of those trays last night. I smile as I recall carrying them both out like some super strong person.

I get into the shower and just let the hot water beat against my aching body. I close my eyes and inhale the steam through my nose. *I wish it were Saturday. Since when does Friday feel like Monday?* I rotate so the hot water massages my back. As I reach for my shampoo, my arms slightly quiver. I look down and see the bruises on my biceps. My own inhale startles me. Dougie's fingerprints are blue and purple imprints on my arms. I stare wide-eyed at my arms. *Dougie doesn't know his own strength. If he saw these bruises, he would be devastated.* The words *difficult to love* flash through my mind. *Maybe I'm the one who has the problem.* I shake my head, not wanting to think more about it.

I finish washing my hair with much difficulty and get dressed as quickly as possible. My shirt doesn't really cover the bruises all the way, but as long as I don't lift my arms up too high, they will stay mostly covered.

I put my ear to Dougie's door. He is snoring. I linger there for a moment as I listen to his breathing pattern. My mind is blank. *He has had such a rough week without work. Poor guy. I should do something nice for him tonight.*

I look at the clock on the wall. *Crap, I'm running late.* I grab my apron and purse and rush out the door. It's a very chilly morning. The grass is wet and has leaked onto the pavement. I should have grabbed my jacket, but I'm already running late. I have a sweater I keep in my locker at work; I'll just have to remember to bring that home with me.

The morning chill makes my nose run. I keep sniffling as I speed-walk down the winding road. My stomach churns as I think about how angry Brian is going to be when I show up late. *I don't want to get into trouble, and I definitely can't afford to get fired.*

I turn the corner and see Brian's car sitting in its parking space. My heart skips a beat. It's 6:09 a.m. *Shoot.* I pick up my pace toward the front door. It's locked. He loves to keep the door locked when someone is running late so she knows that he is aware she is late. *Ugh.*

I pound on the glass. Brian comes to the front door with the look of death on his face. I give him an "I'm sorry" look as he unlocks the front door.

"You're late. Do you know what time it is?" His voice is cold.

"I'm so sorry. I'm sorry. It won't happen again." My voice vibrates as I hold my hands together to beg for his forgiveness.

His face suddenly changes expressions. "Just get clocked in and get to work."

Why the sudden change in tone? Maybe he realizes he has been late before too and that I've waited plenty for him. Either way, I'm just relieved to know that I still have a job. I race to the back room and clock in.

I get my side work done in record time. It's 6:24 a.m. *I definitely need a cup of coffee.* My heart sinks when I see that Brian has already made a pot. *Battery acid it is.*

"Table!" Brian yells from the back office.

I peek my head out from around the kitchen wall. Officer Kipton.

"Good morning." My dimples awaken.

"Indeed it is." His eyes have little sunrays at the creases of his temples as he smiles back.

"Brian told me we had a customer, and I was hoping it was someone nice." *I'm relieved none of Dougie's friends decided to pop in this morning. Not that any of them ever have, but I'm okay not seeing any of them until next Thursday.*

"Well, I'm glad you think I'm nice. Most people think officers are, well, a pain in the rear."

"Ha. Well, I suppose."

"Then again, most of those people are doing something illegal." He gives a quiet chuckle at his cop joke.

"What would you like to drink this morning?"

"Coffee, please."

"I'll be right back." *Crap, Brian's acid coffee pot is still full.* I pour Officer Kipton a cup and walk back. "Sorry, the coffee is a bit different this morning."

As he reaches for the cup, his cologne floats in my direction: he smells like a fresh spring in the middle of the mountains—*not that I know what that smells like, but I imagine it smells like this.* Refreshing. Calming.

He takes a sip of the acid. "Hmm, it's okay." I know he doesn't mean it. It tastes awful. I doubt he would complain either way.

"You want your same?"

"You remember what I had?"

"Yep, sure do. Eggs, bacon, toast-dry, and hash browns, right?"

"Exactly. I'm impressed. I can barely remember what I had last night."

"Well, I guess it's a talent only servers have, huh?" I feel my dimples poke through a second time.

As I ring in his order, I see him sit up straighter. I can feel his eyes on me, his warm stare embracing me. I look down at my arms: my sleeves are popped up, and my bruises are shockingly dark against my pale skin under the florescent lights. I don't dare make eye contact with him as I drop my arms down to my sides and walk back into the kitchen.

I grab my sweater out of my locker. I'd better ask Brian if it's okay to wear it since it's technically against "code."

I find him sitting in his office. "Brian?"

"What?"

"I'm pretty cold. Can I please wear my sweater over my shirt today?" I hold my breath, waiting for his response, praying he says yes.

His silence drags on. "Yes. Just today," he adds.

My body sighs with relief. I quickly pull my sweater over my bruised arms.

Edward is already in the kitchen cooking up Officer Kipton's meal. "Is this the cop, again?"

"Yep. How did you know?"

"Same order, same time."

"How much longer?"

"Now." He places the order up in the heated window.

"Jeepers, that was fast! It's only been three minutes!"

"Like I said, cops creep me out; I don't want to piss this dude off."

"Thanks." I grab Officer Kipton's plate, take a deep breath, and walk out to his table.

"Can I get you anything else this morning?" I smile.

His face is warm. His eyes are wide, like he is trying to look into my soul. I glance down at his food. "Enjoy." I smile at his food before turning to go back to the kitchen.

"Sara, wait." His soft voice is filled with such concern it makes me tremble. I feel myself swallow.

"Yes," I practically whisper back. I don't turn around to face him; rather, I turn my head over my right shoulder and stare at the ground.

"I …" his voice gets choked up. His voice makes me tremble more. "Are you okay?"

"I'm fine. No need for concern." I feel my voice unintentionally raise an octave.

"Sara, please …" His voice trails off. I can hear in his words that he is searching for what to say.

I can't bear to look into his eyes. I'm okay, but his voice and his eyes—they make me second-guess myself. I love Dougie, and he loves me.

"He did that to you, didn't he?" His voice is so warm and gentle, yet he is accusing Dougie of hurting me.

"*He* is Dougie. Dougie wouldn't ever intentionally hurt me." I feel my voice getting stronger as I continue staring at the ground next to the table. "He loves me." I proclaim the word: love. I know he loves me.

Officer Kipton is quiet as he carefully selects his next words. "Love doesn't bruise. Love doesn't hurt." A fleeting image of my parents flashes through my mind.

"Dougie has never hurt me. This conversation is over. Enjoy your meal."

"Sara, if you don't get out of this—"

"Stop it. Right now," I say, cutting him off. "Stop. If you can't respect my personal life as my personal life, maybe you should stop coming in here for breakfast." My voice is so stern it sounds as if I'm hearing someone else talk using my voice.

"I'm sorry. I'll stop. I like coming here for breakfast and talking with you. I apologize." His voice slightly quivers as he tries to backtrack.

"Thank you." I smile at the ground before heading back to the kitchen.

His words agitate me like chipped fingernails on a chalkboard. Love doesn't bruise. *Does Dougie intend to bruise me? No, how could I even let that cross my mind! He just doesn't know his strength.* I tidy up the already tidied salad toppings.

"Table!" I hear Brian's screech from his office.

I check on Officer Kipton as I go to greet my new table. "How is the food?"

"Good. Thank you." I place his bill facedown on the table. "Sara, I—I'm sorry. It's not my place."

It isn't his place to interfere in my relationship. "Thank you. Have a good rest of the day."

"You too." I sense him trying to look into my eyes, but I avoid his. I shouldn't need to defend Dougie to anyone.

I walk over to my new table. "Hi, how are you today?"

"Fine, thank you. You?" A girl around my age with similar build and beautiful long black hair smiles from under her oversized gray hooded sweatshirt.

"Great, thank you. What can I get you?" I watch her eyes shift to the door behind me as another customer walks in. She almost seems scared for a split second. I look over my shoulder. "Morning, Steph."

"Morning," she says to us both.

"Um, I'll just have a coffee and a plain English muffin please."

"Sounds good. It'll be right out."

I fill up a cup of coffee and ring in her English muffin. I hear Edward holler the muffin is up. I grab her food and head out to her spot. I place her coffee, food, and bill facedown on her table. "Enjoy."

She peeks out at me from under her hood. "Thank you."

I turn to walk back to the kitchen. I glance over my shoulder again at the quiet girl sipping her coffee. I shake the thought from my head that I should know her. I've never seen her before. I find Stephanie in the kitchen eating her breakfast. "How's it going, Steph?"

"Meh, not too bad. You?"

"It's going. I could use a nap." I laugh. "I have a feeling it's going to be a long day."

"I hear ya. I was up late with the hubby, you know." She giggles.

"Oh my goodness, Steph." I smile more out of embarrassment.

I peek out from behind the kitchen counter to check on the hooded customer, but she is walking out the door. I walk over to her table. She ate half the muffin and drank half the coffee. She left me ten dollars on a three-dollar tab. *Maybe it won't be such a long day after all.*

My sweater tightly stays around my arms for the remainder of my shift. I hear Brian whispering to Ashley about me just as I'm about to leave. I know they are talking about me because she keeps staring over at Stephanie and me. *I really hope they aren't talking about my sweater, or rather, what's underneath my sweater. How would either of them know anyway? No one was here to witness my early morning conversation with Officer Kipton. The last thing I need is for Ashley to start some rumors about me.*

The sun is throwing its rays upon my path back home. I leisurely walk back to Dougie's, taking some time to enjoy the smell of summer. The birds are chirping as if to play their music just for me.

My mind cannot help but wander back to this morning's conversation with Officer Kipton. I can't believe anyone would think anything other than the best about my Dougie. It makes me so angry that Officer Kipton thinks he knows what my relationship is like.

I stop in front of the park. My heart longs to search for my tree, to wrap my arms around its bark. *If I could erase this morning, I would. What if Dougie finds out someone was asking about my bruises?* The very thought of hurting him is too much for me to bear. *He is all I have. I can't ever lose him.*

CHAPTER TWENTY-FIVE

Officer Kipton Pierre

I only see one vehicle in the parking lot; I hope that means Sara is working. It's still dark in the parking lot as the sun is trying to break through the trees, unsuccessfully. I don't know how she can handle walking to work with it being so cold and so dark. My stomach churns as I think of all the accident reports I get called out to on that stretch of road. I fear that one of these days she'll be on the other end of that call. I pray my fear never turns to reality.

I open the restaurant doors to find it completely empty, just as it has been the last couple of times. Before I can holler out hello, Sara peeks her head out from the kitchen prep area. Seeing her face makes me smile.

"Good morning," she calls out to me. Her dimples brighten up my morning.

"Indeed it is." I smile back.

"Brian told me we had a customer, and I was hoping it was someone nice."

"Well, I'm glad you think I'm nice." I can't help but smile a bit wider, knowing she thinks it's nice to see me. "Most people think officers are, well, a pain in the rear."

"Ha. Well, I suppose."

"Then again, most of those people are doing something illegal." I laugh at my own joke, forgetting that's how I met her—when she illegally ran the red light. I hope she forgot about that too.

"What would you like to drink this morning?"

"Coffee, please." She seems so happy this morning; it's hard to draw my eyes from hers. Is it too soon to hope she left Douglas?

"I'll be right back." She goes and grabs the coffee in the kitchen. I look around to see if the manager is poking around anywhere. No. I look at the security camera and stare at it for a good five seconds. Maybe if he's sitting in his office, he'll know I see him.

Sara comes back. "Sorry, the coffee is a bit different this morning," she says, wrinkling her face.

I test it. "Hmm, it's okay," I say. It takes everything in me not to make a bitter face as I gulp down my first sip. Different indeed. A bit stronger than what I'm used to.

"You want your same?"

"You remember what I had?"

"Yep, sure do. Eggs, bacon, toast-dry, and hash browns, right?"

"Exactly. I'm impressed. I can barely remember what I had last night."

"Well, I guess it's a talent only servers have, huh?" Her smile is absolutely stunning. I watch her walk away to ring in my order. I take another sip of the bitter coffee, and without thinking, I wrinkle my nose and rub my tongue on my teeth. I look back up to make sure she didn't see me doing that. She isn't looking.

I see her reach to the top of the screen to input something; an invisible force punches me in the gut. The air in my lungs is sucked out, and panicked concern rushes in. I feel myself tense up as the anger running through my body forces me to sit up straight. *He* did this to her.

Again. Her glistening white skin is painted with black and blue lines—impressions of fingers wrapped around her entire arm. *How could he hold her so tight?* The fury running through my every cell makes me want to wrap her in my arms and take her somewhere safe, away from here.

She looks down at her arms and quickly drops them to her sides before walking into the kitchen and out of my sight. *What do I do? What can I do? Why doesn't she just leave him? Can't she see he doesn't love her?* Love doesn't bruise. Of course, I know the answers to my questions. Domestic abusers are so manipulative that their victims never see the change; it's a slow fade. Strong women pose a challenge to these sick twisted men, so they manipulate their prey into unrecognizable weaker versions of themselves. I know there is no known way to make the victim clearly see what is going on. I choke on this realization.

Why isn't there training? Why isn't there a simple answer to saving her? Even if she never wants to see me or hear from me again, everything that I am tells me I must save her. Is it because she is a victim that I feel the need to save her? I've always wanted to help people, but no one has ever infiltrated my personal life, my mission, like she has. I hold in the tears that want to spring from my eyes. Seeing her hide her pain shreds my composure.

Sara comes out of the kitchen, wrapped in a pink sweater, carrying my food. "Can I get you anything else this morning?" Her face is smiling, but her eyes are not.

She looks down at my food before I can finish my thought. "Enjoy."

As she turns away, I softly beg, "Sara, wait."

"Yes," she whispers. She looks over her right shoulder and down at the ground, with her back still facing me.

"I ..." I can hear myself starting to get choked up. I take a deep breath to compose myself. "Are you okay?"

"I'm fine. No need for concern." Her voice slightly squeaks, giving herself away—a sign she is lying.

"Sara, please ..." I hear my voice trail off as I try to think of how to handle her delicate state. "He did that to you, didn't he?" I am consumed with worry for her and with revulsion for Douglas.

"*He* is Dougie. Dougie wouldn't ever intentionally hurt me," she begins to whisper, then loudly asserts, "He loves me."

How could anyone want to destroy someone so pure? "Love doesn't bruise. Love doesn't hurt." My words plead with her to see what I see. I know I'm getting too emotionally invested in this conversation that I'm losing my unbiased reasoning skills.

"Dougie has never hurt me. This conversation is over. Enjoy your meal." She isn't willing to hear a word I am saying.

I need to tell her the outcome if she stays with him. "Sara, if you don't get out of this—"

"Stop it. Right now. Stop. If you can't respect my personal life as my personal life, maybe you should stop coming in here for breakfast." She sounds as if she is going to break.

I can't have her detest me because then I have zero chance to protect her. "I'm sorry. I'll stop. I like coming here for breakfast and talking with you. I apologize." She still hasn't glanced away from that spot on the floor she has been staring at.

"Thank you." She walks back into the kitchen.

I quickly panic and look all around me. I'm relieved that no one else was within earshot. I need to keep my emotions out of this. I rest my forehead in my hand with the realization that I could have just put her in danger by discussing this here where Brian could overhear. I look around again and reassure myself that he could not have heard anything. *He hides out when I come in here. There is no way he heard what happened. That was not a smart move on my part. I need to be more careful because if word gets out that I'm concerned for her, Douglas is going to take out his anger on her.*

As I'm having a mental battle of my own, Sara swings by the booth. "How's the food?"

"Good. Thank you." My eyes follow her as she sets the bill on my table. "Sara, I—

I'm sorry. It's not my place."

"Thank you. Have a good rest of the day."

"You too." I try to get a look at her eyes to make sure she doesn't think anyone else overheard our conversation earlier, but she avoids mine. I don't look behind me as she greets the customer who must have come in when I was replaying our conversation.

Doesn't she know? If she doesn't get out of this—I try to calm myself—he'll kill her.

CHAPTER TWENTY-SIX

Sara Olivia Scott

Dougie is already cooking us dinner by the time I get home. My favorite: hotdogs on a charcoal grill, baked beans, and potato chips. "Wow! What's the occasion?" I give him a hug hello.

"Can't a guy do something nice for his lady?" He smirks.

"Absolutely! Let me get changed out of these clothes, and I'll be right down."

"Don't be too long. Dinner is almost served."

I change out of my pancake smelling attire and into a pair of jean shorts and a T-shirt. I grab a quick look in the mirror and panic when I see the bruises on my arms. I had completely forgotten. I switch the T-shirt for the long-sleeve he gifted me. *There. Nothing to worry about.*

Dougie has the patio table set. Two plates, one hotdog on mine and two on his, baked beans, and a few chips on my plate. He also has a bottle of beer next to his plate and a bottle of low-calorie beer next to mine. "What's this?" I inspect the low-calorie beer.

"I thought you might like that. I know you are trying to lose weight, so I figured I would help. Take a sip." I do. "What do you think?"

"It's not bad. Thank you!" *How sweet. My favorite meal and a low-cal beer.*

"What's with the winter gear? It's hot out here!"

"Oh, the long sleeve? I was a bit chilled. Plus, when the sun hits the fabric, it keeps me toasty warm." *Does he know I'm bruised?*

"That makes sense. Well, let's toast to us." He holds up his bottle.

I clink my bottle to his. "What about us?" I smile.

"I think it's about time I tell you something. Something serious." A smile is still painted on his face. I get excited. *What does he want to talk about?*

"I want you to know, Sara, I love you."

I bite my lower lip to contain my smile. "Dougie, I love you." We clink our bottles together again. He leans over the table and kisses me.

"This is the life, isn't it?"

"This is the best life," I agree. *Well, the best that I will, could, or ever have …*

"Also, there's another surprise."

"What?" I am already trying to control my smile.

"What do you think about moving in here, permanently?"

"Really? You want me to stay here? Even with the new school year?"

"Yes."

"Wow, I don't know what to say. I would love to. Wait, how would I get to school?"

"We can work out the details later."

My stomach flips inside. *Am I excited? I've never moved in with anyone. I was raised not to live together before marriage, but hey, where else am I going to live?* I refuse to let my brain acknowledge the home I have waiting for me in Duelm.

We exchange our giddiness throughout our meal.

"Another toast?" He holds up his second bottle of beer, as I do with mine. "Maybe it's time we bring this to the next level as well."

"What do you mean? Moving in?"

"No. The next level physically."

My heart freezes. *Physically? What does that mean?* "What do you mean?"

"Maybe you sleep in my bed with me." I'm not actually sure of what I should say. He knows I'm more of an old-fashioned gal. Living together is already pushing the envelope for me.

"I … I don't know what to say." I gulp a ball of air. "I'm not sure I'm quite ready for that. This is all very sudden." I'm trying to talk it out.

"You don't want to sleep next to me? All I'm asking is for us to fall asleep next to one another. That's it. But hey, if you don't want to fall asleep next to me, you know, that's up to you. I guess I'd be okay with that." He takes a sip of his beer and looks down at his empty plate.

"I didn't mean it like that. Of course I would love to fall asleep next to you. I … I just don't want you getting the wrong idea. You know, when we first started dating, I … I meant what I said about saving certain things for when I'm married."

He clears his throat as his eyes fill with tears. Sniffling, he explains, "I see. It's just that I love you. You love me. I can't save it for marriage since it was taken from me. I was hoping you would help me clear that. When you love someone, you should want to be with them."

I completely forgot about him not being able to *save* it for marriage. "It's not that I don't want to be with you. I do. It's just—I think some things should wait until we have been together a little longer." Like married.

He nods his head and wipes his tears, trying not to let me see. My heart breaks. *I love him. I do. I guess when I love someone, falling asleep next to him shouldn't be a big deal.* "Dougie, I love you. I would love to fall asleep in your arms every night. I would love to move into your room, but only if you don't think it would be too tempting to still stick to my beliefs on certain things."

He looks up and smiles at me. "Really? You will fall asleep next to me in my bed?"

"Yes. I would love that." His tears dry fast, and his eyes beam with excitement. *Perfect.*

"Sara, even though you have some flaws, like all people, I would never want to be with anyone else."

"I don't ever want to be with anyone else either." *He's right. I do have flaws. I'm so lucky he still loves me.* I sense myself starting to bite the inside of my cheeks. *Why did I have to make all of that so awkward?*

"By flaws, I just mean that you need to loosen up a bit and let others in. Ya know. Not loosen up as in get fatter, but loosen up as in stop overthinking everything. Let me be the man. I'll do the thinking for the both of us." His eyes twinkle at me as he downs the rest of his beer.

I stop biting my cheeks. *I do need to just trust him and stop worrying. It would be nice to just be taken care of.* "You're right."

"I'm always right," he laughs. I laugh too. Not always, but a lot.

The sun goes to sleep, and we call it a night. I go upstairs to my room. I feel my body slightly tremble, knowing I won't be sleeping in my bed anymore. As I reach into my suitcase for my pajamas, it feels as if things have been slightly moved around. *Hmm, I must have bumped them or something.* My pajamas are on the bottom right side of my main suitcase as opposed to the bottom left side. I quickly change in my own "guest" room and then go into Dougie's room. I keep my bra and panties on under my pajama top and bottoms.

An idea pops into my head as I hold my dirty clothes from the day. I grab a clean bra, underwear, T-shirt, and shorts. I carry them with me into his room.

He is already under the covers, with his bare chest and boxers peeking out. "You sleep in your boxers?"

"Yes. Otherwise, I get too hot. What's in your hands?"

"I have some of my clothes. I figure I could maybe put some of my stuff in one of your dresser drawers."

"Oh, yeah, just move some of my stuff over."

This is the perfect time to have that conversation about the bottom drawer. He didn't specify which drawer I should use. I'd feel so much better knowing about those cards in the bottom drawer. "Perfect. I'll make room." I smile. I reach for the bottom drawer and pull it open. The cards are still there. "What are these?" I pick up the cards.

"What are you doing? Not that drawer!" He is up and out of bed, standing next to me. "That is my own personal stuff." He rips the cards out of my hand. My fingers drop my clothes and cover my face. I feel my body tense as I crouch even lower … waiting. Nothing.

I open my eyes. He is just staring at me. "What are you doing?"

"I … I don't know." I feel my cheeks turn pink with shame for even thinking …

"Did you think I was going to hit you or something?"

"No." *Was that a lie?*

"Well, I'm sorry. I didn't mean to yell. It's just this bottom drawer is my drawer only. It's full of my own personal stuff from my past, and I prefer no one looks at it."

"Sorry," I whisper while picking up my clothes.

He reaches down and wraps his arms around me. "I love you. Just don't go in my bottom drawer." He smiles as he kisses the top of my head.

That was definitely not the response I was expecting. Now I'm even more curious. "Which drawer do you want me to use?"

"The top one." I make room in the top drawer for my stuff. He's already back in bed, waiting for me to crawl under the covers. I join him. He reaches for his light and shuts it off.

"Goodnight, Dougie,"

"Goodnight." I turn over on my side and feel him curl up behind me as the big spoon. Dougie's arm around my body, pulling me close to him, makes me feel like he won't let anyone get to me. His voice interrupts my thoughts: "Sara?"

"Yeah?"

"Why did you pick the bottom drawer?" My body freezes. I try to think. "Did you hear me?"

"Oh, sorry, I was falling asleep. What?"

"Why did you pick the bottom drawer?"

"I figured you wouldn't have to bend down to get your clothes as much. No one likes being at the bottom." My own words convince me that that is why I picked the bottom drawer.

"I don't mind being on bottom." His chuckles softly as he pulls me closer and kisses my ear.

"Ha-ha. Cute. You know what I mean."

"Maybe I do, but maybe you don't."

I push the thoughts that want to bombard my exhausted conscience out of my mind. Those thoughts are for another day when I'm awake enough to think.

"What the heck?" I feel Dougie fumble at my bra. My eyes open wide. "Why are you wearing a bra to bed?"

"I always do." That's a lie. I don't want to hurt his feelings by telling him it's because I don't want to tempt him.

"That's not smart. That's dangerous for a woman. As your man, I have a duty to keep you out of danger." His fingers, in one quick movement, unsnap my bra. "There you go. Go ahead and slide it off."

My lie didn't cut it. I don't have any other backup story, so I take my bra off under my pajama shirt. I toss the bra to the ground. His arm, which was previously draped across my stomach, now reaches around me and holds my unsupported chest.

"Night," he whispers, getting closer to our already glued-together bodies.

I steady my breathing and try to keep myself from over-reacting. *I just need to stop overthinking. He told me the same thing earlier tonight. I put my hands on his chest when we snuggle. It's only fair he gets to do the same.*

I awake to find Dougie with all of the blankets. My legs and arms are frozen. He is curled up with the blankets wrapped tightly around him and his back to me. I don't want to wake him. It was nice falling asleep in the same bed.

I sneak out of bed and go back to my room to throw some sweats on. I turn on the coffee pot and get some cereal. "Why are you up so early?" Dougie yawns, walking down the stairs.

"I slept like a rock. I was ready to get up for the day."

"Is the coffee ready?"

"Not yet. Want some cereal?"

"Yes."

We enjoy our cereal with our coffee while sitting in front of the television. Snuggled up on the couch, we watch a few movies for our lazy Saturday. Just as we are about to watch a do-it-yourself program, Dougie's phone rings. He runs out of the room to grab his phone, which is still in his room. I can't really hear what he is saying, but he seems happy.

He comes down a few minutes later in his work outfit. "That was my boss." His smile is wide. "They fired Gary, which means I'm the new foreman. Guess this means I'll be working sixty-hour weeks again, and that starts now."

"Oh, that's good news!" I'm happy he's happy.

"I've got a few minutes to get to the job site. I'll see you when I get home. Don't wait on me for dinner. I'll probably go out with my new employees." He gives me a kiss on the lips before running out the door. I wave, but he doesn't see me.

Another day to myself. I really don't like being alone; it's so lonely. I look at the time. 11:11 a.m. *I should go for a run before it gets too warm.* I throw on my running shorts and a long-sleeve shirt. Just as I'm about to leave, my phone rings: "Brenda calling" reads across the screen.

"Hello?"

"Sara! It's Brenda. How the heck have you been, stranger?"

"I'm great. You?"

"Fantastic! I haven't heard from you all summer. What the heck?"

"Sorry! I've been working a ton, and Dougie and I spend the other time together."

"Gotcha. I was actually calling because I'm having a party this Thursday night and wanted you to come. I'm actually having it at my new apartment, and you need to come join us."

"Where is your new apartment?"

"Right next to school! Jenna and I just signed the lease yesterday."

"Wow, I didn't even know you guys were getting an apartment. That's awesome. I would love to come. I'll have to check with my job to get Thursday night off, and I hope Dougie isn't working either."

"Yeah, both of you need to be here." I take down her address and promise I'll try my best to make it to her party.

I pull on my running shoes. *I'll just run up to work and request Thursday off.* The temperature is in the mid-70s when I head out the door for my run. My pace is relatively good—probably ten miles per hour as I make it to the restaurant in record time. I walk around the building a few laps so I can catch my breath before going in.

Jeremy is working. He says there is no problem with me taking Thursday off, so he marks me down in the "time off" book. Stephanie is there, so we chit chat about the party I'm going to on Thursday night. She's been bored all day. I guess it's too nice out for people to want to eat at a restaurant that doesn't have a patio. Just as she finishes saying that, a ten-top, meaning a table of ten people, is seated in her section. I wish her luck as I head back out.

I start my run back. I can't help but smile knowing I'll get to see my friends this Thursday. It's been weeks since I saw any of them.

The sun is scorching hot as I opt to walk the rest of the way home. I don't even let myself glance at the park as I pass it—it's too tempting knowing solace rests in the cool shadows of the trees.

With it being much too humid to be outside, I pull down a book from Dougie's computer shelf and occupy my time in the chilly, air-conditioned comfort of his living room. After reading for hours, my eyes tire. I decide to crawl into Dougie's bed at 9:30 p.m. His text says he will be out late and that I should not wait up. I'm sleeping when he awakens me a little after midnight as he stumbles into bed.

"Hey," he burps.

Mid-yawn, I ask, "Have fun?"

"Yeppers. Night." He lies down with his back to me and passes out in seconds. Literally, seconds. Too tired to inquire further, I roll over and fall back to sleep. I'm glad he didn't notice I'm wearing my bra under my pajama top.

Sunday is a lazy day for the both of us. Dougie stumbles out of bed past noon. I'm two hours into reading a book curled up on the patio chair.

"Hey."

"Good morning." I smile. "Someone have too much fun last night?"

"Ugh. The guys that work for me are big-time partiers. I just wanted to come home and curl up with you, but they wanted me to stay." He smells like stinky perfume.

"No worries. I went for a run and then got some reading done. Did you have fun?"

"Yeah. They will be a crazy bunch of guys to work with."

"Are they the same people you usually work with?"

"No. The boss doesn't promote someone to be the boss of his previous coworkers. He says that never works out well. This is a whole new bunch of guys." He goes inside and turns on the coffee pot. He fills his cup and rejoins me outside.

"So, do you have to work late this Thursday, boss-man?"

"No, why are you so excited?"

"Well, I got the night off of work because Brenda—do you remember her? She's having a party at her new apartment, right next to school. She wants us to go. What do you say?"

He sips his coffee. "I told the guys I would hang with them this Thursday. You know Thursdays are my nights with the guys. Plus, you should be working." Dougie looks annoyed with me.

"But I haven't seen any of them in weeks. Plus, taking one night off isn't going to be a big difference. I'll make up for it in tips another day."

"Well, first, it is a big deal. That means someone else is going to be waiting on the guys and me. And second, did you pick up a different shift?"

"You can come with me. She wants us both there. No, I didn't pick up a second shift. I figured I'd just be cheerier and work on getting better tips the other days."

His deep sigh tells me what he's going to say. "I'm not leaving my guys hanging, sorry. I guess that means you may as well work since you don't have a way of getting to the party."

He's right; I don't have a car. "I can ask Brian for my shift back when I go in tomorrow." I swallow my disappointment before it can show.

• • •

Brian is in a foul mood when he pulls into the parking lot at 6:11 a.m. He slams his car door shut. I don't say a word when he unlocks the front door. I try to sneak in behind him without setting him off. We need a bomb squad for his explosive outbursts.

I clock in and decide I'd better not ask him to manually correct my time card since it was he who was late. Edward shows up right behind me. "What's Brian's deal? I just heard him slam his office door."

Shrugging, I whisper, "I'm not sure. I didn't want to ask."

"Good call." He starts up the grills.

At 6:30 a.m. on the dot, Officer Kipton comes in and sits down in my section. Before I can grab the pot of coffee, Brian peeks his head out from his office. "Is that the cop?"

"Yes."

"What the hell are you standing around for? Get him served and out of here." He hides in his office again. It's funny how weird Brian gets around officers. I quietly laugh to myself after I make sure my back is turned to Brian's spy camera. I know he's watching.

I walk out to greet Officer Kipton. "Good morning!" His hair is wet. He smells delicious yet again as his cologne or shower gel or whatever the heck it is floats around him.

"Good morning." His smile makes me smile bigger.

Between his smile and his scent, he actually appears quite charming. I hadn't really noticed before now.

"Enjoy the beautiful weather this weekend?"

"Yes, I did. Dougie and I grilled out. What about you? Did you do anything fun?"

"Gizmo and I had some good runs in the park."

"That does sound fun. Do anything else fun? Visit family? Watch a good movie?" I don't know why I am asking him all these questions, but I feel that maybe I should make an effort to get to know him better since he comes in here quite often.

"Ah, well, both my parents are actually gone. I don't have any siblings or anything, so

Gizmo and I keep each other company. And I'm not a big movie person."

"I'm sorry. I shouldn't have asked."

"No need to apologize. They died years ago. I've been on my own for a while."

I realize that I'd better change the subject, quickly. "Why aren't you a movie person?"

"I like getting outside and doing things. I have a hard time just sitting still for a couple hours watching a screen."

"Not me." I laugh. "I could sit all day and watch movie after movie."

"What's your favorite movie?"

"My favorite? I couldn't even tell you. I have too many! I'm a sucker for chick flicks and comedies. I hate horror movies."

"If I was a moviegoer, I'd probably stick with comedies, but I don't know if I'm a chick flick kind of guy."

"Ha, I suppose most men aren't. It's near impossible to get Dougie to watch a chick flick with me."

He smiles. "Even though I didn't watch any movies this weekend, Gizmo and I had a blast. The trees in the park shaded us from the heat. We even went for a swim in the lake."

"The one in the park?"

"Yeah, it's perfect for swimming. Not really a ton of fish, and the water is pretty clean."

"I'm jealous. That does sound fun!"

I pour him a cup of my coffee. "I'm assuming you want coffee?"

"Yes, please."

"Don't worry, this is the good stuff."

He takes a sip. "Yes, it is. Why does it taste different depending on the day? Do you guys serve two different brands?"

"Well, if you promise not to tell my boss on me, I'll tell you."

"My lips are sealed. I can show you my badge if you need me to."

Laughing, I reassure him the badge is not needed, yet he points to it on his uniform anyway. "Our coffee is prepackaged, but the serving amount is too much, so it tastes like battery acid when you put the whole pack in. I cheat and leave a couple tablespoons or so in the bag and quickly toss the evidence. That way, the brew is just better overall."

He nods in agreement. "I think I like your way better." He smiles. "I wasn't going to say anything, but the coffee, hmm, has been a bit bitter before."

"Shh!" I put my finger to my lips and smile. "So, what can I get you this morning?" I see his eyes looking behind me, and I turn to see Brian peeking out. He gives us a quick smile and disappears.

"He seems like an odd man." Officer Kipton wrinkles his brow.

"He is different. I think he's scared of cops," I chuckle.

"Ahh." He just smiles. "Is he doing something illegal that he should be scared of us?"

"He's just weird." I doubt Brian is smart enough to be a criminal.

"I think I'll have the same thing I had before."

I'm grateful he changed the subject. I don't want Brian to overhear me talking about him.

"Perfect, let me ring it in." As I turn to leave, I hear someone fling the front door open. Ashley comes stomping in. She takes a quick look at Officer Kipton and then at me before stomping into the back.

Curiosity takes over, and I tiptoe to the machine to ring in Officer Kipton's order in hopes of hearing what is going on in the back.

"What the hell?" I hear Ashley yelling in Brian's office before the door closes and muffles their voices.

Twenty minutes later, Officer Kipton finishes his meal. At about the same time, Ashley comes out of Brian's office. I don't even want to know what went on in there. She seems happier.

Brian trails behind her. "Is the cop still here?" he asks.

"Yes. He's just finishing up his meal."

"Good." He smiles. "Edward, get Ashley some breakfast. Just make her what she wants, cause I'm not going to ring it in."

Ashley gives me a snooty look and tells Edward her order. Brian seems to be in a better mood now, so I figure I should ask about Thursday. He comes back into the kitchen prep area.

"Hey Brian, can I actually work Thursday? I don't need it off anymore."

"No! I get your shift." Ashley looks at Brian.

"No, Sara. You took the day off, and that's that. You shouldn't take a day off if you want to work it." Ashley gives me a victorious smile.

"Okay. Just thought I'd ask."

I walk back out to Officer Kipton's table. "You going to be making this trip more often? I've seen you in here a lot lately. Either you are getting sick of donuts at work or you haven't had time to get to the store."

"Yes, I do plan on making it in here more often on account of the great service." His smile makes me forget about Ashley's snide little expression.

"Well, good. It's nice having regulars."

"Well, you have a great day. I'm sure I will see you later, Sara."

"Have a good day, Officer Kipton."

He turns before opening the door. "You can call me Kipton. You don't always have to say Officer Kipton." He smiles.

"Okay, Officer Kipton." I smile. It's a hard habit to break.

I'm relieved he never brings up Dougie.

• • •

The week quickly passes. Officer Kipton doesn't come in on Tuesday or Wednesday. Stephanie is out sick most of the week. Dougie is working long days. He already put in thirty-six hours in the first three days of the week. At night, we both pretty much pass out from exhaustion, but just being able to sleep next to him makes me feel loved. The bruises on my arms fade, as does my memory of the evening altogether.

Dougie has not brought up Thursday since we talked about it Sunday. As he is filling his coffee mug, I come down the stairs to remind him I am not working the evening shift. "Sweetie, don't forget I won't be there tonight."

"I know. I hope you aren't too bored tonight." He smiles as he shuts the door behind him.

I know it's early, but I figure I should text Brenda and let her know I can't make it. I crawl back into bed.

Just as I'm about to drift off to sleep, my phone buzzes. "It's settled. Erick will pick u up. Text him ur address. See u at eight." I didn't even think to ask one of them to pick me up. I quickly text Erick my address, forgetting it's 6:00 a.m. Surprisingly, he texts me back that he will be here at seven thirty to pick me up. I guess things do work out.

I sleep in until noon, something I haven't done in a long time. I feel like a child on her birthday, so excited to see all her friends. With hours to spare, I lace up my running shoes. As my feet hit the pavement, I can't help but speed up my pace just thinking about tonight. I want to look extra pretty tonight since I haven't seen everyone in a while.

My feet bring me to the park. No vehicles in the parking lot. I know Dougie worries about me running alone, but if no one is here, he has nothing to worry about. Plus, the sun is blistering hot. I enter the park and feel my soul start dancing inside me. I know I shouldn't run to the tree, but I have hours and hours to myself.

It's hard to remember where my tree is. The tall trees appear much taller than I remember. I feel my leg brush up against a prickly bush. "Eek!" I jump back. Blood starts to trickle down my leg. *Dangit. How am I going to explain this to Dougie?* There aren't prickly bushes alongside the highway. Before panic sets in, I look up and see the lake. The water's surface glistens like diamonds; who doesn't like diamonds? My childhood inner-princess winks.

I think of my conversation with Officer Kipton on Monday. He went swimming in the lake and said it was clean. As I near the water, I look around and confirm no one else is out here. I take off my T-shirt, shorts, socks, and shoes. *What remains is practically a swimsuit, right?* I feel sort of rebellious and free out here, just nature and me.

How did I miss this lake before? The water is warm from the sun's heat but cool and refreshing at the same time. I decide to try my side-stroke and swim out to the middle of the small lake. I can't touch the bottom of the lake anymore, so I do a surface dive to see how deep it is. I touch the bottom and push myself back up. Ten feet seems about right.

Just as I come up for air and open my eyes, I see Officer Kipton and Gizmo at the other end of the lake, the one next to the trail. He is only wearing his navy blue boxer briefs. Gizmo—well, he isn't wearing any clothes. I know I shouldn't be looking, but I'm in a stunned state and can't quite peel my eyes off of them.

Gizmo sees me and comes jumping into the water but stops when it reaches his neck. I remain motionless aside from quietly treading the water to stay afloat. Officer Kipton still doesn't see me. He walks into the lake, and when the water reaches his waist, he stops. "Hoooly!" He stops himself from cussing, then starts laughing.

"Guess you weren't expecting anyone else to be in here, huh?" I nervously shout.

"I'll say you surprised me. I didn't see you." He must be acutely aware of his only item of clothing as he quickly gets into the water up past his waist.

"I surface dove to the bottom. When I came up, you guys were here."

"I see." He's still half-chuckling.

I know I should feel completely awkward with a half-naked man in the same lake with me, but I don't. Oddly, I feel even safer with him in the lake. No creep is going to get me while a police officer is out here.

"Do you want us to leave? Were you looking to be alone?"

"Nah, it's okay. Practically swim suits, right?" Now I'm trying to calm myself after I just realized I'm in my neon pink sports bra and black undergarment.

"Ha, yeah. As long as you aren't uncomfortable sharing a lake, Gizmo and I just need to cool off." Gizmo is testing himself, trying to see how far he can go into the water before freaking out and jumping back. The water only reaches his knees and elbows. *Do dogs have elbows?*

"Are you sure you're okay if we stay in here a bit?"

I stop thinking about Gizmo's elbow knees and answer. "No, it's fine. I had the same idea. After you told me how clean the water was, I figured it was the perfect place to cool down." *Or clean out a cut.*

His smile is contagious. He grabs a floating stick and throws it for Gizmo to chase after. Their happiness makes me want to join them. Had I actually been wearing a swimsuit, I might have; however, this is not the case.

My eyes involuntarily notice his six-pack abs, sculpted biceps, and farmer's tan. He is quite handsome in a dorky sort of way. Before I can finish the thought, Dougie's face appears in my mind. He would be livid if he knew another guy was in this secluded lake with me ... even though it's just Officer Kipton.

"Well, I better get back to my run." My conscience sets in. "I've got a party to get ready for."

"Very nice. Where is your party?"

"My friend is having a party at her new apartment back at school. Somewhat of a house warming party." I'm still very aware of my neon pink bra boldly illuminating my wet, pale body.

"Well, have fun tonight."

As I turn to swim back, I hear him add, "Be safe. Lots of drunk drivers out on the roads lately."

"Such a police officer." I smile as I swim back to my side of the lake. I turn around to make sure he isn't staring. Just as I suspected, his back is to me.

I quickly get out of the water and yank on my shorts and T-shirt. Fidgeting to get the fabric to straighten on my damp body, I tug harder. *I'm glad he isn't looking because I'd be embarrassed if I couldn't get my clothes on. All the more reason I need to run like Dougie said.* The extra pounds around my waist are making this difficult. Over my shoulder, I see Officer Kipton still swimming with his back to me. After I finally succeed with my shirt and shorts, I opt for a nearby log to pull my socks over my feet; it's too difficult to balance while fighting with cotton. My socked feet easily slide into my shoes. He is still looking away. My heart warms, knowing he isn't trying to steal any glances at me.

"Thanks." He must know I'm referring to his not looking.

"No problem. See you tomorrow, Sara."

I unknowingly smile at his words. My feet carry me away from the lake at a decent pace but rapidly slow to a leisurely walk after my shoes grow soggy from my dripping undergarments. *Was it weird I was in the lake at the same time as Officer Kipton? What would Dougie think? I left as soon as he showed up. I don't think I did anything wrong.*

The water from my bra creates a wet print on my T-shirt, which quickly fades beneath the toasty rays. I look down at my leg, which is starting to burn where I scratched myself earlier as sweat beads on my legs. Pants will be an easy solution to hide the scratch until it heals. I don't want Dougie to get concerned I was in the park alone … well, kind of.

It's 2:30 p.m. when I open the door. *Perfect! I have enough time for a long shower and to do my hair. I know it's not likely, but I wish Dougie would get home from work before happy hour so we could spend some time together. I'm a little jealous Ashley will be waiting on him and his friends tonight since she's overly flirtatious; hopefully, with Brian there, she won't be so attention-deprived.*

It's 6:15 p.m., and my hair is curled, makeup is on, and my outfit is perfect. The image in the mirror brings my parents' renewal of vows rushing back to me. I remember watching Momma get her hair and makeup done as I squirmed with excitement. She was still a beautiful queen the day I graduated. She started to cry when I walked out in my gown with my curls poking out from beneath my cap. Even Daddy got choked up. My smile brightens as I remember his words. "My princess is all grown up. We are so proud of you."

"Daddy and Momma, your princess is still here," I say to the woman in the mirror. I look away before my tears have a chance to fully form and ruin my makeup. *I wish my prince were here to escort me to this ball. I hope Dougie is enjoying himself. It looks like he is having another late night at work and won't get to see me all dressed up.*

My disappointment quickly dissipates as I hear someone at the door.

"KNOCK, KNOCK." I rush downstairs to the front door and see Erick grinning through the peephole.

"Yowsers! Who is this beauty?" He greets me as I open the door.

"Ha-Ha. Aren't you funny." I chuckle, giving him a hug.

"Seriously, I don't know who this is." He looks at me.

"I don't look different."

"No, but I forgot who you were since it's been a million years." I lock the door behind us.

"Oh, stop it. I've been busy working and busy spending time with Dougie."

"Where do you work?"

"A restaurant up the street from here."

"Cool." He opens his door, pausing half in and half out of the car. "By the way, your dude lives in the middle of nowhere. I drove past this place and ended up at some restaurant up the road." My heart momentarily freezes as I think about Dougie. I hadn't had the chance to tell him Erick was going to pick me up. "Thank goodness there was a cop in the parking lot who told me where the heck this place was."

A cop? Was it Kipton? "Hmm. What was the cop's name?"

"I don't know. Peer or something."

Pierre. It was Kipton. "Was the cop just sitting in the lot or something?" I ask as indifferently as possible. I try to stay calm as I wait for Erick to finish buckling his seat belt and answer.

"Umm, yeah. He was just sitting in his squad, probably hoping some drunk would be dumb enough to get in their car so he could catch them."

I nod in agreement. *That's why he was there. He's a cop, duh, Sara. It's his job to watch the city.* I quietly chuckle to myself for even having thought he may be there to watch Dougie.

"You okay, Sara?" Erick breaks the silence as he watches the dark, winding roadway.

"Yeah. I was just thinking. I was supposed to work tonight, but I was able to get the night off."

"I know. That's what Brenda said. Too bad your guy couldn't come with."

"Yeah." I shrug. "I wish you guys could have bonded, but he couldn't get out of his prior commitment thingy." No need for them to know he is just hanging out with his friends. I'm glad Erick didn't go inside and find Dougie there.

"Yeah. Well, tonight is going to be pretty awesome. Brenda has been bragging about this new apartment for quite a while. It'll be nice to have a place to crash after a wild night this fall."

Erick and I catch up on what we've been up to this summer, and before we know it, we are at Brenda's new place. "Thanks for picking me up. I really appreciate it."

"Of course. You're one of the gang." I forget how much I enjoy spending time with Erick and Brenda. If I had siblings, I imagine this is how they would be: people to call my "gang."

Brenda doesn't answer her phone to let us in, which means she's probably already a few drinks in. We finally make it into Brenda's apartment after waiting five minutes for someone to exit the complex so we can sneak in. Brenda stumbles over to us when we make it inside. There are approximately fifteen other people occupying the small living room that spills into the kitchen.

"Sara! Erick!" She puts an arm around each of us. "Hey everybody, Sara and Erick are here!"

I hear a handful of "Hey's" and "Hi's" scatter throughout the apartment.

"Hey, girlie. This place is beautiful." The apartment's decor looks like it has been taken directly from a fancy furniture magazine. It really does. If I remember correctly, Brenda comes from quite a bit of money.

"Yeah. Looks good, Brenda. Now where's the beer?" Erick's mission is obvious; after all, he was always a participant in Melanie's Thirsty Thursday.

She points to the keg in the kitchen, and Erick bolts towards it.

"So, Sara, why does Dougie get you to himself? Huh?" She's clearly intoxicated.

I chuckle and give a joking eye-roll, "Because we're in love."

"Whoa! Love! We need something to make a toast over here." She hollers to her guests, implying we each need a drink. "Sara and Dougie are in love!" Some tall, lanky guy hands us each a beer. Brenda holds her red cup up to mine. "Cheers!"

We clink our plastic cups together and take a sip. "I wish we got to know your Doug more. I've only met him like once."

"I wish so too, but he couldn't get out of his plans tonight. He would love to see everyone again." I take a sip, remembering the last time we went to a party. *He didn't think any of my friends liked him. I guess he only really knew Melanie.*

"Lame! He's missing out. Next time. When you move back, he'll have many more parties to go to." She gulps half her cup.

"Actually, Dougie and I are officially going to stay living together." *And I can't wait!*

"What?" Erick steps out of the kitchen with two cups of beer in his hands. "Isn't that a bit fast? How are you going to get to class if you don't have a vehicle?"

Why is he interrogating me? "We've been together for over six months now. It's the natural next step. As for class," I say, shrugging, "I'll worry about that later."

"Well, good for you!" Brenda joins in my excitement.

Erick shakes his head and goes back into the kitchen.

"Ignore him," Brenda huffs. "He doesn't have anybody, so he doesn't know what love is."

I give her a smile in agreement.

"So, are you guys going to get married?"

I hadn't even thought if Dougie was planning to propose. I suppose he may have thought about it. After all, we are living together, have said "I love you," and are sharing a bedroom. Marriage is the next step. "Maybe. I'm not really sure," I say more to myself than to Brenda as she begins to slurp a second cup of beer.

The evening goes by quickly. I enjoy a few beers but stop when I start to feel tipsy. I don't like the feeling of being out of control. Plus, I have to work early tomorrow morning. I look at my phone. It's 11:15 p.m. I should probably get back home. I seek out Erick and ask, "Hey, what time were you thinking of leaving?"

"Whenever. Need me to drive you back, right?"

"Are you okay to drive?" His eyes look slightly glossed.

"Oh yeah. I have only had a couple beers."

"Are you sure?" His speech seems pretty normal.

"Yeah. Just give me fifteen minutes, and I'll be ready."

Twenty minutes later, we say goodbye to Brenda and the "gang." Erick blasts the air conditioner and the music. He also rolls his window down to keep him "concentrated" on the road—his words, not mine. I'm getting sleepy and can feel myself half-drifting off. After what seems like a five-minute ride, Erick touches my shoulder, and I spring upward in my seat, startling us both.

"Whoa! Sorry. You were sleeping. I was just letting you know you're home."

I rub my eyes. He is parked in Dougie's driveway, which means Dougie is still at the bar. "Sorry. You just scared me. I didn't realize I had fallen asleep."

Erick chuckles. "That's okay. Have a great night. It was fun seeing you again, Sara."

"Thanks for driving me, Erick. I miss you guys."

"No problem, anytime."

I get out of the car, but before I can shut the door, Erick practically whispers, "Ya know, we all should really hang out more often. You're kinda secluded out here."

"I agree. We should hang out more often." I look around. It's so easy to see the stars out here because there are so few lights. "I like it out here. You can actually see the stars." I smile back.

"Just be careful, okay?"

I look at him and smile. "Always. Thanks again." I shut the car door. *He is definitely what I always imagined a brother to be.*

I unlock the front door. As soon as he sees I'm safely in the doorway, he backs out of the driveway. I give him a wave before locking up and heading upstairs for bed. *I'll tell Dougie in the morning.*

CHAPTER TWENTY-SEVEN

Sara Olivia Scott

My alarm clock goes off after what feels like minutes since I fell asleep. I turn it off and roll over to see Dougie's spot empty. *Didn't he come home?* I drag myself out of bed and downstairs. I relax when I see him passed out on the couch. Covering him with a blanket, I tiptoe back upstairs and get ready for the day.

He is still snoring when I close the front door behind me. The morning air is brisk, making me cough when I first inhale. I wrap my sweater around me and hustle to work. *I hope Erick made it home safely. It was late when he dropped me off.* I reassure myself that I would have heard if something happened.

It's 5:59 a.m. when I arrive. Surprisingly, Edward is already in the parking lot. Just as I walk up to the front doors where he is standing, Jeremy pulls into the lot.

"Morning," I call out to Edward. "Where's Brian?"

"Hey. He's on vacation."

"Morning, Jeremy." I smile as he gets out of his car. He gives me a quick nod hello and unlocks the front doors. He doesn't seem too happy about working so early this morning.

"Do you have to work tonight too?" I ask.

"Yep. Open to close until Brian gets back next Wednesday." He looks worn out.

"Bummer." I clock in and get a quick start on my side work. It's Friday, so I assume Officer Kipton will be in soon. He seems to eat at the restaurant on Mondays and Fridays. I make my special coffee brew and wait for the carafe to fill enough for me to pour myself a full cup. The kitchen prep area is a complete mess this morning. Before I can mentally complain further, a light goes off in my head. *Ashley worked last night. I don't understand how someone can be so carefree about her job. I know I shouldn't judge. I was lucky to have the parents I did because they taught me to always do my best; maybe she wasn't as lucky.*

At six thirty on the dot, Officer Kipton opens the front door. I smile, knowing the morning will pass more quickly now that I have someone to talk with.

"Morning!" I greet him with a cup of coffee. I involuntarily blush remembering our encounter in the lake.

"Good morning!" He smiles back with a newspaper tucked beneath his arm.

"Indeed, it is," I laugh, pouring him his coffee.

"Ha-ha. Indeed."

"You are in luck because today I've got the special brew."

"I was hoping so. This morning came much earlier than I expected." He takes the coffee mug from my hands before I can set it on the table.

Earlier? That's right, Erick told me there was a cop in the parking lot. "Did you have to work last night?" I try not to sound suspicious, expecting him to lie.

"Yes, sure did. I was on watch, actually, out in the lot here. We've had some complaints of drunk drivers leaving on Thursdays, so they assigned me this place."

"Drunk drivers?" I can't help but worry that these may be the people I'm serving. I know there is a law that says the company that serves drunks could be on the line if they were to get in an accident or a DWI.

"Yeah. Someone called in a few cars last week that appeared to be swerving. My sergeant wanted to make sure they have someone patrolling the area." He takes another sip of his coffee. "But that stays between you and me. And this is delicious this morning." He gestures towards the coffee that he is still holding in his other hand before taking another sip.

"Why, thank you. I can actually take the credit for the coffee." I wink. Before I can take his order, Ashley comes in. My facial expression must show I am surprised because she just scowls at me.

"Seems she could use a cup of your coffee." His joke is only loud enough for me to hear.

"Ha. Yeah, maybe." I feel my dimples peek out as I imagine Ashley actually being in a good mood. "Are you going to have your regular meal?"

"Yes, please."

"Okay. I'll ring it in and be right back."

I ring in his order. Before returning to chitchat with him, I go into the kitchen to sneak a sip of my coffee. "Hey, Ashley." I test what kind of mood she is in.

"Hey."

"I thought you were on vacation with Brian?"

"Pshh." She mutters something under her breath that I can't hear. "Yeah, it's a guys-only vacation."

"Oh." She seems hurt that she was not invited. "Well, that's stupid. Why would someone want to go on a vacation with just their friends?" My attempt at cheering her up doesn't seem to be working.

"I don't know. Men are stupid."

"Did you at least make good money last night?" She must have been given Dougie's group.

"Oh yeah." she smiles. I can't help but feel her grin is slightly malicious.

"Good." I feign a smile. I grab my coffee and go back to talk with Officer Kipton so I can't get drawn into her web.

"So, was last night successful?"

"What do you mean?" He puts his paper down.

"Did you catch any drunken bad guys?" I keep the inquiry light.

"No. Everyone was behaving himself." His cup is empty, so I go back to get the pot. *Himself? Singular?*

I refill his cup. "That's good."

"Wait, don't you work Thursday nights?"

"Uh, well, usually. I took last night off because one of my friends from college, Brenda, had a party," I holler to him as I put the coffee pot back in the kitchen prep area. No other customers are in the restaurant, so I don't feel bad for talking so loudly.

"Oh yeah, I remember you saying that yesterday. It sounds like it was fun."

"Yeah, it was." I refill my cup. Ashley is just staring at me while sipping her coffee.

I rejoin Officer Kipton. "So you must be tired today then?" he asks me before taking another sip from his cup.

"No, not really. I'm not much of a drinker. I like staying in control. I hate the feeling you get when you drink too much." I'm suddenly very aware of my own words. First, I'm not of legal drinking age. Second, *I like being in control …*

"That's the smart way to do it. More people should think that way. That sort of thinking keeps people safe."

KATE G. PHILIPS

"I'm sorry. I saw that you were reading the paper. Did you want me to leave you to your paper?"

"Oh no, that's fine. The paper is a backup plan in case there is no one to talk with."

"Good." I glance over my shoulder to make sure Ashley isn't standing right behind me. "Because I don't really feel like visiting with my coworker today," I whisper.

"I think we all have those days."

"So what is a normal day like for a police officer?" I take a sip of my own coffee.

"Well, it's … I don't know," he chuckles. His eyes sparkle. "I guess it always starts with roll call, then I go out on tour, and it ends with paperwork if it's exceptionally busy."

"What kind of calls do you get?"

"An assortment: car accidents, a couple robberies here and there, some domestic disputes, you know, the typical police needs."

"I can't imagine always having to go into the face of danger every day. I bet your girlfriend goes nuts with worry." As soon as the words fall from my lips, I realize I am probably out of place, even assuming he has a girlfriend.

"Well, that has been an issue in the past. Also, probably why I'm single." He takes a sip of his coffee. "But it's not as dangerous of a job as most people think. My job is to protect people and keep them safe. So that's what I do."

I hear Edward call my name from the kitchen. "That must be your food. I'll be right back." I excuse myself to grab his food.

I set his steaming hot food down. "Need anything else?"

"No, thanks. This looks perfect."

"I'll let you enjoy before I bug you some more." I enjoy talking with him. It passes the time more quickly than sitting in the back while waiting for customers.

I join Ashley in the prep area so Officer Kipton can enjoy his meal before it gets cold.

Halfway through his meal, he gets a call on his radio and has to abruptly leave. I don't even get a chance to say goodbye, so it must be some emergency. Another twenty-dollar bill is left on his table. I smile. He must make a lot of money since he generously tips me.

The day crawls by. I only get ten more tables before Jeremy cuts me from the floor. As I'm rolling my bin of silverware in napkins, Ashley sits across from me to start rolling her bin.

"So, are you going to be giving up your Thursday night shift again anytime soon?"

"No. I'm not planning on it. It was just last night."

"Bummer."

"Why?" I know she is trying to lure me in. I'm even more disappointed in myself that I'm letting her get to me.

"I just made really good money. That table of guys you usually wait on—they are really good tippers. I mean, really good." Her emphasis on the word "really" irks me more than usual.

They have never really tipped me. Dougie always tells them I'm his girl so they can save their tips and just pay their tabs. "That's good," I lie, slightly out of jealousy.

"They are all just so funny. They ordered shot after shot after shot."

Now I know she is just trying to ruffle my feathers. "Yeah, they're a fun group. Have a great rest of the day." I finish rolling my last set of silverware. My patience is dwindling at an alarming rate.

Dougie is home when I get there, which is odd because he's supposed to be at work. "Hey, sweetie." He's curled up on the couch with his blanket covering him, exactly where he was this morning.

"Hey."

"Are you okay?"

"Yeah. Had to call in sick. I've just been lying around."

"I'm sorry. Too much fun last night?"

"No. I just don't feel well."

He looks hungover. "I'm tired too. Can I get you something? Gatorade? Water? Soup?"

"No, I'm fine. Why are you tired?"

"You know that party Brenda had last night? Well, Erick actually picked me up so I could go." I try to report in as monotonous a manner as possible.

Dougie's color rushes back in his face. "You went?" He doesn't so much ask me as he demands.

"Yeah." I quickly add, "Everyone else was disappointed they didn't get to see you, but I told them you already had a commitment."

His eyes make me very aware that I'm kneeling on the ground next to where his head is lying on the couch. He sits up. "Why didn't you tell me you were going?"

"Well …" I feel like a child getting in trouble for doing something wrong. I try to explain. "I told Brenda I couldn't go, and then she said Erick would just pick me up. You were at work, so I figured I'd just tell you when I saw you. I was actually hoping to see you before your happy hour."

"You have a phone." His words are flat.

I guess I was wrong; he would have preferred I texted him. He stands up, and his blanket falls to the ground. He lets out a deep exhale.

I stay kneeling on the ground below his waist. This low to the ground feels safe.

"I'm sorry. I didn't think you would care." I honestly didn't.

"You didn't think." His voice starts to scare me.

"I'm sorry, Dougie." I hear my words pleading. "I'm sorry. I won't do that again."

"Why didn't *Brenda* pick you up?" His emphasis on her name tells me it's not so much the party as the fact that Erick picked me up that is causing him to grow irate.

"Because it was her party. Plus, Erick lives like ten minutes from here, so it was closer for him to get me."

"So you know where he lives?" *Yep, definitely an oversight on my part.*

"Well, not really. I've never been to his house." This conversation is not going in the right direction. I can feel his fury building. "It's not like that with Erick." I try to calm Dougie.

"Not like what?" His voice hurts my ears.

"It's not like I like him. He's just a friend."

"If you don't like him and he's just a friend, why are you trying to explain it?" He takes his bottle of water off the coffee table and whips it at the wall. It hits a picture frame of a zebra, and both fall crashing to the floor. Luckily, neither actually break. "If he was just a friend, you wouldn't feel the need to tell me that, now would you?"

"I'm just trying to make sure you know it's not like that. I love you, Dougie. I wanted you to go, but I knew you were with your friends. Erick was able to pick me up—" Instinctively, I hold my arms up to cover my face. I'm too late. His palm is hot against my cheek.

"What? What the hell is this? You want to fight me?"

"No!" I cry, still hiding behind my arms. "I ... I want you to know I only love you. I didn't mean for it to sound like I care about Erick."

"If you don't care about him, then never see him again!" His screaming pierces my ears and shakes my core. Tears spill from my eyes. Darnit.

"Please stop yelling. I won't ever see him again. I don't care about him." My cheek burns as I force my arms to stay where they are instead of rubbing it.

"Hell, Sara! Why do you set me up like this? Why do you purposefully try to make me jealous?" He yanks my arms down from my face. I don't look at him; I stare at the coffee table. "Look at me, damnit!" His hand grabs the hair on the crown of my head and yanks my head upward, forcing me to stare at him.

I stare at his nose so I don't have to see the anger in his eyes.

I don't know what he saw in my eyes, but his tone abruptly changes. "My gosh, Sara, you are shaking." He crouches down next to me. My body stiffens in its position. I'm hesitant to move as I'm not sure how long he'll be apologetic.

"I'm sorry." He cries, wrapping his arms around me. "I'm sorry. I'm the worst boyfriend ever," he wails. His tears don't drip into my hair, but I hear them in his words. Motionless, my body remains sitting in the same position.

"No ... no, you aren't. You are a great boyfriend. Stop being so hard on yourself." The words fall from my lips in a soft whisper. *I just want to console him. This is all moving so fast. I can't keep up with the direction of what is happening.*

"It's"—he pauses—"it's just the thought of you leaving me. I can't bear it. I don't know what I would do."

Is he really saying this? He's afraid of losing me?

"If I ever lost you, I would kill myself. I used to cut myself, and I would do it again if you left me. I wouldn't want to live in a world where you aren't here with me."

My heart breaks at his vulnerable confession. *He used to cut him-self? He'd kill himself if we were separated?* My eyes can't help but glance at his arms; I've never even noticed any scars. I don't see any. I know he saw my eyes glance at his arms.

"Sara, I would kill myself if you left me," he states matter-of-factly.

"Don't ever say that!" I warn him. "I can't live in a world without you, Dougie. You are my only family. I have no one." It's true. Without him, I'd be completely alone in this world.

His crying quiets as I hold him. We rock back and forth, embraced on the floor, until my face dries. He looks at me with wide eyes. "I'm sorry. I didn't hurt you, did I?" He looks like he is on the verge of crying again, yet his eyes remain bright white and clear.

I don't want to see him in any pain. "No, you didn't hurt me," I lie. My teardrops burn my irritated cheek, but I keep my arms tightly embracing him.

"Good." He half-smiles and kisses my cheek.

I refrain from flinching as his hot lips sting my exposed raw wound. If he ever knew it hurt, he would hurt himself; he just said that. If he cuts himself, it will be my fault for driving him to that point. I must stay strong for us both. I need him, and he needs me.

Stinky perfume clogs my leaky nose as I rest my head on his shoul-der, still sitting on the ground. I finally recognize the stench. Ashley's perfume. Without thinking, my lips ask, "Why do you smell like Ashley?"

"Huh?" He pulls away from our close embrace.

"That smell. She must have worn a lot of perfume last night because I can smell it on you." I forcefully chuckle to keep things airy.

"Are you trying to say something?" His eyes are void of feeling.

"No, I can just smell it. That's all. She stunk up the restaurant this morning with the same perfume."

248

Dougie's head cocks to the left slightly. "She smells like ass, and that stench carried with her last night."

I can't help but probe, especially after she tried to make me jealous with our conversation earlier. "She sure does love your group of guys."

"You think I'm cheating?"

"What?" *What is he talking about? That wasn't even crossing my mind. I just wanted to see if she was flirting with him; she loves to give men half-hugs in her low-cut shirt to bump up her tips.*

"Is that what you're trying to say?"

"No." It really wasn't. "I was just reminded of her telling me how much fun she had last night with your group, and the smell reminded me of our conversation."

"Yeah. She was taking some shots with us. She's crazy. Chaz was trying to get with her, but I told him Brian was already with her."

"Gotcha. Yeah, Chaz doesn't want to get Brian upset for flirting with Ashley; I think he's very protective of her."

"What's wrong with being protective?"

"Nothing. I just don't want Chaz to get himself into an awkward position."

"Yeah, he wouldn't." Dougie stands up. "I'm going to shower to get this stench off."

"Good luck." I smile.

"Maybe you should join me and help me to remove the stench like a good girlfriend."

My stomach rolls. "Maybe another time," I lie. *Maybe when we're married. We already had this conversation.*

"I guess I'll have to try and scrub this stench off all on my own. I bet Ashley would help."

My stomach flips. *He has to be messing with me.* "Why are you messing with me?"

"You can't blame a man for trying." He grins before leaving to go upstairs. "Just keep that in mind!" I hear him holler as he ascends the staircase.

I guess I can't blame him for trying, but would he really ever consider Ashley? I'm suddenly very unsure if he is satisfied with me. *He's mentioned my weight a couple times. Ashley is at least five pounds lighter than me around the waist, and her cup size is much bigger. Why am I even thinking of this?*

I rub my cheek. I forget about Ashley as my own guilt and doubt pour in. *Why do I upset him all the time? Do I purposely like to get him upset? Maybe I'm doing it without realizing it. I'll try harder to be more attentive to his needs and my stupid words. Am I enough for him? Do I need to let him be more physical with me? What if I am not enough? Am I underreacting? Am I overreacting?*

What do I want? I want someone in this life so I'm not alone. I need to be better at loving. Love always trusts. Love never fails.

CHAPTER TWENTY-EIGHT

Sara Olivia Scott

Dougie and I always grow closer after we have a disagreement. After I awake, Dougie requests I delete Erick's phone number from my phone so he knows I'm serious about him, and only him. I do so to appease him. I let him look over my shoulder as I secretly try to memorize Erick's phone number before selecting "delete."

"Let me take a look at your phone." I hand it to him. I watch Dougie as he deletes Joshua's phone number, a guy I studied with in my physics class. *That's fine with me because I doubt I'll ever have a need to speak with him again since I'm done with the class. If this is what it takes for Dougie to trust me, he can delete the numbers. Plus, I only have a handful of numbers in my phone.*

"Why does your phone book say 'Daddy cell'?"

My heart leaps inside my chest. "Don't delete that!" I scream as I rush into the living room with our cold beers.

"Why do you have your Dad's cell in your phone book? He's dead."

I realize it's a bit odd to keep my parents' phone numbers programmed into my cell as they have no need for cell phones where they're at now; however, I still have their cell plans up to date so that I can call their phones and listen to their voices whenever I want. In November, after their accident, I used what money I had saved in my bank account to ensure their plan was paid for at least the next year. *I've lost them. I'm not ready to lose their voices too.* Their home answering machine is also still up and running. Late at night, when I need to feel them close, I call their phones so I can hear them talk to me. "I know. I still can't bear to delete their numbers."

"Well, it's kinda crazy. You know that, right?" Dougie's eyes make me feel like maybe I need help.

"I know." I take a gulp of water.

"I'm going to delete them. You're acting crazy keeping them. It's creepy. It's not normal to want to call a dead person's phone."

"No, please don't. I—"

"Done. I deleted it. I'm going to delete 'Home' and 'Momma's cell' too. I'm helping you. Trust me."

I yank the phone out of his hands. He wasn't kidding. He did delete the names. *Do I remember their numbers? What if I can't remember them? 651-45 ... 45 ...*

"Are you seriously going to cry? I'm helping you. You have me. You have my phone number. I'm alive." He puts his arms around me. "And I can actually talk to you."

"But ... that was all I had left."

"It's been a long time, Sara. It's time for you to move on. You're lucky I'm here to help you. If someone else saw this, they would have you committed." His tone is empathetic, but his words are accusatory.

Am I insane? 651-45 ... no, it was 651-53 ...

"Look at me." His voice is curt as his hand gently pulls my chin up and in his direction so he can look into my eyes. "Just say thank you. This will help you in the long run." He takes the phone from my hands and sets it down on the coffee table. "It's done. It's time for you to accept this."

2

I can't help but feel he just severed my last tie to my parents. My eyes return to the television. Choking back my tears, I chug the entire bottle of beer he opened for me earlier. Right now, I need an escape.

Fifteen minutes pass. His eyes weigh on my aura, but I remain focused on the television. "I'm still waiting."

The beer has set in, and I feel lighter. *Maybe I was being a bit crazy keeping their phone numbers in my phone.* "Thank you." I pause. "Sorry."

"You're welcome."

Dougie gets up and grabs another beer from the kitchen. He grabs me another one as well before joining me back on the couch. "I'm just so happy I'm the one who found the phone numbers. Seriously, if someone else found those …"

Is it really that bad to want to hear their voices? Maybe it is creepy, but their voices calm me. I remain quiet, unable to respond to his comment.

"You're lucky I love you, my crazy lady."

"I know." *651-42 … Wait! I have their phone numbers saved in my planner.* I bite my lip to keep my realization from outwardly showing; I can't have Dougie know I still have their numbers.

"Why the sigh?"

Did I sigh? "I guess I'm just relieved I have you." I smile back, kissing his lips to keep him from seeing the flicker in my eyes. *I have you and my parent's voices.*

• • •

On Sunday, we stay in pajamas all day and watch movies. We don't dare discuss my parents' phone numbers again, but I do plan to reprogram them into my phone under coworkers' names. *Momma can be "Stephanie," and Daddy can be "Brittany;" their home phone will be "school admissions." Problem solved.*

• • •

Dougie works late on Monday. Officer Kipton never came in, which has me somewhat concerned about whether everything is okay since he left so abruptly on Friday. *Oh well, nothing I can do.* It's lonely in Dougie's home with him working such late hours. *Thank goodness for a good book!*

Tuesday is yet another solo day, as Dougie has to work well past my bedtime. I have no energy to go running, making me officially lazy. I opt to finish reading the book I found yesterday.

It's Wednesday. This morning, Dougie had breakfast already made for me for my walk to work. It's those sweet gestures that make me so happy he's my boyfriend. Even though we have some difficult times, Momma always told me a marriage, or, in my case, a relationship, is a bit like a roller coaster. There are ups and there are downs. Stick through the downs, and you'll go up again.

I hope that Brian will be in a better mood since he will have just gotten back from his guy vacation. I devour my cream cheese-covered bagel before I even arrive at the restaurant. Brian's vehicle is in the lot, and the front door is unlocked. It is surprising to find that he is actually here on time and that the front door is unlocked. He must be in a good mood. I clock in at 6:00 a.m.

"Hey!" I smile to Brian.

"Hi."

"Did you have a great vacation?"

"How did you know I was on vacation?"

"I talked with Ashley last week."

"Was she still pissy about it all?"

What does he expect me to say? "No." I turn and start brewing my coffee. "Why?" I ask, trying to pretend like I wouldn't know why.

"Oh, no reason. I'll be in the office. When Ashley gets in here, tell her to come see me there."

"Sounds good." *Had he not talked to her when he got back home yesterday?*

Edward rolls in ten minutes late and starts prepping the food. He gives me a nod hello but doesn't say anything.

I look at my phone. It's 6:40 a.m., and no one is in the restaurant. I hear the front door open and assume it's Ashley. When I peek out, I see Officer Kipton opening the front door for Ashley.

"Good Morning." I smile at them both, more so at him.

"Indeed." He smiles as he sits in his usual booth.

Ashley mumbles, "Hey," as she brushes past me.

"Brian wants to see you in his office," I call over my shoulder to her. She doesn't acknowledge me, but I assume she hears me since she heads towards his office. Officer Kipton is sitting in his spot, smiling over at me. I can't help but smile back at him. His sunrays are beaming from his eyes this morning.

"Your brew this morning?"

"Sure is." I grab him a cup of coffee. I'm relieved to see him, especially since he left in a hurry on Friday and didn't come in on Monday. "Everything okay?" I put his cup in front of him.

"Yeah. You noticed I was gone Monday?"

"Yeah. It was dead in here." I'm thankful the faint bruise that was on my cheek Monday from my Friday disagreement is gone today. "I just figured you hated the service."

"Hardly!" His grin is growing. "That's why I am here on a Wednesday."

"Well, it's a nice surprise. Are you going to have the usual, officer?"

"You can just call me Kipton, Sara." He laughs. "And yes, please."

"Okay, Officer Kipton." I punch in his order and go into the kitchen to make sure Edward knows the order is the officer's.

"Cop?" he asks before I can even tell him.

"Yep." I smile. "Maybe he keeps coming in here to make sure you're arriving on time for your job." I joke around.

"The cop is here, again?" Brian inquires as he comes out of his office with Ashley.

"Yeah," Edward hollers.

Ashley is smiling ear to ear. "Jeesh, he sure does come in here a lot," Ashley hisses as she pushes past me to grab a cup of coffee. Brian grabs one as well, and then they both head back into his office. I hear her mention something about him always coming in to sit in my section, but I choose to ignore her jealousy.

Edward has Officer Kipton's food up in record time. I deliver his food to him, unable to keep from being nosy. "So, where did you disappear to?"

"Every couple of months, the academy has some 'ongoing learning' classes we can enroll in." He pauses to put pepper on his eggs. "I chose to take a class since it had been a few years. I forgot it was last weekend."

He takes a bite of his eggs just as I ask him, "What was the class about?"

Chewing slowly, he looks at me and holds up his pointer finger to let me know he is chewing. His eyes hold mine as he swallows. "Domestic abuse," he softly answers without taking his warm eyes off of mine.

Surely, I'm not in a bad situation. Dougie and I have our fights, but that doesn't apply to me. I've never been put in the hospital like those poor women with bad men are. He just got a bit upset a few times. I nod my head up and down. "Was it helpful?"

His eyes are like honey, sweet and embracing.

"Very."

"That's good." I look at his full plate. "You may want to continue eating before your food gets cold."

"It'll be fine. It always comes out really hot anyway." We both feel the silence between us as I stand at the edge of his table and he sits in his booth with his fork in hand.

"What did you learn?" *I'm not sure why I am asking this. Maybe what he will say will reaffirm that Dougie isn't the guy he thinks he is. Maybe this will have shown him that he was wrong about our relationship! I hadn't thought of this before.*

In my eagerness to hear his response, hoping that it will match my prediction, I miss what he says.

"What?"

He clears his throat. "The abused usually end up dead"—he pauses—"or in jail."

Why is he looking at me so tenderly? "That's awful." *I don't wish to speak on this any more.* "I'm so happy I don't ever have to deal with something like that. Enjoy your meal." I feel his eyes follow me into the kitchen. *Jail? Why would the abused end up in jail?* I ignore the question, not wanting to give any more attention to this topic.

He sure left in a hurry on Friday for class; he must have been really late. Odd, since he doesn't seem like the kind of guy who would forget stuff.

"Cop gone yet?" Brian asks.

I didn't get the chance to talk with Officer Kipton much more because an actual party of five was seated in my section, taking up most of my time. "Yeah, he just left. Why?"

"I hate cops. They stink. They're pigs." He wrinkles his nose.

I smile on the inside, remembering what Officer Kipton said weeks ago: the people who hate cops are usually the people doing something illegal. I wouldn't be surprised if Brian was doing something illegal. I know Dougie and him are close and go way back, but I think he's a complete weasel the more I'm around him.

I shrug. "He seems okay."

CHAPTER TWENTY-NINE

Douglas J. Adams

Dougie's dark eyes glisten in the moonlight.

Thursday night.

"Dougie, want to grab a smoke out back with me?"

"Sure, Brian. Give me a sec." I follow him out back. Sara is busy with her other tables and doesn't see me get up.

We light up. "I haven't had one in a while. Sara has never seen me smoke, and I can just see her getting all hoity-toity if she found out," my chuckle echoes.

"Doug, I actually need to talk with you about something, man. You know you are one of my guys, and I'm just watching out for you, right?"

"Why so serious? Has Sara been doing a bad job?"

He takes in a deep drag. "I just thought you should know a cop keeps showing up in the mornings when she is working. First, I'm wondering if he's onto our little agreement." He takes a long drag. "Second, Ashley told me that Sara and the cop were talking about some party and that he seemed to know a lot about her."

"What the hell does that mean?" My voice cuts through the night's air.

"I'm just saying, man. I'm not saying anything, but if that was my girl, I'd make damn sure to keep an eye on her. I just thought you would want to know."

"And what makes you think he's trying to look into our little operation here?"

"The other day, he looked right into the camera at me. I swear he knew something."

"Just stay calm. Cops don't know nothing." I take a drag. "You think my girl is taking an interest in this cop?"

"No, but Ashley seems to think he may be taking an interest in her."

I take a longer drag. "So, you … you still have some of that R2, Bry?"

"Yeah. I got some. Just don't tell me how you use this forget-me pill, okay?"

My smile and fifty bucks solidify our agreement.

I take my packet and tuck it neatly in my pants' pocket before flicking the bud onto the ground and stomping on it with such force that I see Brian jump.

CHAPTER THIRTY

Sara Olivia Scott

At 6:30 a.m. on the dot, I hear the front door open. I peek my head out, expecting to see Officer Kipton this Friday morning. "Dougie!" I shout. I wipe my coffee-ground covered hands on my apron and run over to him. "What a great surprise!" I beam, giving him a kiss.

"I just thought I'd surprise my sweetie."

"It's a perfect surprise." I give him another kiss. "Where do you want to sit?" He walks over to where Officer Kipton always sits and takes a seat. I hear the door open behind me and see Officer Kipton come in. He smiles at us.

"Good morning," he says as he passes by both of us to a different booth, one he's never sat in.

"Morning. I'll be right with you, officer," I greet him as he walks past us to a booth a few tables down from Dougie. I notice Dougie's eyes following him from the entrance until he finds his table behind Dougie's. "Want coffee, sweetie?" I smile at my man.

He pulls me in close and kisses me. "Now that I have some sugar, coffee would be perfect."

I giggle at his corny pickup line. "I'll be back." I walk over to Officer Kipton. "Coffee today?"

"Yes, please." He gives me a half-smile.

I give Dougie his coffee first and then deliver Officer Kipton's. "You going to have the usual?" I ask Officer Kipton.

"Yes, please." *He doesn't seem to be in a talkative mood today. That works since I'd rather talk with Dougie while he is here.*

I go back to my Dougie. "What would you like, sweetie?" *I wonder if he noticed Officer Kipton is the same cop that showed up to the house that while back? No, why would he remember that?*

"Biscuits and gravy, extra gravy." He seems really happy. *Good, I hope that means he didn't recognize Officer Kipton. That would be uncomfortable.*

"Okay. I'll be right back. I'm going to ring it in, and then I'll come sit with you."

As I am ringing in their orders, Brian meanders onto the floor and sits down across from Dougie. I can't hear what they are saying, but I figure I'll let Dougie talk to his bud. I grab the coffee pot and go to refill Officer Kipton's cup. He seems out of sorts today.

"Everything okay?" I ask as I top off his cup.

"Yeah," he nods. "Beautiful day." I'm fairly confident he's watching Dougie and Brian from the corner of his eye, even though he's looking at me.

"You sure? You seem somewhere else."

"Sorry. Last night was a long night. You should check the other guy's coffee." His voice is emotionless. *He knows who the other guy is.*

I go back to Dougie and sit next to him on his side of the booth. Brian gets up to leave.

"See ya later, Bry. Thanks." He gives him a wink. Brian eerily smiles at us and then saunters over to Officer Kipton.

"Good Morning. How is the coffee?" Brian asks Officer Kipton.

"Perfect."

"Great. Enjoy your meal when it gets here." He smirks at all of us one last time before walking into the kitchen.

Sometimes he is so creepy.

"I can't say I've ever seen Brian actually talk to a customer." I smile at Dougie. "And what was with the winking thing?"

"Oh, he's just trying to recruit me to his poker night."

"I'm just so happy you are here this morning. I could get used to this." I lean into him, giving his arm a hug.

"Yeah. Me too." He kisses my hair.

I give both the guys their food and sit with Dougie as he eats. *I feel bad I am not sitting with Officer Kipton, but Dougie never comes in for breakfast, so this is a special treat.* Officer Kipton finishes his meal faster than usual. As he leaves, he tells us both, "Have a great day," on his way past our booth.

"You too." I smile at his back as he goes out the door.

As soon as Officer Kipton exits the front door, Dougie puts his napkin on his plate. "I'd better get going too, sweetie. I'm going to be really late to work."

"Thank you for coming in! You definitely made my day."

He pulls me in close and kisses me. "See you tonight." His grin looks mischievous.

• • •

I get home to find Dougie already home and cooking in the kitchen. "What are you making?"

"It's a surprise?"

"You are just full of surprises today." I shine.

"I know. What can I say? I'm the best boyfriend ever." He grins.

"You are. You are, indeed." *Indeed.* I think of Kipton this morning. *I hope I didn't hurt his feelings.*

"You going to go change into something pretty?"

"Ahh, so you want me to dress up, huh?"

"Yeah. I put something out on our bed I thought would look good."

How sweet! He organized everything for tonight. Is it our anniversary? I try to remember our first date. I calm when I realize we've been dating for over seven months. *He must just want to do something nice.*

A black minidress is lying on the bed. He already cut the tags off. I check the tag—he knows my size. *How did he know my size?* I look at my suitcase. *Ahh, that must be why my clothes were moved around before when I was looking for my pajamas. How romantic.* I switch into my new dress and reapply my makeup. I want to look gorgeous.

The lights are off, and the patio door is open. He has one candle flickering above the spaghetti dinner waiting on the table. Dougie has already poured us each a glass of red wine. He hands me my glass. The opened bottle sits on ice next to his chair. My heart melts.

"I'm speechless. This is so … beautiful."

"You look sexy in that dress. Mmm."

"Ha-ha. Why thank you." I twirl around once for him.

"Come sit down."

I take my seat across from him. "So what's the occasion?"

"Can't a boyfriend do something nice for his girlfriend?"

Is he going to propose to me?

"I propose a toast." He holds his glass up.

I take mine and hold it up next to his. "What are we cheers-ing?"

"To us." His eyes twinkle in the candlelight.

"To us," I agree. We both drink. He drinks half of his glass before setting it down. He looks nervous.

"Are you nervous?"

"About what?"

"Oh, nothing." I smile. I feel my stomach flutter at the thought of being engaged.

"Let's just enjoy the nature surrounding us. The silence of the night."

"That sounds bea—"

"Shhh," he whispers. "Silence."

We eat our spaghetti in complete silence. As the sun sets, the stars begin to pop out. It's harder to see his eyes with the single candle. The light flickers with the breeze that passes through the dense air.

The crickets are making their odd music as the tree frogs croak. Evening birds are singing their babies to sleep. I look up at the stars and back at Dougie. I can tell he is looking at me, but I can't really see his eyes.

"Can we talk yet?" I whisper.

"Not yet. Let's just enjoy this perfect evening." He empties the rest of the bottle of wine into my glass. The wine hits me quickly. I feel slightly drunk, which is really bizarre being that I have only had one glass of wine. I've already forgotten about a possible engagement. I'm just enjoying this moment, this surreal moment in time.

Dougie gets up from his chair and takes my hand. He blows out the candle and guides me inside through the dark house. I'm grateful he is holding my hand because I'm feeling off-balanced after all the wine. Things start to feel slightly pixelated. He leads me upstairs and onto the bed. I don't really remember going up the stairs. I'm sitting on his side of the bed. I don't remember walking into the room.

He lights some candles in the room. I steady myself with both hands on the bed. I hadn't ever noticed those candles before. "Dougie," I whisper.

"Shh." He puts his finger to my mouth. "No talking tonight." His eyes swallow me in darkness.

I feel his hands roam. His mouth is heavy against mine. He unzips my dress. I try to push his hands away from the zipper, but my arms feel floppy and uncoordinated.

He pushes me onto the bed as my dress falls to the floor. His body is heavy, lying on top of mine. One of his hands grabs both of my wrists and pins them down above my head. It almost feels like I keep closing my eyes, but when I reopen them, a lot of time has passed. A candle's flicker shows me his eyes are somewhere far away. Everything is happening so fast. I feel like my brain is skipping information. *I shouldn't have drunk all that wine. The wine was so strong. I shouldn't be this dizzy, this weak …*

My words escape my mouth as I feel his hands tugging on my panties, "No, Dougie. I don't want to do this!"

He continues to hold my wrists as he pulls his head back and stares at me. "If you really love me, you won't fight."

My gut wrenches. I can feel my eyes struggling to stay open as my brain battles an imaginary sleep.

"You love me, don't you, Sara?" His eyes cut into me.

I can't answer. I can't move. I'm paralyzed. I can't move my arms or my legs. Everything comes in and out of focus.

"Then shh," he whispers in my ear.

I try to wiggle as everything is spinning and changing colors around me. I can feel that pit in my stomach growing and swallowing me. "No, Dougie! I love you, but I'm not ready." My words sound slurred.

"I said don't fight what's going to happen. You love me. Stop being a selfish tease. People who love their boyfriends don't do that. Now be still and quiet. I know you really want this; you just don't realize it." I feel spit from his lips fall on my face as he articulates his words. His hands grasp my wrists tighter.

This is not how I wanted this. I can't keep my eyes open. Things keep coming in and out of focus. I want to scream and push him away, but no more words escape my mouth.

My body involuntarily flinches.

I lie still, unable to decipher my reality, unable to grasp the evils of this world.

CHAPTER THIRTY-ONE

Sara Olivia Scott

I'm wide-awake. The candles burnt out. Wax leaked over the holders and onto Dougie's dresser. He's snoring. I know his bare backside is facing me, but I don't look.

My fingers are clenched tightly around the one sheet he left me to sleep with. He's been sleeping for hours. Things kept going in and out of focus all night. Things became clear a few hours ago, but I dare not move. I don't want to wake him.

My mind is blank. Everything is fuzzy. The wine has long worn off. I can move my hands again, but I don't attempt to move them. I'm not sure if it's fear that now paralyzes me or guilt or anger. I'm not sure what I feel. I can feel my mind start to build an invisible wall to block out what I don't want to accept. What I can't accept.

Even with the wall, I can't help but try to remember how everything happened. I know he said if I loved him, I wouldn't fight him. *He must know I love him, especially now. Did I try to resist him? I don't remember. What if I did? What if I didn't?*

He's right. I do love him. I'm going to end up with him. This is normal for a couple. He knows. He's much older than me. He knows more about this relationship stuff. I recall him saying I was selfish. A tease. Am I a tease? Do couples really just do what the other one wants?

He twitches. I remain frozen. Waiting. He continues to snore. I sigh and continue breathing silently. *This is what is supposed to happen. I love him. He loves me. I love him.*

Sleep won't come to me. I've been waiting for it, praying for it. It's not coming. I try to take a deep breath as I feel the panic rise. I feel like I'm suffocating. My chest rises and falls faster. I count to ten to try to slow my breathing. One, two, three, four, five, six, seven, eight, nine, ten.

As each minute passes, the haze trails behind me as I reenter realization.

My brain won't calculate the equation that lurks at every corner. It can't. *I need my Dougie. He's all I have. He loves me. I love him. What happened was a result of too much wine. And it was the natural next step. He wouldn't have done that if I really didn't want to on some level. That's love.*

Love! My tree. My tree! I can feel my chest rise and fall faster. *I should get some air. Cool air is needed. A walk outside is the perfect solution.* Suddenly, I can't resist the need to get some fresh air. *I'm suffocating in here next to him. I just need to get out and breathe some fresh air. That will help me clear up things.*

I slowly roll out of bed, one foot at a time. With my feet on the floor, I lean forward to roll myself off the mattress. He's still sleeping. The sheet is half stuck beneath him, so now I'm standing, completely unarmed. My naked body is exposed. No shields. All my clothes are out of sight. My naked body quivers as I stare down at it. I hold in the sob that wants to escape from deep within my lungs. My hand covers my mouth so as not to wake Dougie.

My footsteps are soft and tingly as I tiptoe out of his room, shutting the door partway behind me. My exposed body has no shield as I go down the hallway. I pull on my neon pink sports bra, a tank top, and bottoms from my suitcase. I grab my socks and shoes so I can put them on outside. My legs wobble as I quietly descend the stairs, praying they don't creak and give me away. I scribble on a piece of scratch paper that is left on the kitchen counter, "Gone for run. Be back. Love you." The word "love" looks funny spelled out. I've only written that on notes to my parents. It feels like a lie as I write it out. *Love keeps not records of wrongs.*

The sun is beginning to sprawl through the treetops and onto the pavement. My feet try to run, but my legs still quiver beneath me. I walk, thinking of nothing but walking. My head still hurts. It's pounding. I ignore the pain. I purposefully only allow my brain to focus on taking one step, then another, and another. My breathing slows and steadies itself.

My feet lead me to the park. It's empty. It's early, even for a Saturday. I stay on the path. Maybe a path is better. A path always leads somewhere. As I walk, my feet feel like they can't breathe. Impending doom feels like it's taking over. I stop and look down. The dirt looks cool beneath my shoes. I take off my socks and shoes and carry them in my right hand. I let my toes dig into the moist dirt. I push the impending doom feeling away. *I'm only going to focus on the present, not the past.*

The dirt is cold against my bare feet. As I walk, I feel twigs and small rocks cutting at the bottoms of my feet. I keep walking. I try to ignore that my heart and soul feel numb. The birds are chirping extra loud this morning. I hear them fluttering from tree to tree, as if they are following me.

Again, I feel panic rise inside me, wanting to escape from deep within. "Focus only on walking, Sara." My words fall from my lips with an exasperated whisper as I talk to myself. I try with all my will to concentrate only on walking.

The trees are towering over me, but not my tree. My lungs hiccup for air. I feel my breathing pick up pace. The sun is only scattered; it's not pieced together like it should be. Things feel like they are closing in. Some of the path is unlit, hiding in the darkness. The path is getting harder to see, and the trees are getting harder to see. Everything is going blurry. I see blue. My breathing momentarily calms. Blue must mean water. I remember the lake. I try to run. I want to be at the water's edge with the cool droplets on my face. I feel like I need that cool water on my face like a body needs air.

One foot in front of the other, I run. I watch my shoes go flying as my hands come crashing down with me as I trip over a stick and hit my head on a fallen branch. I feel a hard and pointy rock against my right palm. I'm numb to all pain. I know I should feel it, but everything is closing in around me. I look up. The water is close. I push myself up. I see black spilling into my eyes. I brush it away but it keeps coming. Ten feet. Five feet. I fall to my knees at the water's edge. Everything is blurry. I can hear my own body gasp for air. I crawl into the water. My hands and legs feel jolted in the freezing water. I splash the water on my face. Splashing isn't enough so I crouch down and surrender my face to the water. My tears are hidden in its safety. My sobs are muffled in its depth. No one can hear me. I'm free to scream under the suffocating waters.

I run out of air to push from my lungs, so I allow my body to break the water's surface. My eyes are clearer, and the black redness has stopped spilling into my sight; I feel it drip down my temples.

I don't have the energy to sit on all fours. I crawl back towards the water's edge and lie down on my back. The water blankets my body, keeping my face uncovered. My muscles finally relax as cool water skims over my resting body, splashing my face with its ripples. I listen to my breathing slow down. I close my eyes. *I won't make it to my tree, but I know it's here with me. It's watching over me.* Soon, I feel its comfort.

Twigs crackle in the distance. Deer and squirrels play; they are free to live their lives. Sleep wants to consume me, but I know I have to get back.

Time passes without measurement.

I surrender. Silence. Stillness.

A loud crackle from a branch breaking jolts me back to consciousness.

"SARA!" A voice rips through the silence, running towards me.

Where am I? My head bobs in the water as the rest of my body remains submerged and motionless.

"SARA!" The voice is closer. It's getting warmer.

I force myself to sit up just as Officer Kipton kneels down beside me. His eyes are wide with terror. "Are you okay?" he practically yells, exasperated and out of breath.

The horror in his tone frightens me: "Where the hell am I?" I try to push the fear down. *Officer Kipton is here. Think, Sara.*

He blurs out of my mind as I orientate myself. *I'm in the lake, in a sports bra and running shorts. I must have gone for a run.*

My memory drifts back to the present. I take in his presence, which is like warm honey.

He is talking, but I do not understand him. I'm consumed by his eyes; it's like he's looking at a dead person. *I'm alive, right?* I test my voice. "Warm honey."

"Huh?"

Thank God! I'm alive. I allow myself to close my eyes to help me remember. I came here to get fresh air. I was tired. "I … I fell asleep." I talk out loud to myself as I open my eyes.

His eyes are still wide with fear. "In the water? What are you doing in the water? Thank God you didn't drown!"

He grabs at his shirt, peeling it off his sweaty body. I watch as he quickly dips the bright blue fabric in the water and rinses it, dips it and rinses it, dips it and rinses it until it's free of his sweat. He gently holds it to my head.

"What happened to your face?" His voice remains alarming, but his eyes are calming down.

Is this a dream? No … I recall a bit more clearly. "I went for a run. I got dizzy and tripped over a stick and hit my head. Maybe. I don't know. I just needed to cool off, so I came into the water. I must have fallen asleep for a second."

"I think I need to get you to the hospital." His eyes search the area.

"No, no," I reassure him. I reassure myself. "I'm perfectly fine." He rinses his shirt and puts it on my head again.

He lets out a loud exhale. "You scared me. I … I thought something happened to you." He is clearly overwhelmed with concern … for me.

"I'm sorry. I'm just tired. I haven't slept for a couple days." I listen to my own voice trail off as my memory tries to swallow me. I push down the memory that forced me to get out of the house to begin with.

"Would you like to drink some water?" He holds out his water bottle for me. I take a sip. I see my wrists are slightly bruised. I flinch. I shake my head, trying to erase the memory of Dougie holding my wrists. *He couldn't have known it hurt. He couldn't have known I didn't want to do that.*

Officer Kipton interrupts my internal dialogue. "Are you okay?"

I sense myself pausing too long. "Yes. I'm just tired." I push yesterday's memories out. I know Officer Kipton is talking, but I can't hear him. *I need to focus on deciding what to do with my thoughts.* As I tell myself I'm not going to think about it, I can feel the anger rise. *I don't want the anger fighting the fear.*

I don't let my eyes accept the bruises on my legs and forearms. My heart and brain are dueling it out. I hear myself moan, which makes Officer Kipton stop talking. Nausea surfaces. "I'm going to be si—" *Too late.*

I throw up on my own lap. At least I'm still in the water. *Puke water now.*

He keeps his cool, wet shirt on my forehead. He doesn't make any remarks about being disgusted. Dougie may have.

"I am taking you to the hospital, Sara."

"No. No doctors. I just have the flu."

"Please, Sara. You need help." His plea hugs my heart.

"Please, Officer Kipton. Please just sit here with me. Please let me just sit. Quietly." My eyes don't have any more tears to spill, but I hear my voice shake as if it is crying.

He respects my wishes and sits with me. Occasionally, he redips his shirt and places the cool fabric on my head.

I don't throw up again.

I feel safe with him here by my side. I know I shouldn't be sitting here with him. I should be with Dougie. I decide I'm not going to go over this again in my head. *What is done is done. I need to keep my life together.*

"Please help me up."

"I'm concerned you may have a concussion. Throwing up is a sign of a concussion."

"Please, officer. Just help me to my feet." I have no energy to argue.

As I lift my arms from the water, he turns white. He sees the bruises too.

I watch his eyes scan the rest of my body and rest upon my legs, also covered in bruises. He doesn't say a word. He merely turns his head and looks over his shoulder. I can't see the expression on his face, but I notice his body trembling ever so slightly. His lack of composure almost breaks my heart. I push the realization away before I crack. I told myself what is done is done.

I don't rush him to help me to my feet. His hand is still holding his dripping shirt to my forehead, while the other hand is covering his mouth. The seconds drag by.

Without saying another word, he helps me to my feet. We hear branches breaking in the distance, and he whips his head around.

"Probably deer," I say. "They have been running around all morning." I vaguely remember hearing cracking twigs earlier when I first got to the water's edge. I look around. The sun is hot. "What time is it?"

"Eleven," he says, his voice cracking.

"Oh my gosh!" I feel myself slightly trembling.

"What?"

"It's just, I came out here at seven. I didn't realize I fell asleep for so long. Dougie is going to be worried sick!"

His body stiffens at my words. I divert my attention from his water-filled eyes. *What do his tears mean?* I bite my lower lip to refocus my attention.

"I'll drive you home and then we can go to the hospital."

"I'm not sure that's the best idea." *Dougie has been extra jealous lately, and I don't want him to get the wrong idea. After all, it's not like this is serious. Just a little bump and some bruises.*

"Why not?"

I can't say why out loud. My words stay hidden.

"Look, I'm a police officer. As an officer, I can't just leave someone who could be dehydrated with a concussion to walk along a roasting hot highway. I'm not going to let you risk your life. I have a duty to take care of you—of everyone."

I look up at him. He is still holding my arm. "I'm fine. You can put your shirt back on. Sorry I got it dirty."

"No need to apologize. Please, if you won't let me take you to the hospital, let Dougie."

"I'll discuss it with him." *No, I won't.*

"Thank you. Are you sure you are okay to walk?"

"Yes. I'm fine now. I'll take care of myself." The words feel like a lie as they roll off my tongue.

"I'm just happy you're okay." He rinses his shirt and wrings it out before putting it on.

I look down. My shoes and socks are neatly stacked next to us. "Thanks for getting my shoes and socks."

He looks at me. "Huh?"

"My shoes and socks. Thank you."

He looks down at them. "Those were there when I got here. I came running over to you."

"Oh, I must have picked them up before. I was quite dizzy." *I thought I dropped them. I remember seeing them fly through the air. How hard did I hit my head?*

"Would you like to hold onto my arm as we walk back?" He holds out his arm. Water trickles down from his wet shirt.

"Thanks." I smile. I wrap one arm around his and hold onto his forearm with my other hand. We walk in silence through the winding path. *I'm relieved that he realizes there's no point in arguing with me about the hospital, even if I did slightly mislead him about going. I'm a big girl.*

Neither of us look at the obvious bruises that cover my body. Sometimes passion can leave bruises. As soon as the word *passion* pips into my head, I feel a wave of nausea roll up my stomach. I shake my head to get my thoughts out. I can feel the lake glistening at our backs as my tree watches over us. We slowly make our way along the winding path.

I walk in silence, leaning into his arm for support. I'm still quite faint. Minutes pass. No longer able to resist the urge, I glance up at him. He's biting his cheek. I know he saw the bruises. We both know. *I'm glad he doesn't say a word. I can't deal with his paranoia, especially now.*

I allow him to drive me home. Officer Kipton pulls up to the bottom of Dougie's driveway. The red dragon is still in the driveway. I'm still much too dizzy to try and walk further without assistance. He holds his arm out for me to grab and escorts me to the front door. "Thanks," I whisper.

"If you need anything, call. Please." Instinctively, I know his plea is not merely for today.

I smile as if to agree. "Thank you." I open the front door. He turns and walks back to his squad car. I wave goodbye.

I shut the door behind me and lean up against it. No movement in the house. *Dougie must still be sleeping. It's almost noon, so it's likely.* I tiptoe up the stairs and go straight for the shower. *I'd rather clean myself up before checking on Dougie.*

As I step into the steam, I can't help but wonder why Officer Kipton was in his squad car. I hadn't even paid attention to what he was wearing. *Was he in uniform?* I finish scrubbing the dirt from my feet. I resist the urge to curl up in a ball and fall asleep on the shower floor. Just as I finish towel-drying, I hear the front door open and close.

I wonder where Dougie is going. I look in the mirror. The scrape on my face looks better. I pull some shorts and a T-shirt on before opening the bathroom door. "Sweetie?" I call out.

"Yeah, down here."

I join him downstairs. "Are you going somewhere?"

He is sitting out on the patio with a cup of coffee. "No. I just opened the front door because I thought I heard something. I just read your note, but you were in the shower. What time did you leave for your run? I didn't even hear you." I walk closer. He hasn't said anything about the cut across my forehead.

I sit down across from him. "I left early. Like seven-ish."

"And you just got back?"

"Funny story. I was running, tripped over a stick, and hit my head. I think I passed out."

"Are you okay?" He looks at my forehead. I could see the cut a mile away. He's just noticing it.

"Yeah. I'm fine now. I just passed out near the lake."

"You were in the woods?"

I fear my words will fall on the eggshells he's laid. Swallowing, I say with as much confidence as I can muster, "Yeah. I figured it was so early that no one else would be out. It's safest that way."

I sense his intense gaze. *Is he going to get mad?*

"Well, I'd really prefer you not go alone at all. What if something had happened to you? Thank goodness you came to and were able to find your way out. But those woods are massive. Someone could get lost in those." His words scare me. *I guess I am lucky. What if Officer Kipton hadn't found me? Should I tell him about the officer? He doesn't need to know.*

"Yeah. I think I'll stay out of the woods. I'm going to grab a cup of coffee."

Before I can get up to go into the kitchen, Dougie reaches across and puts his hand on mine.

"I'm glad you finally showed me how much you love me last night. With more practice, you can love me more."

His words momentarily make my skin crawl. I feel angry and scared and guilty all at once, but all I can do is smile. *At least he knows I love him.*

But I feel dirty. I feel water trying to well up behind my eyes. I quickly stand up and face the kitchen before I close my eyes tight and take a deep breath. *Breathe Sara. You did the right thing. That's what partners do.*

I get up and go into the kitchen to pour myself a cup of coffee. Dougie didn't seem to notice my bruised wrists. *Good.* Steadying myself up against the counter, I take another deep breath. The dizziness is dissipating. I pour coffee into my cup and remain there just a few more moments.

As I gather my last nerves, I can't help but notice his tennis shoes under the kitchen table. Fresh, wet mud clings to the grooves in his soles.

CHAPTER THIRTY-TWO

Sara Olivia Scott

Brian hums as he pours himself a cup of his bitter coffee. "Why, good morning, Sara." His smile mentally makes me shiver.

"Morning."

"Do anything fun this weekend?"

"Yeah. Dougie and I hung around the house Saturday. On Sunday, we went for a walk and went to see that new action movie. I can't remember the name. What about you?"

"Sure did. It was fantastic. Ashley and I went up north to a cabin she rented."

"Cool." I pour myself a cup of his crappy coffee.

I finish my side work just as Officer Kipton comes through the front doors. Brian smiles as he grabs his morning plate of food and says, "Better greet the new customer."

I bring a cup of coffee out to Officer Kipton. "I'm sorry," I say, setting it down, "but this is the awful stuff."

"That's okay. I come more for the service." Without skipping a beat, he quietly asks, "Are you doing okay?"

I touch my forehead. The cut has scabbed over and doesn't look as bad. "Yeah. Thanks again for everything," I whisper so Brian's ears can't hear me.

"Please don't thank me. You don't need to. I'm just thankful you didn't drown. You scared me half to death."

"I scared myself," I confess.

I ring in his usual order. As soon as Brian's pot of acid runs out, I volunteer to make the next batch. I bring Officer Kipton his favorite coffee with his meal. "Enjoy. I was able to brew a good cup for you." I wink. I feel Brian's eyes on me.

As I walk into the back, Brian pries, "Are you giving him good service?"

"Of course. I always give good service."

"Good." He pours himself another cup of coffee and goes back to hide in his office.

Everyone seems so on edge lately. There must be a full moon coming or something. "Hey, Edward, is there going to be a full moon?"

"I don't think so. The weirdos were here just a couple weeks ago."

Hm. Maybe it's the heat. With nothing else to do in the prep area, I decide to visit with Kipton. "Do anything fun this weekend?"

"Not much. Gizmo and I went for a run yesterday. I was relieved not to find anyone lying in the water." He smiles.

"Ha-Ha. Funny," I chime in.

We both sense the words he isn't saying but wants to. I know they sit on his tongue, wanting to escape. I'm relieved he keeps them there.

"Not too much," he adds. "Just enjoyed the beautiful weather."

"Very nice. I took it easy too. Didn't want to risk passing out again from running."

"Have you been eating enough?"

"Yeah. What I normally do."

"You just look really small. I thought maybe you passed out from low blood sugar." I can tell he is trying to act nonchalant. "Please tell me you got checked out at the hospital with Dougie." The concern radiating from his eyes is comforting.

"I didn't get checked out. I felt fine after I showered. Plus, I was thinking about it. I forgot to eat breakfast that morning." *It could have been something else, but I'm not going to allow my brain to work on that equation.*

He finishes his food and pushes the plate a few inches away.

I grab it. "Let me get this out of your way." I take the plate and bring it to the kitchen. I bring back his bill. "Ya know, it's nice getting to see you in the mornings." I smile. He is so welcoming. I can't help but feel protected.

"I enjoy it as well. Gives me something to look forward to." He smiles. "Plus, the coffee, ya know, it's the best in town," he laughs.

"Well, have a great Monday. I hope you come back Friday."

"You too. I'll be back. Please don't let me find you passed out by the water's edge." He forces a smile. "But seriously, please be safe, Sara." He puts on his police hat. *I've never seen him wear his hat before. He looks so official.* He throws me a smile, his sunrays beaming from his hazel-green eyes, before he gets up from the table to leave. "I'll see you Friday."

• • •

I get home to find Dougie sitting on the couch. "Short day?" I ask, hoping he wasn't required to take additional time off.

"It was too hot. I didn't want any of my guys dying of heatstroke."

I give him a quick kiss hello. "Good call. You are always so sweet."

He grins. "I know."

I turn to go change, and he grabs my hand.

"Miss me already?" I joke, hoping he is not in one of those moods.

"Come here, sweetie. After all, you just said I was so sweet. I think I need some more sugar." He pulls me in close and kisses me forcefully. I feel my nerves rattle as I wonder what he's planning. We haven't really spoken of that night. I still don't know what to say.

I pull away. "I really need to change."

He sticks out his lower lip. "But don't you love me? I'm in need of some love."

I reach for my mouth. "I think I'm going to be sick."

His face crinkles, and he lets go of me. I run upstairs and into the bathroom, locking the door behind me.

Must be the stomach flu. I don't dare leave the toilet in case I throw up again.

"Are you okay?" he hollers up the stairs.

"I think I have the stomach flu," I call down.

"Yuck. I hope you don't give it to me." I hear him shuffling some things. "Feel better."

"Thanks."

"Mind if I go out with Chaz?"

"Go for it. Have fun." I hear the door close before I even get the words out of my mouth. *I should have asked for some ginger ale.*

An hour passes, and I don't throw up again. In fact, I feel fine now. I go into the guestroom and lie down. *I'm sure Dougie wouldn't want me in his bed if this is the flu.* My suitcase is chaos. All of my clothes are mixed up. I dig through the heap and find a pair of shorts and a tank top. *Perfect.* I crawl under the cool, crisp sheets and close my eyes. "It's the stomach flu, Sara, just the stomach flu," I say to myself.

I pull out my cell phone and dial Daddy's—I mean Brittany's cell phone. "Hi, you've reached Brian Scott. Sorry I missed you. Please leave a message after the tone. Thanks." I miss Daddy.

I call Momma's cell, or rather Stephanie's cell phone. "Hi! This is Rose. Sorry, I can't get to the phone right now, but leave a message and I'll call ya back. Many blessings." Oh Momma. *Why did you guys leave me so soon?*

I call the home phone, which is saved as "School administration." "You've reached the Scotts. We are unable to get to the phone right now." Momma's voice is so cheery. Daddy chimes in. "So leave a message, and we'll call you back." This is my favorite of their three messages.

I try to remember my conversations with them, but it's all fading. *What would they say to me right now? I haven't a clue.*

I don't address the equation that continues to linger beyond my thoughts.

I delete my phone history so it doesn't look like I just called anyone. *Better safe than sorry. I don't want to get Dougie upset.*

Sleep falls upon me, but rest is distant.

Dougie gets home a few hours later and checks in on me. "Feeling better?"

"Getting there." I feel fine now. Must have been a one-time thing. That can happen; it can strike just once. It definitely was not my nerves. My stomach flutters.

"Well, feel better. I'm going to watch some TV. Night."

"Night." I don't blame him for not wanting to get closer to me; if it is the flu, I don't want to pass it on.

Tuesday morning comes before I can complete my dream. I can't even remember what I was dreaming, but it was delightful. I shut off the annoying alarm. *If I have the stomach flu, I'd better not go into work and get anyone else sick.* My brain tries to give me a reason to go back to bed. Plus, no one shows up until Stephanie and Ashley are both at work on Tuesdays. I call Brian's phone. I get his voice mail. "It's Sara. I have the stomach flu and can't come into work. Sorry."

I know guilt lurks around the corner for that, but I haven't seen a doctor. I can't be sure I don't have the stomach flu. Guilt goes somewhere else. I fall back to sleep.

The sun's heat on my face awakens me. *I should probably get out of bed and move around.* I look at the clock. It's 12:05 p.m. I check Dougie's room. Empty. I head downstairs. No notes. *He must be at work.* I open the fridge and grab a slice of lunchmeat and cheese. I skip the bread. The television is playing old romantic reruns. *This is clearly the right day to call in sick.*

Dougie gets home around seven. "Hey," he says, walking in, keeping his distance. "Are you still contagious?"

"No." I give him a half-smile. "I feel much better. I just needed some rest today."

"When did you last barf?"

"Last night."

"Okay." He comes closer to me. "I bought Chinese food. I figured you would probably make yourself some soup."

"Yeah, I'll probably make some later."

"What are you watching?"

"Old romantic movies." I smile. "I'm such a sap."

He smiles. "Wanna watch baseball instead?"

"Sure." *I don't really care what we watch.* "I was getting tired of all the sappiness."

"Did you shower today?" he asks, probably to make sure I'm germ-free.

"Yes, and I brushed my teeth."

"Good. I just didn't know. You look sick without makeup on."

I hadn't realized I forgot to put any on. "I completely forgot to put it on."

He doesn't say anything more about it. I get up, make myself some soup, and join him back on the couch. He eats his chow mein, and I eat my chicken noodle soup as we listen to nine innings of baseball.

"I'm going to call it an early night again."

"You sleeping in the guest room again? Or do you have your energy back?" My stomach flutters again.

"I think I'd better sleep in the guest room one more night until I have my strength back."

"Night."

Brian was not happy with me Wednesday morning. "You should have called me the night before if you were sick."

"Sorry. Did a customer come in early?"

"Well, no, but that's not the point. You better thank Ashley for getting here at 6:45 a.m. to cover your butt."

That is her start time. "I will," I say. "Sorry." I'd rather he just stop yelling at me and go hide out in his office.

"You feeling better?" Edward asks through the heat lamp-covered counter.

"Yeah. Thanks, Edward."

I get three tables before Brian cuts me from the floor. I'm pretty sure he cut me early because he was still angry I called in yesterday, and he wanted to give Ashley more tables. I don't really care either way.

I get out of the restaurant at noon. The walk home is quiet. The sun isn't painfully hot. I try to make my brain avoid the topic I know I need to address. Intimacy. I know he is going to want me to allow him to be intimate tonight. My stomach flutters. *That night, I did tell him I loved him, right? I don't actually remember. I wish I hadn't had so much wine. He hadn't done anything wrong. He couldn't have known I was …*

I hear a car speeding down the winding road behind me. I hear Officer Kipton's voice in my head: *Accidents.* I move over onto the grass beside the road and look over my shoulder as I continue walking. I watch the car pass me. *I think he just told me that to scare me. Well, it's working.* I decide to stay in the grass, just in case. I don't rush. I just walk at a slow pace, enjoying the freedom of an open road.

My stomach flutters as I light Dougie's candle on the patio around seven o'clock. I try to ignore the butterflies. Dougie will be home soon. The flutter-flies whirl some more. "This is what someone who loves someone does," I whisper to myself as I put the pizza slices on their plates. "I love Dougie," I whisper as I pull two beer bottles from the fridge. "I—"

Dougie opens the door. "You what?" He smiles as he sees me preparing dinner.

"I have a surprise for you." *Surprise.* That's what he said. I push that night out of my memory.

"I love surprises." He drops his cell phone on the counter and pulls me in close. *I'm not going to fight. I love him. I need to show him that I love him.* I surrender to his lead.

CHAPTER THIRTY-THREE

Douglas J. Adams

"Brian, let's go out back and grab a smoke."

"Yeah. Meet you out back. Let me get 'em out of my office."

He meets me out back.

"Need some more R2?"

"No. The stuff you gave me last time worked fine." I step closer to him. "Was *he* here this week?"

Brian fumbles getting the cigarettes out of the box. "Yeah, but man, I don't think you need to worry about—"

"That's all I need to know. Keep it." I didn't come out to smoke.

That woman is gonna pay.

CHAPTER THIRTY-FOUR

Sara Olivia Scott

Just as I finish ringing in Dougie's group's order, Brian comes in from smoking out back. "Sara, can I see you in my office?" He seems nervous.

My stomach drops. He has never called me into his office. "Yeah." I follow him into the back.

"You can shut the door."

I look around as I gently close the door. He has nice, expensive furniture in here. *I expected this place to be a dump. How can he afford expensive stuff like this?* As the door clicks, I'm reminded I've never been alone with him in a small room. "Did I do something wrong?" my voice cracks.

"Oh, no. I just wanted to ask you"—he pauses and sighs—"I think maybe you should take the rest of the night off and get some rest."

Some rest? What did I do wrong to be cut from the floor early? "Am I in trouble?"

He looks up at me, eyes widening. "I hope not," he says, forcing a smile.

My stomach drops again. *I must have done something to get him angry … or Ashley.* "I still work tomorrow morning though, right?"

"Yeah. Of course. It's just been slow in here, and I'm over on hours, so I need to cut some shifts early the next couple of weeks." I feel myself relax.

"Okay. I'll get my side work done. What about the tables that I have?"

"I'll have Marie pick up those."

"Okay. Why didn't you just tell me this out there?"

He scrunches up his face as if to ponder if he should tell me. "I don't want the other employees knowing we are over on hours. I can't have people get worried and jump ship."

"That makes sense. I won't say anything," I reassure him. "Thanks, Brian."

I feel his eyes on me as I open the door and gently close it behind me. *That was weird. Uncharacteristic of him.*

I finish up my side work. *I really hope he wasn't lying and that he just needs to cut hours.*

As I roll my last set of silverware, Dougie's table's food is up. I balance all the plates on two trays and deliver their orders.

"Sweetie, want anything else?"

"Hmmm." Dougie smirks. "I'll let you know what else I want."

He sounds tipsy. "Well, Brian cut me from the floor because he is over on hours, so Marie is taking over for me."

"Are you kidding? Now we gotta tip her?"

I shrug. "Maybe not. If you're just going to order beers and whatnot, you probably don't have to."

"Well, where is she?" He looks around.

I look behind me. "Probably in the kitchen right now. That reminds me. I need to refill my salt and pepper shakers. I'll say goodbye before I leave."

Twenty minutes later, I finish topping off the condiments. I find Brian in his office and ask him to clock me out. "And you are sure I'm not in trouble?"

He gives me an impish smile. "Nope. Cutting back hours. Have a *good* night." His emphasis on *good* sends chills up my back. *I hate it when he's creepy.*

Marie is already flirting with Chaz. She's working on a tip she probably won't ever see as I walk back out to say goodbye to Dougie. "Hey, guys. I see you have met Marie." I smile at her.

"They sure are a fun group!" She smiles back at me.

"I know. The best." I look at Dougie. He seems distanced. "You okay, sweetie?" I whisper into his ear.

"I'm great. Just great." He avoids my eyes.

"I'm going to head home. Want me to wait up?"

"I'll be home later. Yeah. Why don't you wait up? I won't be long."

"Would you rather I just wait here with you?"

"No. It would kinda kill the 'guy' time. I'll see you at home."

I give him a quick kiss on the cheek as he's looking at his phone. "I'll see you later. I love you," I whisper again into his ear.

"Yeah." He always acts so macho in front of his "guys."

It's already dark outside. Looks like a thunderstorm is rolling in. The breeze is quite chilly. I glance around the parking lot. No squad car. *I guess the police department doesn't need an officer guarding the doors this Thursday night. Too bad; a ride home wouldn't be so bad.*

I feel a raindrop on my nose as I step out onto the road. I hope the storms hold off until I get home. Another drop falls on my head. I pick up my pace.

I look up. No stars. I never realized how difficult it would be walking this winding road when it's so dark. Usually the moon lights my path, but I feel blind. Not that I'm scared of the dark, but I am most definitely not its biggest fan. I would use my cell phone's light, but I don't want it getting wet.

The few droplets multiply as I listen to the rain creeping up behind me. Each droplet comes shooting out of the dark sky. I take my apron off and try to hold it like an umbrella above my head. I start jogging.

My path is momentarily lit up as a streak of lightning jumps across the sky. My nerves await the crackle that is sure to follow. BOOM! It strikes something nearby. I start running. *I hope my tree stays safe!*

The rain hurts as it hits my back, pushing me forward. Faster. My legs ache as I exert as much energy as my body will give. The wind whips my back harder. I gain my second wind and pick up my pace.

Headlights follow behind me, nearing me with every step I take. I move over ten feet into the grassy area that borders the road. I hope it's Dougie or Officer Kipton to give me a lift. I don't turn around. I keep running, hoping the car will slow behind me if it's one of them. The car goes zooming past, spraying my face. I can taste the mud on my lips. There is no point in keeping my head covered anymore, so I use my apron as a towel to wipe my mouth and face. I'm already soaked and dirty, so I wrap it around me as a jacket. Hopefully, my chattering teeth will calm down. The rain pelts against my face, washing away the rest of the mud my apron didn't get. *At least it counts as a shower, right?*

I make it home in record time. I fumble for my keys with my frozen fingers. I unlock the door and jump inside. The wind tries to blow the raindrops in after me, so I slam the door shut and lean up against it. I take a deep breath as I finally reach my shelter. My legs throb, and my chest hurts. It burns from panting.

Ten seconds pass before I catch my breath. *I'd better dry off, or Dougie may get upset that I'm dripping water everywhere.* I reach to set my keys on the table to the right of the door next to the kitchen.

I'm mid-reach when something catches my eye from the living room. I glance over. A shadow appears out of the darkness and pushes towards me from the couch. I open my mouth to scream, but fear paralyzes me. My legs feel like there are 100-pound weights holding them in place. I sense the water pooling around my feet. My left arm is glued by to side. My right arm freezes, holding the keys, unable to drop them in the bowl. My chattering jaw falls silent. *Who is it?* Hostility and hatred radiate from this dark figure. Its evil pierces my inner, stunned self.

Scream, Sara. Turn around and run outside. RUN! My mind tries to get me to move, but my body won't inch. My heart thuds so loudly that my ears want to pop. The dark shadow stops ten feet from me in the hallway. I can't see who it is. I feel lightheaded, like I may pass out at any moment.

Lightning tears through the patio door, exposing the shadow. I see *it* holding a knife. The realization that I may die flashes through my mind. *Why can't I run? Why can't I scream? Why can't I do anything?*

"What do you have to say for yourself?" The voice cuts through my ears. The figure takes a step closer to me. Nine feet separate us.

"Dougie?" My body wants to relax, hoping he's playing a prank, but the sharpness in his words keeps me frozen.

"Expecting I was someone else?" His words slice through the silent air that stands eight feet between us as I hear him take another step.

"Wh … What are you doing?" I find my quivering voice.

He takes another step closer. And another. "What? My girlfriend not excited to see me?"

He stands six feet from my dripping, still paralyzed body.

"What are you talking about?" His eyes are now visible, but they are darker than his shadow. Black diamonds glistening in the dark.

My right hand unfreezes. I slowly, without making a noise, reach behind me for the doorknob while still looking straight at him. I fumble to unlock the door but can't seem to get my hand to grasp the handle; it keeps sliding off. The doorknob clinks, giving me away.

"Greased doorknobs make it hard to get out, don't they? Why don't we play a game? Let's call it the truth game." He takes another step closer. His voice is strange and wicked. It's not my Dougie's voice.

My adrenaline breaks through my paralyzed state, and I frantically turn to try harder to get the doorknob to open. I grab it with both hands. I can't get a grip on it. I know my back is to him, but I need to get out! Clink. Clink. Clink. I can't get it to work.

"Why don't you tell me what you really do when you go running?"

"Huh? What are you talking about?" I talk as I keep trying to get the door to open. *Maybe he will snap out of it. Maybe he is just trying to scare me.* I finally get the doorknob to turn and open.

But before I can open the door, he stomps towards me, closing the gap and slamming the door closed with his left hand. His hand pounds on the door with such force that my ears ring. I feel his breath hot on my neck. I feel the presence of his body towering over mine. I whip around.

His right hand grips a twelve-inch knife as his left hand grabs my throat. He starts to close his hand tightly around my throat, squeezing out what little air is left in my lungs. I claw at his wrist, trying to break free. He squishes me up against the closed door with his hip, not loosening his grip on my throat. "Don't lie to me again. Answer me. Tell me the truth!"

The man who is inches from my face is a stranger. His body is Dougie's, but those dark eyes I've caught glimpses of before are energizing this beast. He releases my throat. I double over for air. My ears hear me gasping, struggling for every breath. I force myself to stand up as I keep gasping. If I can explain, maybe I will have time to get out.

"I. Go. Runni—"

WHAM! His left fist stings my open jaw, throwing me to the floor. My ears hear my own gasp.

CRUNCH! His boot kicks my ribs with such force my body involuntarily rolls over onto my back. Multiple cracks come from within my body. Sharp pain stabs me from the inside. SMASH! I feel his boot hit me in my opened jaw. My voice is drowned out by the thunder, but I can feel it escaping my broken jaw through my own blood-curdling scream. I scream louder in hopes that someone will hear me.

"SHUT UP!" His steel-toed boot kicks my jaw again.

My hands grab my jaw. The lightning-bolt pains shooting through my face are unbearable. I stretch my legs out. He's standing over me, one foot on either side of my body. My foot touches the closed door. TAP. TAP. TAP. My shoe taps the door. I'm so close, but I can't reach it. He stands between the door and me, laughing.

No one can hear me.

I can't get out.

I stop screaming. *No one is coming for me. No one can save me.*

The wickedness of his laugh echoes through the hall now that my screams have stopped.

His laughing stops.

"Stand up," he orders.

I don't think my body will. My words are hiding. I don't think I can even talk. I lie there, unable to catch my breath and unable to comprehend what is going on.

TAP. TAP. TAP. My shoe hits the door. *So close.*

He grabs my left leg and yanks it over my body to rotate me around. I kick at his hand with my right leg. I use all the might I have to hurt him so he stops hurting me. My attempt is feeble. He drags me further down the hall. I kick harder. My foot makes contact with his hand, causing him to drop my foot. Before I can move my legs, his heel comes crashing down on my right leg. Immediate numbness replaces the sensation in my leg. The pain radiating through my abdomen and face steals any energy I have left. I can't move.

I watch, unable to control any of my movements, as he grabs a hold of my left foot. He drags my body further. I reach out to try and grab at anything I can. I just feel my hands slide down the hall. He stops in the middle of the hallway. I hear my foot thud on the ground as he drops it. His stiff body crouches down next to me.

"I know you have been with *him*."

Him? I want to ask who him is, but my jaw won't move.

"You don't think I know you've been lying to me? I know you guys have breakfast together. I know you guys meet up in the woods. I've witnessed all of this. Yet, you think you can lie to me?" He spits as he enunciates every word coming from his mouth.

Silence swarms the empty space around us as he stares at me, waiting for me to answer.

"You can't even be honest with me, can you? I know you went through my drawer. There was an oily fingerprint on my cards. Hmm, who could that have been?" The sarcasm in his voice gives me a flash-back of him asking about his burger's cheese. He spits again in my face as I feel his saliva fill my paralyzed, opened mouth.

He puts his face up next to mine, our noses touching. "After everything I did for you."

With agonizing movements, I summon the power to whisper and force my jaw to move. "I've never cheated. I loved you, just you." I hear the whisper echo down the hallway. I don't love this man. I loved Dougie.

His eyes are unchanged.

"Don't you say that! You aren't worthy of saying that!" He spits in my face again before standing up. He walks into the living room. My eyes scan to see how far away the front door is. It's ten feet away. I try to move my arms and legs. I can't move. A moment later he returns.

"If you really love me, you'll let me do whatever I want to you." His wicked laugh tears through my broken body, clawing at my soul. "You were a toughy. I even had to use a little help to do what I wanted to innocent little Sara." His sadistic laugh scratches at my ears.

"I'll be nice one last time, even though you're a fat, lying bit—."

"STOP IT" my voice cuts him off.

His eyes meet mine. "This time, you won't get the drugs to numb the pain." He puts the knife in his belt and bends down. "You may have one last word." He grabs my oxford shirt with both hands and rips it off. The buttons scatter across the room. "What is it?"

This is the end.

This is my end.

I think of Daddy and Momma. *I'll be seeing them soon.*

I cry out to the world above me in hopes that they will come and save me. "Daddy! Momma!" I beg the universe to let me go now. *Just let me die.*

"They're dead, you crazy prude. But I'll tell you what. I'll send you to them."

He grabs his knife from his belt. He wraps both hands around the handle and slowly lifts his arms up, taunting me.

"You'd like me to make this quick, wouldn't you?" He gives a jabbing motion downward but doesn't touch my body with the blade. He lifts his arms up. Wicked laughter fills the room.

"But first, we are going to have a little more fun, Sara." A demonic smile spreads across his face.

I've never known this stranger standing over me. My body won't move. I know my limbs are twisted and not working. I'm trapped in my own body. I'm a prisoner of my human self.

He cuts off the rest of my clothes with his knife. The blade is cold. As he cuts the clothing, I feel the sting of the blade against my skin.

I know I won't see tomorrow.

I wish I could fast forward to the end. *Let it be over. I want it to be over.*

I push out his laughter. I push away what he is doing to my body. I disconnect from my flesh. I let my mind go and force my body to shut down. I allow myself to let go. I will myself to shut off. I imagine myself at the lake. I feel myself sink into the water and willingly breathe it deep into my lungs. I know it's the end. I stop fighting. I imagine myself breathing in more and more water as I watch my body drown.

My eyes bring me back to the present moment as cold metal tears into my already pained body. I watch as he pulls the knife out, dripping my blood on my broken skin like paint splatter.

God forgive—

Total Darkness.

CHAPTER THIRTY-FIVE

Officer Kipton Pierre

My alarm sounds much too early. It's only 6:00 a.m. After a night of tossing and turning without more than a couple hours of sleep, today is here. I'm not sure why I couldn't get a good night's sleep. I'm usually out when I hit the pillow. I sleep like the dead. *Maybe it was the storms that kept me awake.* This time of year, there are frequent severe storms. *Yeah, that's got to be it.*

Thankfully, it's Friday, which means I'll get to see her bright face in a short while. I've been counting down the days until I get to see her bright eyes and that beautiful smile. After the scare at the lake, I don't think I could stand another day without seeing her. I want to see her and make sure she's doing okay.

Maybe she'll have left Douglas. I can always hope.

I smile thinking of her dimples. There's something about that gal …

I jump in the shower and race through washing my hair so that I am not late to the restaurant.

The air is brisk and smells of worms. Thunderstorms are always a joy to listen to, but I wouldn't mind if the worms stayed underground after the rain stops. Their scent always makes me queasy.

The air is eerily still this morning. Crows squawk and dive-bomb the worms that are lost on the pavement. Sunshine hides behind the gray clouds that fill the sky.

I can't help but feel something is *off* this morning. *Did I forget something?* I'm wearing my uniform. My taser, cuffs, and gun are around my belt. I've got my badge. I'm wearing my hat. I look in the mirror. I didn't shave, but it's not Saturday or Wednesday, so that's not it either. *Cell phone?* I feel my back pocket. *Check. Oh well.* I look at my watch. It's 6:20 a.m. *I'd better hurry.*

The restaurant has a single car in the parking lot, like every other morning. My stomach dances as I pull open the front doors. I look around. There's no cheery Sara to greet me. She must be in the back, so I just grab my usual spot. Again, I attempt to keep from smiling as I wait for her to greet me good morning. I look at my hands to steady my excitement.

I feel someone's presence in front of me, but when I look up, it's that shrewd-looking manager. My brow involuntarily wrinkles. Before I can say anything, he greets me. "Hi there, officer. What can I get you this morning? Coffee?"

"Ah, yeah, coffee would be fine." He turns to get my coffee. *Is she in the restroom? Maybe running late?*

He sets my coffee down in front of me. I look at it so I don't appear too eager. "Where, um, where is Sara?"

His face is blank. "That would be nice to know. She hasn't shown up yet."

I look at my watch. It's 6:31 a.m." *She's never late.* "Did someone try to call her?"

He crinkles his face. "Yes. She didn't answer. I called Doug too. He didn't answer either. They are probably just spending some time together."

My stomach churns.

"You wouldn't have a problem with that, officer, would you?"

His smirk sparks a fear that I've been ignoring for weeks, ignoring because Sara begged me to. "What does that mean?" My voice is calm and to the point.

"Well, it's just that Dougie knows you seem to request Sara's section every week."

"She's the only one working when I eat."

"Well—"

I aggressively stand up to interrupt what he is saying. My coffee spills on the table from my abrupt movement. "As an officer, you need to tell me what you know right now." His face goes white.

"I don't know anything. I just told you. It's just weird that you come in here and ask for her section for breakfast every day. That's all."

"She is the ONLY one working when I get here!" I'm getting pissed off.

He avoids my eyes. "She's probably just running late. I had to send her home early last night, so she's probably just oversleeping." He looks like he may pass out.

"It's not like what you think it is. It isn't her I'm watching! Where is she?" My voice is so loud my own words sting my ears.

"I don't know." He shrugs. I believe him.

"If she shows up, you call the station right away. You got that?"

He nods.

I run as fast as my legs will carry me out to my squad. *I don't care if I just gave away the fact that I've been investigating his restaurant. I don't care about that guy. I don't care about the possible drug bust.*

I choke back the fear that is lurking around every corner of my brain as I start up my squad. I radio in. "This is Officer Pierre. I'm headed to 863 Sunrise Court, Newport, Minnesota 55055, on suspicion of domestic abuse. Send back up and ambulance ASAP."

I don't care if this is an overreaction. I've got this weird pit in my stomach. I know something isn't right.

The sirens wail as I speed 70 … 80 … 90 miles per hour down the winding road. I feel the car losing traction on the turns, but not enough to flip it. I need to remain calm.

God, don't let this be it, I pray. *Not her.* Each second is precious. I press down harder on the accelerator.

Three minutes pass. I screech to a halt on Douglas's front lawn. I jump out of the squad, leaving the door open, and run to the front door, gun drawn. I pound on the door. THUD! THUD! THUD! No answer. "OPEN UP," I scream. A neighbor opens her door across the street. "You see anyone leave this house?" I yell over my shoulder.

She yells, "No!" before quickly shutting her door. There isn't time to wrap my hand; I punch the glass window next to the door and reach in to unlock it. It's already unlocked. The handle is all greasy. I slam open the door.

I'm in a horror movie.

My inhale is cut short as my eyes focus on the blood smeared down the hallway. "SARA? Douglas?" I shout out. My voice bounces off the walls without a response.

Gun pointed forward, I maneuver into the kitchen. Everything in the house is thrown about, flipped sideways, and turned upside down. The small kitchen table is up against the fridge. Four chairs lie scattered throughout the kitchen, some of them broken. The cabinets are emptied, and broken dishes are on every surface. Blood is splattered everywhere. It looks fake. Too surreal. My gut tells me this isn't fake.

Maybe she defended herself. I hold onto that hope. *Maybe she stopped him, and this is his blood. I step back into the hallway.* My eyes see a small handprint smeared down the hallway to the living room, like a person was dragged. All I hear is the sound of my breathing. I feel the inevitable truth closer with each step I take.

I turn into the living room.

Life stops.

Her naked, limp body lies motionless on the carpet. *Is she dead?*

I holster my gun as I take the five steps that separate us. My soul screams as I kneel down beside her. Ripping my shirt off, I wrap it around her blood-soaked abdomen. But blood is seeping out from everywhere! I check her pulse. There is so much blood. I'm shaking too much to tell if it's her pulse or mine that I feel.

"Sara!" I scoop her upper body into my arms as I kneel beside her. "SARA!" my voice cries out, trying to see if she will awaken.

I check her pulse again. My hands are trembling too much to tell if she has a pulse. There is just so much blood. Her once-white oxford waitress shirt lies torn on the ground, now red in color and soaked in her blood. Her black pants are shredded on the ground as well. Her legs expose cuts and abrasions from her thighs to her shins. Her bones look twisted. I look for something to cover her bottom half with. I see a blanket on the couch and grab that while still holding her. I cover her lower half. I won't let anyone see her bare like this.

Tears fall from my eyes. *Please God, please let her be okay.*

I listen to her open mouth to see if I can hear her breathing.

Purgatory. Hell.

I can't tell if she is breathing.

I don't notice the paramedics run through the front door. Randy comes in behind them. The paramedics take her from my hands. I watch, helpless, as they lay her flat on the ground. I sit there next to these strangers, unable to move. Waiting. Praying. They pound on her chest. One of the paramedics starts mouth-to-mouth as another does CPR.

My eyes stay focused on her. She isn't breathing. *Breathe, Sara. Breathe.*

I feel Randy's eyes on me. His voice commands me to move back. I ignore him. *She needs me.*

Minutes pass like hours. I can't tear my eyes away from these men pounding on her chest to make her breathe. They remove the shirt that covered her broken body and zap her. One paramedic checks her pulse again.

"She has a pulse! It's very weak, but it's there. I'm not sure how much longer she has. We need life flight here NOW!" one of the paramedics shouts.

Everything else turns to white noise. *Pulse. She has a pulse. There is hope.*

I feel Randy's hand on my shoulder, but I can't take my eyes off her. Her frail body is just lying on the floor. I try to go to her, but Randy pulls me back by my shoulder. "Let's get some air, Kip."

I don't move. "She needs me," I argue.

"Let them do what they need to." He pulls on my shoulder to follow him outside. I follow.

"I think you need to take a step back, Kip. It's not your fault."

I don't say anything. *How can I? Why aren't they covering her naked body? No one should see that.*

"You're just going to get in the way."

No one knows *who* she is to me. I don't answer him. I stand, watching through the opened patio door as they hook her up with all of their medical equipment. I hear the helicopter in the distance.

Randy puts his hand back on my shoulder. "Kip, it's not your fault. Hopefully, she'll pull through. But, you know, these types of things sometimes just happen."

"Stop it!" I turn to face him. His expression quickly changes as his eyes meet my face. "She isn't just anyone!" I yell out into the much-too-quiet world around us. "I love her!" *I love her. I love Sara like I love breathing. I love Sara like I love being an officer. I love her.* This realization sends a tremor through my body. "I need her to be okay. I should have gotten her away." I can't choke back my tears. "I should have made her leave him … I always knew this could happen."

The thought of her body lying limp, twisted, and exposed when I came in cuts into my stomach. I turn away from her unconscious body. I throw up into the bushes next to us. I can't breathe between my nausea and sobs.

My mind goes haywire, replaying everything I know about her. That day at the lake, she threw up on herself. It's because he beat her body and soul until she … I throw up again. I knew he was hurting her. I should have just taken her away, even if she didn't realize he was hurting her. *If she dies, this is my fault. This is all too much. I should have done something. I should have just picked her up in my arms and ran. Ran her to safety.* I hold my face in my hands, my hands stained with her blood. I can't stop myself from falling into this downward spiral of thoughts.

The sound of the chopper pulls me back to this moment. The helicopter lands in the front yard. Dust and twigs fly down from the roof of the home. Darting through the house, I watch them load her body into the copter. Looking over my shoulder at Randy, I give him my own command. "Randy, I'm not leaving her side."

He does not say a word.

"Find *him*." I look at Randy. I know backup is searching the rest of the house. The rest of the team will get here soon. He will not get away.

I signal for the pilot to wait for me. I run to the chopper before sergeant can object. Her body doesn't move as I jump in. I take her cold, small hand in mine. *She is just sleeping,* I tell myself.

Salt trickles down my face and onto my hands. My hands soaked in her precious blood. My hands hold hers beneath me. *This can't be the end. Not hers.*

CHAPTER THIRTY-SIX

Officer Kipton Pierre

Day Seven.

The doctors don't know how long she will be in this coma or if she'll even awaken. It's taken the doctors days to address each of her injuries:

Concussion

Skull fracture

Lacerated eyebrow with six stitches

Lacerated lip with five stitches

Broken jaw now wired shut

Fractured right ulna and radius with second and third metacarpals hairline fractured

Seven broken ribs. Two had to be removed because they were shattered

Punctured and collapsed lung requiring surgery. Chest tube removed yesterday

Stab wound lacerating the spleen. Partial splenectomy performed

Bilateral tibia and talus fractures of her ankles requiring
open reduction and internal fixation surgeries

Knee fracture, for which they have not done surgery yet

Numerous small lacerations to her face and limbs
that did not require suturing

Countless contusions and abrasions

Signs of sexual trauma

The image of her broken body haunts me to this day; her innocence taken from her and her body left exposed for anyone to see.

I haven't left her side for more than thirty minutes in the last seven days. Randy guarded her door during the times I needed food or a shower. I don't trust anyone else to protect her. The shock has worn off, but guilt has replaced it. I'm not sure I'll ever forgive myself for not getting to her sooner—weeks sooner.

The staff here is incredible. The first six days she was in the ICU, they allowed me to sit outside her door during non-visiting hours. Now they have set up a chair that turns into a pullout chaise for sleeping in her surgical ICU room. Most people aren't allowed to sleep in the ICU guest chair, but they are making an exception for me. I'm allowed to shower in her private bathroom, which she hasn't used. I haven't left her bedside in the last thirty-four hours.

Randy and the staff bring me food when I need it, but I don't have much of an appetite.

Her heart is much steadier. I think it's growing stronger as the days pass; the doctors haven't said anything about that, though. The doctors were very concerned about pneumonia as a complication of her lung, but today she is breathing on her own, which is a good sign; it is also the reason they are allowing me to stay in here.

Sergeant won't let me in on the investigation, but Randy keeps me informed. He has swung by the hospital daily to check on me and give me updates on the case. Yesterday, he told me it wasn't looking good but didn't give any other details.

Thankfully, sergeant won't let Douglas near the hospital until the investigation is closed. Randy told me yesterday that Douglas, Chaz, and Brian, the weasel from the restaurant, were brought in for questioning. The precinct let them go for lack of evidence to hold them. That was yesterday. They are roaming free—for now.

I push away the anger because I know Sara needs me.

The door opens a crack.

"Hey, Randy."

"Hey, Kip. How's she doing?" he whispers.

I look at her and then back at him. I motion for us to talk outside. In case she can hear us, I don't want her to worry about anything. God knows she's been through enough.

As soon as the door quietly closes behind me, I tell Randy the good news. "Well, she's now breathing on her own." I smile as I deliver the good news. My hope flickers.

"Good, I'm glad to hear that, Kip."

I nod in agreement. "So what's going on with the case?" I whisper. We aren't supposed to discuss the case since sergeant wants me out of it, but Randy and I go way back.

"Honestly, Kip," he says, looking down at his feet and shaking his head before looking back up at me, "it's not good."

I take a deep breath, trying to keep the anger out. Rage is a powerful emotion. I need only positive energy around Sara.

"Kip, Douglas is claiming someone broke into his home and was trying to rob it when Sara must have gotten home. He's claiming that he spent the night at his friend Chaz's house. We've brought everyone in for questioning—Douglas, Chaz, the rest of the bozos they hung out with on Thursday, as well as the restaurant manager. They are all saying the same thing. We even interviewed Douglas's neighbors, and they are all saying his car wasn't in his driveway at all that night."

My loud exhale prompts Randy to pause.

"This is bullsh—" I stop myself. "We both know this guy did this to her." I take some more deep breaths to push the rage away. "But what about the rape kit?" *There has to be DNA from him to prove he's the monster.*

"The doctor advised a condom was used. We don't have DNA for the rape."

"That fuc—"

Randy interjects, "I know, Kip. But this guy's smart. He puts on a good show. He even had real tears and all. This guy thought this through before he did anything. No one heard any screaming or anything like that. No one saw anyone come or go from the house." His voice trails off.

"There was a thunderstorm." I connect the dots. Of course, no one heard her screams or the thrashing of furniture. Nausea consumes my body with this realization. I hold it back. Glancing at her closed door and drawn shades, my eyes fill with tears. I didn't think I had any more tears to give.

The last seven days have been purgatory—no, hell. *I just need to know how this will turn out. Is she going to live, or is she going to die?*

My mind immediately jumps to when she told me about her parents' deaths the Monday after I noticed her bruised arms. She hadn't wanted to talk anymore about Dougie, so I inquired about her family. *A young woman with no family; she was the perfect victim for him. Monica had a family.* I shake my head. *Monica escaped this. I should have told Sara about Monica. I know I couldn't because of confidentiality laws, but what does that matter now? What does it matter if she doesn't live? If only I could go back in time.*

My mind jumps from one thing to another.

Is she going to live? This unanswered question gnaws at me, haunting me. *I have no control over the outcome. I'm helpless. I've done all that I can do.*

I would trade places with her if I could.

"Kip." Randy's voice pulls me back to the present. "I'm going to do everything I can for you guys, but you need to understand this sneaky bastard, he may have to wait for his next life to get what he deserves. I haven't even sat down with the DA because we don't have enough."

They always seem to get away. It's not fair.

"Did they find the weapon? DNA on the weapon? Was there DNA on her clothes? Anything?"

"No weapon. They've concluded it was a knife, but we haven't found anything. He didn't have any knife sets in the house when we searched it. As for DNA? Sure, it's everywhere, but it's his house. She was living there, so his DNA was already on her clothing. She was seen serving him Thursday night at the restaurant. So that doesn't prove anything."

"Do they know when she was stabbed? The doctors won't tell me. Was forensics able to determine when the attack started?"

Randy pauses, debating on whether or not to tell me.

"Well?" The eagerness in my voice demands him to go on.

"Thursday evening. Probably around ten or so."

I should have been patrolling that night. Although no one was assigned to the restaurant's lot, I had been keeping an eye on it the last couple of weeks. I took that Thursday off because I was so tired. *Why the heck did I let myself relax on the couch? I would have been able to prove he left.* "What about the restaurant? Has anyone tried to find anyone who was dining there that night? Did someone check receipts of credit cards or checks used to pay for meals so we can track down who may have been there to see him leave?"

My hope is quickly extinguished. "The manager claims their system shut down, so they only accepted cash that night from six on. No one has come forward with any information."

Before we can discuss anymore, a nurse approaches us, and we immediately cease our conversation. "Officer Kipton?"

I look at her. "Yes?"

"You have a phone call. She says her name is Melanie."

Randy stands outside Sara's door, guarding her.

I follow the nurse to her station. "Hello, this is Officer Kipton."

"Officer Kipton, my name is Melanie Anntomp. I'm Sara's friend from college. I … I just found out what happened to her. How is she doing? Can I fly out and visit her?" I fight to keep the tears on her end of the line.

"Friend from college?" I haven't let anyone see her; she doesn't have any family, and I can't trust anyone outside of Randy right now. "I'm sorry, Melanie, but I am unable to disclose her condition to any non-relative. How exactly do you know her?"

"I was her roommate. Well, we lived together for the first semester. I moved home after her parents died because I wanted to be close to my family. Is she alive? Please, please. I need to know how she is!" The desperation in her voice sounds sincere. My instincts tell me she is telling the truth.

"I'm going to run a security check on you, and if you pass, I'll call you back. I'm sorry, don't take any offense. It's just that I don't know who we can trust yet."

"I get it. When can I expect to hear back from you?"

"Give me two hours." I get her full contact information.

Randy assures me he will get her information ran right away. Once he's done, he will come back with dinner for us.

I open Sara's door after Randy leaves. Her chest lifts up and down. Relief. I like to make sure she's breathing. Sitting in the chair beside her bed, I take her hand in mine. My eyes grow heavy as I listen to her better-yet-still-struggling inhales and exhales.

The door opens. I jump up from my chair, dropping her hand from mine. I instinctively reach for my gun until I realize it's just Randy.

"Sorry." I exhale. I flip my holster cover back down. "I must have dozed off." I rub my face with my hands.

He nods for me to join him outside in the hall. I follow. "I got us burgers and fries with Melanie's report. She's clean. I already contacted her and let her know she has the green light to visit."

"Thanks." I rub my eyes again before taking the burger and fries. "You're a good friend, Randy. I don't know what I would do without you." He hands me a cup of coffee. "I'm serious. Thank you."

"Don't mention it, Kip. You are like a brother to me. We'll get through this. She'll pull through." We both know the future is unknown, but I appreciate his words anyway.

CHAPTER THIRTY-SEVEN

Officer Kipton Pierre

Day Ten.

Melanie flew out two days ago. I'm happy Sara has someone like Melanie in her life. She and I got to know each other pretty well these past two days.

Hearing her say she was the one who introduced Sara to Douglas was extremely difficult. She cried as she told me. She barely knew Douglas but thought he was sweet. She blames herself. We both realize he has not been convicted of any crime yet, but the pieces don't add up to a burglary either.

After some thought, I thanked her for the role she has already played in Sara's life. Had she not introduced Sara to Douglas, Sara would have never moved out to Newport. If Sara had never moved out to Newport, I never would have met her. I don't tell Melanie this, but I wish she had never introduced Sara to Douglas; of course I wouldn't know her then, but her life never would have been put in danger's path in the first place.

My life without Sara: Dull. Incomplete.

But a world without Sara: Empty.

I promise Melanie I will keep her informed of Sara's condition. She promises me she will report her condition to the rest of Sara's college friends. A few others have called for an update: a kid named Erick, a girl named Brenda, and some others. I'm just glad I have someone who will keep her real friends informed. Sara needs friends at a time like this, even if they aren't authorized to visit her in the hospital. Genuine prayers and good thoughts can perform miracles.

Sara is sleeping peacefully in her unconscious world. Her body has started to heal. The bruises have hit their worst and are on the mend. I swear, I even see some color in her cheeks. Even as she heals in this unknown dimension, my heart invests more in her every day. I am consumed with dreams of her opening her eyes and living her life.

I realize that she may never love me. But my love for her extends beyond any earthly explanation. I don't expect anything from her in return for my love. All I want is for her to be happy, to have the life she is worthy of having. I can't fathom living in a world where she isn't smiling with her bright eyes and bold dimples.

I smile as I imagine her awaking from her extended slumber. I want nothing more in life than for her to wake up. I'll protect her for as long as she allows me to.

• • •

Day Eleven.

Randy called me when he got into work this morning and asked me to check on Gizmo, who's been staying with him. I guess Gizmo has been whimpering the last few nights. Randy seems to think it's because I haven't really seen Gizmo since the incident. Sara's taken priority.

Even though I don't want to tear myself away from her side, I know I need to check on my Gizmo. Randy meets me after work to take over security outside Sara's door. I should only be a few hours.

It's been eleven days since I've stepped foot outside of the hospital. The sun shouldn't be shining—not until there is a reason for it.

Gizmo is sitting in Randy's front living room chair as I pull into his driveway. He sees me park the car and get out. I can't help but smile at how excited he is to see me. I open the door, and Gizmo leaps on me before I even open the door all the way. I crouch down next to my excited puppy and let him lick my face. I hold him in my arms. "I've missed you too, bud!" Gizmo pushes his head into my abdomen, giving me hugs. I can't help but laugh. My laughter turns to tears as I hug my buddy.

An hour passes, and we both calm down. Even though she isn't at my side, she's never left my thoughts. Gizmo lies sleeping in my lap, exhausted from all his excitement. Knowing I've been gone for longer than I anticipated, I wake him up to say goodbye. I give him a kiss on his forehead and shut Randy's door behind me. He looks sad, sitting in the front chair and staring out at me from the front window. "I'll be back," I say to him from inside my squad car. I know he can't hear me, but I feel like saying it anyway.

Dispatch screeches through the squad's speakers: BEEP! BEEP! BEEP!

"Squad 3220 and other available units respond to 863 Sunrise Court. There's a report of shots fired, and suspect has fled the residence. One victim, male, in his late-twenties, injured and possible DOA. Suspect does not live at residence and forced his way inside. Suspect is described as wearing a gray hooded sweatshirt, a mask, jeans, and being approximately five feet five."

CHAPTER THIRTY-EIGHT

Sara Olivia Scott

Day Thirteen.

My toes and fingers tingle with the sensation that they have been asleep for a long time. I wiggle my fingers to assist them in waking up. Heavy bandages weigh me down. Opening my eyes takes every bit of energy that I can summon. It takes a minute for things to come into focus.

His sunray smile embraces me.

I'm safe.

Warm honey.

CHAPTER THIRTY-NINE

Monica Chant

Permanent red marker stains his last Hallmark card.
"I forgive you." Now that you know what *hurt* is.

END

If you or someone you know is in danger, please reach out for help. If in immediate danger, call 9-1-1. The National Domestic Violence also has an anonymous hotline at 800-799-7233. You can text START to 88788.

You are worthy of respect regardless of how "prudish" others may view you. You are worthy of respect regardless of how many people you previously had intimate relations with. You are worthy of respect regardless of your past. You are worthy of respect because you are important. Please don't be like Sara and stay until it's too late. Your life isn't worth that gamble because you are "more precious than rubies" (Proverbs 3:15).

You are important. You are worthy. You are loved.